Readers love *The Great Wall* by Z. ALLORA

"I am very excited to check out the next books when they come out and definitely recommend this book and author."
— Rainbow Gold Reviews

"The growing love is sweet and strong despite all the difficulties."
— Diverse Reader

"Overall, a good start to a new series, and I can't wait to see where the series goes from here."
— OptimuMM

By Z. ALLORA

The Craving
Illusions & Dreams
The Librarian's Rake

ENTWINED DREAMS
Lock and Key
Secured and Free

MADE IN CHINA
The Great Wall
The Temple of Heaven

Published by DREAMSPINNER PRESS
www.dreamspinnerpress.com

The
Temple
of Heaven

Z. Allora

Published by
DREAMSPINNER PRESS

5032 Capital Circle SW, Suite 2, PMB# 279, Tallahassee, FL 32305-7886 USA
www.dreamspinnerpress.com

The Temple of Heaven
© 2018 Z. Allora.

Cover Art
© 2018 PL Nunn.
http://www.plnunn.com
Cover Design
© 2018 Paul Richmond.
http://www.paulrichmondstudio.com
Cover content is for illustrative purposes only and any person depicted on the cover is a model.

Trade Paperback ISBN: 978-1-64080-549-1
Digital ISBN: 978-1-64080-548-4
Library of Congress Control Number: 2018930552
Trade Paperback published July 2018
v. 1.0

Printed in the United States of America
∞
This paper meets the requirements of
ANSI/NISO Z39.48-1992 (Permanence of Paper).

To Mollie Murphy,
Thank you for sharing your brilliance with me.
Your support and empathy has been invaluable to me
(even if you won't just tell me the answers).
You've helped me regain my voice
and taught me how to draw boundaries…
I'm forever grateful.
Many hugs, Z.

ACKNOWLEDGMENTS

A HUGE thank-you goes to my editor, Desi, and the entire Dreamspinner team who help untangle Z.-speak. Without you, I'd be lost… and so would the readers.

Much appreciation to Lane, Rory, and Thursday who named the K-pop group: Symmetry.

Thank you to Eden, Danny, and Angela S. for your feedback and your love for Jordon.

Sending huge hugs to my Pretty Ones on Facebook, my Z.-bies in my Yaoified Love group, and to all my readers. I hope you enjoy *The Temple of Heaven*.

Finally, a thank-you to my love, which is woefully inadequate whenever I think about how grateful I am for you. You are my everything. Thank you for making our life such an adventure. You proved to me insta-love is more than real. All my love… always, Z.

CHAPTER 1

Dear Future Husband,

Maybe it's silly that I've been writing and drawing pictures for you since I was twelve years old. I know currently you don't exist in my world, but you're never far from my thoughts. I'm convinced you're somewhere out there waiting for me. At night I catch myself looking at the stars, wondering if you're seeing the same sky... making the same wishes I make.

I wonder if you'll love me as much as I know I'll love you.

God, this is dumb. I should stop, but I'm lonely, and I can share things with you I can't tell anyone else.

Sometimes I fantasize about what you'll look like. I don't really have a type, but I do appreciate—

Jordon's cell vibrated with a notification.

Following the alert, he checked the in-box on his laptop. *A new Made in China clip. Yes!*

He sprawled out on the red leather couch outside the Dark Angels' practice room. His brother would be in there for at least another hour, so he might as well enjoy his beloved band. He cast a gaze toward the closed door. Make that his *second*-favorite band.

He followed the link to Youku, the Asian version of YouTube. Humming a few bars of a Made in China song, he waited for the video to buffer, then hit Play.

His laptop screen filled with the bass player chasing the keyboard player while the drummer and lead guitarist made music accenting the silliness. The twenty-second clip ended with a brief flash of the singer chuckling and holding a mic. He asked in English, "Now are you ready?"

Fuck, yeah! Jordon was more than ready as that deep voice reached inside him and soothed empty spaces. He pulled at the front of his suddenly too-tight jeans because he couldn't pretend Tian Di's androgynous sex appeal didn't flip all his switches.

God, what was wrong with him? Crushing on the singer in a band. Was there anything more clichéd?

He grabbed his sketch pad and pencils from his bag, then started to draw. He was on his fifth sketch before he realized he'd done one study after another of the singer.

Damn, he needed to stop or check into a groupie recovery program. He went back to his laptop, but instead of returning to the letter he'd been writing, he allowed the sirens to call him to the other videos of Made in China.

Jordon had seen each video and snippet about a hundred times, but he rewatched the trailer clips of the South Korean game show *Knock Your Socks Off*. Made in China would compete against the reigning champs from Korea. Of course, Made in China had no shot at winning the rigged game show, but the exposure for the band would be great, and watching them play Rip Tear or Suck and Blow would be… stimulating. He couldn't wait for someone to post the episode.

Clicking through the videos, he came to his favorite trailer of the band. Goddamn, Youku limped along, taking forever to load. When the clip finally finished buffering, Made in China's driving sound blared out of his computer and slo-mo images of the band posing for pictures morphed into individual head shots of each member.

Then the picture twirled into a still of the drummer and the lead guitar player. They hugged and blushed in a way that almost made Jordon gag with its sweetness—or was that just him choking on jealousy? Their foreheads touched while they stared at the space between them as if they were going to share their first kiss. The tabloid blog rumors painting them as lovers must be true.

The screen image morphed into the bass player holding the keyboard player by the hair. Far from struggling to get away, the keyboardist wore a demonic smile of lustful joy.

Jordon's breath caught. Those two were totally hooking up.

The band's singer, Tian Di Zhao, reappeared on the screen in a long red jacket with an embroidered white rose pattern running along each side, tight black pants, and knee-high boots. His raven hair cascaded in gentle waves over his shoulders and down to the middle of his back. His eyes were closed, and he held a white rose like a microphone. Some might label his high cheekbones, delicate mannerisms, and lean body more feminine than masculine, but Jordon's fingers itched to draw the perfection of him.

Biting back a moan, Jordon wet his lips and tried not to be envious of the petals that caressed the singer's full red-lipsticked lips. Tian Di's long lashes fluttered, and he opened his mesmerizing brown eyes. He stared into the camera with such longing that Jordon's heart ached.

The screen flashed to a group shot of the band and then panned in for close-ups on their mouths. Jin, the guitar player, gripped and tore a piece of paper that Styx, the drummer, held between his lips.

Jordon's stupid heart triple-timed its beat when Tian Di's glossed lips came into focus. He clamped his straight white teeth down on the paper before tearing a piece away from the drummer. He turned to Li Zhehao, the bass player, whose mouth grazed his chin before severing the paper close to Tian Di's mouth.

Indigo Young spun Li, playfully subdued his struggles by wrapping him in an embrace, and then kissed him full on the mouth. After a long lip-lock, Indigo pulled back and blew the slip of paper out of his mouth.

Ah, Asian bands understood fan service.

The clip ended with the two couples hugging on either side of the singer. Tian Di glanced to his right and then to his left. Finally he stared directly into the camera and gave an empty look that gutted Jordon. Tian Di grabbed for a microphone as if it was the only thing consistently there for him.

A silly need to be there for Tian Di slashed through Jordon's soul. Yeah, like an international star like Tian Di Zhao wanted Jordon Davis to rescue him from the loneliness of falling into bed with his worshippers. Jordon dismissed his feelings as a crush.

Who wouldn't have a wicked case of heat over the guy? Tian Di had the voice of an angel and looks to match. He wasn't just a pretty face. Jordon had listened to Tian Di's interviews—okay, quite possibly Jordon heard or read every interview the guy had ever given—and Tian Di presented himself as quiet, intelligent, and driven, with a tease of irresistible hidden depths.

His deep speaking voice held more confidence than Tian Di showed onstage. Knowing the music industry, the Tian Di Zhao Jordon thought he knew could all be branding. Made in China didn't have the benefit of a record label or management behind them dictating an image.

Indigo was no stranger to the music scene; his father was well connected in LA. According to Dusty, Jordon's oldest brother, who knew just about everyone and everything, the guy's father was a guru who worked tirelessly behind the scenes, setting the direction of many pop icons. Maybe Tian Di's persona was a creation—so Jordon might be crushing on someone who didn't exist.

Why did Jordon always overthink things?

Tian Di was hot and provided Jordon with jerkoff fodder. Wasn't that enough? Why did he have to take his fantasies further? Why couldn't he revel in some mindless sex? Everything in him rebelled against that idea. Maybe that would explain his lack of experience and his silly need to write to a nonexistent husband.

He clicked on the link to Tian Di's website. No new pictures since the last time Jordon checked... yesterday.

There were cute pictures of Tian Di as a kid of five or six. One or two of them showed him as an awkward teen—maybe he hadn't grown into his height—but everything else was still in the range of delicious. Jordon scrolled through the numerous head shots. And the rest were posed pictures of Tian Di around Hong Kong and Shanghai.

God, what would it be like to be curled up in his arms? Maybe reading or watching a movie. He'd love to kiss those lips and maybe even stroke his cock.

Right. The way Jordon's brothers kept him sequestered ensured that type of encounter would never happen even though Made in China was going to be the opening act on the Dark Angels tour. His brothers were the biggest cockblocks in the world. Not only were they overprotective, but seeing their successful relationships set the standards pretty high for what Jordon expected in a partner.

He couldn't dwell on the fact that Made in China had been signed for the entire Asia leg of the *Life's a Drag* tour, because it was like letting the artist Pollock loose inside Jordon. His mind melted into all spatters of happiness and vivid colors. He'd get to meet the man who had haunted his dreams for well over a year.

Maybe he and Tian Di would hit it off. *Ha! What a freaking imagination.* He should stick to art. Tian Di Zhao probably wasn't even gay, or if he was, he wouldn't be into Jordon. *Whatever.* It was a great daydream.

The practice room door banged open, but no one appeared.

Jordon put his computer aside and grabbed his sketch pad. Maybe sitting outside while his brother and the Dark Angels practiced wasn't the best time to contemplate all the things Tian Di's glistening lips invited Jordon to do.

No, definitely not the best time.

He looked around, and his gaze landed on one of his abstract pieces that hung outside the practice space. Over the last several years, Jordon's canvases had replaced and now dominated the area. Some were earlier abstracts he'd given the band and original sketches from the first Dark Angels manga he'd penned backstage at one of their shows.

He opened his work sketch pad and paged past the character sketches of the various designs he'd yet to draw into his Manga Studio program. His characters were born on paper with pen, an essential step for Jordon to connect with his subjects. Only fully realized images found their way into his computer.

Angel strutted out, followed by Darius and Dusty. Angel pointed to Jordon's computer. "You perving on our opening act again?"

Jordon was compelled to cut Angel down. He had known his brother's best friend forever, and Angel had always been good to him. Maybe the overcompensation was to ensure Angel never discovered that at twelve Jordon had crushed on him for an entire year, or that he had wished to be more confident like Angel. Eh, or maybe God put Jordon on earth to keep Angel Luv's ego from overwhelming the band.

"Nah, listening to your replacements." Direct hit, if Jordon could go by Angel's injured expression. "You do know Made in China's singer has a larger range than yours?"

Dare rushed over and hip-bumped Angel. "Hey, in terms of size, I've got no complaints. Besides, their singer's good, but he's not Angel Luv."

Angel shrugged and gave his boyfriend a sparkly smile for a moment. "The guy's amazing, which is why Made in China will be opening our show. And I wish them every success."

"Don't forget about the drummer." Jordon winced at Dusty's frown. Why did he still play the role of the bratty kid brother? Damn, but every interaction forced him to slip into the familiar role and into saying words scripted years before.

Dusty admitted, "The kid's impressive. No doubt."

"Yeah, but he doesn't have your experience." Jordon tried to find something Made in China's drummer didn't have over his brother.

"Ha-ha. Yeah, I'm close to another birthday. Thanks for reminding me." Dusty waved him off.

Damn it, Jordon needed a tongue transplant. "No, that's not what I meant. You know how to drive the crowd with the drums. It's because you can read them, and you got that from years of experience in front of an audience."

Dusty twirled his drumsticks. "He'll learn. Made in China is still relatively new."

God, Dusty's easy agreement, which helped Jordon's careless words cut him, made Jordon sick.

Robin came into the room, fixing his hair, with a smirking Josh. Robin's gaze zeroed in on Jordon. "Who needs a cuddle?"

Ever since the night Jordon's mother had thrown him out at age sixteen, Robin, the keyboard player for the Dark Angels, seemed determined to give him some much-needed mothering. He loved that Robin didn't just accept him, he celebrated who Jordon was and, best of all, who Jordon was trying to become. Robin even knew two of Jordon's deepest secrets, and he didn't tell anyone, not even Josh.

Josh growled, which forced Jordon into an automatic response. He raised his hand like he desperately needed a pass to the bathroom. True, there used to be pleasure in making Josh jealous, but baiting him stopped being fun a while ago.

Just another thing Jordon did out of habit. Maybe he needed to figure out a way to break these patterns.

Robin settled onto the sofa next to him and murmured low enough so no one else could hear, "I loved your—I mean, Sakura Rose's latest volume of *Tricks and Treats*."

"Thanks. I mean, yeah. It's good work. But Sakura's having trouble with the next story." That was a damn understatement. Jordon sighed, shut his sketchbook, and set the pad aside.

Robin eased Jordon's head down into his lap and played with Jordon's hair. "I'm sure Sakura Rose will figure it out. Sakura is extremely talented."

Jordon drank in Robin's kind words. "Sakura Rose has hit a major creative blockage… I've heard."

Why couldn't Jordon admit to his brothers he'd been drawing for a Japanese yaoi publishing house since he was sixteen? It wasn't like Dusty or Zack could ground him. For fuck's sake, he was twenty years old. But the confession would be delivered with an admission he'd lied by omission, or at least wasn't honest with them. They'd be disappointed in him and hurt. Avoidance was easier.

"I'm sure SR will find a way." Robin patted Jordon's cheek with a little frown and a glint of determination in his eyes, like he'd fight the dragons of artistic constipation for Jordon.

Josh crushed in next to Robin and threw a territorial arm over Robin's shoulder. "Who are you talking about?"

"A yaoi artist I really enjoy." Robin didn't exactly lie, but his inventive use of the truth made Jordon feel shitty nonetheless.

He inhaled Robin's vanilla-lavender calming scent—which was always mixed with Josh's—and found comfort. Even though Jordon's brothers kept him like a sequestered nun, he'd always enjoyed Robin's platonic touch.

What did Tian Di smell like? He probably smelled edible. Now was not the time to think about the deliciousness that was Tian Di.

Jordon jumped off the sofa and knocked over his sketch pad in the process. It landed on his latest storyboard for *Tricks and Treats*.

Josh grabbed the sketch pad from the floor and stared at the scenes of Tricks on his knees providing a *treat* for one of the main characters. "This isn't for a Dark Angels manga, is it?"

"No. It's for something else I'm working on." He snatched the pad back and clutched his secrets to his chest.

Josh was way too perceptive to have missed the "SR" scrawled at the bottom of the sketch; his look of understanding was clear in his gaze. *Shit.*

Some silent communication went back and forth between Robin and Josh until Robin caressed Josh's hand, then turned his attention back to Jordon. "Any new Made in China videos?"

"Yeah, actually, there's a couple. One is a trailer for a game show they'll be on, and a few others are just silly." Jordon loved when someone shared his… interest.

Josh shifted and patted the place between him and Robin. "Well, let's see it."

Jordon eased back down and clicked on the Rip Tear trailer with the speed of a skilled stalker.

By the time the clip ended, Dare, Dusty, and Angel had all squeezed in around him and his laptop, watching the trailer.

"Hey, wait. Let's see this one again. It's my favorite." Angel reached over Dare and Robin and tapped the curser on a music video.

The video opened. Made in China took to the darkened stage in traditional Chinese opera costumes, each band member standing in a spotlight, holding traditional instruments. The bottom left identified the song as "Evolution."

"Evolution" was the first video Jordon had showed the Dark Angels. Angel credited the band's viewing of "Evolution" as the moment that convinced them to consider Made in China for an opening act for their upcoming tour. Jordon should be content knowing he helped draw attention to Made in China's talent, and if his involvement impacted his crush in a positive way, all the better.

The video started with flutes and plucking strings on a *ruan*, or Chinese guitar, accompanying Tian Di as he glided toward center stage, trailing the hem of a light pink embroidered robe across the floor. Colorfully stitched birds perched on cherry blossom branches covered the expanse of silk. As he reached the spotlight, he thrust his arms up, and white waterfall sleeves shot out of the jacket and into the air before the silk gracefully fell in ripples at his sides.

Flowers dangled from the ornamental sticks holding his ebony hair in a knot at the back of his head. His makeup blurred the line between Goth and Chinese opera, heavy black eyeliner making his eyes appear huge.

How many times had Jordon caught himself sketching Tian Di Zhao?

He couldn't deny he was drawn to gender ambiguity, Goth, and tradition. Maybe he tried to capture Tian Di's essence so he might be able to understand why a man half a world away enchanted him.

"Geez, if I didn't know he was a guy…," Dare said to no one in particular. "The singer's movements are graceful, and the way he wears that kimono—"

"In China it's robes," Captain Know-It-All Dusty corrected.

Angel pulled Dare against him. "He's got a voice, no doubt about it."

Dusty shook his head during an unexpected drum solo that cut into and around the traditional flute and ruan. "I can't imagine doing that in those heavy robes."

As if the statement was a decree, the traditional Chinese clothing vanished with a bit of choppy editing. The band appeared, wearing black T-shirts and jeans, playing their usual instruments. The beat increased in intensity and speed.

"I love how they keep the same melody while rockafying it." Robin's label of the style was accurate.

The guitar, bass, and keyboard gave the song a driving, almost heavy metal sound.

"The evolution is really good. Get it? 'Evolution' is the name of the song." Josh apparently got Dare's meaning, because they fist-bumped.

Beep.

At the simultaneous announcement of a text message, Angel and Dusty pulled their cell phones out of their pockets.

"Fuck!" Angel glared at his phone.

"She'll fix it," Dusty said.

Jordon's stomach dropped. "What?"

"One of Made in China's band members is having trouble getting a visa for travel outside of China because his mother wasn't married to his father when he was born. Apparently certain paperwork and identification cards are necessary to get a passport."

Josh scoffed. "What kind of backward shit is that?"

Robin petted his hand. "It's how they do things in their country."

CHAPTER 2

TIAN DI stared at his computer screen, glad the bedroom door remained shut so his bandmates couldn't hear his mother. Why did he let his guard down?

"I am serious, Tian Di. When are you going to cut your hair? You look more like a woman than your sister!" Tian Di's mother complained for the second time in the three minutes of their Skype video chat.

And he hadn't even called her.

"Mother," Tian Di and his sister said in unison.

His older sister, Zhang Min, scrunched in close to their mom. She was the only reason he stayed on the call. She had always been on his side, and he'd always been on hers.

The ongoing long-hair battle he'd won only after moving from Hong Kong. The memory of being physically dragged to the barber and having his hair hacked off still made him break out in a cold sweat.

Refusing to accept his long hair proved to be only a symptom. Most of his family refused to deal with his attraction to men. Somehow the length of his hair was connected—in his mother's head—to his sexuality.

"His hair is beautiful, Mom. Leave him alone." Zhang Min stopped glaring at their mother to smile at him. "Tian Di, did you get the hair oil I sent, or did customs snatch the bottle?"

Zhang Min remained the only one in the Zhao family who accepted everything about him. She'd been the first one he'd told when he figured out he liked guys. She'd hugged him while he tried not to cry, and then she shared her secret collection of yaoi with him. He'd realized he wasn't alone in the world, and his life could get better; he just needed to be patient.

"Yes, I got the oil and the spearmint candy drops, thanks. That's why I'm calling. To tell you the hair oil works great and smells incredible." He called Zhang Min on her day off, which she usually spent reading. Their mother must have popped in for one of her surprise inspections.

His mother leaned closer to the screen and looked past him into his bedroom. "It's midday. Why didn't you make your futon yet?"

Tian Di looked back at his bed, which he didn't return to futon sofa form unless he expected company. His comforter lay straight enough, though one pillow happened to be out of place. Thankfully, he'd put away his mangas. He certainly didn't need her to spy his collection of yaoi.

"Just doing some stretches. I used the pillow." He wouldn't tell her for what, and was glad nothing else told tales on him.

"You need a woman to clean up after you. Are you dating a nice girl yet?"

What he craved was a nice *man* who was orally inclined, and then he wouldn't have to worry about the flexibility of his spine.

Zhang Min rolled her eyes. "Mother, Tian Di is gay. He won't be dating—"

His mother folded her arms across her chest. "No, he just hasn't met the right woman. *Nánrén sìshí yī duǒ huā, nǚrén sìshí dòufu zhā.*"

Tian Di winced at the sexist proverb, which meant men of forty are a blooming flower; women of forty are dregs of bean curd.

Zhang Min grimaced. "Well, good to know. He's got a long way before he turns forty. Thankfully, I'm still a few years away from being disgusting bean curd."

Their mother seemed unconcerned with how her arrow pierced both her children. "Let me go stir the dumplings."

He waited until his mother left the room. "You could be one hundred and forty years old and you would never be bean curd."

Zhang Min laughed. "I'm not worried about it. Though she needs to join us in this century. Taiwan is getting close to legalizing same-sex marriage. Times are changing."

Tian Di spun his silver ring with the musical notes circling the band. He wore the ring on the same finger that was believed to be directly linked to the heart. The ring was not only a declaration, but a reminder. Music was his first and only love.

The life he chose did not leave room for more than a temporary someone to fill the void. After all, no one would drop everything to go on tour with him. Or who would tolerate being separated for months at a time? No, even if China's mainland legalized same-sex marriage, he wouldn't get his hopes up.

"The world is changing, but you know she will never accept it or me. She's like most people who deny and hope everything different disappears." He tried not to let people's ignorance get to him. His mother's attitude only reinforced why he needed to get to Los Angeles or someplace where being gay wasn't just tolerated but accepted as no big deal.

Zhang Min waved him off. "Well, I'm not going to support her delusions."

Those were the delusions most of the country held. Beliefs many gay Chinese men held… even if they did enjoy sex with men.

"Did you meet anyone yet?" she continued.

"Other than my right hand?" And a few random men at the club. It was depressing. He twisted the ring reminding himself of his choice: music over love. "I'm focusing on my career."

That sounded less pathetic than he had given up on love.

She grinned at him the same way she had when he was ten. "I can't believe you're going to be on *Knock Your Socks Off*. I love that show. What game are they making you play?"

"Suck and Blow." Game, ha! More like sucking face on TV. The object was to pass a playing card between players by only sucking and blowing the card. Many times, the cards accidentally on purpose would fall and band members would kiss.

"Your singing career is starting to happen."

"And I can't let anything screw up my music." If Tian Di wanted to be successful, he needed to keep singing as his top priority. Nothing could stand in the way. Once he became a success, he'd do things he wanted to.

His mother bustled back into the room and reclaimed her spot next to Zhang Min. "Why don't you come work for your father?"

"Mother, you know I can't." He had no interest, nor did he have any talent for business.

His mother whined, "Tian Di, please consider coming home. Your father made a good position for you in the family business. You'd be director of sales, have your own apartment, car, and driver. Everyone would welcome you home."

More like welcome him into an empty life of make-believe and misery, which would include a wife and a child. No, he wouldn't settle for a lie. At fifteen he came out to his parents, but if they couldn't hear he liked men, the fault didn't belong to him. His mother had blamed his attraction to men on his love of yaoi and bootleg videos of Western movies.

"Mother, you know I can't. Besides, the band is doing well." For the first time, that wasn't much of a stretch.

"What kind of life do you have? Take the position; then maybe your sister could focus on finding a husband so she can have a baby before she's too old."

Zhang Min sighed. "I love working."

"And she's good at marketing," Tian Di added. Zhang Min had made a name for herself in their family's company. She always had been a force of nature.

His mother *tsk*ed. "A woman should be raising children and taking care of the home."

Tian Di's mother avoided stepping into the twenty-first century by refusing to hear anything that didn't reinforce her outdated beliefs. Her enduring motto was "respect tradition." Too bad if that didn't promote happiness.

"Argh, there's no winning this argument. Call me later, Tian Di." Zhang Min stomped away from the computer.

His mother's hand fluttered to her chest. "I don't understand."

"I know, Mother. I will speak to you soon. Tell Father I wish him health." Tian Di ended the call before his mother could say his father would want nothing from him except an acceptance of the position Tian Di had been offered.

Tian Di popped another melt-away spearmint that Zhang Min had sent, then grabbed the bottle of expensive hair oil and sniffed. She always spoiled him with presents, and he did the same whenever he had money. He put a coin-sized drop in his palm, ran the fragrant oil through the strands, and brushed until his hair shone.

Time to check on his bandmates.

He meandered out to the living room to find his bandmates sprawling, perched, or pacing. He kicked Indigo's feet off the coffee table and dropped onto the sofa next to Li.

Indigo glared at Tian Di and put his bare feet back on the table, one at a time with a thud. He pulled Li closer to him. "About time you joined us."

It hadn't even been a year since he'd moved in with the other members of his band, but he couldn't decide if living with the guys was a blessing or a curse. They were great, and he enjoyed having a group of friends, but Indigo Young could push his buttons way too easily.

Jin yanked at his naturally blond hair as he paced, driven by nervous energy he normally reserved for playing his guitar in front of a pack of screaming fans. "Guys, I'm so sorry. I didn't know the government would give me trouble about traveling outside of China. I didn't know the salon just paid off the Suzhou officials for my work visa."

Two weeks and this bit of stress continued. They had their big break and were so close to making their dreams come true, but paperwork could stop everything.

Ashen-faced, Styx eased Jin's hands out of his hair and dragged his boyfriend to the couch. They'd been through so much already; they didn't need more anxiety.

Indigo growled, "I don't understand this fuckery. What century are *you* people in?"

Did the guy think harsh words could change the way things were?

Indigo constantly defining the differences between China and America had gotten old. Tian Di had been born and raised in Hong Kong. He understood the differences better than most. "*You* people? You're starting to sound racist."

Indigo rolled his eyes. "I'm just as Asian as you."

"Though much more insulting." Tian Di said the words in English to ensure Indigo didn't misunderstand. Tian Di wouldn't let Indigo's talent and connections stop him from speaking the truth.

Indigo glared. "Come on, Tian Di, this is bullshit! Just 'cause Jin's mom had him without being married to his father, he can't get a visa or a passport?"

Jin groaned, jumped off the sofa, and tried to wear a track into the wooden floors again.

"Come on, let's remember *Knock Your Socks Off* decided to film on location in Suzhou, so we bought some more time to figure this out." Funny how helping a guy save face in Suzhou's only gay bar got Made in China this incredible gig. Apparently the relationship Tian Di helped the producer of the show secure had been going well enough, because he willingly agreed to shoot the South Korean TV show in Suzhou rather than cancel the band's appearance.

Jin halted his circular trek around the room and wrung his hands. "This is going to screw everything up with the Dark Angels."

Indigo shook his head. "I'm telling you, my dad said the Dark Angels' management hasn't contacted anyone else to open their shows in Asia. They want us."

Tian Di begrudgingly gave Indigo points for rarely talking about his famous father and for wanting to earn his own place in life. But honestly, Tian Di wouldn't have an issue with Indigo accepting parental help.

Styx dragged Jin back to the couch and threw an arm around him. "It will be okay. We'll figure something out."

Tian Di wasn't thrilled to have his dream threatened either, but someone needed to be the voice of sanity and calm. "Jin, what exactly did the Dark Angels' manager say?"

Jin shook his head. "She said she'd deal with it but didn't say how."

Indigo trained his glare on each of them. "What is she going to do? Just bribe the government officials to get you the right paperwork and stamps?"

Probably....

Li spoke up from beside Indigo. "We still have a couple weeks until the game show. Let's focus on doing the best we can on *Knock Your Socks Off*. Shall we practice the two songs we get to play?"

TIAN DI couldn't help but chuckle at Styx's grumbling as he slid into the limousine sent by *Knock Your Socks Off*. "I don't know why the producers sent over a car for us. We live right across the road from the SCAC. We could walk like we always do."

Everyone else slid into the plush seats with a smile.

The producers decided the Suzhou Culture and Arts Center served them better than Shanghai, probably because the venue saved the show money.

Indigo leaned back in the limo, hands behind his head. "Get used to it. Want this luxury treatment. Let the pampering motivate you."

Styx grabbed Jin's hand and in a strong voice said, "There's only one thing I need."

Jin rested his head for a moment on Styx's shoulder.

Tian Di enjoyed seeing how Jin and Styx were together. He ignored the ache in his heart that tried to make him crave the impossible.

"We're going to be great," Indigo proclaimed as the limo pulled up to the front of the SCAC.

"How can you be so sure?" Styx shook his head and stared out the window.

Indigo chuckled. "My opinion is simply a fact that hasn't been proven… yet."

Having had enough of Indigo's damned American arrogance, Tian Di swung open the car door. It was still early, so the neon of the bird's nest building didn't burn his retinas with its colorful light display. He stepped out to a screaming line of fans.

Wow! The band had been recently filling the Biergarten restaurant, but this number of screaming fans catapulted them into another dimension.

Indigo jumped out next. Eyes gleaming as he drank in the fans' appreciation, he elbowed Tian Di and gave a quick wave. Then he reached back to help Li out of the limo.

The piercing shrieks died down a bit when Jin and Styx tumbled out. The crowd must have realized Made in China wasn't the band they were waiting for, but still a respectable part of the crowd applauded and some even yelled louder.

Tian Di shook himself out of his wonderment and followed the rest of the band. He hiked the red-carpeted stairs, and a fan held back only by a rope shoved an autograph book at him. "Tian Di. Please!"

She knew his name. His name. He recognized the woman as someone who came to listen to Made in China about three or four times a week. Wow. "Who should I make this out to?"

"Me!" She laughed.

He stared at her and drew a blank. Had he ever spoken to her? "Um, yes, how do you spell—"

"K-I-M." She bounced in place.

He wrote: "To Kim, it's always a pleasure to see you in the audience. May you always hear the music." He drew a heart and signed *TD*.

She squealed and gave him a quick hug.

The rest of the guys waited at the top of the stairs for him.

Instead of letting them escape, Tian Di stepped forward. He put on his stage persona and smiled shyly at the crowd. "Thank you so much. We're going to give everything we've got today because we love you."

The crowd roared back.

The band followed his lead and waved before they slipped inside.

AFTER A couple of hours of primping, Made in China stood in the wings offstage.

Symmetry, the band they were competing against, brushed past Made in China. A couple of the members made eye contact with Tian Di. He wished they hadn't. Their sympathy and pity did nothing but irk him.

Hell, Tian Di understood the game, both this one and the music industry, and he willingly opted to participate. He'd signed up and entered this spectacle with open eyes. The only difference between Made in China and Symmetry was... Symmetry had played the game a bit longer.

Symmetry zoomed to the top of South Korea's boy bands in part due to their sweet melody but mostly due to their good looks. They were no strangers to mastering the many games a band needed to play to survive. Their members represented most of the stereotypes: two bad boys, two shy guys, two pranksters, and two talented singers. Symmetry could be exchanged for any of the other large boy bands that raced into the hearts of their young fans.

Tian Di pushed away how close stardom came to irrelevance and focused on the cameras swirling around, unseen by the audience.

The crowd screamed for each and every one of the eight members of Symmetry as they were introduced.

Tian Di's Korean language skills might be minimal, but judging by the laughter of the studio audience, the MC of the show made yet another joke at Made in China's expense. The translator in his earpiece didn't bother to translate the tease. Maybe it was a good decision, considering the tenseness of his bandmates.

The big screens around the theater translated into Chinese for the locals and English for the expatriates living in Suzhou. Not as many expats as in Hong Kong, but definitely a large population settled in Suzhou due to some major European companies. Western ideas and values hammering against some of the Chinese traditions helped reinforce that Tian Di's own beliefs were not insane.

Sebe, the band's teenaged would-be manager, started his pep talk. "Remember you're not going to win the competition. Your prize is the opportunity to be memorable. Get people talking about Made in China."

Styx groaned.

Indigo jumped in, "We do need to do some sucking and blowing—"

Idiot. Tian Di continued the explanation, "We play the game, do two songs, and then Symmetry will play some music. No problem."

Sebe used a lint roller to remove the specks of dust on their black T-shirts and jeans.

Styx stared at Jin and then at Tian Di. "They really do want us to play that game?"

Poor guy must have been hoping for a last-minute reprieve. Tian Di shrugged. "The fan service buys us two songs in front of a huge audience. Just accidentally drop a card or two and do mouth to mouth on Jin."

Tian Di slipped on his long, embroidered jacket, setting him apart from the other guys who were all in black. Indigo bitched at him to keep his brand consistent. His marketing-expert sister agreed with the advice.

The hair and makeup people descended upon them to attack with brushes and sprays one more time.

After they vanished, Indigo huffed out a breath. "Just have fun, Styx."

"I'm here to play music. I'm not here to kiss on TV." Styx ran his twitching fingers through his perfectly tussled mop of hair.

The stylist rushed back to slap Styx's digits away from the mess he made of his hair, then repaired the damage. She slinked back into the shadows but remained on guard.

Styx sighed. "My little sister watches this show."

Jin took Styx's smacked hand and pressed his lips onto the knuckles. "You already prepped your family, right?"

Twirling his drumsticks, Styx nodded. "Indigo did. He chatted with my dad for a long time."

Indigo waved him off. "He mostly asked about expensive cars, but I made sure he understood the concept of fan service and giving the audience what they wanted. And yes, that does mean you're here to lock lips. Get the fuck over it. If you want fans, you need to earn them. Sex sells music."

"Not helpful, Indigo. Styx, Jin said your parents were excited about you being on TV," Tian Di pointed out, hoping the encouragement made a difference.

Styx stared at the floor.

Indigo chimed in with "Yeah, come on. You said your dad even gave you advice on how to deal with the game. Make them proud and play kissy face with Jin."

Tian Di rested a hand on Styx's shoulder. "Just stay on the end near Jin… away from Indigo. I hear he's a sloppy kisser."

Indigo smirked. "You wish you knew, Tian Di. Styx, we're here to get fans. This is the way to accomplish that feat. So drop a card or two. I'm sure you won't mind kissing Jin."

Styx's face got even redder. It might have been a miracle he had any modesty after living with Indigo, who had made it a top priority to give Styx a degree in every aspect of the gay world beyond China.

"Don't pay attention to the audience. Think of Jin and have fun." Tian Di slapped the unconvinced Styx on the back. "You got this."

Jin leaned in and whispered something.

Styx nodded eagerly, then widened his eyes. His frown turned into a smile.

Edging closer to Styx, Jin winked at Tian Di over Styx's shoulder.

A stagehand clapped quietly. "It's time. Places. Four, three, two, go."

Li led them out onto the stage and in front of what felt like the whole damned world.

Tian Di passed Indigo and wedged himself between Indigo and Li. He wasn't sure why, but he did.

Symmetry gave Made in China enough applause to appear sportsmanlike as they took their place on the other side of the MC.

Tian Di got into his lead singer mode. He kept his eyes down and shifted from foot to foot as if he were nervous. Staring at the ground, he hoped to appear shy as they stood waiting in line for the silly game of Suck and Blow to start.

It wouldn't benefit his career for fans to figure out sucking face wasn't the only thing he liked sucking. To say he had an oral fixation wouldn't be an exaggeration, and if he didn't need to protect his voice, he'd probably smoke three packs of cigarettes a day or suck—but this was China, not LA.

Tian Di pieced together the information as the MC explained the game rules. "The band able to suck and blow the best...." The MC waited for the crowd to "oh" and "ah." "Um, suck and blow the most *cards* wins."

The wise guy gave his oversized whistle a blow, but the only translation Tian Di received in his ear piece said, "Begin." As if he couldn't have figured out what the shrill sound popping his eardrums meant.

Some members of Symmetry sat out the game to keep the teams even. They bounced around the stage and rallied the crowd.

Styx leaned over and with the necessary suction, picked up a card, then shifted it to Jin. Jin slowly pursed his lips and blew away the queen of hearts before he planted a big kiss on his boyfriend's lips.

Nice! Way to pull the attention to Made in China.

Styx blushed and his hand fluttered to his mouth as if the lip press were a big surprise to him. Styx must have decided to ham it up, because he shrugged to the audience, and then he and Jin shared a quick smile. The audience ate the affection up.

Damn, Styx and Jin fit together like puzzle pieces. Tian Di's heart clenched. He coveted the deep connection they had. Each touch, look, and kiss they shared served only to remind him of everything he lacked in his life. A couple of years ago, exchanging blowjobs with a fanboy would have been more than enough to satisfy him, but now… he was lucky to be flexible.

He had never been so long between men. He wasn't picky. Young and old, Tian Di found reasons to enjoy whoever offered to spend time with him. Though things had changed over the last year. The last guy he'd been with, while skilled, left him feeling empty afterward.

He could barely believe it, but he craved more than casual encounters. Maybe living with people who really loved each other highlighted how fleeting and inadequate the passing pleasure had become. He twisted his ring to remind himself of his goals.

Styx sucked, latching on to the eight of spades, and turned toward Jin.

The audience got louder as Jin tucked his fingers into Styx's belt loop and tugged him close. Jin grazed his lips across the card as if he were kissing Styx, and then he turned to blow the card to Indigo's lips.

Indigo sucked the card away from Jin, turned toward the camera, and wiggled his eyebrows. He grabbed Tian Di's waist.

Tian Di tossed his hair over his shoulder.

The audience sighed.

Indigo glared at him.

Whatever. Tian Di tilted his head to the left and pursed his lips in the best pout he could manage so he could receive the playing card from Indigo's lips. He ignored the angry daggers Indigo threw.

Tian Di sucked the card against his mouth. He could see Styx and Jin working on their next card.

Stepping back, Tian Di bumped into Li, who steadied him. "Come on. Give me a card! Symmetry is winning."

The scoreboard displayed two to zero.

Tian Di blew the card to Li who sucked the card and got it into the basket. They scored a point.

Jin passed the next card to Indigo, which he transferred without incident to Tian Di.

Wanting to build the drama, Tian Di turned nice and slow, giving the camera big eyes, and even fluttered his lashes. He leaned toward Li and couldn't prevent the ace of diamonds from falling to the floor, causing him to plant his mouth on Li's.

Li's lips were soft, his kiss thorough, though mechanical. The kiss held affection but lacked passion. It appeared to be nothing like the kisses Li exchanged with Indigo.

The crowd clapped and stomped their feet, unaware there was no chemistry between them.

Putting a hand over his mouth, Tian Di playfully batted at Li.

Li's eyes flashed amusement.

The onstage monitors showed young women had jumped out of their seats, screaming like they'd won the lottery. Some hugged the person next them, and a few even started to cry.

Success. That was what this game was all about: fan service.

The game continued, and after half a deck of cards, even Styx appeared to relax and get into the spirit of silliness. He dropped the card right as Jin sucked, and their lips touched. He clung for a moment.

Tian Di was sure when the program aired, there'd probably be hearts around their heads at every mistake, which would be shown in slow motion. He was good with the games... right?

For fuck's sake, was this worse than blowing your way to the top? At least with a suckfest, once the guy in charge shot off, Tian Di could rinse out his mouth and put the incident out of his head. But these damned pictures would be following him throughout his career... however, this show would be enabling that career, so he needed to deal. He had to keep his eyes on the prize.

More cards, less kissing, and Made in China fell into a rhythm, their time almost up.

Indigo sucked the card from Jin and turned to Tian Di, a question in his eyes. Everyone had dropped a playing card except the two of them.

Tian Di cocked an eyebrow slightly to lay the dare at Indigo's feet.

Indigo dragged him close by the shoulders, lowered his mouth to Tian Di, and blew the card at him. The jack of diamonds hit Tian Di in the nose and fell to the floor.

Tian Di laughed right before Indigo pressed his mouth onto him.

Indigo's lips against his couldn't be called a kiss. Even though they were touching lips, somehow Indigo turned the kiss into a power struggle.

Tian Di wouldn't be outdone by Indigo. He jerked back and put a hand over his lips as if that could hide what happened. Using big eyes, he stared out at the crowd, causing a bit of mayhem in the audience.

He didn't want to admit Indigo's and Li's kisses were the most intimate thing he'd had with a man in recent memory. A piece of him wanted to drop to his knees and blow Indigo's boyfriend right there in front of him. More because he could, and less because he wanted to.

The MC blew his giant whistle and named Symmetry the winner. Big surprise. The translation across the huge-screen TVs said the game had finished.

As soon as the cameras stopped filming, Indigo got in his face. "What the fuck was that?" He gestured wildly at Li.

Tian Di wrapped him in a hug. "Careful, man. There are too many eyes on us."

Indigo's gaze followed his as he assessed the audience, who were taking snaps of their interaction. He fake smiled. "Yeah, yeah. You're right. But if you suck face like that again with Li—"

"So I guess a blowjob is totally off the table?"

Indigo patted him on the back a bit too hard, and ended the hug. Turning his back to the audience, Indigo growled, "If you ever kiss *my* boyfriend again like he's *yours*, I will take you apart."

Tian Di couldn't help but point out the basic fact that their relationship was open. "Unless you give your permission?"

"That will never happen. Though I can make you sing in a higher range for the rest of your damned life." Indigo smiled with sweetness before glancing over at Li.

The MC waved them back into line.

A scratchy translation of "commercial break over" pierced his eardrum.

"Congratulations to Symmetry!"

The bands formed two lines and shook one another's hands as if they'd played a basketball game.

The MC clapped with the crowd and Symmetry filed off stage.

Lights cut out.

Tian Di's earpiece demanded, "Sing."

So much for a setup.

He stalked to center stage through the inky blackness to the edge of the spotlight.

The rest of the band got their instruments together. Preparing for a show in the dark was a skill perfected at the German restaurant.

Tian Di paused and opened himself. When he got Indigo's signal, he stepped into the light, letting everything good in the world slam into him, propelling him to reach out to the audience with song. He grabbed the mic and sang, "Neon-lit streets only highlight my loneliness and doubt."

Styx came in with a soft drum beat, followed by Jin plucking his guitar and Li laying down a bass line, and Indigo held the melody together with his keyboard. The band supported the soft sensuous mood of the song.

Lyrics flowed out of Tian Di, even as tears tracked down his cheeks. He allowed his desolation and despair to overwhelm him as the words in the song described. "Everyone has a love but no, not me."

He sang, letting everything he never thought he wanted invade the lyrics. "I can yearn, but it cannot be. I'm not free, and you never wanted me...."

The music carried the sadness of unfulfilled need.

He poured all of his sadness into the song until he sang the final words to a silent theater. "Never before and never again." Dropping his head, he let the tears fall.

The music died.

The roar from the crowd erupted and clutched him tight. He drank in the appreciation.

A stagehand ran out and handed him a tissue. Why? Oh. He carefully wiped away his tears without screwing with the eye makeup.

Pulling himself together, he changed gears and belted out a song Indigo usually referred to as one of their anthem rock songs.

The crowd jumped to their feet, singing the words that flashed across the screen right along with him.

He touched his ring, drinking in love and acceptance.

What a feeling. This was why he tolerated the loneliness of his world.

CHAPTER 3

JORDON FELT restless and constricted. He craved a bit of freedom to do things on his own schedule. To gain liberation, however, he would need to take the right tone in addressing his oldest brother.

He wandered into the kitchen. Both Zack and Dusty were making lunch. "Oh, hey. Those look good. Can you make me one?"

"Of course. Wasn't sure if you'd be down for lunch; I didn't want to bother you. Zack was just going to bring one upstairs to you later." Dusty added more slices of bread to the lineup on the counter. He slapped on cheddar cheese, turkey slices, tomato, and lettuce. On two he put mustard, and for Jordon's, he put a special sauce Zack found at the deli near his side of town.

Zack rewrapped all the lunch fixings and muttered at the refrigerator's disorganized state—at least according to Zack's way of the world. "For clarity's sake, using the labels I put in the fridge to guide you both to put things back in the right place isn't harmful to your health… and it might save your life."

Jordon rolled his eyes at Zack's threat.

Dusty gave Jordon a small grin and a conspiratorial wink.

Sliding onto the barstool next to Zack's usual spot, Jordon asked, "You off today?"

Zack continued shuffling things around the refrigerator. "Nah, I've got a roadie meeting later this afternoon, but I wanted to stop by to make sure you were packed and ready for Asia."

"What? Why?" Jordon shouldn't bother asking. He knew why.

Zack gave up on the organization, and he took his seat. "Um, 'cause I've helped you pull your shit together before every single tour."

"I can pack myself." He could. He should. He would….

Dusty focused on him. "Have you?"

"No…." Jordon hated to admit he hadn't even thought about packing. He needed to get better with the details of his life.

"No worries. I've got your back." Zack took out his phone and waved it. "I've got your packing list from the last tour right here, with the things you wanted me to make sure you didn't forget. We've got thirteen hours before we head to the airport."

Well, here was the segue served on a silver platter made of overprotection and micromanagement. Jordon exhaled hard. "I'm totally not ready to go."

Dusty nodded. "Zack said he'd help you pack, and I'll take you shopping if you need to pick up anything. Remember, this tour is longer than usual."

"I know, but I have storyboards due to the publisher. I also have a painting that's giving me hell, and if I can just focus, I can finish everything if I didn't have to leave so soon."

Dusty hesitated in placing the final sandwich on the plate. "What are you saying?"

"Do we have any chips?" Jordon hoped the redirection would give him space to spit out his words.

"I'm not even going to mention there are six open bags of the same kind of chips." Zack pointed out the epic fail as he foraged through three more cabinets on the potato-chip scavenger hunt. "And two of them don't have clip closures on them."

Jordon chuckled. "High crimes and treason. Hey, that's what happens when you abandon Dusty, Justin, and I to live at Obsessive Compulsives R Us—"

"It's just wasteful to open so many bags." He glared at Jordon and Dusty while he condensed the six bags down into one. Then he added a handful of salty crunchy deliciousness to each plate. He clipped the bag with the care of a surgeon and returned the chips to where he designated their spot should be.

"Jordon?" Dusty slid Jordon's plate in front of him. "What were you saying?"

Shit. Here goes. "Well, I was thinking maybe I could just stay here for a couple of days longer."

"What? Alone?" Zack's shock was clear. "You don't like staying in the house by yourself."

True. He'd probably lock himself in his bedroom studio before it got dark. Justin had restocked his minifridge with his favorite orange soda and string cheese. He could hole up for a few weeks and be fine. "Look, I need to get over that. Besides, there's a new alarm system now, so if I hear any noise, I can check the cameras. What, you think I'm going to throw a wild party?"

"No, of course not." Dusty rooted around the refrigerator and grabbed two Cokes along with Jordon's Mirinda. He passed the sodas out.

Yeah, why would he? Jordon didn't have many friends in the area, other than the Dark Angels and his brothers. Between his art and touring with the band, he usually didn't bother to make time to spend with others except for his bestie.

"Dusty, seriously, I can manage on my own for a couple of days. Besides, my therapist wants me to figure out ways I can be more independent." He wasn't playing the therapist card for the win, but she *had* asked him to work on being more responsible, learning to identify and share his needs with others.

Both Zack and Dusty stared at him in silence. Hmmm, the nervous coiling sensation that made him want to puke must be the *discomfort* she told him he might experience.

Jordon took a big bite of his sandwich, because hearing himself chew was better than brotherly quiet. The sandwich parted and some of the magic sauce dripped onto his T-shirt. "Argh! Dammit."

Dusty handed Zack a napkin, and Zack dabbed at the drip. Dusty gave Zack some club soda, and he used it to make the spill vanish. "It shouldn't stain but I can—"

"This is an example." Jordon gestured down at his now-clean shirt. This had been the first T-shirt he'd speckled with paint, so he was happy it wasn't ruined, but that wasn't the point.

"Of?" Zack scrunched his face and glanced over at Dusty, who seemed to be just as lost.

"I know how to do laundry. I'm not helpless." Granted, it wasn't until Dusty's fiancé had moved in with them and taught him. Justin showed him how to bleach his whites that had faded into that terrible grayish blah color when he tossed everything in together.

"Laundry is a lot different than traveling for almost twenty-four hours to a foreign country by yourself." Zack paced. "What if something happens before you get on the plane?"

Jordon glared at him. "Zack, I'm twenty years old."

"You're too trusting…," Zack said as if the cryptic code couldn't be cracked.

"I was sixteen and stupid. Going to meet a stranger off the internet like that… was the dumbest thing I've ever done." A ripple of terror echoed through him as all the horrid possibilities raced through his mind of what might have happened.

"You have no idea." Zack's voice broke a little, and pain could be seen in the haunted look in his eyes before he shuttered the expression away behind a glare.

When Jordon had gotten that weird feeling of wrongness and tried to back out of going to the guy's house, the guy hadn't taken the change of plans well. Thank God, Zack had followed him. There had been no doubt the man would have done much more than give Jordon a black eye. "I'm grateful you rescued me, but nothing is going to happen."

"And what if I'm not there, and something happens?" Zack folded his arms.

"If there's an emergency, I'll dial 911. I'm capable of staying on my own for two days. I've got deadlines and one painting I need to finish before I go or it will never get done." Being alone might help Jordon focus on his project, and maybe give him time to figure out the changes he needed to make in his life.

His brothers were great and always there as his safety net. Jordon never had to lift a finger. He was grateful he never went without, but maybe that was the problem. They took care of everything, and he'd let them. "It's just a couple of days."

Dusty studied him and let out a long exhale. "If you're sure, I'll have your ticket changed. You can follow us in two days."

He saluted Dusty. "Fantastic. Thanks."

"This is totally a terrible idea, Dust." Zack could drone on all he wanted; Dusty had the final say.

Jordon couldn't help but flash Zack a victory smirk as he stole the perfect chip off Zack's plate.

A LITTLE after midnight Jordon waved goodbye to his brothers and Justin as they headed for the airport.

Alone at last. It was the first time in years Jordon had been outside of a five-mile radius of his brothers' reach.

Amazing how liberating freedom felt—no one to disappoint… no expectations. He could do things the way he wanted.

The hours slipped away into days of drawing and painting.

Now Jordon stood outside his house. His BFF would be taking him to the airport. He and Gwendolyn Carrow had hit it off when they'd met in an art class.

Jordon tugged on his hood and checked his phone. Maybe he should text Gwen again? She might have forgotten the gate code.

No need. His bestie pulled her silver Camry into Dusty's driveway.

Jordon wheeled his luggage to the back of her car. "Gwen to the rescue. You're a lifesaver."

She jumped out and popped the trunk. "That's what best friends are for. Hiding bodies and trips to the airport."

"Thanks." He tossed his two bags into the car, then hugged her.

She pulled back and peered at his suitcases. "Um… is this all?"

He studied the trunk. "Yup, two bags. Not that I want to give Zack's boyfriend—"

"You mean Master," she added ever so helpfully.

He glared at the reminder. "Whatever the hell the guy is to my brother, I don't want to give him too much credit. But those packing cubes were hella impressive. The number of things I was able to pack—geez, when everything was rolled, contained, and stored in zippered cubes—defied logic."

"We can talk about your new packing fetish later." Gwen shook her head. "My question is where's your carry-on stuff, your travel sketch pad, your laptop, your iPad, your chargers—"

"Shit!" He ran back into the house, grabbed his knapsack, locked the door, and jumped into the car.

"Passport?" She fiddled with the radio.

"I—shit!" Slamming the car door felt good. He stomped back toward the house.

"And don't forget to rearm your brother's alarm system," she called out.

Dammit. No wonder his brothers felt he needed a keeper—he did. No, he needed to remember what his therapist said about how change is a number of small steps. "Thanks, I will," he called over his shoulder.

He found his passport next to where his knapsack had been. Zack must have put it there so Jordon wouldn't forget. He reset the alarm and trudged back to the car.

Again.

"Thanks, Gwen." He tucked his passport into his pocket.

"Welcome. Anything you need." She put her finger out to stop his probably too predictable quip. "Except a blowjob."

"Then why do you offer *anything*?" He feigned the exasperation their interaction required.

"I'm surprised your brothers didn't arrange a car for you." She zipped out of the compound and down the road.

He shrugged. "I told them not to bother. I'd take care of it."

Stopping at the red light gave her too much time to throw a judgmental glare in his direction before she continued down the road. "And you decided not to arrange transportation until three hours before your flight?"

"I was working on a piece… and I had to finish it."

"I get it. Sometimes I—" Gwen rolled down her window and screamed at the car that passed her, "Next time you ride my ass like that, make sure you pull my hair, and you better have used a condom."

Jordon snorted. "You're too funny. Control your—wait, aren't you wearing the same clothes you wore yesterday when I FaceTimed you?"

She glanced down. "Um, yeah. Why?"

"Slut." God, he wished he could be more like her.

"I prefer *sexually expressive*. And why the fuck is it 'good job' if a guy scores, and when I do, I'm a slut? Sexist, much?" She tightened her hands on the wheel.

"Um?" *Good damned question.* "You're right. I'm sorry."

"Yeah, well, fuck you and society's version of acceptable gender roles."

She flared all hot oranges and fiery reds. The exact colors he craved. Dammit, not for the first time, Jordon asked, "Why can't you have a dick? It's such a waste."

"Excuse me? *Waste*? Let me assure you my multiple orgasms reinforce in my mind what's down there is no *waste*."

Jordon put his hands up in surrender. Now he remembered why he didn't say that! "Sorry. I know. I haven't slept, and I'm just… bitter."

"What do you have to be bitter about?" She didn't scoff; she asked like she cared.

"I'm twenty, and what do I have to show for it?"

After stopping at a Stop sign, she turned to give him her wide-eyed "are you insane?" stare. One she used often enough to make him question how off-base she actually was in her assessment. She made a left turn. "Honey, you're a successful artist. You're young, beautiful, and you travel the world with a freaking rock band. Get a grip."

"Eh, successful artist." Right, but he'd had no relationships. Monks probably had more experience than he did. His life appeared great, but he felt like he was in shambles and exhausted by wanting something he probably wouldn't ever get.

"You are. Though I don't get why you don't simply tell your brothers about Sakura Rose."

Yeah, right. Tell his brothers he'd been publishing not only the Dark Angels manga but several series in Japan under the name Sakura Rose? "Not in this lifetime."

"Why not? You're an adult. What will they do? Ground you?"

He glared at her for making valid points. His fear of telling his brothers might be stupid, but it undoubtedly paralyzed him. "No, but.... Look, I've been publishing under SR since I was, like, sixteen, and they'll want to know why I didn't tell them before."

"So?"

He sighed. His brothers were everything to him. "It's dumb, but knowing I've kept a secret like that would hurt them."

His oldest brother, Dusty, would get that apologetic look for being an inadequate guardian, and then he'd give Jordon a sad smile as if his feelings were irrelevant. Not even in a martyrish way, but a real, sliced-to-the-soul way. And Zack, he'd kill him. Jesus, Zack would be pissed, and yell at him. Then—

No, he needed to put the brakes on his guilt and inject reality into his narrative.

Zack would not kill him. Dusty might be hurt, but perhaps it could lead into a real discussion among all of them. A talk they should have had years ago.

At the next red light, she rolled to a stop and shook her head. "Okay, but if you don't tell them, how do you plan to get to that publisher event? Are you going to slip away and go to Japan for a weekend?"

"Fuck if I know."

"Look, you made the commitment, said you'd be there." *Queen of the Freaking Obvious might point out the sky is blue and the grass is green next.*

"Maybe I can back out, tell 'em I'm sick or something." *Sick of being a wuss, maybe.*

"Dude, you're not a little kid anymore. You've got to live your own life." Gwen threw reality at him as if he wanted some.

"I know." Somehow his brothers had this way of keeping him a little kid.

Gwen yelled at a metallic red sports car that zipped in front of her extremely close, "There are restrooms at the mall, but I hope they're closed and you pee your pants."

Jordon snorted. "What the fuck was that?"

"I try to give bad drivers a reason for their poor decisions so I get less mad."

Jordon hated to point out the truth, but…. "It doesn't look like it's working."

"Nah, it totally is." Gwen smirked and then scrunched her face. "Hey, if you've been publishing since you were sixteen, how do your brothers not know? I mean just with taxes and such."

"By the time I was actually published, my first check came after my eighteenth birthday."

"Wow, long time." She rolled to another traffic light. "So you deal with all the Japanese tax stuff?"

Jordon shook his head. "Nah, I hired an accounting company to deal with all the nonsense. Math is hard."

"Tell me about it." The light turned green, Gwen started driving again. "Anyway, I'm going to make a prediction you will get your cherry popped."

"OMG! Don't be gross."

"What? You're going to find someone great. I just know it." Gwen, if nothing else, was persistent.

"Sure." Lots of men wanted someone with no interest in fucking or being fucked, only in sucking, hand jobs, and cuddling. If it got out, the rainbow community would take away his gay card.

"Hey, you know I know things."

He rolled his eyes at the reference to her self-proclaimed psychic abilities and changed the subject. "Whatever. Tell me about last night's one-night stand?"

She put her hands at the ten and two positions on the steering wheel, started looking at all her mirrors, and acted as earnest as a first-year driver. "We're almost at the airport."

"Is this avoidance? Tell me." Had he been so absorbed in his own shit he'd missed hers?

"Whatever." Snarkish responses and her red cheeks added up to something.

Jordon fished. "Maybe last night wasn't a one-time thing?"

She shrugged.

"What? So is he your boyfriend or something?" Jordon didn't approve. Who was this guy, and why didn't she tell him?

"*Boyfriend* is a juvenile term. He's my lover."

"Ew, Gwen! Lover? I just threw up in my mouth. All joking aside… that word is gross."

They both giggled.

"I know, right?" She groaned. "But what do I call him? My man-friend, male companion, maybe my—"

"Is it serious?" His therapist would identify this creepy crawly feeling slithering through him as fear of abandonment.

"Look, I don't know. I've been seeing him for a while, Jordon. I didn't think it was a big deal, but now I really like him."

"Him or his cock?"

After a long pause, she frowned at him, then admitted, "Both, but if I had to pick, I'd choose him."

"Wow." She was serious. The sliver of fear expanded. Would he be replaced? He didn't know what to say. But this was a fraction of how his brothers would feel if they found out he'd kept a secret for years. Betrayed.

"Hey, Jordie. You know I love you, and you'll be my bestest friend always no matter who I'm boning." Her sincerity broke through his worry.

"Yeah, yeah. I know you. Attached or not, I still expect to drive you to the sex shops when I'm eighty-eight, and he better not have any problems with that." Jordon tried to sound tough, but his laughter ruined the effect as he pictured the scene he'd described illustrated on a manga storyboard.

"Of course he won't. I promise I'll be there to point out new flavors of lube for your harem of boy toys."

"I don't want a harem, just one man who loves me, you know? Why is that so fucking hard to come by?" He didn't mean to get depressingly dramatic on her.

"It'll happen."

"Gwen, I don't know what the fuck is wrong with me." He wasn't terrible-looking. Hell, he was actually pretty cute. Though most of the men he'd met were interested in bagging the brother of the Dark Angels' drummer and not Jordon. They wanted to be close to a star, nothing more.

She pulled into the Albany airport. "I'm telling you, start putting yourself out there."

"Oh my God! Remember the last time you dragged me out?"

"You mean the one time six months ago? When you used me as a shield against any potentials interested in either of us, I might add. Yes, I recall the stock of Energizer spiked due to all your cockblocking." She'd bitched at him and made him buy her a thirty-six pack of AA batteries.

"Are you going to tell me I just need to believe and 'it gets better'?"

Her glare had a sting to it. "Fuck you, and yeah. It does."

"Sorry. Look, I'm happy for you, and what's his name?"

"Haru."

"He's Japanese?"

"Yeah. Keep in mind I don't like most people, and I adore you."

"Of course you do. Everyone does." Except Jordon's mother and any guy he'd ever been interested in.

She ignored him. "Hey, even though someone else may be added to my shortlist doesn't mean I love you less."

Damn, when she put it that way, he sounded insecure, immature, and foolish. He opted for the classic Han Solo response. "I know."

She rolled her eyes and laughingly told him, "Fuck you."

He scoffed. "You said we couldn't." In truth, he'd been tempted to try something between them, but she'd been smart enough to stop them.

"Oh please! You're gay, and I'd make a terrible man. I'd come in six strokes, and without the benefit of multiple orgasms, my partners would be quite annoyed."

Jordon cackled. "You'd so roll over after you came, wouldn't you?"

"Hey! Um, well if I could only come once, yeah, probably." She pulled to a stop along the airport curb.

He jumped out of the car.

She went to the trunk and popped it open. "Text me as soon as your SIM card is swapped out for a Chinese one."

Pulling her into a tight hug, he reassured them both, "I will. And tell Haru he'd better treat you right."

"He does."

"Good." Jordon sniffed and geared up to say something sappy and stupid.

"You're nervous about flying alone. I don't blame you. It's a long flight, but suck it up, my friend." Gwen helped him with his bags.

"That's what I said." He extended his luggage handles and slung his knapsack over his shoulder.

She snorted. "I hate you."

"I love you too." He blew her a kiss.

"Jackass." She glared at him. "Passport?"

He patted his pocket. "Right here, bitch... and I use the term in a purely non-gender-specific but absolutely insulting way."

Grinning, she kissed his cheek. "You are trainable. Now go."

He rolled his bags through the terminal door and waved to her once more.

I can do this. The Albany airport's small size made finding the airline desk simple. He stepped into the business-class line.

The ticket agent gave him a questioning "do you belong in the elite line" once-over. He stood his ground on the red carpet with a smile.

She waved him forward.

Jordon pulled out his phone and showed his boarding pass. He even remembered to hand over his passport too. Points. He was totally capable of handling his life.

She stared at his cell and pulled her fiery red glasses dangling on a chain into service. Pointing to the cell phone's screen, she asked, "May I see the ticket for today?"

"What? That's my ticket." He snatched his cell back and stared at the date. *Son of a*—How could this be?

"I'm sorry, but the date of this ticket is yesterday's, sir."

Late by an entire day. How did he do that? Zack and Dusty were going to kill him when they found out. Neither thought Jordon able to travel to Shanghai without them.

Shit, a quick time check showed his original plane wouldn't arrive in Shanghai for another three hours. With the time difference, they didn't even know he'd missed the flight. He would text them as soon as he dealt with this mess. Staying calm, he channeled his eldest brother. "Okay, how do I get to Shanghai?"

She stared at the screen and clicked around. "Well, you can take the same itinerary, although I'm afraid business class is sold out on the Newark to Shanghai flight."

He shrugged. "That's okay. I'll do first class, then."

Her focus remained on the screen longer than seemed good. "I'm so sorry, sir. On today's Newark to Shanghai flight, there is no first-class cabin. All we have left are seats in economy."

"Okay. I'll take an aisle seat in the back. Is there a chance there's a row that's free?" He added a smile and held out his frequent-flyer card. This was no big deal. He'd make the best of the situation.

"I'm sorry, there are no aisle or window seats. It's almost completely booked. On the Newark to Shanghai leg, I have only three middle seats left."

Oh no. Full stop. Changing gears, he worked on keeping the frustration out of his voice. "Um, what about tomorrow?"

"I can get you to Newark, but the flight to Shanghai is oversold in all cabins."

What the heck? "Next day?"

She clicked. And clicked. And clicked. Every shake of her head crushed his hopes further. "I could get you there in three days if you went through—"

He held out his hand. "That's okay. I'll take a middle seat."

The keyboard clicks pecked into his brain, as did her cheery "Newark to Shanghai is only fourteen hours and fifty-five minutes, barring any delays."

He accepted the paper ticket and waited for the attendant to tag his bags through to Shanghai. They'd probably be more comfortable than him.

"Gate A6, sir. Have a good flight."

"Thanks." *Not bloody likely.*

He checked the time on his phone. The original flight he should have been on would be landing in a few hours. Even though he'd told his brothers not to, someone would be at the airport to greet him.

Better get this over with so he could prevent them from an unnecessary trip to the airport. He'd text both Zack and Dusty.

I'm going to be a day later than originally expected. He signed with an artist emoji. When in doubt, blame the art.

An immediate *What?* from Zack and a *R U OK?* from Dusty.

He typed, *Yes.*

Why aren't U on a plane? Zack demanded, as if Jordon wasn't twenty freaking years old.

I'll be there tomorrow the same time.

Dusty asked, *Did you miss the flight yesterday?*

Sigh. So much for avoidance. *Yeah.*

Zack texted, *Did you forget what time you were flying or what day it was?*

He hated the fact he could hear his incompetence and their worry in the words. *All of the above.*

Dammit, he needed to get a grip on his life. *C U soon.* He signed with an angel-haloed dog and trudged over to security.

Though if he thought about this situation, it could be viewed as a success. He encountered a problem and dealt. Not the greatest outcome but the best available. He was going to count it as a win.

The Albany flight landed late, so Jordon ran through Newark's airport to board the flight to Shanghai.

"Um, hi. That's my seat." He pointed to the middle seat between two very large men.

The guy on the aisle huffed, "Of course it is. I can't believe business was sold out."

Jordon sandwiched himself into his place, which was half-taken by the man who already appeared to be sleeping against the window.

Seat-belted in, he reviewed the safety card and imagined how pleased Dusty would be by his caution.

Bing! "This is Captain Morse. I'm sorry to inform you we need to hang tight at the gate. There's some minor repairs required. I'll turn off the Fasten Seat Belt sign for now, but I also have to cut power to the air-conditioning. You might want to shut your window shades to keep the sun out for the time being. I'll be back when I know the estimated push-back time."

A Chinese translation followed.

After two hours, numerous complaints to the unsympathetic flight attendant by his row mates, and a rise of twenty degrees, a *bing* echoed through the cabin. "The ground crew did their fixes. However, they discovered a few other issues. Though the good news is we have the air back on, and we should be pushing back within the hour."

Groans and feet stomping shook the cabin. Jordon tried not to long for the space and comfort of business class. Not to mention a delicious bottomless flute of the fresh-squeezed orange juice they probably handed out.

Forty-five minutes later and *bing!* "Hello, this is your captain. I'm sorry. We must deplane. Our crew can't fly due to time restrictions the delay has given us. The new captain and crew are on their way, though we may be getting another aircraft as well. So please deplane, take all your personal items, but do stay in the boarding area for instructions."

Jordon unfolded himself and stretched. He traipsed up the Jetway and found space near an outlet. He collapsed on the floor, waiting for the man with four devices plugged in to allow him to use some power. His phone battery showed 45 percent.

After several hours, Jordon had finished three pictures. One picture was a straight sketch of the plane, and the other two were more of a manga style. He drew one of him crunched into the middle seat, trying to draw with his elbows touching, and the other was of him happily piloting the plane. He signed each of them *To My Future Husband With Love, Jordon.*

He'd just finished signing the last picture when the announcement finally requested that passengers get in line to reboard the plane.

Ten years must have passed, but Jordon was back on the plane, sandwiched between two new seatmates. *Bing!* "This is Captain Dorsay. Sorry for the maintenance kerfuffle, but as soon as you're in your seats, we can get out of here. We're number seven in line for takeoff."

Jordon didn't scream when number seven stretched into number thirteen. He just took out his iPad.

> *Dear Future Husband,*
>
> *I'm a fuckup. Here I sit on a plane I should have been on yesterday. But I'm so dependent on other people to tell me what to do I didn't look at my ticket, and if I'm honest, I didn't even know what day of the week the flight was or what day it actually was. Maybe this is why my therapist said I needed to take responsibility for my life. She also said I should trust myself; clearly my abilities are lacking.*
>
> *(I just deleted seven paragraphs of whining. I'm going to stop doing that.)*
>
> *No more. I'm going to get a grip of my life. I handled this problem on my own and lived to tell, but it's time I became independent. I want to be the best person I can be before I meet you.*
>
> *Right now, this is the start of a new Jordon. I'm going to be ready when we meet.*
>
> *Lots of Love,*
> *Your Future Husband*

CHAPTER 4

WHERE WAS the idiot? Why would Indigo simply disappear? Made in China had a show in a few hours. Things were finally happening for the band, and the selfish jackass had taken off.

Tian Di hit every bar open in daylight, searching for Indigo. Time for one last-ditch effort. One more stop before heading home to work on a Plan B. Plan B, what he'd do while his hopes and dreams crawled away to die? He walked into the Biergarten.

The asshole sat on the barstool, sipping some pink drink, spinning a little umbrella as if he wasn't destroying Tian Di's chances at a real life. Strangling the band's leader was probably a bad idea but wringing Indigo's neck would feel great.

Tian Di slid onto the stool next to the prick. "What are you doing here?"

Indigo wiped his face, but he still had enough attitude to roll his eyes. He took a swig of whatever was in the glass. "What does it look like I'm doing?"

Indigo Young spoke perfect Mandarin, but his American accent and formal words were hard to follow at times, even for someone from Hong Kong. Though if Tian Di were honest, he didn't make much of an effort; mostly he tried to annoy the Los Angeles transplant not understand him.

"When did you start drinking at noon? We're playing tonight. The Dark Angels and their management will be arriving in a couple of days." If the three little parasols turned over were the number of pink drinks Indigo had, Tian Di would be carrying the asshole home.

Indigo shrugged.

Was strangling him a crime or justifiable homicide? "Some of us don't have a trust fund along with a father who will bail us out of our mistakes," Tian Di growled.

"Fuck you. I've earned my bank account with my royalties off the songs I wrote and composed. And please, spare me the pauper-by-choice act." Indigo's words held none of the venom Tian Di had come to expect.

This was an issue. Indigo might be a self-centered asshole, but he was dead-serious and band-focused when it came to their music. "Come on, Indigo. Did you forget? Tonight is our first night back since *Knock Your Socks Off* aired."

Indigo sniffed and glanced away from his drink. "Li separated the beds in our room."

"So? You two fight all the time." Tian Di knew this because his room was across the hall from theirs. Their makeup sex was rough enough to knock pictures off his wall.

"He never put space between us like this... not since I was old enough to be fucked." Indigo spun the pink parasol.

"You'll make up." Right? They would. They had to.

"You don't know how stubborn Li can be." A small bitter laugh came out with the slurred words. "Do you know, he wouldn't touch me until I wasn't jailbait in the USA? I kept saying in China the age of consent is fourteen, but he wouldn't lay a finger on me... and I made it difficult."

"I bet you did." Tian Di didn't know the full meaning of *age of consent* or *jailbait*, and he wouldn't ask. Though he could only imagine the drama, begging, and seduction a younger version of Indigo would pull.

"He kept saying he didn't want to take my virginity." Indigo shook his head. "I was tempted to lose it with someone else just so he wouldn't have the excuse, but—"

"Why do you sleep with other men?" It made zero sense to Tian Di. If he could find a good man, whom he loved and who loved him back, he'd never want other people.

"I don't *sleep* with anyone but Li."

There was no time to sort the tea leaves. "You know what I mean."

"You mean have sex with other men. I want to keep the excitement." Indigo slurped more of the pink liquid.

"Sounds more like you're keeping the misery."

"No, but Li—"

"*Shǎguā*! He doesn't want other people." Much to Tian Di's disappointment. There had been a time when he would have been pleased to show Li that not all men were total jackasses like the American in front of him.

Some men wanted monogamy and a true love to share everything life threw at them. Hopefully, after he'd established his career and could live in a place with more acceptance, he could have that. Unless Indigo screwed up his chances.

Indigo tilted his head and grinned. "Why'd you call me a melon?"

"You've got the intellect of one. It means you're a fool." Tian Di texted Jin, who'd tell Li and Styx: *I found him. We'll be there tonight.*

Indigo snorted. "Chinese insults are da bomb. They're so stupid."

"You're incredibly insulting. It's—"

"No." Laughing, Indigo shook his head and threw his hands in front of him. "No. Stupid means good. It's slang."

Tian Di promised himself he would never ask if this was similar to taking back slur words, because he didn't care. "Well, saying something is stupid sounds rude."

"Okay. Okay, but I'm paying China a compliment. What's that one insult? Oh yeah, *thirteen o'clock.* That's just a brilliant way to say someone is crazy."

"Whatever." Tian Di would never admit to loving the simplicity of *whatever. Whatever* felt good to say and was the perfect dismissal.

His cell pinged with Jin's text: *Good. Counting on you.*

They were all counting on one another. Without one of them, Made in China was like a pile of rice with no sack.

"Right, whatever." Indigo dragged out the words.

Tian Di pushed the drink away from Indigo's reach. "You're slurring your words."

"I. Am. Not." Indigo enunciated every syllable. "I'm speaking in cursive… and I'm not a melon."

He needed to stay angry at Indigo. "Yeah, you are. I remember what you're like when you drink."

"I rarely drink." Indigo wagged a finger at him.

"Night we first met, you were drunk, and you still don't quite remember what an asshole you were, do you?" Maybe Tian Di did like to taunt Indigo.

Indigo frowned and shook his head. He traced his fingers along Tian Di's leg. "I remember most of it. Hey, maybe you're interested in—"

Tian Di slapped Indigo's hand away from his thigh. "Hands off."

"Come on, maybe that's why you're so uptight. You never get any." Indigo offered sex like one would a handshake.

"I don't want *just* anyone." Tian Di understood why some men didn't look for love. Sex was hard enough to come by, especially for a gay man in China. But he was done settling.

Argh! Indigo's wide eyes and open mouth told Tian Di he'd said way too much. Hopefully, Indigo's drunkenness would prevent the memory from sticking. Tian Di didn't need someone reminding him he didn't have much hope of finding what he wanted. He was in a soon-to-be-famous rock band in Asia. It wasn't like he could afford any kind of attachments that would work against him right now.

His pile of mangas, accompanied by his hand, worked well enough. He bottled the emptiness that mode of operation created and used the absence of happiness in his music.

Indigo rested a heavy hand on Tian Di's shoulder, drawing his attention back. "You just haven't found the right guy… guys. Me and Li could—"

"Right now, there is no you and Li, which is why you're sitting here crying into your flowery pink drink." Maybe that was too harsh.

"Hey, crying doesn't make you less of a man unless your mascara runs, and I'm not wearing any right now." Indigo attempted to chuckle, but the sound caught in his throat. He ducked his head and stared at the floor. "What am I going to do?"

Tian Di couldn't take him back to the apartment yet, in case Li wasn't ready to accept the apology for whatever the asshole had done. "You're going to get sober and come to the nail salon with me."

Indigo slid off the stool. Tian Di steadied him while Indigo tossed several hundred yuan notes on the table.

Tian Di waved to the bartender. "See you tonight."

When Tian Di headed for the boardwalk instead of the street, Indigo asked, "We're walking?"

"Saving on taxi money, and it's a nice day. Not too humid." The sun played peek-a-boo behind the clouds, and the exercise might help move the alcohol out of Indigo's system.

They trudged along the boardwalk around Jinji Lake. Water lapped under the planks, blooming white and pink lotus on one side and big fat goldfish surfacing every few meters to beg for food on the other.

Indigo stopped and stared at the horizon. "Suzhou has grown so much since I've been here. Tall skyscrapers and residential apartments pop up weekly. It's amazing."

Tian Di shrugged. "China has a long-term plan, and the country wants to meet it."

Indigo's movements seemed in control.

Directing Indigo off the boardwalk, Tian Di guided him to a footpath that cut to the sidewalk. Cars, trucks, scooters, and bicycles zipped by on the busy road.

Indigo sighed again, slumping over.

Tian Di couldn't hold his tongue and had to ask, "Why do you want so many other men, Indigo? Li is a great guy. Why isn't he enough for you?"

"That's not it at all. I know how this works." Indigo touched his chest. "Born and raised in LA, with a gay dad, and uncles that changed every season."

"Uncles?"

"My dad would never stay with one guy for very long. He'd get bored, and the uncles disappeared." Indigo shook his head. "I don't want Li to replace me."

"You're not exchangeable." Tian Di would never have guessed Indigo could ever think like that.

He laughed, which ended in a sniff. "That's what my father said when I asked if he'd get rid of me someday too. 'You're not exchangeable. You're my son. I only get one of you.'"

There was too much pain in Indigo's tone. Tian Di couldn't help but try to reassure him. "Not everyone's like that in relationships."

Indigo kicked a stone off the sidewalk. "I can't take the chance. I'm determined to maintain the excitement."

How could he convince Indigo of such a basic thing? "You do know this isn't America."

"Hell, yeah. I notice every damned day," Indigo snarled.

"Well, you know *they* can't be loud and proud here." Tian Di felt the need to point out the obvious.

"They? Tian Di, do you even consider yourself Chinese?"

Out of paranoia—*thank you, Mother*—Tian Di was forced to make sure no one was around to overhear the answer. "Look, I was born in Hong Kong a few years before it was returned to China. I was raised by people who didn't consider Hong Kong to be a part of China. But I do love China."

"Hard to push the genie back into the bottle?"

What? Tian Di lowered his voice. "There's an us-and-them mentality. The stereotype of mainlanders is they're uncivilized, uncultured, and uneducated. Many mainlanders think people from Hong Kong are spoiled by years of democracy and aren't patriotic."

"Never thought of it like that. Do you have problems here?" Indigo asked.

"Not really, but my family hates that I live here. Anyway, that's where the *them* comment came from. But what I was trying to explain is gay people in China are still mostly in a closet because being gay was illegal in China until 1997. It was only in 2001 that the official mental illness list removed homosexuality."

"Yeah, it's one of the reasons my dad left. The police would harass anyone who didn't have the money to pay them off, and at that time he couldn't." Indigo shook his head. "I don't know the whole story, but it was bad for him here."

"Hong Kong isn't much better. In some ways, worse." Tian Di tried not to careen down tragedy lane. He didn't want to relive the trauma of being beaten for being too girly or having a teacher try to take advantage of him. He avoided dwelling on his two unhealthy relationships of the past and a string of meaningless one-off encounters. What was the point of focusing on being a fish trapped in a dry wheel track?

"Is that why you left?"

It was Tian Di's turn to shrug. "One of the men I'd gotten involved with had a lot of influence with the clubs looking for singers. When things ended, he had me blacklisted."

"Fuck, you were blacklisted?"

"It wasn't difficult." Tian Di gestured to himself. "One look at me and the club owners knew the rumors he spread about me had to be true. Bands stopped auditioning me, so I decided to try the mainland."

"Why didn't you just go to America?"

"The plan was to get noticed and get management to help me get there. Immigration is easier when you have the help of a label or agent working on your behalf." He had no clue why he shared this with Indigo.

"Yeah, that's what Li said too."

"There's a lot of walls you need to scale to escape." And they usually felt insurmountable.

"I know." Indigo sighed. "I guess I've had a lot of privilege. I lived in a bubble, and I've never felt this kind of repression. It feels intense to me, like China's this big-assed closet without a door and—"

"Exactly. Keep that in mind the next time you push Li for public affection. This is where Li grew up, so don't judge him by Western standards. You saw the struggle Jin and Styx had, and even now they've got to be careful. You can't imagine what it's like to think there's something really wrong with you or that you're the only guy in the world who likes other guys."

"My dad couldn't stand living here in hiding." Indigo smacked the crosswalk button.

"Well, some of us don't have the luxury of choice."

Indigo groaned. "Yeah, I know."

They trudged the rest of the way to the nail place in silence. When they arrived, Tian Di held the door for Indigo.

Indigo read the sign aloud, "Lotus Nail Salon," as he brushed past Tian Di and entered.

The muted gray of the walls, floor, and ceiling encompassed Tian Di in tranquility. Natural light poured in, filtered only by the sheer white curtains making the line of eight black pedicure chairs and eight black lacquer nail stations gleam. Photos and paintings of lotus blossoms provided the only color, except for the tiers of nail polish bottles, arranged in order by color, making a vivid rainbow.

Silence. The soft melody of conversation stopped. The six women who sat in massage chairs for pedicures stopped talking. The two getting their finger nails done turned and stared. Everything came to a halt. The nail techs stared at them like they were an intruding horde.

No matter how many times Tian Di came to this salon, they hadn't gotten used to a man wanting his nails done. Sometimes it was more intense than being onstage because he had no microphone to hide behind.

Several of the Western women whispered to their nail techs and then to one another. Finally a tanned blonde with a heavy Australian accent asked, "Are you two in *that* band?"

"Made in China?" Indigo supplied in English.

A cute tiny woman with a Korean accent said in English, "Oh, yeah. That's where I recognize you from. The German restaurant on the lake, what's it called… the Biergarten."

The salon owner guided Indigo and Tian Di to the nail tables, announcing, "And their band was just on that show, *Knock Your Socks Off.*"

This announcement was met with clapping, and squealing women pulled Indigo out of his funk, forcing him into a kind of normalcy. He spoke in English. "We're very excited for all the breaks Made in China has been given and could have in the very near future."

The woman with the Australian accent pressed him. "I keep hearing rumors. Who exactly is the band in talks with?"

A nail tech said in uncertain English, "I hear the Dark Angels come here to make tour...."

Whether caused by the alcohol still in his system or strategy, Indigo gasped. "You heard about that?"

That was all the admission the women needed.

Indigo turned on his megawatt smile. "I hope you'll join us tonight at the German restaurant."

All the women nodded.

One woman told Indigo, "I'm going to bring my husband and two women he works with from Sweden."

"I look forward to seeing you in the audience." Indigo gave her a bright smile.

The savvy detective among the group said, "Google says the Dark Angels tour will begin in Shanghai. Is that true?"

Everyone looked to Indigo.

He nodded enthusiastically. "I can't confirm or deny this."

The Sherlock Holmes of the group started typing into her phone, and a few clicks later, she announced, "The tickets just went live this morning. I'm getting mine."

Several women pulled out their phones and busied themselves.

Indigo flashed him a mischievous smile. Ah, a confirmation he played to wrangle in more fans.

Tian Di's nail tech asked, "What instrument do you play?"

He tried to call the expected blush to his cheeks and shyness to his voice. "I'm the lead singer."

The nail tech squealed, "That's great." She sat a little higher in her chair and glanced at the other techs like she ruled over them. "He's the singer."

Indigo leaned in and whispered, "Face?"

"Correct."

Indigo nodded.

Maybe Indigo was finally getting the concept. He'd sat through several lectures on the concept of face. The band tried to give Indigo an understanding that face wasn't about only saving one's dignity. One could give face to a person by allowing them the honor of doing a favor or service for someone deemed important.

Indigo pointed to his nail tech's name badge. "Your name is Mary?"

"My English name is Mary," she replied as she batted her eyelashes at him.

"English name?" Indigo asked in English.

The nail tech looked at Tian Di and said in Mandarin, "Explain to your friend."

"Many people who work in the service industry, such as nails, tanning, hair, restaurants, and hotels, all take on an English name so their customers can say it."

"Hmmm." Indigo smiled at his nail tech. "But what's your real name?"

"Ai," she said low, glancing at the owner, who was more focused on playing Minesweeper on her computer than running the business.

"Pretty. That means lovable?"

"Correct." Mary refocused on Indigo's nails.

As a woman whose English name was Jennifer buffed Tian Di's manicured nails, Indigo grinned. "I guess this is why you're the only one with decent nails in the band."

He nodded. "Usually I visit Lotus once a month."

His technician asked, "Do you want color or a little flower?"

Indigo turned his head.

Tian Di spoke slowly. "Yes, a small lotus on the thumb. Your flowers are perfect, Jennifer."

Indigo asked, "Why are you speaking English?"

"Jennifer likes to practice her English."

Mary massaged Indigo's hand with citrus lotion and asked him, "Do you want any shine or design?"

"Nah, just black polish." After gasps echoed around the room, Indigo grinned at the other patrons and stated, "I'm a true rocker."

The Australian lady who was paying for her nails exclaimed, "Whoop! Damn right you are. I'll be there tonight."

The other women echoed the sentiment of attending tonight's show. Tian Di said quietly, "We would be very pleased to have you."

His sister would have been proud of him, as three of the ladies fanned themselves, while his mom would have started to plan a wedding.

Once he and Indigo left the nail salon, Indigo hailed a cab to take them back to the apartment.

"Hey, thanks for this afternoon. I know you think I'm an ass most of the time, but I appreciate you."

"You're welcome." Tian Di slipped into the cab, careful not to rip the seat's pleather further.

"If there's anything you can do to help me patch things with Li, I'd be grateful," Indigo said in English, probably to avoid being understood by the driver.

When no sleazy double entendre followed, Tian Di believed the sincerity. He answered back in English, "You've got to stop dragging other people into your physical relationship."

"But Li—"

"Li doesn't need or want that. If you don't, then just stop."

The taxi pulled into their apartment complex, and the gate opened. Indigo paid the driver, and they took the elevator to their private entryway.

Indigo kicked off his shoes and rushed barefoot through the apartment door.

Tian Di slipped into his plain red slippers with dragon heads that he parked near the bubbling fountain in the corner.

"Oh… I guess you do like my nails." Indigo chuckled.

Tian Di entered the apartment in time to see Li manhandle Indigo into their room, and called out, "Hey, remember we've got a show tonight."

Indigo poked his head out. "We know. We'll—"

Midsentence Indigo vanished. The door slammed shut, and the bolt engaged a moment later. Scraping of what sounded like beds being pushed together followed a long moan.

Crash! Indigo's broken "Yes!" floated through the door.

Smiling, Tian Di said, "Well, I guess they're making up."

Styx grabbed the DVD remote. The apartment filled with the sound of loud rock and roll.

Jin grinned and gave him a thumbs-up. He glanced at his cell phone. "I think there's time for a bath before the show." Jin strutted toward his room with a noticeable twitch to his hips.

Tian Di had never seen Styx so red.

"I'm… I… um…." Styx's didn't even spare Tian Di a look. Instead he focused on Jin.

"We've got two hours before we need to—" Styx vanished before Tian Di even finished his thought.

Panting loud enough to hear during the breaks of the pounding drums coming through the stereo propelled Tian Di into his own room. Maybe he had time to read a few mangas. He pulled out his favorite

Sakura Rose and some hand cream, unbuckled his belt, and slid down his zipper. Time to relax before the show.

TWO AND a half hours later, Made in China sound-checked their instruments at the German restaurant.

Sebe rushed in and waved them over. The restaurant owner's son took his role of Made in China's management a bit too seriously at times. He was only a teenager but became a force of nature that mowed down everything in his path if it didn't help the band get to where he believed they were headed.

"What the hell? Sebe, we got to finish setting up," Indigo growled in English.

The teen pointed to the closed stage curtains. "The Dark Angels are here. Here. Right now. They'll be in the back."

"Say what now?" Indigo still hadn't stopped grinning nor did he bother to cover the fresh suck mark on his neck from his makeup session with Li. He rushed over to the edge of the curtain and pulled it back enough to see the audience.

"They aren't supposed to be here yet," Styx pointed out the obvious.

Indigo ducked his head back and pushed the curtain to the wall. He nodded as he rejoined the group. "The kid's right. The Dark Angels are sitting in the back corner on the right side."

Tian Di's stomach tightened like he had taken a punch. "Guess they got here earlier than expected."

"Yeah, like days early." Jin pressed his lips together. *Good idea.* Tian Di mimicked the motion to keep his guts inside.

Styx put a hand on Jin's shoulder, either to comfort him or to keep himself upright, because Styx didn't look all that steady on his feet.

Li adjusted the strap on his bass. "If we open for them, they'll hear us play a lot. It's not a big deal."

Indigo stepped in and waved everyone into a formation he called a huddle. "We got this. They wouldn't have asked us to be a part of the tour if we weren't incredible. Styx, your drumming is tight. Li and Jin, your strings will take us anywhere we need to go. And Tian Di, your range is wider than Angel Luv's, so let's just do this."

Sebe had handed Tian Di a glass of warm water. He sipped the liquid, wishing he had put himself on vocal rest today.

Indigo shoulder-bumped him and smirked. "Hey, glad I got my nails done. Li really liked them."

CHAPTER 5

"This is your captain. We've started our descent. We'll be landing in the Shanghai Pudong International Airport, terminal one, in twenty minutes. I'm sorry for the late arrival. Between that mechanical delay, then the runway delay, add the head winds… well, an agent will be at the gate to give passengers connecting information. It's rainy and 19 degrees Celsius or about 66 degrees Fahrenheit. Again, we know you have a choice in airline carriers, and we look forward to serving you again. Welcome to China."

Finally. Thank God. Jordon would get away from the man on his left taking all the available space, and Mr. Both-Armrests-are-Mine on the right. His seatmates from hell had gotten drunk, talked nonstop to each other, spilled alcohol on one of Jordon's sketches, and unplugged his phone so the battery decharged. He'd been grateful when they each took a sleeping pill, until they collapsed on his shoulders. One snoozing ton of deadweight on either side made his body ache. He wiped off his wet left shoulder. *Ew!*

After an eternity, Jordon stumbled off the plane and trudged to the top of the steep Jetway. Every exhausting step reminded him how the estimated fourteen hours and fifty-five minutes had turned into a twenty-four-and-a-half-hour marathon nightmare.

Now he trailed along with the crowd.

Damn, how big is this terminal? How many miles was it to get to baggage claim?

People pushed and shoved to get around him, as if they had to go to the bathroom. He'd have to tell Gwen that totally didn't work when he was sleep-deprived.

The herd of humanity shuffled through something that looked like a metal detector, labeled Full Body Infrared Scanner. Ah, the temperature taker thingy Zack mentioned.

Jordon followed the herd and stood on the escalator. The all-white terminal had soaring ceilings with multicolored hanging mobiles. Boy, how cool it would be to have his art displayed for millions to see—

though no one stopped to appreciate the red metal ribbon that cut across the area they just walked through. How could they not notice the light installation? There had to be tens of thousands of bulbs painstakingly designed to create an ever-changing pattern, so visually pleasing Jordon imagined he could hear the colors.

Shit, that line. That was what everyone else focused on. The slow-moving tail leading to Passport Control looked like the line was a half a mile long if it were unwound.

After an eternal wait, Jordon crossed the yellow line and stood in front of the customs agent.

The man in a crisp olive-green uniform and hat asked in perfect English, "Why are you here?"

"My brother's band is on tour, and I'm attending the shows." Jordon used the reason the Dark Angels' manager had given him. Keep it simple.

"How long are you here?" The agent scrutinized Jordon like he'd broken four laws exiting the plane.

"In China, um… it's a whole tour…." *Shit.* How long would he be in China? It was a simple question. "Um, a few weeks."

The agent studied him. "Less than thirty days?"

Jordon stifled a yawn. He was pretty sure, so he nodded. "Yes."

The agent inspected his passport and frowned as he leafed through the filled pages. He found a blank page, slammed the stamp down, and took the form Jordon had filled out on the plane.

Whew. He bypassed the duty-free stores and saw on a monitor that his plane's luggage would be on belt three. Thankfully, both bags had arrived.

He headed toward the exit, and the agent at the door stopped the family of four in front of him.

Oh boy. Here we go. The agent questioned them in Chinese and then sent them to a different line. The agent barely looked at Jordon and waved him through.

Bursting through the auto-open doors, he faced people lining the forty-foot-long railing separating him from the exit. Some held flowers or balloons, others clutched signs, and everyone scanned the crowd looking for someone else.

Story of his life.

He wished he hadn't told Zack not to come. Getting into a car with a stranger and having to make small talk wasn't high on his list of fun-time activities.

"Jordon Davis" read an iPad sign. He braced himself, only to find Zack holding the device. His brother's fiancé, Andrew Nikeman, stood behind him.

"I told you you didn't have to show up, but I'm so glad you did." Jordon collapsed into Zack's arms.

He let his brother hug him tight until Zack said, "You look like shit. I still can't believe you forgot when your flight was and—"

"Zack. Jordon got here in one piece." Andrew saved him. "But he's probably exhausted. Let's get him to Suzhou."

"You're right, Drew," Zack admitted.

Hell might have frozen over. For the first time ever, Jordon didn't take issue with Andrew's interference.

Zack kept hugging Jordon almost too hard. "I'm sorry, Jordie. I got worried, and maybe I might have missed you."

Holy crap! One growl from Andrew, and Zack not only backed off but he played nice? The whole whips and chains thing they had going appeared to help give his brother perspective and keep him in line.

Zack released him, allowing Jordon to shake Andrew's hand. Jordon mouthed, "Thank you."

Andrew nodded and gestured to the man standing beside them. "This is our driver, Jack. He's going to drive us to Suzhou in his MPV."

Jordon nodded back to the man, who didn't want to shake his hand but only wanted to grab his two bags and knapsack. "Um, thanks. But what's MPV?"

"Multi-person vehicle. It's what they call SUVs here," Andrew supplied, proving once again he was quicker than Google.

The three of them followed the driver to the covered parking garage. They piled into the SUV… MPV.

Jordon lay down on the bench seat. Heaven. He could live in this bench seat, because he was never moving again.

"I saw your boyfriend sing last night," Zack said, low enough that even if the driver did understand English he wouldn't have overheard.

Jordon pushed upright. "Mother of Monet! Do I really need to say it again?"

Zack leaned over the seat to ensure Jordon couldn't avoid his eye roll.

Curiosity tickled Jordon's brain. God, the exhaustion swallowed him, but he remained sitting. He had to know. "How was the band?"

"Made in China has a great sound, and a pretty good following," Andrew commented.

"Even Dust was impressed," Zack added.

Now that was saying something. "Good."

"Tian Di commanded the stage as well as Angel, but in a different way. Hard to describe what he did, though he knew how to work the crowd." Zack grinned.

"So you don't think I made a mistake suggesting them?" Jordon hated himself for needing the validation.

"No, and besides, if Made in China hadn't impressed all the people who scouted them, they wouldn't be on the tour."

Relief eased Jordon's mind. Right, this was business. "But he, I mean, they were good?"

"Excellent." Zack nodded. "They—"

"Zack, don't you think Jordon should get a little rest?" Andrew, the killjoy, interrupted.

Smiling at Andrew like he'd given Michelangelo the lapis lazuli to paint the ceiling, Zack agreed. "Oh, right. It's about an hour and a half without traffic, so get a bit of rest, Jordie."

Andrew held out his hand to Jordon. "Give us your phone, and we'll swap out the SIM card so you can use it here."

Jordon handed over the phone and fell onto his side before they even got out of the airport parking garage.

Fuck! He was going to meet Tian Di Zhao. Good God, it wasn't like he'd forgotten. Eh, the singer was probably an asshole. Most of the guys in rock bands weren't the kind to give Jordon the time of day, and if they did, it was only to get in someone else's good graces.

Though, holy hell, it wasn't often one got to meet the celebrity they'd most like to… orgasm with.

THE ROAR of the crowd was deafening, but it didn't stop Jordon from climbing onstage with Made in China. Tian Di Zhao, the rock god, stood there waiting for Jordon to worship him.

Jordon dropped to his knees in front of his idol. His fingers trembled as he dared to run them over Tian Di's tight denim jeans, which vanished into his over-the-knee boots.

The star of his dreams stripped off his long black intricately embroidered jacket, and the silk puddled to the floor. He stood there half-naked, his long dark hair blowing around him as if he were filming a video shoot.

Oh, Jordon wanted him to shoot all right, but footage of a music video wasn't what he hoped for. He could almost taste the salty sweetness.

He traced his fingers over the outline of every ridge, bulge, and muscle in Tian Di's thighs. Then he danced his fingers along the hidden zipper.

Tian Di started to sing into his microphone.

An arena full of people watched, but Jordon saw no reason not to unzip Tian Di's pants. He wore nothing under them, and everything Jordon wanted access to was right there. Staring up at Tian Di, Jordon licked his lips.

With a thrust of his hips, Tian Di touched the tip of his erection to Jordon's mouth.

The shape was so perfect Jordon might have drawn Tian Di himself. Unlike with his mangas, there was no need to erase for the censors... he only had to suck. Jordon parted his lips to take Tian Di in. He pushed forward so the cock hit the back of his throat, and with his lips, circled the base of the cock, and swallowed.

Throwing back his head, Tian Di moaned. The lyrics got all breathy and twisted. "Jordon. Jordon."

"JORDON? WAKE up. We're at the hotel."

"What? Oh." Shit, that dream was so... real.

Jordon staggered out of the car and waited for Andrew to settle payment with the driver. A railing in front of him overlooked a lake, a row of restaurants lined the street to the left, and the twenty-story hotel stood on the right. Huge potted trees created a walkway leading to the hotel's door.

"We got your bags. You look like you can barely walk." Zack guided him into the hotel lobby.

"I'm fine." He threw his knapsack over his shoulder and got in line at the reception desk.

Zack shook his head. "What are you doing?"

"Duh? Checking in." Jordon did know how some things worked.

"Already done. Here's your keycard." Zack pulled out the plastic and handed the card to Jordon.

"Thanks." Jordon trailed after Zack and Andrew to the elevator.

"It makes you insert your card before the elevator registers your floor number." Zack demonstrated how the elevator worked.

"Got it." Jeez, his brother really didn't think he could figure out even the simplest things.

Zack opened Jordon's room.

"Um, why do you have a second key to my room?"

"How many times have you forgotten or lost yours?" Zack might have a point. "I figured I'd save you time at the front desk, at least once."

"Whatever." It didn't matter, and even if it did, he was too tired to fight about it. Jordon stepped past Zack and into his room.

"Welcome to your classic room. It's got the basics: bed, desk, chair, reading chair, refrigerator, and a microwave." Zack meandered over to the drapery and flung the fabric open. "It's overlooking the Golden Cock Lake."

Jordon tossed his knapsack on the dresser. "What? You're joking?"

"Nope, your singer lives on the Golden Cock Lake." Zack chortled.

Andrew's glower, directed at Zack, appeared to stop the jackassery and make electricity pass between them. "It's actual name on the map is Jinji Lake. Though according to Made in China's self-appointed manager, the locals call it the Golden Chicken Lake, but the translation could be rooster."

"Meaning cock, so—"

"Zack?" Andrew said way too much for just using Zack's name.

Zack stood straighter. "Yes, Drew."

Jordon so wasn't in the mood for whatever this was. "I should shower."

"Meet us downstairs in twenty minutes." Zack focused more on Andrew than Jordon.

"Twenty minutes?" *Shit!* How was he ever going to be ready?

"Yeah, everyone's at Made in China's apartment waiting for you, so no time to jerk off." Zack stalked over to Andrew.

Andrew nodded. The man studied Zack like he had the power of the universe in him. "True. Twenty minutes means there is very little time."

Jordon grimaced. *Not going there.* He hurried into the bathroom, not bothering to let them out.

He took one superquick shower, which forced him to forgo any release. He barely had time to blow-dry his hair. *Shit, what to wear?*

He didn't even unpack. Unzipping his suitcases, he found them empty. What? Had he been robbed?

Opening the closet, he saw all his clothing hanging there, organized by type, then color. He opened the drawers and found his packing cubes unzipped, ready and accessible. Ignoring the fact his brother or Andrew had touched his underwear and how that made him feel like a kid, he grabbed a pair and slid them on.

Stopping in front of the mirror, he stared. Damn bikini briefs might help him remember he wasn't a kid. Not that anyone would see the satiny blue material, but they looked kind of sexy. He'd tried to paint some underwear two years ago, but the paint dried hard and came out scratchy. Hmmm, maybe he could experiment with fabric paint or direct dye and—

His phone beeped. He grabbed the cell and read a text from Zack: *5 minutes.*

Shit! He pulled on a black T-shirt, a pair of black jeans, and pushed his feet into a pair of Vans. Rushing into the bathroom, he grabbed some mousse and worked the product through his hair to accent the waves the way Andrew taught him. After grabbing his wallet, his partially charged cell phone—thanks to his brother—and pulling his leather messenger bag out of his knapsack, he raced out the door.

In the elevator, he texted Gwen: *Travel sux. Many delays. I'm here. Heading to party with dead phone. Kill me later.*

Andrew and Zack were in the lobby, sitting in the stylish gold and apple-green chairs. The furniture complemented the gold carpeting and walls. The concentric circles on the ceiling, echoed in the contrasting orange modern light fixture, struck an odd chord in Jordon. The space tried to be lush and upscale, but failed in the art department.

"Fanboy, much?" Zack pointed at Jordon.

"What?" Jordon glanced down at his T-shirt. *Oh geez!*

"I'm sure they'll be flattered," Andrew said.

Jordon tugged at the T-shirt. "I should change."

Zack shook his head. "We don't have time. Besides, if you look past the stalker factor, it's cute that you designed the T-shirt for the band."

Andrew patted Jordon on the shoulder. "Zack's right. I'm sure they'll be honored you took the time."

"Come on, stan. We should go." Zack gestured toward the door.

"Stan? Dare I ask?" Jordon wasn't sure if he should glare at his brother or not.

"*Stan* is short for stalker fan."

"Funny." Jordon stomped past Zack and Andrew. "And stop unpacking my clothes for me."

"We were just trying to help," Zack called out.

Jordon grumbled. "But I don't need or want that much help."

Zack caught up and handed him cards. "Here. These are taxi cards. You live and die by them here."

What the fuck? "Dramatic much? Meaning?"

"Unless you learned Mandarin in the last few days, you might have a hard time finding your way back to the hotel if you're separated. Drew also took a picture of the hotel card with your phone just in case."

"Okay, thanks." Jordon put the cards in his bag.

Andrew handed him a baggie of stuff.

"What's this?" The package contained a packet of tissue, another hotel card, one hundred yuan, which was about fifteen dollars, soap leaves, a package of wet wipes, and several coins.

"For restrooms. Unless we're in a Western place, you might need it." Zack grimaced as if he'd run into some trouble.

Andrew added, "They usually charge one RMB to use the bathrooms, and many don't have bathroom tissue or soap. The one hundred yuan is taxi or food money for places that don't take credit cards."

"Got it. Thanks." Jordon slipped the package into his bag.

Andrew led them on a walking street out to a six-lane road. "If we took the other path, it meanders along the boardwalk that rings most of the lake. But since you're tired, I thought heading along the main road would get us there sooner. That's the band's apartment building."

Jordon looked in the direction Andrew pointed—at a twenty-six-story apartment building. Tian Di Zhao was just three blocks away.

"Hey, slow down. It's not a race," Zack whined.

"So this is an industrial park?" Taking in the lake, the trees, flowers, and several abstract art statues, it didn't seem like that could possibly be correct.

"Yes. It's the SIP, or Suzhou Industrial Park." Andrew added, "There're some factories, but this area has a lot of apartment buildings."

"What's that?" The building looked like an uneven coil of wire but was somehow familiar.

"That's Suzhou's answer to the bird's nest, the Olympic building. It's a decent-sized theater, according to Dust. Right next to it is the Biergarten, which is the German restaurant where Made in China performs." Zack pointed in the opposite direction. "Farther along the lake is Moon Bay. Drew and I walked around there last night. There are a bunch of restaurants and shops. Why are you going so slow?"

Tian Di is in that building. "I'm not."

They turned down a side street, and one more turn brought them to a guard gate. They went through the pedestrian walkway, which opened into a circular driveway with two tall apartment buildings on either side and a fountain in the middle.

Andrew guided them to the building on the left and pressed 901 in the building's security box.

A sick-sounding buzzer pierced Jordon's ears.

Zack pulled open the door and held it for Andrew and Jordon. The slumped guard didn't even lift his head off the desk. Zack snarked, "Hm, so much for residential security."

Andrew and Zack led him through the marble lobby to the elevator.

Andrew explained, "The guys just buzzed us in so the elevator will go to their floor."

Jordon whistled. "Fancy setup."

"They have a private entrance where you take off your shoes," Zack added.

The elevator opened to an all-gray, swirly marble room with a fountain, bench, a basket of slippers, and a graveyard of shoes.

Zack set out three pairs of slippers. He and Andrew slipped theirs on quickly. "Come on."

"Um, let me check my messages. I'll be in soon." Jordon sat on the bench.

Tian Di was inside that apartment. God, he felt crazed and scrambled. Everything took on a surreal quality that muted the edges of reality—or maybe it was jet lag.

Andrew guided Zack through the door before he could argue or tell Jordon what to do.

Jordon pulled out his phone and stared at the screen. He was a few feet away from meeting Tian Di. What the fuck was wrong with him? Tian Di was a singer. He'd met a ton of singers and some truly famous people. Celebrities didn't scare Jordon, fame didn't impress him or give him butterflies. Somehow Tian Di crept under his skin in a different way.

Maybe he could slip into the gathering unnoticed, quietly introduce himself to the band, claim exhaustion, and go back to the hotel.

Through the door, a woman's words echoed. "Angel, I read that you are bisexual."

"Yup, I am," Angel said.

Jordon didn't need to see Angel to know he was distracted, most likely by his boyfriend. If there was a singer Jordon should be intimidated by, it was Angel Luv, but he wasn't. If anything, Jordon found perverse pleasure in not falling prey to Angel's sexual ooze.

"But, like, now you're dating a man exclusively. What do you think about bi-erasure?"

"Um, I don't know… Angela," Angel answered.

"What's bi-erasure?" a kid, whose voice cracked on the prefix "bi," asked.

"That's when a bisexual person opts for a same-sex partner and society believes the gay community swallows you." This Angela person giggled and continued her educational lecture. "Literally. Or it's when you're dating someone of the opposite sex, and people assume that you're now straight based on who you're with and no longer consider you bi."

"So?" asked the kid whose voice managed to wreak havoc on a single syllable yet again.

"Bisexuality is about who you're attracted to, not who you're sleeping with. Angel, wouldn't you like to be with a woman again? You must miss women." Her voice got flirty at the end.

"No, the only one I miss is Darius when I have to share him with others."

After toeing off his Vans, Jordon slid his feet into the puffy red house shoes. Stylish they were not. However with a bit of detailing…. He scuffed through the door.

The apartment was a vast open space with cherrywood floors, fabulous masks on the white walls, tables piled with food, and black sofas and chairs with people sitting on them. The gathering was to be mostly the Dark Angels, Made in China, and a few others milling around. Most of the band members had their instruments nearby or in hand, and from the bits of conversation, music was the topic being discussed. But no Tian Di.

Angel jumped off the sofa and pulled Jordon into a hug. "Our wayward artist is finally here."

"*Tsk*, I've never been led astray." *What the fuck is coming out of my mouth?*

"I've been trying, but Dusty will kick my ass," Angel teased.

From across the space, Dusty pointed his sticks at Angel. "I don't even know why, but yes, I will. Jordon!"

Dusty rushed across the apartment and yanked Jordon into a tight embrace. "I was worried about you, kid."

"I'm not a kid, and I'm fine." Jordon wondered if he could hide out with his brother and avoid conversation with other people.

"Where's your better half?" Odd to see his oldest brother without Justin.

"Jet lagged. He couldn't sleep last night, so he's lying down in Styx and Jin's room."

Angel pushed Dusty back toward the spot from where he came. "Dust, go back to Styx. I'll intro the kid around."

A bony artist elbow into a singer's middle helped Angel see his error. "Ow! Jordon, I know you're not a kid."

Darius appeared by Angel's side, rubbing the injury. "Jordon, I expect more from you than Dusty."

Jordon snorted and put his hands out in front of him. "Got it. My apologizes."

Grinning, Darius gave him a half-hug back slap. "You look tired. Long trip?"

Still no Tian Di.

Jordon kept his voice low. "Exhausted. I don't want to be rude, but I think I'll say hi and vanish."

"Got it. Trying to work iTranslate while you're sleepy can be dangerous." Darius's smirk added something more to the list of things Jordon didn't want to know about. Darius pressed a kiss to his hand and touched Angel's side with its healing power. "I'll see you in a bit. I think you might need more first aid."

Angel nodded way too eagerly. He threw an arm around Jordon and dragged him over to the sofa he'd abandoned. "Jordon, this is Sebe, Made in China's manager and a force to be reckoned with, and his schoolmate, Angela. Sebe, Jordon's one of the reasons we're here. He's one of those super fans we talked about. He's who the band needs to satisfy."

"Hi." Jordon smiled at Angela—teenager or not, she totally got the double entendre Angel lobbed in his direction.

Luckily, the other kid missed Angel's dirty attempt at humor. Sebe jumped to his feet and shook hands with Jordon like he wanted to realign a dislocated shoulder. "Mr. Davis."

"Just Jordon's fine."

"Pleased to meet you," Sebe said with an accent Jordon identified as German. "That's an awesome shirt, Jordon. Where did you get it?"

Touching the screened art of the Made in China band shirt and trying not to feel like the *stan* his brother had labeled him, he admitted, "I designed the art, then sent it to a company that prints pictures on things like travel mugs, pens, tote bags, and T-shirts."

Sebe might be only a teen, but Jordon saw a future shark. "Have you copyrighted the picture yet?"

"Um, no."

Sebe was too serious for a teen. "Ah, okay. I'll study up on US copyright laws. Would you mind sharing the link with me?"

"Of course not." Jordon tried not to feel stupid he hadn't copyrighted any of his pieces. Another thing he needed to get on, but one thing at a time.

"I love your manga and the art I've seen on your pages. Maybe since you're a fan, you might be interested in—"

Angel waved off the teen. "Sebe, let the guy relax. My guess is he had a flight from hell sitting in the back of the bus."

Where was Tian Di? Had he left his own party?

Even if Jordon hadn't drawn Made in China a thousand times, he'd recognize Indigo anywhere. The Dark Angels had worked with his father, Song Young. Jordon shook his hand. "Indigo Young. Glad to finally meet you. Hope your dad is doing well."

"He's fine, and it's great to meet you." Indigo fell onto the sofa.

"I—" Angel dragged Jordon toward another group. "Rude. Why did you do that, Ang?"

"Because that one can't help but cause trouble and add confusion." Angel pointed to the man, who was talking on a cell phone. "That's Li, his boyfriend, on the balcony. Trust me, steer clear of their chaos."

Jordon exchanged waves with the nice-looking guy as he moved back toward his older brother.

"Let me introduce you…." Angel spoke louder. "This guy is Styx Wong, and he'll replace your brother in a few years as the world's best drummer."

The man put his sticks in his back pocket, and he shook his head. "No. He is a joker. Do not listen." He handed Jordon his name card with two hands.

Jordon took the card, which had two drumsticks on the upper right-hand corner, and Styx's personal contact information. He studied the card for a moment before slipping it into a side pocket of his messenger bag. "Nice to meet you, Styx. I'm Jordon. I'm sorry, I forgot my name cards."

"No trouble, Jordon." Styx pronounced each word with care.

Jordon was grateful Styx didn't appear offended. "The beats you lay down are incredible."

Jin said something in Chinese to Styx. Maybe a translation.

"Thank you. You are too kind." Styx nodded and shook hands with Jordon.

"Styx lit many joss sticks in the temple, praying to be half as good as Dusty Davis. I am Jin Lan, the guitar player for Made in China. Nice to meet you, Jordon Davis."

Jordon accepted Jin's name card and shook his hand. "I love your music. I've heard several of your incredible solos. You understand silence."

"Silence?" Jin cocked his head to the left and then stared at the ceiling.

Damn, I'll remember this pose to use on my next story board. Too cute. So good for—focus on the conversation, not the art in my mind. How to explain silence? "Um, your quiet. You make the guitar stop at the right places, and for the perfect amount of time."

"Thank you. Solos are not only about fast playing. Our teacher taught us you must allow the audience to hear all of what the instrument can do. Um, Tian Di has shown us your work… the art and pictures. You are very good." Jin smiled. Both his and Styx's faces got a bit red.

Tian Di had Jordon's mangas? How was that even possible?

Not ready to go there, especially since Made in China's singer appeared to be absent. "Um, thanks. Your English is great."

"Eh, no. We take English lessons." Jin shook his head. "And Indigo and Tian Di are helping us."

Styx leaned in and confided, "Tian Di's a better teacher."

"I heard that," Indigo called out from across the room.

The conversation and groups reformed.

Styx and Dusty fell into a deep conversation, aided by the iTranslate app, about where the best drumsticks were made. Jin and Darius were talking through their guitar riffs.

Robin came from around a corner, rushed over, and hugged him. "Jordon!"

"Where were you? I didn't see you." *Whine much? I need to stop seeking people to hide behind.*

"We were in the bathroom," Josh answered with a smirk as he smacked Jordon on the back.

Images Jordon would need to brain bleach later danced through his head. Granted, he'd drawn them in various compromising positions at Robin's request, and they were beautiful together, but... no.

Angel said, "I leave you in good hands. I'm going to sit on the balcony with Li for a bit and count traffic accidents."

"What?"

Indigo waved them off. "Lots of minor accidents at this intersection because people don't always stop for red lights."

Angela supplied, "Unlike Western countries, the right-of-way goes trucks, MPV, cars, motorcycles, scooters, bikes, then people."

"Wow, that sounds dangerous," Jordon mused.

"It can be if you don't respect the pecking order." Angela pulled a tube from her handbag and applied some lip gloss. "Want some?"

"Sure, it smells good." Indigo held out his hand.

Instead of handing him the tube, Angela slid into his lap and pressed her lips to his mouth. "There you go."

Indigo leaned away but smiled and eased her off his lap. "Um, thanks."

"Well, Sebe and I have to be going. We'll see you at the show. Nice to meet you, Jordon." Angela swept out of the apartment with far more grace than someone her age should have.

"Tell the guys to text me when they want to meet, and please give Jordon my information," Sebe ordered Indigo.

Indigo remained quiet but eventually gave him a thumbs-up.

Sebe told Jordon, "Remind these guys if they forget to give you my information. I'd like to work with you on a T-shirt design or two." He waved and disappeared out the front door.

Robin pulled Jordon down on the love seat with him.

Josh asked, "Do you want anything to drink, Jordon?"

"No."

"The usual?" Josh asked Robin.

Jordon sighed and wished he had someone who knew what his usual was.

"Yes, please." Robin stared at Josh until he disappeared into the kitchen. "So talk to me. What's new and exciting? Isn't China amazing?"

"I just—" *Holy fuck!*

Tian Di leaned against the corner of the room with a ghost of a smile, making him look incredibly sexy.

Jordon was pretty sure he was going to die.

The blue silk jacket Tian Di wore nipped in, showing off a small waist. Tight jeans displayed his long legs, and his hair flowed over his shoulders like a black river. Even his blue satin slippers were smoking hot and embossed with a navy blue dragon design fit for a prince.

Fuck! He looks exactly as he did in my dream. There were no two ways about it. Tian Di commanded all Jordon's attention, and he hadn't even moved or said a word.

"Jordie, why's your face getting red?" Josh was too perceptive at times. Handing Robin his drink, he asked, "Have you met Made in China's singer yet?"

Jordon stood and focused on not tripping as he stepped toward the living version of his fantasy.

Tian Di pushed off the wall. He was the same height as Jordon, but his essence was all fiery oranges and deep reds, making him appear taller. "We've yet to have the pleasure. It is an honor to meet you, Jordon Davis."

Jordon forced himself to glance away from Tian Di's eyes for a moment to pay respect by looking at the name card he'd just accepted.

He swallowed and held out his hand again. "Um, I forgot my name cards."

"You can put your information directly into my cell." Instead of a manshake and a finger-breaking squeeze, Tian Di gently grasped Jordon's hand. Their palms glided across each other's, making Jordon half-hard.

"Jordon, you should see Tian Di's manga collection. It's quite impressive." Robin's soft voice brought Jordon back to reality enough to realize he should let Tian Di's hand go, but he really didn't want to.

"Oh, I thought you couldn't get that stuff here." Jordon impressed himself with a coherent sentence. Tian Di was even more beautiful up close, he smelled of spearmint, and his hand was soft and warm.

"You can't. My sister buys the books when she's in Japan, and I get them when I visit her in Hong Kong."

Jordon nodded, probably looking like a bobblehead doll. He opened his hand, but the man didn't let go; instead he stroked his thumb against Jordon's knuckles.

Tian Di leaned closer. His hair fell around his face, creating a feeling of privacy. "Would you care to see my collection?"

"Yes, of course." If Jordon's knees didn't buckle and his head didn't explode.

Tian Di led him to a room around the corner. "Come in. This is my bedroom."

CHAPTER 6

BEDROOM? JORDON stepped into Tian Di's room. *God, if this is a dream, let me finish before I wake up.*

Tian Di let go of Jordon's hand to shut the door.

Click.

Pollock splatters and dabs of color in Jordon's mind swirled into a vortex of the greatest bad ideas he'd ever had.

Holy fuck! They were alone. Jordon restrained his weird neediness to reclasp Tian Di's hand.

His heart rate tripled. No one would know if they—

I can't do anything. Dusty and Zack would kill me. It would be crazy. And Tian Di probably doesn't want me anyway—

Tian Di took a small step closer and stared into Jordon's eyes. And then he smiled, silencing all the warning bells in the world.

The crazy desire to get to know the real Tian Di played fast and loose with Jordon's risk-taking equation.

How could he pass this moment by? Jordon longed to know the man who sang lyrics with such emotion. Tian Di's voice had become embedded in Jordon's heart and soul. All the pain and heartbreaking loneliness laced together with the slightest bit of hope. That small glimpse allowed Jordon to believe love could be real. Perhaps he could find his soul mate, and maybe, just maybe, there was a happily ever after for him.

The promise of a fairy-tale ending made Jordon crave… all of it.

A piece of him knew trying to take this further was insanity, but his senses hit overdrive. Perhaps his subconscious had gotten used to the many jackoff sessions starring Tian Di, and now with Tian Di up close and personal, everything in Jordon demanded the reality.

He shoved his hands into his pockets and glanced around the sparse room. It contained a black lacquered armoire with Chinese-style brass door handles, a shiny red desk with a black leather Z-chair pushed underneath, black drapes with a red design slashed across them, and a crimson futon with black pillows. The walls were white and— "Those are Sakura Rose prints."

"Yes." Tian Di nodded.

Jordon stepped over to get a closer look at the black-framed prints. The Japanese publishing company had run a limited number of prints of the cover art of his first book, and two scenes as giveaway prints. One look showed these pictures were no knockoff copies. Jordon's "SR" in gold pen burnished the corner, along with a 28/88. The other print was marked 8/88. Jordon had done a special design under any number with a lucky eight, which meant prosperity and double happiness throughout Asia. His publishing company insisted he skip the unlucky number four, which sounded too close to the word for death. "Wow. You got good numbers."

"Yes. I lucked out on the eights, though there were three released, unfortunately I could only get two." Tian Di sighed, making Jordon want him to make that noise for a different reason.

"Impressive you got two. The publisher didn't want to sell them outright. They had contests, and I heard the after-sales were steep."

"Still are." Tian Di stood so close his body heat raised Jordon's temperature. "But look at the work."

Jordon turned and stared at Tian Di's soft dreamy-eyed expression of admiration. It made Jordon extremely happy, and he was honored he could put that look on someone's face with his work. He'd gotten emails from fans but had never met any.

Tian Di smiled at Jordon. "I've noticed your Dark Angels are drawn in a similar style. Maybe you could sign them for me."

Shit! "Oh? Yeah."

Stepping over to his armoire, Tian Di pulled out a standing file, unlocked the box, and pulled out one of the Dark Angels manga. After he slipped the thin book out of the protective cover, he flipped to a scene similar to the one displayed. "See. Your sketch lines are the same. There's clean strong lines. You and Sakura Rose even use width of the lines to show which character in the scene is more vulnerable, as well as how you show movement."

Jordon shut his mouth. No one had ever picked up on those things. Hell, not even his editors noticed the subtlety until he explained his methods. "Hmmm, really?"

Tian Di continued to study him. "Not that it's bad. I just find it interesting. Even the pace of the stories feels similar, and the... how do you say it? The message is quite Western."

"No kidding?" What the fuck should he say?

Tian Di set the manga on his desk. "I mean no disrespect, and you don't have to answer this—"

"Yes, I'm Sakura Rose." Whew. Amazing how good the admission felt. Jordon exhaled, and a weight lifted with claiming SR's identity.

Tian Di's mouth dropped open. "Um, I was going to ask you if you had studied under Sakura Rose somehow. But I guess...."

Fucknuggets! "Well, Sakura Rose is nothing without me."

Jordon's lame joke only got him an intensified stare and the pleasure of seeing Tian Di's cheeks tint the most charming shade of pink.

"Thank you for telling me." Tian Di's voice wrapped around Jordon, making him feel safe and needy.

Catching himself, Jordon stopped from leaning any closer to Tian Di. "No one else knows except the publisher and two of my closest friends."

"Not even your brothers?" Tian Di's words pushed spearmint-scented air across Jordon's lips.

"No, I—not yet."

Tian Di's gaze dropped. "Why did you tell me?"

Where was this compulsion to share things with Tian Di coming from? "I don't know. I just wanted you to know."

"I'm glad you did. I need to thank you. Sakura Rose's series has sustained me."

"What?"

Tian Di shook his head. "Maybe that isn't the right word. Um, the way you—Sakura Rose—portrays love, relationships, and um, sex... it is wonderful."

Jordon face grew hot. "Thanks. I try."

"You succeed." Tian Di's voice softened as he continued, "And the fact that you're wearing a Made in China T-shirt... this is beyond a dream come true for me."

"I love... the band." Jordon's mouth almost spoke for his heart ahead of his brain. Granted, anything above his flushed cheeks wasn't receiving any blood flow. "When I heard your voice...."

Tian Di shifted closer. "What?"

"I was in my car, listening to a music podcast. They played a poor-quality copy of 'Evolution,' and... man. That song changed my world." He left out how infatuated he'd gotten with Tian Di.

"You really like our music?" There was no coy fishing for compliments in Tian Di's tone, just raw vulnerability.

"Hearing you made me believe life could be okay." Jordon had been driving back from a hookup gone to hell. Another guy being shitty, reinforcing why Jordon rarely bothered to make the effort.

"Sometimes my English isn't as good as it should be. What do you mean?" Tian Di was a mere couple inches from Jordon.

How did he convey the depths Tian Di touched in him? "It's like you understand everything about me."

"Could you explain this more?" Tian Di tucked some of Jordon's hair behind his ear.

Tian Di grazed his finger along the shell of Jordon's ear. *Holy fuck!* Tian Di's touch made Jordon crave him even more. The raw need slamming into him was astounding, and more than a little terrifying.

"You unraveled my confusion, loneliness, and my desire for love." Jordon's voice cracked with need. "You sing my pain and show me the other side is possible. You give me hope and the determination to keep trying."

"We always have to keep believing." Tian Di spoke barely above a whisper.

Jordon's heart screamed *yes* and romance lived. "It's hard sometimes because not many people believe in trying."

Tears sparkled in Tian Di's eyes. "That means a lot to me. Thank you. I want you to know your work calls to me in the same way. I feel like one of your characters simply dying to have someone to love, to know them, and through your drawings you give me that. I mean, them. You allow me to believe, even though I've never had that kind of love, that someday I could. Reading your stories allows me to sing with hope."

Jordon didn't know what to say. He licked his lips and stared at Tian Di.

Tian Di locked gazes with him.

Silent communication of camaraderie passed between them.

Insane, that was what this was—two like souls seeking and hoping to find their other half. As crazy as it seemed, Jordon couldn't deny an overwhelming connection tied them together.

Jordon didn't spend a lot of time with other people. He and Tian Di were cut from the same canvas like a diptych. Two parts of a painting, separated not just by a frame and a hinge, but half a world, though now they were reunited. He couldn't shake the feeling of two halves coming together to be whole.

Tian Di tucked another wayward piece of hair behind Jordon's ear.

The familiarity, which bore a rightness impossible to understand and too powerful to ignore, cascaded between them. Jordon yearned for the promise of perfection.

Tian Di glided his tongue over his full, perfectly shaped lips, making them glisten. "May I kiss you?"

"Yes," Jordon gasped. Was there any other answer?

They were going to kiss. Excitement and nerves battled within him. Should Jordon lean in? Maybe he shouldn't move.

The few times Jordon had followed someone into a back room or gotten into someone's car, the agenda was to get off as quickly as possible. Kissing wasn't usually on the menu.

Tian Di's romantic question of "May I kiss you?" echoed the Sakura Rose scene hanging on the wall. Jordon had captured the two men right before a lip-lock, a moment filled with nervous tension and incredible desire battling to push the protagonists to act.

The same force impacted Jordon.

God, were Tian Di's lips as soft as they looked?

Jordon tilted his head to the side, drowning in Tian Di's brown eyes rimmed in bronze. The flecks of gold made their depths appear endless. He inhaled Tian Di's spearmint breath, parting his lips and hoping to find out what Tian Di's mouth was like on his.

Tian Di bowed his head and leaned closer to Jordon.

Oh, yeah, this kissing thing would be happening.

Closing his eyes, Jordon savored the anticipation.

Tian Di traced his tongue across Jordon's mouth, sending desire spiraling low into Jordon's belly, forcing a pathetic moan to escape.

The gentle touch of Tian Di's fingertips on Jordon's palm invited him to lace their hands together. The gesture filled the empty parts of Jordon, making him long for more.

Tian Di squeezed his hand and pressed against him.

Their breath mingled and the connection gave Jordon confidence. He brushed his lips against Tian Di's mouth.

"Oh!" escaped with the sweetest gasp from Tian Di.

Jordon slid his mouth across Tian Di's again with even better results.

"So perfect," Tian Di whispered before he captured his mouth and kissed him back, sweeping his tongue into Jordon's mouth.

A kaleidoscope of color burst around him. This wasn't Jordon's first kiss, but it was, hands-down, by far the best. Any of his fans would be proud to claim it. Without a doubt this kiss was exactly like the ones he drew for his characters.

There were no demands or taking, only the simple gift of giving. The exchange became drenched in affection, respect, with enough heat to make Jordon want to beg for more. The kiss was everything and yet not enough.

Stroking Tian Di's face allowed Jordon to feel the barest hint of stubble against his palm, reminding him this wasn't a picture for drawing, but reality.

Tian Di tenderly cupped Jordon's face and continued the slide of his mouth against Jordon's.

The tender touch made Jordon's heart expand past capacity, ignoring his brain's cautionary message of "too soon, too soon." He was falling heart-first into Tian Di.

On and on the kiss went. It wasn't nearly enough, but Jordon couldn't tear his lips away from the sweetness to do more.

Tian Di whimpered. No, that had been Jordon making sounds. But he didn't know how to stop his moans, and he didn't want to if quieting meant ending the kiss.

They shuffled over to the futon, and Tian Di stumbled against it. He grabbed Jordon to steady them.

Jordon remained attached to Tian Di's mouth as they fell onto the futon in a tangle of limbs.

Kissing Tian Di forever was a great plan. However, when Tian Di's hands landed on Jordon's ass, while the kiss sparked a continuous explosion of color behind Jordon's eyelids, there were other options to be explored.

Tian Di guided Jordon's hips, making them slide against him. Oh, the friction forced Jordon to writhe over him. None of the numerous dreams he'd had about Tian Di could compete with the reality.

The hands on Jordon's butt tightened, pulling him in and making him grind down harder. The urgency began to spiral out of control. The kiss had gone wild.

Clang!

Armageddon! Jordon jumped halfway across the room.

The door remained shut, but Jordon stared at the wooden barrier, waiting for the hordes to pile in.

Clang! Clang! Thump.

"Styx on drums. They're in the practice room across the hall." Tian Di lay on the futon, hair disheveled, mouth kiss-swollen, and eyes begging Jordon to return.

A Dark Angels' song slipped under the door.

"I guess we should—this would have been a stupid idea to—" Jordon wiped his hands on his pants as crushing disappointment took up residence in his heart.

Tian Di stood and straightened his jacket with swift but elegant moves. "I have a feeling your brothers would be furious."

"Yeah, and I don't want to do anything that would affect your big break."

"It's very sweet you're worried about me. Thank you." Tian Di combed his fingers through Jordon's hair, sending mixed signals.

Not knowing what to say, Jordon went with "You're welcome."

"I'm not used to someone thinking about me first." Tian Di toyed with the shell of Jordon's ear. "I guess we'd only have been setting ourselves on the path of trouble."

"Trouble's bad." Jordon wanted to twirl Tian's Di's midnight strands through his fingers. If Tian Di could run his fingers through Jordon's hair, it was only fair Jordon got the opportunity too.

He skimmed his hands over Tian Di's embroidered silk jacket, inching along until he finally tangled his fingers into Tian Di's curtain of hair. For the love of Buddha, how many times had he watched Made in China's Youku videos, wishing desperately to twine his fingers in Tian Di's hair. He sifted his fingers through the soft length.

Tian Di closed his eyes and leaned into Jordon's stroking hand. "That feels sensuous. Almost as good as kissing you."

"You liked kissing me?" Dumb question, but the words came out of Jordon's mouth anyway.

"Loved it. You're a very good kisser." Tian Di ran his index finger over Jordon's bottom lip.

Some mischievous imp invaded Jordon, and he licked Tian Di's finger.

"Mmmm, Jordon." Tian Di's voice dropped to the husky range of sexy.

"You like that?" Jordon teased his tongue against Tian Di's finger. He sucked the tip into his mouth and then released the finger with a kiss. He'd always wanted to do that.

Tian Di stepped closer and grazed his erection across Jordon's. "Yes."

If wishing could manifest action, Tian Di's pants would vanish. Instead, Jordon did something he'd only dreamed about doing, he pushed Tian Di's hair out of the way, and ran his lips along the elegant column of Tian Di's neck.

Shivering, Tian Di squeezed his eyes shut and held Jordon's mouth against him. "That's incredible. Let me feel your teeth."

"Okay, but I don't want to leave a mark."

"You won't. You won't. Please." Tian Di's careless words were hot and breathy.

Jordon couldn't resist the temptation and grazed his teeth over soft skin, giving Tian Di a little bite.

"Oh, Jordon." Tian Di panted, tilting his head farther.

Jordon couldn't resist the invitation. He licked hard, used his teeth and mouth until Tian Di wrapped his arms around him and trembled.

"Jordon. I…." All of Tian Di's wants and got-to-haves were laid bare for Jordon. And Jordon appeared to be at the top of his list.

He couldn't pretend. As crazy as it was, Jordon couldn't help himself, and confessed, "Me too."

Jordon landed flat against the door. He wasn't sure who moved first, but hallelujah for the stability of the thick wood. "We're being stupid."

"I should say yes and help stop this, but I don't want to. I adore everything about you, and I want this one perfect moment just for me. Can I have that, Jordon?"

Heat flashed through Jordon, as no amount of inexperience would allow him to misread the desire in Tian Di's warm brown eyes. Old fears tried to creep into his head, but Tian Di's spearmint breath calmed him, allowing Jordon to wrestle his worries back.

There was no denying Jordon longed for everything Tian Di wanted. The single best fantasy in his world could be his, if only for a while. He didn't have the strength to turn down the offer.

In that second, Jordon decided several things. This was indeed a bad idea for both of them. Though it didn't matter how little time they spent together, Jordon's feelings were real. Tian Di could have this moment and as many moments as he wanted with Jordon. But if Jordon didn't kiss Tian Di again right now, he would die.

Jordon reached under Tian Di's silk jacket, tugged him in by his belt loop to pull him closer.

Tian Di pressed and shifted. Denim rubbed against denim, causing sparks of heat to catch between them.

Oh, fuck yeah. Jordon's hard-on stabbed against his zipper, wanting freedom. The voice screaming, *Bad idea! Abort! Abort!* had been totally overshadowed by Jordon's *I don't fucking care* erection.

God, maybe he should have taken time to jerk off in the shower before coming to the gathering. How long had it been? *Shit.* Days and days. He'd gotten tangled in a project and now he'd embarrass himself in front of someone who, on a good day, could probably make him come without even touching him.

He closed his eyes as Tian Di leaned in, but no kiss.

Tian Di swept his wet tongue across Jordon's mouth.

Two could play. Jordon opened his eyes and turned his head the other way and licked his tongue across Tian Di's.

Fuck! Stroking over Tian Di's tormenting tongue sent lightning crashing back through him. Jordon's cock throbbed as if it had been licked instead of just his mouth. He thrust his hips to get a bit more friction.

Going to come. Need to stop. Artists. Leonardo Da Vinci was born 1452 and died 1519. Wassily Kandinsky, his dates were what? 1886? No, 1866 to um... 1944. Claude Monet lived between 1840 and 1926. The master of The Birth of Venus *was Sandro Botticelli. He was born in 1445 and died in 1510. There. Okay.*

Tian Di tightened his hands around Jordon's waist and wiggled against him.

Fuck it all! Any patience Jordon had gained got lost again.

Jordon tantalized Tian Di's mouth, willing his lips to part. He was gratified with a whimper as Tian Di's lush lips parted for him. Jordon took full advantage and drew him into a kiss.

His mouth fit Tian Di's like a puzzle piece snapping in place.

Tian Di rubbed his pelvis against him restlessly. Tian Di licked, danced, and tangled his tongue in Jordon's mouth, leaving him breathless.

Jordon could kiss Tian Di for the rest of his life, but that might be short if he didn't figure out how to do more. What would Tricks do? The sexually expressive main character in his *Tricks and Treats* series would know exactly how to act.

Pressing his hips closer to Tian Di, Jordon squirmed.

One of the Angels' rock anthems seeped into the privacy, making Jordon second-guess, so he peeked at Tian Di. He found the answer to his unasked question in Tian Di's small smile.

Tian Di steadied Jordon's hips, guiding him in a sliding rhythm that had Jordon almost begging to come. "If you keep that up—"

Whispering, Tian Di asked, "What's going to happen?"

Delicious excitement chased through Jordon. Cupping Tian Di's ass, he shifted closer and moved faster. "I'm going to come."

Rocking harder, Tian Di moaned, "Just a little more."

Jordon kissed him and squirmed over Tian Di's bulge.

Tian Di broke their kiss and hissed, "Yes."

No stopping the foregone conclusion. Jordon's cock throbbed as waves of pleasure radiated out. The orgasm was so blissful he didn't even care about coming in his pants. He rubbed happily against the most beautiful man he'd ever drawn.

Jordon trembled against a writhing Tian Di and found intense satisfaction far beyond orgasm in his relaxed smile. "That was—"

"Incredible." Tian Di stirred in his arms to peer at him with dreamy eyes.

Another Dark Angels song seeped into their haven.

"Yeah." *Whew!* Jordon hadn't been the only one to lose control while still wearing his pants.

A small smile played on Tian Di's lips. "Can I take you to dinner?"

Trying not to appear shocked but unable to play cool, Jordon answered immediately, "I'd love that."

"Tonight?" Tian Di glanced to the door.

Jordon did a little happy dance inside at how anxious Tian Di was to spend time with him.

Tian Di corrected, "I mean, um, tomorrow? There's a party happening right out there, and we can't leave for a dinner date... right?"

A date? Woo-hooo! The desire to indulge them both and sneak out warred with Jordon's mission to act like an adult. "Yeah, it might be seen as tacky...." But, oh, so tempting.

They stood there smiling at each other. "We should probably clean up.... The bathroom is right outside this door."

Not wanting to go, Jordon reminded them both, "Oh, I didn't sign any of your manga."

"Gives you a reason to come back."

"I'd love any reason to come... back." Jordon loved the blush spreading across Tian Di's cheeks. He'd discovered a new way of coloring, only way better.

CHAPTER 7

TIAN DI stared at the text he'd just typed to Jordon.

Thanks for the wonderful night! That was an understatement. He'd never felt such a connection with someone. He added, *If you are free before dinner, maybe I can show you Suzhou?*

There. That didn't feel desperate or pushy. Offering to take a foreign visitor sightseeing wasn't like his awkward dinner invitation.

Jordon was already asleep. He'd get the text in the morning and wouldn't notice the time and date stamp. Tian Di hit Send.

His phone vibrated before he could set it aside. It couldn't be. It was.

I'm free!

I didn't mean to wake you. Tian Di's heart danced happily.

How could he not adore this man? Jordon Davis was everything he imagined Sakura Rose to be, and more. He didn't know Jordon at all, not really. There were only a few people Tian Di actually wanted to spend time with, and none of them fit him so well.

An almost instant text rattled Tian Di's phone. *I'm up... very up if you know what I mean.*

Oh-ho. Jordon had a bit of spice to him, and Tian Di loved it. Before he could think of what to type, his cell indicated another text.

My brothers gave me a sleeping med. It hasn't kicked in but has made me loopy. I was sketching.

What were you sketching?

You. I shouldn't say that. But you, you, you.... God, you're beautiful.

Tian Di was used to people hitting on him with empty compliments, but with Jordon... there was a sincerity that touched him and made him blush.

Thank you.

No, like I knew you were pretty & sexy, but you're beautiful. There's just something about you. It's weird. I feel like I've known you 4ever!

It wasn't odd to him at all. Maybe lying alone in the dark gave Tian Di the courage he needed to confess something.

I feel that too.

A giant, happy-face emoji with heart eyes filled Tian Di's phone screen and was followed by, *Glad we exchanged numbers. I'm rambling.*

You are jet lagged and it's 1 in the morning.

I'm usually up late. Sometimes I don't sleep for days, there's too much to paint. Zack (brother) says I'm 20 lbs. of crazy in a 10 lb. bag. LOL

I think you're a 1000 kilos of wonderful!

The next text vibrating Tian Di's phone read *OXOXOX* followed by *Do you know what O & X mean?*

Hugs and Kisses. OXOXOXO back!

There was a pause. Tian Di tapped his ring against the phone. Had Jordon fallen asleep? Maybe he should—

Another text vibrated. *But this is stupid for your singing career.*

What?

Us.

Tian Di twisted his ring. It felt tight.

There was no denying Jordon's point. Them getting involved invited trouble. It might be career suicide, and he knew his career should be more important to him than someone he'd just met, but… if Made in China worked out, some people would think it was because he had played the whore to curry favor. If it didn't, they'd blame him for blowing their chance. *So you don't want to see me?*

It scares me how much I want to see you, spend time with you, kiss you….

Tian Di shivered. *Me too, Jordon.*

I guess we're going to be stupid. Jordon's honesty was irresistible.

I am good with that. And he really was.

So, sightseeing tomorrow morning?

Yes. 8 tomorrow morning? Was that too early? Maybe he should—

Great! It's dumb but I miss you already.

Wow. Tian Di hadn't taken sleeping pills laced with honesty, so when he texted back *Me too*, he had no excuse.

Night came through with an artist emoji.

Get some sleep. Have honeyed dreams. Tian Di's grandfather would always say that when he tucked him and his sister into bed.

Jordon responded with *I will if I dream of you.*

So sweet. Nothing like the men he'd known. It was the first time he felt he could share all of himself and wasn't made sorry for doing so.

ZHANG MIN shifted closer to her computer screen. "You look different, Tian Di. Why are you calling so early?"

Maybe a video chat with his sister wasn't the best idea, but he couldn't stop his smile from widening.

"Zhang Min, what do you mean?"

She sat back and folded her arms in that stubborn way of hers. "Either you're super excited about the tour starting or you've met someone."

Tian Di might burst if he didn't tell her. "I met someone."

"And?"

"He's sweet, funny, smart, talented, and it's a really bad idea."

"With this gush of affection, I think you've already fallen for him."

Had he? "It's too early for that. He's the younger brother of the Dark Angels' drummer."

"How young?"

Not the issue. "He's twenty."

"Old enough, but that's still setting yourself on fire and hoping there's enough water to put out the flames."

"I know." Tian Di sighed. "I'm seeing him in a few minutes to show him Suzhou."

She stared at him for a while. Many emotions crossed her expression, from excited to worried, ending on resigned. "This is your big musical break, and I know you don't want to ruin your chance."

"It's everything I've worked for my entire life." He dropped his head into his hands as his heart screamed it wanted Jordon.

Zhang Min nodded. "I know."

He peeked at her, hoping she might help him sort out the crazy. "But I really like him."

"Keep in mind you just met this guy." She could always be counted on to be practical, and she wasn't wrong.

"I know." He was compelled to add, "It's hard to describe. I feel like he's meant to be mine. It's insane, but I can't stop thinking about him, and it's as if there was nothing before him that was even remotely important."

Zhang Min's mouth dropped open, and she stared at him. "You sound like Ye Ye."

Their grandfather had told them stories of when he first saw their grandmother and he knew right then he would make her his wife. She gave him a fine chase, but after fifty-eight years of marriage, her eyes still sparkled when she glanced in his direction. Tian Di didn't think that would ever exist for him.

He opened his mouth and closed it before he said something dumb.

Zhang Min tilted her head and studied him. "Maybe this is the real thing. Spend time with him and see."

Tian Di wished he could hug her, because that was what he needed to hear.

"Do what will make *you* happy. Text me later." She signed off.

He grabbed his bag and headed over to Jordon's hotel. Zhang Min's words chased around his brain. She had never been traditional, but telling him to focus on his own happiness before the greater good, that bordered on sounding like Indigo.

To date the Dark Angels' drummer's baby brother would make Tian Di crazy! What was he thinking? His selfishness could wreck Made in China's big break. One word from the manager and no American record label would ever touch Made in China or him again. The band would sputter out of existence, and him with it.

No, this was just sightseeing. It would be rude not to show someone from a different country around Suzhou. It—

There he was. Tian Di's heart triple-timed.

Jordon stood outside his hotel, leaning on the railing overlooking the lake. The early morning sun's angle silhouetted him in gold, making the waves in his hair catch the light and sparkle. He turned as if he felt Tian Di's closeness.

"*Zǎo ān!*" Jordon said good morning in Mandarin with the most precious American accent.

Every logical and rational intention disappeared. Tian Di tried not to quicken his steps, but failed. "Wow, Chinese. You've been studying?"

"Nah, that's where my language skills end. I see my objective as helping you refine your perfect English." Jordon's grin shoved any fear of playing with trouble out of Tian Di's head.

Tian Di chuckled. "Have you had breakfast?"

Jordon glanced quickly at the hotel as they strolled past. "Um, no. I just left a note under Zack's door and slipped out."

Warning bells blared. "Are you hiding that we're—"

"I'm just not advertising our little adventure. I think it would be best, don't you?"

Hating that he was right, Tian Di changed the subject. "We can go to the 7-Eleven store before we go to the subway."

Uniformed school kids trudged past, showing only a little interest in Jordon, which suggested they went to the International School. They didn't give a second glance to Jordon's blond hair.

Tian Di held the convenience store door open for Jordon.

"Oh, look at this. It's just like back home, only the products are different." He stared at the bags of potato chips. "Spicy crab? Cucumber? Shrimp chips? This is amazing."

"I'm going to get us some buns. This shop gets their bao from a Singaporean expat, and they're delicious." Tian Di bagged two buns.

"I'll get the drinks. Preferences?" Jordon asked as he headed toward the refrigerated section.

"A green tea." Even though he would have preferred something else, his grandmother would be pleased. She taught him having green tea at least once a day could prevent many diseases and problems.

Jordon grabbed a green tea and a rose tea, which made Tian Di smile.

At the register, Tian Di paid because Jordon gaped openmouthed at the condoms behind the counter. He turned toward Tian Di looking for answers. "This package is called Jizz Boom. These are labeled Yummy Covers. And this has lines to measure…."

"How much." The man behind the counter tried to explain in English to Jordon.

Tian Di waved off the helpful clerk. He guided Jordon outside.

Shaking his head, Jordon frowned. "I'm sorry. I didn't mean to be an ugly American, but the translations caught me off guard."

"Yeah, I guess I don't think in English, so I don't even process the exact translation, but Yummy Covers…?"

Jordon snorted. "I don't mean to be immature, though that cracks me up."

"It's okay. Once I saw a note over bathroom urinals: 'Sharp forward and show your civilization.' I burst out laughing, and between the looks from the other men and one older man who called me thirteen o'clock, which means crazy, I ran out of there." Using a napkin, Tian Di reached into the bag, and handed a warm bun to Jordon.

Their fingers brushed. Memories of what those tentative fingers felt like on Tian Di's body made him want them driving him insane again.

The way Jordon grinned at him, Tian Di was certain Jordon knew what he'd been thinking.

"Thanks." Jordon examined the outside of the bun. He broke the bun open and sniffed the meat.

"It's barbecued pork. The buns are baked daily and are delicious." Tian Di demonstrated by biting into his, and he groaned as the soft, doughy bun gave way for the sweet meat flavor that exploded over his tongue.

Jordon stopped dead and shook his head. "God, Tian Di. Please don't make those sounds out here. I want to hold your hand really bad, but I know we can't."

Maybe the admission that he'd affected Jordon shouldn't have pleased Tian Di so much, but it did. "Come on. The train won't be crowded this early."

Jordon walked a few steps and bit into the bun. "Mmmmm, these are so good." He covered his mouth and talked around the food.

It was Tian Di's turn to wish Jordon wouldn't torture him in public. He focused on eating and sipping his tea.

Tian Di waved to a group of about a dozen women doing tai chi. Many waved back with their red fans once they went to the top of their pose. "I usually join them a couple of times a week."

"Maybe I could sketch one of the classes," Jordon mused, but kept pace with Tian Di.

They finished the pork buns and drinks, tossed the trash, and stepped into the quiet, yet still bustling, station.

Jordon glanced around the relatively new station. "It's so modern."

Tian Di led Jordon to the machines on the wall to purchase a subway pass. "I guess a seven-day pass is enough?"

"Seven days never felt this short before," muttered Jordon.

Tian Di was now more driven than ever to pack decades of fun into the few hours they had today.

Jordon accepted the colorful subway card and traced his finger across the artwork of the skyline. He glanced up with emotions that tore at Tian Di's heart. "This is going to be hard, isn't it?"

Nodding, Tian Di said something his grandmother always said. "I feel like a mouse in a broom store with too much rice scattered on the floor."

Tilting his head, Jordon asked, "Meaning the broom shop owner is going to sweep away the rice before the mouse eats his fill, right?"

Tian Di stared into Jordon's watery, emerald green eyes. What could he say? "There's not enough time in the world to have all the rice I want... with you."

"Attention! Line 1 is arriving," the station speakers blared, nipping the romance of the moment.

Sighing, Tian Di waved him forward. "Come on. That's our train."

Swiping their cards across the machine made the gates open. They jogged down the stairs and stepped into an almost empty subway car with time to spare. Even though there were plenty of seats available, they sat side by side.

Jordon pressed closer than necessary, but Tian Di wouldn't complain. He drank in the heat of Jordon's lean body. A throat clearing yanked Tian Di out of all the wonderful things he could do to Jordon's body. "Um, so I haven't even told you where we're going."

"I'll go anywhere with you."

No games. No pretense. Jordon's straightforward honesty terrified Tian Di, because he had an overwhelming need to get used to Jordon's sincerity. "I thought since the Suzhou Museum hours begin at nine, we should get there when the doors open."

"Sounds great. I love museums. Usually I go with Zack or Justin."

"Now, Justin is your brother's...."

Jordon quietly said, "He helped raise me after my mom kicked me out."

"Kicked you out? Why did she do—" Tian Di shut his mouth, shocked at how he could ask such a personal question like he had the right to know.

The train slowed to a stop, and the only other two people in their car got off.

Tilting his head toward him, Jordon said, "She kicked both me and my brother Zack out for being an abomination."

"Abomination?" Maybe Tian Di's translation or definition was off.

"I guess telling her I was gay while her church group was over wasn't the best choice." Jordon sighed.

Not seeing any cameras, Tian Di moved his shoulder bag so he could hold Jordon's hand under it, wishing he could ease the pain. "My mom refuses to acknowledge... *anything* about me. It's not the same, but that's one of the biggest reasons I left Hong Kong. I couldn't live in the box my family had built for me."

"I'm sorry." Jordon's sincerity touched a place inside.

"I have my sister who accepts me, and I still visit my family, though I know they won't accept… me." Tian Di left it at that.

Jordon squeezed Tian Di's hand and touched his musical note ring. He stared down at their interlocked hands. "Sweet ring."

"In China, during some wedding ceremonies, people put their ring on their index finger since that's a meridian, or place that connects directly to the heart."

"Oh, this is how you tell everyone you married music?" Jordon smiled at him. "It's very *Phantom of the Opera* of you."

"What?"

"Nothing. Dumb reference. The lead of the play has a choice between music and the man she loves."

Music over love. That had never even been a question until Jordon. How could a few short hours with someone change Tian Di's outlook so dramatically?

Tian Di swallowed. "That used to be an easy choice for me…."

Jordon's lips parted—

"Attention. Now arriving at Lindun Lu," the speakers called out.

Tian Di was almost relieved to not hear Jordon's response. Everything spun too fast, but he didn't want the feelings to end.

"This is us."

They left the train, hiked up two sets of stairs, and stepped into the heart of downtown Suzhou.

Jordon did a 360. "Wow. This is impressive. High-rises, a busy six-lane road, and a buttload of department stores."

Tian Di smiled and pointed across the road. "That's one of Suzhou's walking streets, meaning there's no car traffic, or at least there shouldn't be. There is a temple in the center, souvenir shops, restaurants, tailors, clothing shops, and more department stores."

"It's funny. I knew China was modern. I've been to Beijing, but it's still surprising." Jordon stared at the cars honking their horns as they zipped past a man pedaling his pedicab, hauling a couple of older women.

Tian Di waved off the offer of a ride and led Jordon down a side street. "That's the Lion Grove Garden. There's a rockery maze, pond, and a hundred-year-old teahouse. We… I mean, you, should see it before you—"

Jordon's shoulder bumped his. "Just so you know, I'll be on the whole Asia leg of the tour."

Things brightened a little bit. More time. "Yeah? That's great."

They turned down onto another walking street.

Stopping dead, Jordon shook his head and stared at the museum. "What an incredible legacy. This building is said to be one of I. M. Pei's final designs. Look at the clean shapes of white outlined by the black roofs."

Tian Di fished for words. "The building is very traditional for Suzhou, but—"

"Somehow modern and sleek." Jordon traced his fingers in front of him like he was drawing the building in the air.

"Yes, exactly." Tian Di enjoyed having someone other than his sister finishing his thoughts.

"The simplicity gives the building a crisp clarity that... wow, the man was a master."

"I. M. Pei did the glass triangle at the Louvre, right?" Maybe Tian Di should have studied to be a better tour guide.

"Yeah, the glass symmetric triangle was his design." Jordon snapped some pictures from every angle Tian Di could imagine.

"I guess architecture is really the art of buildings." Tian Di had never made that connection before, but seeing the world through Jordon's eyes, he couldn't miss it.

Jordon grinned at him. "Yes!"

Jordon's cell rang. After looking at his phone, he exhaled and answered. "Hey, Zack.... No. No, I'm fine. I'm just going into the museum. I have my wallet and the hotel keycard. No. No, you don't have to meet me at the museum. Don't you want the day to spend with Andrew? Nah, I'm good. Really good. Yes, I'm fine. I'll catch you later."

"One of your brothers?"

"Yeah." Jordon huffed out another puff of air—hard.

Tian Di wasn't sure what that was about, so he changed the subject. "They're opening the doors of the museum."

"Cool." Jordon grabbed his arm and pulled him to the short line of yawning tourists.

After their bags went through the metal detector, they headed inside.

The art propelled Jordon forward. He stood in front of one of the museum's treasures, read the English placard, and then said, "This is the

Pearl Pillar of the Buddhist Shrine. It's a thousand years old, and was found in the Ruiguang Pagoda. Stunning. It looks like it's almost four feet high."

"Yeah, about 1.2 meters. The main body is carved in wood." Tian Di tried to recall what Li had told the band from his guidebook when Indigo insisted Made in China needed a field trip. "If I remember this right, the shrine's base is octagon-shaped and is supposed to remind us of the eight custodians of Buddhism."

"Are you Buddhist?"

Tian Di shook his head. "No. My grandparents are, though."

"Look at this piece. The artistry of the dragons chained and cuffed right at the top is incredible. Look at the personalities of each of the figures, and the eight silver lions. This is mind-boggling if you think about the tools the artists had to create with at the time." Jordon circled the glass-enclosed relic.

Tian Di pointed out, "Look at these sections. They're dripping with gold, silver, pearls, jade, and crystal."

Jordon took some pictures with his phone.

Across the room a dragon plate with one of the talons scratched out caught Jordon's eye.

He followed.

"Why did they wreck the plate?" Jordon's horror of art harm rang out loud and clear.

Tian Di remembered this one. "In ancient China, dragon claws represent the classes of people. Three talons were meant for ministers and officials, and during a couple of the dynasties even for commoners, four was designated for nobility, and five was reserved for the emperor. This plate had to have been stolen from the emperor's court, and then the thief tried to hide their guilt."

Jordon's mouth hung open.

They spent two hours drifting from treasure to treasure, and Tian Di had never appreciated any museum anywhere more.

Seeing Jordon happy did things below the waist to Tian Di, while the unexpected euphoria in the region of his heart surprised him. It was even more fulfilling than pleasing his sister.

Jordon gave him a new view of what he was looking at and discussed the techniques behind some of the creations. It couldn't be helped; Tian Di stared at Jordon more than any of the other treasures.

JORDON BEAMED at Tian Di like he was the keeper of magic. "Thank you for taking me to the museum. Where to now?"

"Since Suzhou is the Venice of the East, we could walk along Shantang Jie. The street snakes along one of the canals and is probably one of the oldest in Suzhou. They recently restored the entire area."

"Sounds great." Jordon had such an easy way about him.

Tian Di led him to the mouth of the Shantang's canal.

"Wow." Jordon stopped to snap pictures of the weeping willows dripping in the canal. Traditional wooden boats were no longer used to ferry goods along the canal, but tourists looking for a taste of ancient China formed a line to ride the boat.

Jordon took pictures every few steps, and they meandered over a stone bridge.

"Shops!" Jordon beelined to an embroidery shop.

"Suzhou specializes in embroidery." Tian Di smiled as Jordon touched the stitched mythical animals, birds, and symbols.

"Here, here. You try. You try." The shopkeeper abandoned her TV drama to push an embroidered jacket at them.

Jordon tried the jacket on, but the maroon did nothing for his coloring. He examined the material with a frown. Maybe he recognized it wasn't silk, but a poly blend that would probably fall apart after three wearings.

As the shopkeeper fished around for another one, Tian Di whispered, "If you want, later we can go to my tailor and get you a custom jacket. You can even design the embroidery."

"Really?"

Tian Di handed the dismayed shopkeeper back her items. Once they left the shop, he said, "A lot of these shops cater to tourists and aren't trying to win repeat customers. They may not have the highest quality."

Jordon nodded. Tian Di liked that he didn't condemn the entire country based on a few folks trying to make a bit of yuan.

Going in and out of the shops with no lag inspired Tian Di. "You seem to like shopping as much as I do."

"I love seeing new things. Usually you can tell something about the people by their handicrafts, art, and souvenirs." His cell buzzed again. "Sorry. Let me text him back."

After a few minutes, Tian Di followed Jordon into the government-owned Suzhou No. 1 Silk Factory and Embroidery Store. All the patterns were displayed on the wall, and each was available in bedding and clothing. There was also a room filled with wall hangings.

The price jumped by a 300 percent markup, though everything was certified authentic and made by local artists.

Jordon whistled. "No fakes here. Feel this silk."

A pretty saleswoman came over to them. "Hello, I'm Kathy. What can I help you find today?"

"Just looking," Jordon muttered and slid away. "Tian Di, check this out."

Tian Di and the woman followed him into the room of exquisite wall hangings, ranging in size from a postcard to wall murals.

Jordon's phone rang. He gave a quick "Sorry" and answered his mobile. "Zack, didn't you get my texts? I'm fine. I'm at the Silk Factory. Just shopping. Yes, I'll get lunch. See you later."

Kathy whispered in Chinese, "Where is your friend from?"

"America," Tian Di answered in English. Before she could offer him a kickback for getting Jordon to buy more, he hurried to Jordon's side. "That's gorgeous."

Jordon traced his finger over the colorful tail feathers on the wall hanging. "I've always loved phoenixes."

Tian Di ignored the price tag. "The work is well done."

Kathy inserted herself between them. "The artist is a local man from an embroidery family. His family has been embroidering since the Ming Dynasty."

"Cool." Jordon continued searching the walls and stacks of embroideries and pulled out those pieces that required closer inspection.

Tian Di had a great time watching Jordon. He figured out Jordon admired vivid color mixed with precision. Jordon stayed clear of the primitive embroidery, preferring the refinement Tian Di appreciated.

Jordon leaned into Tian Di. "Zack said I should ask for a discount. Though the sign says no discounts."

"Depending on how much you're buying, she might give you 5 to 10 percent off."

"I guess it doesn't hurt to ask." Jordon turned to Kathy, who lingered close by. "If I were to get several pieces, would you be able to do a discount?"

Kathy pointed to the big sign. "I'm sorry, sir. No discount... unless you were buying at least five pieces."

Jordon grinned. "I am."

"Then 5 percent."

"I'm buying seven smaller pieces, and three wall hangings, so how about 15 percent?"

Wow. Tian Di was impressed by Jordon's guts.

Yuan signs danced in her eyes as she calculated the zeros. "Which ones?"

Jordon pulled seven pieces from the tops of piles without hesitation. He pointed to the wall hanging of two dragons with the balls between them, symbolizing the world. "I'm interested in those two, and one of the phoenix."

"Of course, sir. We can deliver them to your hotel."

Jordon looked at Tian Di.

Tian Di answered his unasked question. "Since this is a government shop, it's safe to assume your purchases will arrive."

She countered Jordon's offer. "Ten percent discount, sir, and I'll deliver for free."

Jordon gave Kathy his hotel details.

Smiling, Jordon held the door open for Tian Di and whispered, "I would have settled for 8 percent."

They strolled to the end of the canal.

Tian Di started to lead him back toward the main area of downtown. "Are those art supply stores?"

Looking across the street, he gestured to the shops. "I never noticed them, but yeah."

Jordon rushed inside. Ten minutes later, he'd purchased brushes, inks, an ornately carved ink block, a fancy swan water dripper, and paper.

Tian Di asked, "Do you know how to do brush painting?"

"You mean watercolor?" After Tian Di's nod, Jordon admitted, "Only a little."

"Would you like to meet an artist of brush stroke?"

"Yeah!"

Tian Di made a quick call and then told Jordon, "My friend said she'd be home this afternoon if you're interested to visit."

"Yes, that would be great."

He confirmed the meeting and disconnected the call.

Jordon stopped. "This has been such an amazing day. Thank you."

Tian Di felt too many things, so he waved Jordon off and changed the subject. "I met the artist, Chin Yu Fan, in the park doing tai chi. She used to be an art professor at Suzhou University." She'd been impressed how well he handled his fan.

"I can't wait to meet her."

AFTER LUNCH and a quick stop at the tailor shop where Jordon drew an amazing dragon and phoenix design for a jacket in deep forest green, they went to the artist's apartment.

Chin Yu Fan flung open the door. Her height always surprised Tian Di. The artist barely reached his chest.

Tian Di spoke Mandarin to Chin Yu Fan and shook her hand. "Greetings to you, Aunty."

She turned toward Jordon and grinned. "He's pretty like you. The blond hair, very nice, and those eyes. Those green eyes are special, just like jade."

Jordon tentatively smiled back, clearly having no clue as to what she was saying.

Before Tian Di could stop her, she pushed her fingers right into Jordon's hair. "Very nice, but too long for a boy. You should take him to get a haircut when you get yours cut."

Jordon widened his eyes, but he didn't duck away. He held out his hand. "Nice to meet you."

She grabbed his hand and held it against her arm. "So white. His skin...."

Jordon slipped his arm down and caught her hand in his. "*Ni hao ma*, Fan *lǎoshī*."

"Oh, Tian Di. I can't believe my ears. How does he know the word for teacher in Mandarin?"

Tian Di shook his head and translated for Jordon.

Jordon reminded him, "Some of my characters are from China."

Tian Di told Chin Yu, "He's an artist who studies all about his subjects."

"Oh, come in." She fluttered her hands to usher them in from the hallway.

He admired how easily Jordon slipped off his shoes and into the slippers Chin Yu Fan provided.

"Thank you for meeting with us. I'm grateful you'll consider giving Jordon a lesson."

"Yes, thank—"

She held up a finger to Jordon and dashed into her kitchen.

Chin Yu Fan reappeared, holding out a chopstick to him.

Tilting his head, Jordon studied the implement. Muttering something about the karate kid, he carefully accepted the chopstick.

Chin Yu Fan nabbed his hand and scrutinized his fingers. She appeared to be assessing his finger placement as well as his grip. One nod later and she dragged him into her office studio.

She pointed to chairs, and once they were seated, she scurried around gathering supplies. Returning to the newspaper-covered desk, she laid down a book and a sheet of paper. She paged through the book and stopped on a colorful picture of lotus with a dragonfly resting on a petal. Blocking out all but a few petals of the lotus, she told Tian Di, "Tell him to only see a portion of the picture. Piece by piece he will paint the rest."

Tian Di translated.

Jordon listened.

"Watercolor is about water. The ink colors the water. You layer the water and the color deepens." She taught and Tian Di transferred the knowledge.

This continued for the next hour. Jordon painted a dozen lotuses, sometimes with Chin Yu's hand-over-hand assistance.

Watching Jordon work fascinated Tian Di. Jordon's focus narrowed to the task in front of him. He picked up the technique easily.

Jordon drew lotuses in various positions with surprising accuracy. "But why can't I do the lotus my own way?"

Tian Di filtered down Chin Yu's almost hostile answer and translated, "You need to follow those who were before you. You don't change what isn't broken."

"It's art. My job is to break the rules, to go beyond them and make new ones," Jordon muttered.

Chin Yu Fan might not have understood Jordon's words, but she could read a pout. She said in English, "No. You do the right way. One way, this way."

Jordon sighed. "Yes, Fan lǎoshī."

She X-ed out the lotus Jordon had drawn that was different from the picture in the book. Pointing at the page, she said, "Now do."

Following the picture, Jordon replicated how the lotus flower was depicted, line by line.

"Good." She petted his hair and then left the room.

Jordon grabbed a scrap paper and drew a variety of lotuses, none of which was a reproduction of the image in the book. He grinned at Tian Di like he'd won some great victory and slipped his artwork under the newspaper.

Chin Yu returned with tea and watermelon.

"Xiè xie ni, Fan lǎoshī." Jordon's Mandarin with a heavy American accent shouldn't be such a turn-on.

After they ate and drank, Chin Yu had Tian Di translate how the picture would go through a preserving process and could be picked up at a later time.

Jordon smiled.

Tian Di gave a grateful goodbye to Chin Yu. Once he and Jordon were on the elevator, he readjusted his pants.

Jordon caught him and asked, "Um, problem?"

"Between your American accent and watching you lose yourself in art—let's just say these jeans have never been this much of a challenge."

Laughing, Jordon shoved his hands into his pockets. "This has been an incredible day. Thank you."

"I feel like I'm trying to jam decades into a day." The elevator doors slid open. Tian Di put his hand over the doors to ensure they remained open while Jordon stepped off. He followed.

They meandered down the street in silence toward the train station. Never before had Tian Di wanted to hold someone's hand so badly.

Jordon looked at his cell phone. "Oh, I forgot about your show tonight. You should be resting or something."

Tian Di kept smiling even though he knew his band would be freaking out. "The train will get us there with plenty of time to spare."

On the train, Jordon checked his messages. He growled. "I got a bunch of texts from my brothers."

"Is everything okay?"

Jordon sighed and moved a tiny bit closer to Tian Di. "Yeah, they just want me to go to the teahouse show with them tonight."

Tian Di's heart dropped. He'd been looking forward to Jordon being in his audience tonight to show off a little. "You can go. It's not like it'll be your only chance to see me—I mean, Made in China."

"No." Jordon typed onto his phone with speed as he rocked in his seat. "I told them I'm going to see you sing, and that's final."

He could sense the tension and stress this decision caused Jordon, but he didn't say more. "This is our stop."

Tian Di walked him to the hotel. "I guess I'll see you in a bit."

"Good skill," Jordon said.

"I thought Americans say 'break a leg.'"

"Most do. I don't. I hope you sing to the best of your ability." Jordon held out his hand.

Tian Di shook it and pulled him in for a backslapping man-hug that felt odd, especially since he just wanted to cuddle.

Jordon turned his face and licked a spot—on Tian Di's neck.

Shoulder-bumping Jordon, Tian Di claimed, "You're a demon."

"Nah, maybe an imp, though." Jordon waved and then sashayed into his hotel.

A quick check of the time showed Tian Di he needed to forego his shower, and he headed directly for the German restaurant.

Of course, Indigo was there to snap at him. "Where have you been? You're late."

Jin, Styx, and Li stopped fussing with their instruments and stared at him.

"If by late you mean being on time, just not around to help you set up, then I'm late. Ask me if I care."

Indigo stood straight and his fists were clenched. "I don't need to ask you. I can see—"

Li stepped in front of Indigo. "Hey, knock it off. We're all uptight. But Made in China is happening."

Tian Di nodded. "Sorry, man."

Indigo growled. "Yeah, if he doesn't screw it up."

"Indi," Li pleaded.

"What? He's playing with all of our futures." Indigo gestured with his head toward Jin and Styx. "We got a whole lot riding on this. Let's not fuck this to hell just 'cause you want to get your dick wet."

Hurt morphed into anger almost quicker than Tian Di could register the emotions. "That's not what this—"

Indigo raised his hand. "Don't, okay? Just don't."

Guilt slashed through Tian Di. He didn't want to fuck up Made in China's chance, but he wasn't willing to walk away from Jordon.

CHAPTER 8

JORDON SIGHED as his phone vibrated with another text. Which brother worried too much this time?

Where R U? Zack's text had a demanding ring to it.

Saying "none of your fucking business" and "you're not the boss of me" wasn't adult. He texted, *I'm fine.*

Just like the sixteen times he'd told them before. Why didn't his brothers think he was capable of walking a few blocks to the German restaurant?

Dusty texted, *Are you there yet?*

U should have come with us! I hear it's a great show! Zack's whine came across even over the text.

Miss me that much, Zack? I think your anal elf should entertain U better.

Don't call Andrew that, both brothers texted.

LOL. Jordon threw an emoji with double middle fingers up.

When our tea show is done, we'll come get U to walk back with you. Dusty made the coddling sound reasonable.

No! Jordon texted back as quickly as his thumbs would hit the keys in the right order. *I can get back on my own. I got here fine.*

There was a pause. Zack and Dusty consulted with each other.

Zack texted back, *Breakfast tomorrow,* along with a glaring emoji.

Yeah. Okay.

Dusty texted, *Call if U need me. Have a good night.*

U 2.

Jordon turned off his text notifications and stepped into the restaurant. He surveyed the wall mural of windows. Interesting idea, although to create the feel of a German town they were in need of perspective, and maybe a few different colors, unless the artist was going for ironic....

"May I help you?" The hostess wore a crisp business suit, which ran counter to the traditional Bavarian dirndl dresses of the waitresses.

He pulled his focus away from the flat wall paintings. "Oh, yes. I'm here to hear the band."

She embodied adulthood with her no-nonsense professionalism, reminding him he still failed the basics of Adult 101 when it came to his brothers. "Drinks or dinner?"

"Um, I guess drinks. But could I see a menu?" Maybe he'd get an appetizer or something.

She collected three menus. "Of course. This way, please."

With a final glance at the mural, he tried to leave his ideas of improvement at the door. He followed the hostess to a large group of women.

All attempts at adulthood fled screaming. Without his brothers to run interference, he wasn't up to making small talk with band groupies. He preferred to drool quietly. "Oh, um, could I sit toward the back?"

The hostess led him toward the back. "You can sit at any of these tables."

He picked one in a shadowy corner and skimmed the extensive drink menus she'd left with him. The legal drinking age in China was eighteen, and his brothers weren't here to stop him, so he focused on the wines.

What did he know about alcohol? He didn't much like the taste. Once Justin had mentioned sparkling wine was his favorite. Hmm…. Forget recognizing the wineries. The wines were written in English letters but he probably couldn't say them—save for one.

When a bubbly waitress bounced over, he tentatively ordered, "I'll have the sparkling white from the Great Wall."

To his surprise, the waitress didn't card or chastise him for ordering wine. She asked, "Anything to eat? Pizza, french fries, pretzels, or—"

"Pretzels would be great." The pretzels seemed Germanish, though he was in China, so maybe that was odd.

Soon his wine and a wooden tree with six freshly baked, salted pretzels hanging off the branches arrived. At the base of the tree were six vividly colored dipping sauces. "Enjoy."

As he tried a soft, warm pretzel in the minty green sauce, the group of fans caught his attention. From their appearances, they were a mix of locals, tourists, and expats; mostly women, but some men were in the group. A woman stood in front of them reading the other fans an article about Made in China going on tour.

Other restaurant patrons dug into huge portions of veal, steak, and ribs or drank at the bar.

Somewhere around the time Jordon developed an addiction to the salty treats with the orangey sauce, the lights dimmed.

"As you've heard, our band is going on tour with the Dark Angels." The announcer's familiar voice cracked a little. Was that Made in China's would-be manager?

A shiver of excitement ran through Jordon. He was going to hear Made in China in person. More to the point, he got to watch Tian Di strut around stage. His inner fanboy raced to the surface.

The speaker cried out, "Please give a warm welcome to Made in China!"

The fan group stood and cheered. Jordon jumped to his feet and joined in.

The curtain opened and the band took the stage, followed by Tian Di, who demurred and dragged his feet to the spotlight front and center. "You've heard the news. We want to thank all of our fans. This wouldn't have happened without you believing in us."

Jordon stood and clapped with the rest of the crowd. When everyone else sat, so did he.

Tian Di bowed his head. The music started slow, then erupted into a wild mix of instruments. Tian Di's strong voice penetrated through the chaos and into Jordon's heart.

This wasn't Jordon's first concert, not by a long shot. Looking around the restaurant, he noticed the space was tiny compared to the Dark Angels' smallest concert venue, though "damn amazing" didn't even cover the sound. Within minutes, the band involved all of the crowd in their electricity. Even the men at the bar turned and watched the show.

The Youku videos didn't do them justice.

Tian Di had the mythical *it* factor agents always sought. He sparkled and beamed. His shy demeanor appeared innocent and sweet, but then he morphed into this confident demon whose strut spoke of dirty things he'd do while twisting the bedsheets.

The band was the total package. They had the sound, a look, and actual talent. The musicians in each of them strove for perfection, and they found completion in one another. The band members merged and became better as the night wore on.

The lights dimmed from bright to dark in a nanosecond, but when you have a teen running the lights, you forgave errors.

Toward the end of the set, Tian Di stepped closer to the edge of the stage. "If you'd allow me, I'd like to dedicate this next one to someone very special. This person, along with all of our fans here in Suzhou, helped us on our path. Jordon, this one's for you."

No one had ever dedicated a song to him. It was to him? Of course it was. Tian Di had even given a small smile in his direction.

The words of the song touched Jordon, not because of the lyrics, but because of the emotion that accompanied them. Raw need tore directly into Jordon's soul and filled him with something it must be too soon to name—though he felt it nonetheless.

The crowd broke into thunderous applause, and Jordon stood with most of the audience, clapping.

After the first set, the stage dimmed. He wasn't sure if he should go backstage or—"Robin, what are you doing here?"

Robin slid into the seat across from Jordon's. "I popped out of the teahouse show to see how you were doing. And, oh my, I'd say you're doing rather well. He dedicated a song to you."

Positive his face was the color of lava, Jordon couldn't deny it. "Yeah."

"You really like him," Robin stated more than asked.

"Yeah, we spent the whole day together, and the time with Tian Di was pure magic. Perfect. I can't explain—"

"Maybe more than like?" Robin was never afraid to get to Jordon's truth.

Jordon shook his head, but he wanted to nod. "I… isn't it too soon?"

Smiling, Robin rested a hand on his heart. "Love doesn't tell time the same way we do."

"It's just that—oh, Robin." Jordon probably had emoji hearts covering his eyes, answering better than words. "We went to the museum and talked. I felt like we were in a movie. We strolled along a canal and shopped. He arranged an art lesson for me. Tian Di simply gets me. It's easy with him."

Robin squeezed his hand. "I'm happy for you. I look forward to getting to know him. But you probably want to text your brothers."

Jordon shook his head and huffed. "Are they losing it?"

"When you didn't answer a question fifteen minutes ago, Zack imagined you'd been kidnapped."

He didn't know whether to laugh or scream.

"You're their baby. It's hard for them to see you as an adult. Give them some time, but unless you want company, text them back." Robin hugged Jordon and slipped back out.

Jordon begrudgingly looked at his texts, responded to both brothers' numerous questions, and to Justin's nonquestion question.

"THANKS FOR waiting for me." Tian Di led Jordon out of the restaurant and onto the boardwalk.

Jordon felt guilty about Tian Di cutting out after he spoke with Made in China's fan group, without helping the band pack their equipment, but he was too greedy to forego the time.

"No worries. I get how rock stars are in demand." Jordon had to tease, if only to see Tian Di blush. The dusky rose revealed by the streetlights would be a difficult color to replicate in paint.

Tian Di ducked his head. "I know it's nothing like the Dark Angels' following, but I want to show my appreciation. These were our core fans before anyone really knew we existed. It's truly special of them to care so much about us."

"It is—look!" Jordon stopped at the railing to point out Suzhou's neon skyline-lit bridge. "Wow. I also love the buildings topped with pyramids. The architects here use the city as a canvas."

Tian Di gestured to a path along the lake. "Care for a walk?"

"Sure."

Tian Di put a hand on Jordon's back and guided him across the street.

Jordon kept in step with Tian Di and let their shoulders rub as much as possible.

"I think it's amazing how you have Western restaurants like Pizza Hut, KFC, and Burger King next to Coach, Gucci, and other expensive designers."

There were many different shops, selling toys, souvenirs, clothing items, pastries—every shop demanded Jordon's attention. A rainbow of neon splashed everything with color.

"This area is called Harmony Times Square. It was built to give the rich a place to shop."

"You know, American kids used to be told to finish their dinner because there's poor children in China with no food."

"There was a time that might have been true, but there's a saying here now: We used to work to be a good person. Now we work for money, and money's better. Capitalism became the emperor."

"If you judge wealth by expensive cars, I'd say China's doing okay."

"True."

They turned the corner of a building. Jordon stopped dead. "Wow."

"That's the Sky Screen." Tian Di pointed to the LED screen scrolling above them in a gentle wave.

Tian Di led him over to a concrete bench, which allowed Jordon to keep his eyes on the screen. "It's three hundred fifty meters long. Right now, there's only two others in the entire world, but this one is the largest."

"It's fantastic." Jordon stared as digital fish swam overhead, and then the scene morphed into a field of vivid wildflowers with butterflies fluttering about.

Tian Di rested flush against Jordon. His body started making suggestions he might not have even been aware he was issuing.

Jordon could have watched the screen all night, though not when there might be other invitations to act on. "Um, do you want to come back to my room… and hang out?"

Tian Di pressed his lips together. "Yeah, but I need to shower."

"You can shower in my room. I don't mind." What was he thinking? Other than wanting to wash Tian Di's back… and other things.

Tian Di scrunched his face and shook his head. "I think your brothers might."

He was an adult and didn't need their approval. "They aren't invited."

Jordon tried to feel bold and daring in inviting a man back to his hotel room. However, those feelings were buried beneath a lot of shit Jordon didn't want to sift through right now.

Tian Di's breath hitched. "I want to… really I do. Maybe too much so—"

Decision made. "Me too. Come on. Let's go."

Jordon held out his hand to pull Tian Di to his feet.

There was a slight hesitation, but Tian Di clasped on tight and held his hand a bit longer than necessary.

No more words were needed. They rushed back to the hotel and took the elevator to his floor. Jordon couldn't help but look down the hall at Zack's door.

He breathed a sigh of relief when they got into his room undetected. He engaged the secondary lock on the door.

Jordon turned, and Tian Di was right there.

Was it hot in here? He rushed to the thermostat. Nope, it was on and set to 20 Celsius, which was about 68 Fahrenheit.

"Um, the bathroom's right in there." Jordon pointed to the bathroom.

Tian Di brushed past him, lighting fire to the place he touched. "Thanks."

Jordon stumbled to the bed and sat. He should stay put.

The bathroom door remained cracked open. That wasn't an invitation… was it? Maybe it was, and if he didn't accept the invite, would Tian Di think he rejected him? If he did—

The water turned on.

A shirtless Tian Di peered out. "The shower stall is huge."

For an endless moment, neither of them moved, Jordon's gaze trapped in Tian Di's.

He'd never done anything like this in the past, and his nervousness stole the awesome.

Tian Di raised his arm to lean against the doorframe, almost posing for Jordon.

As a reflex Jordon assessed the figure in front of him. Tian Di's chest was smooth, and his sepia nipples pebbled against the room temperature. His torso tapered into a narrow waist, with just the slightest hint of a treasure trail drawing Jordon's gaze lower. His black jeans clung to everything important. He looked better than any character Jordon had drawn.

There was definitely an offer on the table.

Desire slashed through him, forcing Jordon to freeze and just gape at temptation. The man he'd drooled over for well past a year stood in his bathroom, offering to do God knows what… with him. Right now.

Tian Di gave a small, inviting smile and disappeared into the bathroom.

Jordon shifted and sat on his hands. *Holy Fuckenstein!* He should get in there and… and what? What did one do in shower stalls with insanely hot rock stars?

The steady sound of the water changed from hitting the tile to hitting flesh. Tian Di's naked body was right behind the partially open door.

Jordon wiggled and adjusted his jeans, but that didn't do much for his comfort. Why couldn't he just go in there and join Tian Di? God, he was such a wuss.

There had to be some kind of protocol.

Grabbing his cell, he checked the time. Even with the time difference, it was after eleven in the morning in the US, so Gwen should be up. She'd know. He texted, *Tian Di is in my shower.*

Why aren't you with him?

This was a bad idea. *I don't know.*

Is the door open?

Jordon looked over and reconfirmed. *Yeah.*

That's an invitation. Get on that!!! texted his one-woman cheering squad to get him laid.

I don't know. Jordon sighed. Sometimes she couldn't see past her own comfort.

Didn't you two already have the intro orgasm?

Too late. Water's turned off. Later.

He's clean now, so your mission should be to get him dirty.

He sent a thumbs-up, signed his text with an artist emoji, and set his cell on the nightstand.

"Um, do you have something I can borrow to wear?"

All the witty come-ons Jordon had once practiced were sucked out of the room, much like his brain when he turned to see Tian Di wearing a towel like a sarong around his waist.

His wet hair dripped down his chest. Droplets cascaded where Jordon ached to touch.

Tian Di stepped closer.

The hotel's orange blossom-scented bath gel enveloped Jordon.

"Or I can just stay in this towel for a bit." His voice spun around Jordon forcing the deluge of horny thoughts to get etched into his must-do-list. Though Jordon hadn't a freaking clue how to bring any of them to fruition.

He wanted to say something brilliant and witty; instead he nodded.

Tian Di tugged Jordon off the bed. "I've wanted to kiss you all day. May I?"

Tilting his head, Jordon groaned, "Please."

Tian Di licked his own lips then glided his wet mouth against Jordon's. He hadn't embellished the memory of Tian Di's lips on his. Sparklers danced beyond Jordon's eyelids, and he needed to hold tightly to Tian Di's bare shoulders to stay upright.

The kiss broke through any restraint Jordon had. He twirled his fingers in Tian Di's wet hair and tugged.

Tian Di rewarded the action with a moan and a breathy "Yes."

Fingers toyed with the top button of Jordon's jeans, requesting permission. Jordon pulled back from Tian Di's delicious mouth.

Worry skated through him. What was Tian Di asking? How far did he want to go?

Before Jordon could figure out the underlying question, he thrust his hips toward the questing fingers. Then he trailed his mouth along Tian Di's neck, drinking in the groan of desire that escaped Tian Di.

Tian Di ran a teasing finger along the button fly of Jordon's vintage jeans. He popped the first, second, and third buttons open.

"Teeth," Tian Di begged as he pressed his neck against Jordon's mouth.

Nipping just enough to get those little sexy gasps of want out of Tian Di built Jordon's confidence. If he could make Tian Di needy, he could do anything.

But he missed that gorgeous mouth and needed a kiss. His fourth button opened. He pressed his mouth against Tian Di's and took another toe-curling kiss as the fifth and final silver disk slid out of its buttonhole.

Tian Di ghosted his hand over Jordon's arousal, trapped under his silky underwear, tantalizing him with the possibilities that chased away his doubts. "Yes?"

The light touch drove Jordon insane. Still not sure of the question, only the answer, he whispered, "Yeah." *Hurry!*

Jordon traced the top of the towel secured with only a tuck. One pull and Tian Di would be his. He'd never been with a naked man before, and the reality started to melt his mind.

He cupped Tian Di through the towel and dispelled the myth Asian men were lacking in the size department. Capturing Tian Di's mouth again, Jordon let the kiss give him courage to toy with Tian Di's cock through the damp towel.

Everything in him coiled.

Tian Di's hand had entered his pants and continued to tantalize him.

Jordon wanted to do so many things. Though at the same time, he froze with indecision.

Tian Di tormented the reason out of him with talented fingers gently caressing his asscheeks over his underwear. Once Tian Di slid Jordon's pants down, Jordon wanted the offending barrier off to give Tian Di more access.

"Mmmm, sexy" was Tian Di's only comment on Jordon's silky underwear. He skimmed his hands under the purple material, touching Jordon's bare ass. If the silk had been sensuous against his skin, Tian Di's hands on him were a ton better.

Tian Di caressed Jordon's ass as he worked the underwear down.

Jordon stepped out of them. He might have been naked from the waist down, but there was no embarrassment that could get past his arousal.

He ran his fingers around the hem of the towel and peeked at Tian Di.

Licking his lips, Tian Di begged, "Please."

With a flick of Jordon's wrist, Tian Di's cock escaped the confines of the towel. The terrycloth dropped to the floor.

A beautiful, unwrapped Tian Di stood in Jordon's hotel room less than a foot from the bed.

Tian Di took Jordon's shaft in hand and gave him a slow stroke.

"Fuck." Jordon gasped for breath.

Polishing his palm over the wet tip, Tian Di licked Jordon's neck, making him whimper.

God, all he wanted to do was come like crazy.

Marc Chagall lived 1887 until 1985. Oh, fuck! Picasso, 1881 to 1973, not 1975. Oh, my God, I'm going to come. Stop! Van Gogh was born.... Focus on Tian Di.

Jordon pushed back from the edge and closed his fist around Tian Di's cock. Tian Di's felt different from his own. Thicker?

He lowered his eyes to see what he touched. Tian Di's foreskin rolled over the top of his cock and back down. *Mm....*

The foreskin glided with ease across the crown to cover the wet tip, then slid back down, bringing the slick along the shaft.

Jordon glanced back up at Tian Di's face.

Grinning, Tian Di licked his hand and began matching Jordon's strokes.

A groan escaped because it was impossible to hold back. This was better than any fantasy Jordon had ever had. He was incredibly aroused, and his horny need began to overwhelm him.

Miro.... Miro, when did he live? Tian Di. Fuck!

"You close?" Tian Di panted and stroked Jordon at the exact speed he craved.

Jordon groaned, "Yeah," as his hand kept working Tian Di. His body tightened and started the climb.

"I love how breathy you get. It's extremely sexy." Tian Di pushed his hair back and crowded in close, placing sweet kisses on Jordon's throat. Soft, wet lips caressed the column of Jordon's neck.

That was fucking it. The tender affection tossed him beyond the edge. No amount of artist recall could pull him back.

Jordon whispered, "Coming."

He warned as if it mattered. Nothing could have stopped the wave of pleasure as the orgasmic bliss rushed out from his middle down to his toes.

Tian Di grunted in response and stroked him a little faster, making the ecstasy soar higher.

Jordon felt each and every pulse his body released, and just as Jordon floated down from the heights of heaven, Tian Di thrust as if Jordon were the only one capable of satisfying him.

The curtain of hair fell forward and brushed across Jordon's shoulders. Tian Di trembled.

Jordon stroked faster and gave him no mercy.

Groaning in surrender, Tian Di came in Jordon's hand. He crashed face-first into Jordon's shoulder.

Jordon slowed the strokes when Tian Di's spasms ended, and hugged Tian Di as they tried to catch their breath.

They remained entwined, held together by something more than their mutual need to get off.

Tian Di nuzzled Jordon's neck and stifled a yawn.

A need to take care of his exhausted lover flooded Jordon. He wiped them off with the discarded towel, settled Tian Di under the bed covers and tucked them around him.

"Where are you going?" Tian Di reached for Jordon.

"I'll be right there." Jordon used the coffee maker to make Tian Di some chamomile tea.

Tian Di accepted the warm cup with a sniff. "No one but my sister has ever made me tea."

Jordon kissed his fingers and traced the bruises Tian Di sported from his bites. "I'll make you tea whenever you want."

The promise hung in the air. His expression screamed that he was not only aware of what was happening between them but could see their connection in vivid Technicolor.

Just when Tian Di opened his mouth, Jordon spit out, "You have to protect your voice."

"Thank you." Tian Di wiped a hand across his face and sipped the tea.

The reality hit Jordon. Tian Di was in his bed... naked. Should Jordon go *au naturel* too? *Fuck it!* If he wanted to sleep nude next to Tian Di, he could. He tossed his shirt to the floor and slipped under the covers.

Tian Di arched an eyebrow but didn't comment.

Jordon took the empty teacup and set it on the night table.

They rolled into the middle of the bed, facing each other. Tian Di resettled the blanket over Jordon's shoulder and combed his fingers through Jordon's hair.

Snuggling into Tian Di, Jordon felt relaxed, content, and jubilant.

Tian Di cleared his throat. "I don't know why, but I feel like I've known you forever."

"Me too." Jordon was relieved to hear him speak the words.

"And I know it's too soon, but I don't care. I want you in my life... forever."

There was nothing else for Jordon to say except "Me too."

CHAPTER 9

BANG! BANG! Bang!

Ripped from an excellent dream, Tian Di snuggled into the warm body next to him. He didn't want to move.

"Hey, Jordie! Open up."

Jordon had remained cuddled in Tian Di's embrace all night, but now he stiffened like a board. He shifted out of Tian Di's arms and had the look of a truck driver with no brakes and a broken horn coming to a red light.

"Er… that's Zack," Jordon whispered as he frantically searched the room for clues to make sense of how any of this was possible.

The door pushed open a few inches, but the secondary lock caught and refused to allow entry.

"Why's your door latched?" Zack's voice echoed into their private oasis.

Jordon wrung his hands and muttered frantically, "I'm not ready to deal with my brothers yet."

Tian Di hated the fear of discovery in Jordon's eyes. He pointed to the other side of the bed. A finger to his mouth told Jordon he'd hide.

Knowing what needed to be done, Tian Di slipped over the side of the bed, slid under, and lay flat. Though if he were honest, some of his willingness to vanish was out of self-preservation. The one thing he'd learned from his father was that success depended on everything being handled in the right way. Finding his naked ass in Jordon's bed wasn't the way to accomplish the endgame. A dead Tian Di couldn't figure out what was between them.

Thump! Thump! Thump! "Jordon!"

Jordon muttered, "Jesus, let me get pajama bottoms on."

He loved that Jordon had gone to bed naked. The access made their middle of the night release marathon easy.

Tian Di had never met anyone so into touching. Jordon seemed to love stroking off together as much as Tian Di did. His gentle hands gave complete satisfaction. He appreciated that Jordon had cherished caressing him and hadn't demanded more from him.

Jordon stumbled across the room and unlatched the door. "What do you want, Zack?"

Zack burst into the room. "Why did you put the security lock on your door?"

"I guess I heard there were a lot of jackasses who would just use their key and barge in. Can you imagine that?"

"Nope. You've never double latched it before."

Jordon growled. "Zack, I'm twenty. Isn't it time you start treating me like an adult?"

"Um… yeah, but what if… you needed help and I couldn't get to you?"

"Zack…."

"Yeah… I mean, I know you're twenty, but shit happens."

Tian Di didn't think Zack sounded all that convincing.

"Zack… your brother's fine." Another voice, probably Zack's boyfriend, Andrew.

"He'd be even better if you stopped barging in on him." Tian Di could imagine Jordon with his arms folded across his chest and a look of determination in his eyes.

Zack snorted. "Fine, I'll try, Jordie. But come on, get dressed."

"No," Jordon snapped.

"What do you mean, no? You can't sleep all day. You'll never get rid of jet lag. You can come out with Andrew and me."

"No." Jordon sounded like he had injected a bit of steel to his decline.

"Are you sick?" Zack's tone suggested he'd never been told no by Jordon.

"No, I'm going somewhere with Tian Di…."

Sometime in the middle of the night, Tian Di had suggested he could take Jordon to Zhouzhuang. Though at the time they'd both become interested in something other than ancient water towns, so no decision had been made other than they wanted to touch each other some more. He couldn't wait to share the water town with Jordon.

Silly excitement wound around Tian Di's gut as he imagined showing Jordon the ancient place.

"What? No." Zack sounded confused.

"Yeah, he mentioned a water town, and I want to go."

Zack sputtered, "We can take you, and—"

"I want to see it with *him*." Jordon wasn't backing down, and defiance crept into his voice.

Zack gave an exasperated huff. "But—"

"Zack, let your brother spend time with Tian Di."

Jordon cleared his throat. "I had a lot of fun with him yesterday."

Tian Di grinned and wanted to add, "And early this morning."

Zack sighed loudly. "You know he's a singer, right?"

"And…?" Jordon seemed to be daring him to finish that thought.

"What if he's using you?"

That was exactly what Tian Di feared people might assume.

"Using me? For what? Made in China's already got the opening act. It's a done deal."

Tian Di wished he could ease Jordon's sting from Zack's words.

"Jordie, you know not everyone is—"

"Oh, I see. Is it that hard to imagine a beautiful man would want to spend time with me?"

He thinks I'm beautiful. That made Tian Di's world right. Although, he was hiding under a bed, so how right could it be? And even worse was that the concept hurt Jordon.

"Tian Di seems nice," Andrew said.

"He's great. I really had fun. He's smart, funny, and—"

"Doesn't he need to practice or something?" Zack asked a fair question.

"For the love of Buddha, stop being the human version of a headache. Made in China is off until Beijing."

Zack scoffed. "Well, I don't like it."

Jordon chuckled. "I can tell. But I'm sure Andrew can keep you busy."

Andrew mumbled something that sounded like "and tied up for hours," but Tian Di must have misheard.

"Fine. Please text me so I know you're okay." Zack's words were mumbled, so it suggested they were hugging.

"Oh, um, Zack." Jordon cleared his throat. "I want the extra key."

"What? But what if you get locked out?" Zack's shock over the request appeared to be an overreaction.

Jordon sighed. "Well, then, I'll have to drag my ass to the front desk and get another."

"I don't want you to have to do that. If you left your key, it means you're probably exhausted and you shouldn't have to go down to the front desk."

"It's not really a big deal." Jordon put a bit of steel in his voice.

"Yeah, but you'd be tired and—"

"Zack, listen to what Jordon is saying. He's twenty and doesn't need you holding an extra key anymore. That made sense once, but it no longer does." Tian Di was glad Andrew reinforced the idea because Zack didn't respond to what Jordon communicated.

Zack *tsk*ed. "But—"

"Give your brother the key." Andrew appeared to be the voice of reason.

"Fine. Though if you get locked out, remember you'll need ID to get a new key, so if you forgot your wallet, text me... but what if you lost your phone?" Zack asked the question like there was no solution.

"Zack, you can't get to the floor without the key, so I wouldn't get past the elevator. If I got mugged—"

Zack gasped. "God forbid. Don't talk like that, Jordie. Please...."

Jordon huffed out a breath. "All I'm saying is the front desk can call you or Dusty, and I can be verified."

"Oh, right. I... just worry." Zack muttered the last bit as if anyone could miss that fact.

"Yes, I know." Jordon sighed. "I'll be fine."

Zack sighed. "I know. Look, have fun today and text me."

The duo left the room with only a minimum of mumblings from Jordon's brother.

Jordon locked the deadbolt and hit the latch on the door. Ten seconds later, he peered over the side of the bed, biting his lip. He was all kinds of adorable. "Sorry."

Tian Di kept the sheet swathed around his hips. "You okay?"

"Yeah, I—" Jordon's cell phone danced across the nightstand. He stared at the screen and shook his head. "Text from my other brother. Dusty says I can go to the gardens with Justin; that's his fiancé."

Tian Di didn't want him to feel obligated. "If you want to—"

"No! Um, no, I want to spend the day with you. I mean, if you still want to." Jordon frowned and stared at the floor like the abstract pattern had done him wrong.

Tian Di rose from the floor. Sitting next to Jordon on the bed, he threw an arm around him. "I definitely want to spend every moment with you."

Jordon turned to gape at him.

Too much? Probably not, since last night he'd made his *forever* wishes known. He shook his head. "I hope that doesn't scare you, but I don't enjoy games. I really like you."

A cute pink rushed over Jordon's face. He leaned into Tian Di's shoulder and whispered, "I really like you too."

Tian Di's heart soared.

"Let me tell Dusty and Justin that I don't need a babysitter." Jordon typed on his cell.

HE AND Jordon took separate showers. Tian Di squashed his disappointment, because he certainly didn't want to push Jordon. If he had to guess, he'd say Jordon didn't have much physical experience, though that only made everything they did more special.

They slipped out of the hotel and got into a taxi. Jordon handed the driver a taxi card with the name and address of Zhouzhuang on it. The driver gave him a nod and sped along the highway to the water town.

"Thanks again for letting me borrow some clothes." Not only did Tian Di not want to put on the sweaty clothing he'd performed in, but there was a real thrill about wearing Jordon's clothing. He wanted to see Jordon in his clothing too. It was what boyfriends did in the movies Indigo watched.

"It's great we're about the same size. I'm glad I brought several different versions of the Made in China T-shirts. I might be obsessed. Their lead singer is hot."

"Yeah?" Taking pleasure in Jordon finding him *hot*—and beautiful—made him smile.

"Definitely." Jordon smirked and glanced down at his Made in China design. He'd drawn the band in a manga style.

"We're here." Tian Di paid the driver and then helped Jordon out of the taxi. He bought entrance tickets.

Jordon accepted the ticket. "Thanks. So how old is Zhouzhuang?"

"Zhouzhuang is the oldest water town in China. The town was built during the Ming and Qing dynasties." Tian Di realized Jordon probably had no clue when that was, and clarified, "The Ming Dynasty was from 1368 to about 1644 and the Qing Dynasty started right after until 1912."

"Wow. But these buildings look new?" Jordon pointed to the tourism buildings lining the street leading to the ancient town's entrance.

"Yes. They're not part of the original town, though built in the same style." He handed in their tickets and hip-bumped the bar to get through the turnstile.

Jordon stopped to read the sign denoting Zhouzhuang's importance for the trade of food, silk, and arts and crafts in the south of China.

They meandered down the first cobblestoned alley. A canal on their right was lined with weeping willows drooping into the still water, and on their left were all manner of shops and bustling crowds.

"Amazing." Jordon stumbled on the uneven steps leading to a kite shop, and Tian Di steadied him.

After a quick smile and a squeeze to Tian Di's arm, Jordon was lost to the colorful silk that raced around, covering the entire shop. Tails dripped from the mythical beasts hanging from the ceiling.

In an odd way, it made Tian Di proud that Jordon could find the quality among the souvenirs. It was fascinating to watch the artist in Jordon come out as he admired the artistry that went into making the kites and went straight for the ones created by the master craftsmen.

Jordon bounced out of the shop and on to the next. Tian Di joyfully followed, drinking in Jordon's enthusiasm.

A couple of shops later, a man pounded out sesame candy, and another worked a manual machine twirling taffy. Jordon appeared enamored with the process. Tian Di rushed into the shop and purchased a chunk of the sesame brittle and a small pouch of the taffy.

Jordon devoured every piece Tian Di handed him. Covering his mouth, he said, "So good. Usually I prefer chocolate, but this is delicious."

They strolled past several antique stalls where vendors were hawking all kinds of things—pottery shards made into pendants, incense burners in the shape of dragons, knockoff pocketbooks, pashmina shawls, and paintings. Many of the pieces were made to look old, though some of them looked like things from his grandmother's cabinet.

Outside a shop, a man sat on a blanket he shared with his long grass creatures. The man twisted and wove grass into a dragon. The bulk of his inventory specialized in crickets and grasshoppers, but there were also butterflies and birds.

Jordon studied the man's technique as if he were memorizing each movement. Tian Di found a Zen relaxation to the weaving of the grass, and only Jordon's claps of appreciation woke him.

After wandering a little longer, Jordon's stomach growled.

"Let's get an early lunch," Tian Di suggested. "That power bar we split wasn't enough for breakfast."

"You got that right." Jordon rubbed his stomach.

"And at this time of day, we'll beat the lunch crowd." Tian Di picked a traditional but popular restaurant. The eatery sat on the canal bank under a giant weeping willow. One wall was lined with relatively clean tanks filled with fish in a predinner swimming state. The waitress led them to a table overlooking the canal.

Jordon beamed with excitement. "It's like we're in ancient China. I love this!"

Curls of satisfaction wound around Tian Di at making Jordon happy.

The menu was in Chinese. Tian Di asked, "Do you want me to translate the menu?"

Shaking his head, Jordon said, "Nah, surprise me."

"Anything you can't eat?"

"No. I'm usually good with most things."

Tian Di scanned the menu. "Do you like pork? Wanshan pork hock is a specialty of this town."

"Sounds good."

"The pork is very juicy. I'll order that and—"

"Where you from?" the waitress demanded rather than asked.

Jordon smiled. "New York. Upstate, near Albany."

"Ah, New York… the Big Apple."

"No, about three hours away from the city."

The waitress ran her fingers through Jordon's blond hair. "Nice."

Annoyance trickled through Tian Di. He understood she might not have seen a lot of blonds, but no one in Hong Kong would ever have been so bold.

Jordon stared at her with his enormous green eyes.

She put her arm against his and rubbed his biceps. "So white. I want."

Tian Di explained to her in Mandarin, "You're making my friend uncomfortable," even though Jordon seemed unfazed by the attention.

Grinning, she asked Tian Di, "He want a wife? I'll give him a baby."

Biting his tongue, Tian Di decided to order. "He'll pass. I want to order the special pork, vegetables, and rice. Please bring the rice with the meal."

Her stomp suggested she understood he was dismissing her with their order.

"Sorry about that," Tian Di apologized to Jordon.

"No need. I know I stick out here. I've noticed the picture taking." Jordon leaned over the table. "Though the whole 'I want your skin' thing creeps me out in a *Silence of the Lambs* way."

Tian Di chuckled, understanding the reference. His sister called him in the middle of the night for a week to whine about that particular movie keeping her awake.

Jordon looked right and left, and with a serious expression said, "All I'm saying is, if she brings me body lotion and says 'it puts the lotion on its skin,' I'm out of here."

Snorting, Tian Di nodded. "Deal."

Jordon's cell vibrated. "Argh."

From the irritation on Jordon's face, Tian Di didn't need confirmation that it was probably one or both of his brothers checking on him.

"I canceled breakfast with them and you'd think I've been abducted by aliens." Resting his head on his hand, Jordon admitted, "I guess it's my own fault."

"What do you mean?"

Jordon sighed. "When I was younger, I made the mistake of trying to hook up with a stranger. He was much older and much scarier than I expected. Apparently he preyed on young guys."

A sick fear went through Tian Di. There were too many terrible things that could have taken place to the precious man in front of him. Compelled he asked, "What happened?"

"The man didn't like that I chickened out on going to his house, so he punched me. He might have tried to force me, but Zack rescued me before anything too bad happened."

That explained a lot of his brothers' need to protect him. Tian Di grabbed his hand across the table and squeezed. "I'm glad, though the whole experience must have been scary."

"It screwed with my head. I've been in therapy for years. Probably one of the reasons why I've never had a real relationship." Jordon frowned.

"It's terrible that happened to you." Tian Di wanted to protect him too.

Jordon straightened his back.

Tian Di recognized Jordon didn't need or want to be coddled, but supported and respected. "I'm impressed how well you dealt with it."

The smile that lit Jordon's face told Tian Di he was correct.

"I'm trying. Now if I could just get my brothers to remember I'm twenty and not five, I'd be set."

Tian Di caressed his hand, trying to send reassurance through his touch.

The waitress returned with their meal. "Wanshan pork, vegetables, and rice. I learn English."

Jordon smiled. "Your English is great. Way better than my Chinese."

She laughed and set the dishes on the table.

Ignoring the curious looks the waitress gave them, Tian Di gave Jordon's hand one last squeeze and released it to do surgery on the pork. He was sure Jordon didn't want any part of the layer of fat that had to be at least fifteen centimeters thick. He served a juicy piece of pork, vegetables, and rice to Jordon.

"This looks incredible." Jordon took his chopsticks and tore off a piece.

A bit of the juice ran down Jordon's chin, and with great effort, Tian Di didn't lick his face. He dabbed at the drip with his napkin. "You've got something here."

"Thanks."

AFTER LUNCH, they continued their exploration of the ancient water town. Tian Di took a lot of pleasure playing tour guide for Jordon. "This is the Double Bridge. See? There's one bridge over the large canal and a connecting one over the side canal."

Jordon stopped to take some pictures. "Can we take a picture together?"

"Sure." Tian Di smiled for the selfie.

Holding his phone up high, Jordon took several snapshots that included them, the bridge, the canal, and a boat drifting beneath them.

"This is one of the scenes you'll see on postcards and on embroideries depicting the four seasons." Tian Di gestured at the canal.

"Let me just send a couple to Gwen, my best friend back home." Jordon's fingers danced over his phone. "She's a textile artist. You know, she promised me I'd meet someone special on this trip."

Tian Di froze.

Jordon grinned. "I can't wait to tell her… I did."

Tian Di would welcome all the wrinkles his mother promised he'd get by smiling.

THEY CONTINUED to amble through shops and artist studios.

Jordon watched the snuff bottle painters with fascination.

"Could you ask him to show me what he's using to paint with?" Jordon requested.

A couple of quick translations later and Jordon was decorating the inside of the bottle like a pro.

Tian Di purchased Jordon an ornate phoenix on a bottle. One side had the bird bursting into flames, and the other side had the vivid bird taking flight. He had no patience and gave the present immediately.

Jordon accepted the small gift and gave him a hug. "Thank you. I love it. I feel like this is me right now. Like I'm unstopping the bottle, and I'm—"

"Silk comforters?" the woman in the silk bedding shop asked.

Tian Di smiled. "Do you—"

"Want silk comforters?" the shopkeeper asked in English.

Jordon poked his head into her shop, shrugged, and stepped inside. He accepted the silk cocoon she handed him, then pointed to the poster on the wall of a silkworm eating a mulberry leaf, spinning the cocoon, a pot boiling the cocoon, and then people stretching the silk.

She took a semi-unwound cocoon, tossed it on the table where some silk was already stretched out, and called for her assistant.

The two women proceeded to pull and stretch the layer across the table until it lay over the current one.

Jordon pointed to the price on the wall. "I heard about these. Is that the price?"

Tian Di turned so the woman couldn't see his lips. "It's a good price, but it's still too high. We can get the comforters for 30 percent less."

"I'd like to get seven of the two-kilograms and seven of the three-kilograms. That way the comforters can be added or subtracted based on the weather."

Jordon never thought of just himself. Tian Di asked, "For your friends?"

"Yeah, and a set for you."

"You don't have to—"

Jordon said for Tian Di's ears only, "I know, but I like the idea of keeping you warm."

"That's not a challenge for you," he muttered and then turned to focus on the shopkeeper. "My friend wants seven two-kilograms, and seven three-kilograms. What's your best price?"

She punched a number into her calculator and handed the device to Jordon.

He stared at the digits, which were even higher than her posted prices, then handed the calculator to Tian Di.

In Mandarin she told Tian Di, "I will give you a free one if you make him buy at the shown price."

Tian Di smiled. "I will be happy to take my friend two stores down and get him a better price."

"No need. No need. You drive a hard bargain." She grabbed the calculator, tapped the numbers again, then handed it to Jordon. Still, the price was higher.

Tian Di shook his head and started to steer Jordon toward the door.

"Okay, okay." She handed over the calculator with a reasonable price.

"Thank you." In Mandarin Tian Di said, "We will pick the comforters up on our way back. And we will weigh them."

She glared, having her final trick taken from her. "Okay, okay."

No one was going to cheat Jordon if Tian Di could prevent it.

WOMEN IN traditional blue linen tops with frog closures paddled the tourists along the canal, singing as they drifted by in flat-bottomed boats.

Catching the look of interest on Jordon's face, Tian Di asked, "Would you like to go for a boat ride?"

"Yes, please," Jordon squealed, causing some people to stare. A couple of them snapped some pictures of him.

Tian Di guided him down the cobblestone alleyway that led to the boat launch. The wooden boats were piled together, a dozen deep, with their blue canopy tops. Tian Di paid for the tickets and asked for a singer to ferry them. He recalled from his first journey to Zhouzhuang that the women navigating the canals were like jukeboxes. Passengers needed to give money for the songs.

Tian Di hopped onto the boat and slipped their fair captain a tip.

He turned back around to assist Jordon into the wobbly boat and then settled him onto the bench. Since they were tourists, it was acceptable if they sat together so they could both face forward. Though any excuse to be close to Jordon was a good one.

The woman hopped to the back of the boat and paddled the oar in a figure eight pattern. The boat glided under a bridge and into the main canal.

"This is gorgeous. I love the view from the water." Jordon snapped a ton of pictures, capturing the white stucco houses with the black roofs and red lanterns hanging off the side, a woman washing her clothing in the canal, fishermen with birds, and weeping willows dangling over the water.

People waved and snapped pictures of them… well, of Jordon.

The attention didn't faze Jordon. Maybe being raised by a famous rock star prepared him for being a curiosity in China. Jordon posed with a smile and gave a peace sign.

Tian Di pointed out the open water sheds. "Those are holiday floats."

"Cool. They do parades on the water?"

A soft song erupted behind them. The tip worked. "Yes."

"What's the song about?"

Odd that she would pick that to sing. "It's an old song about falling in love… how the feelings can be overwhelming, but then the couple settle into a steady happiness… that grows over the years."

Tian Di hummed along.

"Please?" Jordon nudged him.

"I haven't warmed up and I just ate, but can't say no to you." He added his voice to hers.

There was applause from the canal banks and from the boat behind them. Someone called out in English, "We should tip you."

Tian Di smiled and sang another duet. This time the song was about trying to keep your lover forever. It didn't take much to infuse the lyrics with emotion. If anything, Tian Di needed to hold back.

Even though Jordon didn't know Mandarin, tears sparkled in his eyes, and he wore a lovely smile that touched Tian Di's soul.

Making Jordon smile was just about the best thing in the world. Actually, anything to do with Jordon had become Tian Di's favorite thing in the world.

AFTER THE canal, they wandered back through the alleys and into some more shops.

"Shall we stop for some tea?" Tian Di led Jordon to one of the traditional teahouses.

"That would be great." As soon as they entered, Jordon seemed bemused by the dark wood interior. He peered out the window overlooking the canal and squealed, "Koi!"

Tian Di tingled. He loved the intenseness of how Jordon experienced life. He ordered Longjing tea and snacks.

Within a couple of minutes, the waitress set the tea and snacks on their table.

"Thank you," Jordon said in Mandarin, deliciously accented by his New York tones.

Tian Di spoke as he prepared the tea. "We always use hot water to rinse the cups, then add the tea leaves to each cup, and wash those.

He added the tea leaves and swirled the leaves in a little water, then covered the teacup with the lid. "You want to pour out the water, not the awakened leaves."

Jordon scrutinized the contents of the cup. "The leaves have unfurled, and it smells so fresh."

Pleased he noticed, Tian Di explained, "These leaves are from the first flush. We're lucky to have gotten first flush this late in the season."

"Flush?"

Tian Di filled the teacups with hot water and checked the time on his cell. "A flush is a tea harvest. The first flush usually makes the freshest, purest cup of tea because the youngest leaves are picked. Each flush has a unique flavor based on the type of tea, and some can taste the difference."

"Tea sounds complex," Jordon mused.

"It can be, but tea is about how it tastes. Longjing tea is from Zhejiang Province near Hangzhou. There's a proverb: Heaven has paradise and on earth we have Suzhou and Hangzhou."

"That's a lovely saying." Jordon's stare made Tian Di's cheeks heat.

"It's not an exact translation but you get the meaning." He checked the time again. "Um, it's been about two and a half minutes. Try the tea."

Jordon took off the lid and stared at the long leaves still floating on top. He tilted his head and scrunched his face. "How do I—"

"Like this." Tian Di demonstrated by adjusting his teacup's lid and used it as a filter so he could sip the tea through the partially covered cup.

Copying him, Jordon exclaimed, "Wow, that tastes like a meadow."

Tian Di chuckled.

Jordon shook his head and added, "A good meadow. I don't know how to describe the taste other than green."

"It does." Tian Di pushed a plate filled with nuts, sweetened rice cakes, and preserved fruit in Jordon's direction. "Try something."

Jordon cautiously surveyed the plate before picking a rice cake. He nibbled on the treat. "It's sweet."

Pushing down the need to hold Jordon's hand, Tian Di brushed a crumb from the corner of Jordon's mouth.

Their gazes locked. It was clear Jordon wanted many of the same things Tian Di did right here and right now.

Breaking the stare, Jordon asked, "Do you mind if I sketch you?"

What? The why didn't matter when Jordon's eyes sparkled, and he practically vibrated in his seat. "Sure."

Jordon pulled out his pencils and pad from his bag and set to work. Five minutes later, he turned the sketch pad over to show Tian Di. "What do you think?"

It was hard to believe both Jordon's talent and the way Jordon saw him. His longer hair added to the feminine portrayal, but he didn't appear fragile. Jordon had captured Tian Di's steel core, which hadn't allowed society to reshape who he was.

He didn't know what to say. Eventually he asked, "May I see the others?"

"Um… sure."

Tian Di flipped the sketch pad and found another of himself. He was onstage singing, looking very much like a rock-and-roll god he'd always wished he could become. Turning the pages, he found himself sitting, staring out a window, and even one of him sleeping with the sheet dipped down low on his waist.

He studied Jordon, whose cheeks were tinted bright red.

Jordon took some of the rice cake crumbs and dropped them out the open window to feed the koi. "I couldn't sleep. If you keep turning pages, you'll see some scenes."

"What are these?"

"I know it's stupid, but I draw places I've gone and things I've seen for my future husband."

Tian Di gasped. "You're engaged?" This was the first he'd heard of this other man.

Jordon shook his head. "No. No. I know it's dumb, but ever since I was little, I believed that someday I'd find someone and we'd spend our lives together… and since he wasn't with me, I didn't want him to miss all the things I'd seen or done before I met him."

Tian Di wanted to raise his hand and volunteer with such enthusiasm he could barely restrain himself. He settled for saying, "That's the sweetest thing I've ever heard. Any man would be extremely lucky to be able to call you his."

As long as *he* was that man.

There was a lingering silence as Tian Di studied Jordon, who considered the table.

When Jordon finally raised his gaze and met Tian Di's, he asked, "Do you think things work out the way they're supposed to?"

More than anything, Tian Di wanted what was growing between them to come to fruition, but there were so many odds against that happening… against them. Made in China's success could be jeopardized if Indigo's dire warning could be believed. Jordon lived half a world away, apparently with overprotective and possibly controlling brothers. Tian Di's mother would continue to try and convince him homosexuality was simply a Western concept meant to confuse young people.

Though nothing could contain the hope trying to burst from his heart. "Chinese people won't talk about lost causes because there's no benefit in doing so. We say it's like climbing a tree to catch a fish."

Jordon sniffed, and the light in his eyes was dimmed by the glistening tears threatening to spill down his cheeks.

"My brothers have always said if you want something bad enough, you find a way." A tear fell and tracked down his cheek as he smiled.

Tian Di didn't know what to say.

Pointing to the weeping willow dangling over the canal with long hanging branches, Jordon said, "Maybe you just have to pick the right tree."

Tian Di grabbed Jordon's hands. "Do you want to climb a tree with me?"

Jordon sniffed again and nodded.

Trying not to crush Jordon's hands, Tian Di squeezed them. "It won't be easy, but—"

Jordon's cell phone danced across the table. He ignored his phone and declared, "I want this."

"Me too."

THEY ROAMED back through the ancient town and collected and weighed the comforters. Tian Di convinced Jordon to accept the shop owner's son's help in carrying the comforters to the exit. Jordon generously tipped the kid.

Jordon pulled out a ring of taxi cards and started to flip through them. He shook his head and asked, "Hey, instead of me playing with taxi cards, could you translate where we want to go?"

"Of course." Tian Di explained the order of the stops and their final destination to the taxi driver as they filled the trunk and passenger seat with comforters.

The remaining space in the back seat became filled around Jordon and him. Tian Di appreciated the excuse to press close to Jordon.

Snuggling a bit closer than necessary, Jordon sighed as they were whisked to his hotel. He dropped his bundles at the front desk with requests to deliver a set to Zack, each of the Dark Angels' couples, himself, and their manager, Megan, then raced back to the car. "I escaped before either of my brothers waylaid me."

A quick stop at Tian Di's apartment allowed him to drop off the comforters Jordon gifted him. He avoided the band by not going into the apartment; he simply set the bedding to the side of their private hallway and left.

Jordon exhaled. "Whew! I feel like we got away with something."

The taxi took them to the far side of the lake and turned into the first parking lot.

Tian Di translated what the taxi driver said. "He'll drop us off here for the restaurant so he doesn't get stuck in the traffic."

Jordon was lightning fast with his wallet and paid the driver.

Tian Di piloted Jordon away from the chaos of people and cars to the path along the lake. The wooden boardwalk led through a garden to the famous restaurant De Yue Lou.

The restaurant's interior was exactly how Tian Di remembered, all lush cherrywood and lots of windows overlooking the lake. Dark tables were scattered through the room, with a lazy Susan on top. Or at least that was what Indigo called the spinner.

Once they were seated, he told Jordon, "The restaurant does the Suzhou specialty of squirrel fish."

Jordon snorted. "That sounds terrible."

Could he be any more adorable? "No. Imagine a mango turned inside out."

Jordon shifted forward and grinned at Tian Di. "So it's not a squirrel?"

Laughing, Tian Di shook his head. "No. The fish is cut into cubes but remains attached to the skin. They turn the fish inside out and deep fry it, then add peas, crystal shrimp, and sweet and sour sauce. It's delicious."

"Hmm. I guess I like sweet and sour, and I trust you. I'll try it." Jordon kept his arms folded, and he remained suspicious until the watercolor paintings distracted him.

Tian Di ordered when the waitress came over.

"Look at how a few strokes of color are used to make the petals." Jordon studied the picture closest to their table. "And the dragonfly's determined expression is impressive."

Now that Jordon mentioned the dragonfly's expression, Tian Di could see the personality and character shine through. "I really love how I can see things differently through your eyes."

Jordon fluttered his long lashes breaking their extended stare. "Um, tell me what it's like singing in Made in China?"

"I love our music. I'm beyond excited about the tour. Who wouldn't be? I cannot believe this is going to happen. I have wanted this since I was six years old singing into my sister's hairbrush." Tian Di closed his mouth on the gush of words.

"How are the other guys?"

"Styx, Jin, and Li are great and very talented. I consider them friends."

"And Indigo?" Jordon's gaze narrowed on him.

Tian Di chuckled. He had no doubt Jordon was perceptive. "Indigo is extremely gifted, and when it comes to business, I trust him completely."

Jordon grinned. "Though his wild reputation precedes him. Ha, even Angel warned me about him."

"Wow, that is saying something. I guess I wish he could be... less wild." Was that too vague?

Jordon tilted his head, encouraging him to continue.

"Li is a great guy, and, well, Indigo should focus on being a better partner." Tian Di didn't want to tell tales, but it irked him that Indigo didn't appreciate what he had.

Twirling one of his chopsticks through his fingers, Jordon mused, "A lot of people have open relationships."

Tian Di shouldn't have been surprised Jordon understood the issue. It made him wonder. "Would you ever want that?"

Jordon sat upright. "An open relationship? Nah, seems like a lot of drama to me. You?"

"No. I only want one person in the tree fishing with me." Maybe Tian Di shouldn't be so honest.

Jordon's cheeks colored to a pink, and a smile brightened his face. "Good, because I don't share well."

The American adage of honesty being the best policy was one to live by.

Tian Di asked out of curiosity, "Have you met Indigo's father?"

"Song Young? Yeah, he was involved with the Dark Angels, especially early on. The guy is a genius. Dusty and Angel credit him for putting the Dark Angels on the map." Jordon poured Tian Di and himself tea.

"Thanks." Tian Di mused, "It must have been incredible to grow up in the music scene."

Jordon wobbled his head. "Dust kept me and Zack out of it, for the most part."

Not being able to imagine the excitement and access Jordon had, Tian Di asked, "Was it strange having a rock star for a brother?"

Giggling, Jordon claimed, "I wouldn't know."

Tian Di snorted and then cracked up, drawing the attention of other diners. He restrained his mirth by covering his mouth.

Jordon waited until Tian Di regained his composure and then said, "Nah, it wasn't weird. I loved traveling with the band because I like their music, got to hang with my brothers, and I've gotten to see some great museums."

He could see Jordon focusing on the positives. "What about school?"

"Dusty got me a tutor who was ruthless. My online sessions would last for a year every day. Not for nothing, but I think I should have a PhD in everything." Jordon gave him a lopsided smile.

"Was it lonely? Not going to school and traveling all the time?" Tian Di didn't have the greatest experiences in school, though he would have been lonesome without any interaction with other kids.

Jordon swirled the tea in his cup. "I had my brothers, my art, Robin...."

Tian Di had noticed the connection Jordon had with another member of the Dark Angels. "You're close to the keyboard player?"

"Yeah, when I came out—" The waitress delivered their squirrel fish with sides of broccoli and rice, along with a knife and fork for Jordon. "*Xiè xie.*"

The waitress smiled and said in English, "Your Chinese is good."

Jordon inclined his head and returned his skeptical attention to the fish. He turned the plate around again and again, studying their dinner.

Tian Di bit back a laugh and served him a large piece of fish along with some shrimp and peas. He spooned some of the sweet sauce over the fish. "There shouldn't be any bones in that piece, but still be careful."

Ignoring the knife and fork, Jordon used his chopsticks to try the fish. "Mm, that's delicious. It's like a sweet and sour blooming fish."

"A what?" Tian Di spooned some rice onto Jordon's plate.

"There's a restaurant in the States that does this same process to an onion." Jordon served Tian Di some broccoli.

"Interesting...." Tian Di had hoped to hear what Jordon started to say before the food arrived. He lowered his voice and encouraged him. "You were telling me about coming out?"

Jordon swallowed and then took a sip of tea. "Oh, yeah. Robin threw me a party when I came out. It was the same night my mother had just kicked me to the curb. Well, I mean she packed my things and took me to Dusty's. She dropped me on his doorstep like a flaming bag of—sorry."

"That's terrible." Tian Di couldn't imagine. As distant as he had become with his family, they had never disowned him.

Jordon sipped more of his tea. "Yeah, it was horrible. I was hurt and devastated, but Robin turned a band dinner into a coming-out party for me."

Tian Di refilled Jordon's teacup and tried to piece together the foreign concept. "He gave you a party because you admitted who you were?"

"Basically. My world had imploded. Even then, I never wanted to be a burden to Dusty or Zack, but I knew my mother's decision would impact them negatively."

"Negatively? I don't know your brothers well, but neither of them seem to think taking care of you as a negative." Tian Di didn't want to overstep, but he didn't want Jordon to continue carrying false beliefs.

Jordon frowned. "Maybe *negatively* is the wrong word."

"What happened after you were dropped off?"

A small smile turned Jordon's lips up. "Robin calmed me down, put green eyeliner on me, and then made all the Dark Angels celebrate me. Angel even sang me a song."

"A song?"

"Angel changed the words to 'Over the Rainbow.'" Jordon leaned forward and said, "He sang something like this." He whisper-sang,

"Somewhere over the rainbow….
Your prince waits there….
Among the men that I've heard of
Once in a lullaby.
Somewhere over the gaybow
Men are hot,
And your wet dreams, you dare to cream
Really do come true."

Tian Di tried to imagine what impact such words and support would have had on him, and couldn't. "What amazing friends you have."

Jordon sniffed, and his eyes welled with tears. "As upsetting as that night was, Robin and every one of the guys helped me find the joy in being me. And if I'm honest, Robin's better at mothering me than my own mother ever had been…."

Tian Di wanted to hug him and take away all his pain. Not being able to do that without causing a scene, he said, "I'm sorry that happened to you, but I'm glad you have Robin and your brothers."

"Me too. Most of the time. But it's hard with my brothers, though, sometimes."

Having seen the overprotection, Tian Di understood, but Jordon seemed to want to share more with him. "What do you mean?"

Jordon ate some rice and broccoli. Then he said, "They basically raised me, and I'm so grateful, but both Dusty and Zack still see me as a kid. You've seen how they check on me constantly. They plan most things for me and take care of the details of my life. I admit I've let them. It was nice, but now it's time they start seeing me as an adult. I've been trying to do things differently. Be more responsible. I need them to see me as a grown man capable of running his own life."

Tian Di was not sure what to say other than the obvious. "I have always seen you as a man… a quite lovely one."

The smile that reached Jordon's eyes said Tian Di had found the right words. "Thank you."

"It surprised me when you said your brothers didn't know about Sakura Rose," Tian Di confessed, hoping it didn't upset Jordon.

Jordon shrugged. "I think part of the reason I never told them about Sakura Rose was because I was desperate for some independence. And everything I did under this pseudonym was all mine."

"I can certainly understand that. It's probably one of the reasons I never wanted to go into the family business." Tian Di wanted a slice of the world that belonged to only him.

Eating a bit of fish, Jordon focused on his plate, then glanced at Tian Di. "Funny, now I need to figure out how to tell them, because Sakura Rose needs to go to Japan for a dinner event with my publisher. I can't just disappear, so I'm going to have to deal with it."

"If there's anything I can do to assist…." Tian Di would do anything to make Jordon's life better or easier.

"Thank you. The more I get to know you, the more I want…." Jordon waved his hand between them.

"Me too."

AFTER A tasty dinner, Tian Di pointed across the lake. "Do you want to walk to your hotel?"

Jordon nodded. "Yeah, we're just on the other side of the lake."

Tian Di escorted Jordon to the boardwalk that circled in the direction of the apartment. A breeze coming off the water cooled the air enough to make it pleasant. Crickets chirped. Early dragonflies hung low, predicting tomorrow would be humid.

He didn't need to speak; just walking close to brush arms and shoulders with Jordon was almost enough. They ambled past empty playgrounds, sculptures, and restaurants.

The neon rainbows off the restaurants and buildings chased shadows in vivid color across Jordon's blond hair, making the strands magenta at one point. They passed the vendors selling ice cream and bottles of water. The strains of "Hotel California" spilled out into the night from the bars and pubs catering to expats and tourists.

He couldn't resist humming until the music evaporated.

"I love your voice," Jordon confessed in that breathless way of his.

Tian Di had to have a little more Jordon, so he veered them off the path, down to a solitary pavilion. Hidden in the shadows, he finally pressed his mouth to Jordon's.

The ache in his soul eased as Jordon moaned, deepening the kiss. His tongue swept into Tian Di's mouth, erasing rational thought. Jordon tasted like the peppermint candy he'd sucked on after dinner, and happiness. Tian Di could stay right here forever and be content.

A distant horn hauled Tian Di back to his senses. "Shouldn't do this here."

"The hotel." Jordon pointed at a distance that seemed impossibly far, but they picked up their pace and hurried.

CHAPTER 10

JORDON LEANED against the opposite wall of the elevator and stayed pinned there. He ached to touch Tian Di but settled for anticipating what was to come.

Hopefully, both of them, and soon.

Tian Di had a hungry look that excited and worried Jordon.

What were Tian Di's expectations of him? Could Jordon meet all of Tian Di's needs? What were they going to do?

Jordon didn't snap out of his head until the hotel door clicked shut.

Tian Di latched the secondary lock, spun into Jordon's arms, and planted his lips on him.

Yes! The embrace had been worth waiting for and chased away his worries.

Ending the kiss, but pressing closer, Tian Di whispered, "I wanted to do that all day long."

"Me too."

Tian Di ran his hands up and down Jordon's back, massaging the remaining tension away. He slid his hands down to Jordon's ass and pulled him in tight, forcing their erections to nudge against each other.

Sparks ignited, but Jordon wasn't sure what to do. Maybe he should—

"You mind if I take a shower again?"

"What? Oh, um, yeah. It was pretty hot today." Jordon could probably use one too.

Tian Di smiled, giving Jordon a come-hither look, and then stepped into the bathroom.

This was it! Second invitation. Step up! Why did his internal voice now sound like Gwen? Well, he'd do her proud.

Jordon tripped on his own feet getting to the bathroom. "You have enough towels?"

"Yes. Thank you." Tian Di unzipped his jeans.

Facing away, he pushed down his jeans, exposing an incredible backside. He stood, glanced over his shoulder with a grin and stepped under the shower.

The cascading water danced along Tian Di's body.

Jordon followed the rivulets beading and running down Tian Di's back and over his ass. His raven-colored hair morphed into liquid silk.

Watching a man unscrew a tube of liquid soap shouldn't have been a turn-on, but the way Tian Di worked to uncap the top was shower porn.

"Mmmm, they changed the gel to sandalwood." Tian Di's moan wrapped around Jordon, making him need more.

"What? Oh, um, to what?" Jordon shouldn't be standing in the bathroom, gawking at his guest. Maybe he could offer to wash his back, or anything else that might require attention.

"Smells good." Tian Di turned and held the tube out for Jordon to sniff.

Inhaling was difficult while panting. *Go figure.* "Yeah."

The need to sketch Tian Di rode him hard. His therapist pointed out that art was how he distanced himself from the world, but under these circumstances, it was a way to merge with his subject. Ink and paper would allow him to capture this moment. "I long to draw you."

Tian Di turned toward him. "I would rather you touch me."

Even if the offer could be twisted into a way that could be misinterpreted, his body sent a clear message. Tian Di wanted him.

Jordon craved Tian Di. The day only reinforced how much that was the case.

Fuck it all.

"May I join you?" His voice cracked.

Tian Di reached out a hand. "Please."

In record time Jordon stripped out of his clothing, took Tian Di's hand, and stepped around the glass shower barrier.

Now what? Oh my God! He was naked in a shower with Tian Di.

Tian Di was a work of art. Jordon's voice broke when he told him, "You're so beautiful it hurts."

Shit! Note to self: Don't say everything that pops into your head.

"Thank you. I find your blush adorably perfect."

Disregard last note and tell Tian Di everything.

Tian Di shifted closer to the wall, allowing water to pellet Jordon. The warm water woke him out of his stupor.

Jordon ran his fingers through Tian Di's damp hair. They were alone… and very naked. What should he do?

Studying him, Tian Di confessed, "I've never taken a shower with anyone before."

"Me either. I don't know whether I'm supposed to soap you up or...."

"Get me dirty?" Tian Di's voice dropped an octave.

"Was that a request?" 'Cause one peek down below to their waists showed they both wanted to do delicious and filthy things to each other on the quick side of now.

Tian Di held out the tube of shower gel.

Palm up, Jordon accepted the sandalwood gel Tian Di squeezed with a trembling hand. That gave Jordon assurance enough to stroke his soapy hands along Tian Di's shoulders and down his chest, then rest them on his hips.

He wasn't sure who moved first, but Jordon found his mouth plastered onto Tian Di. Tongues, lips, and mouths all tangled, making him crave more. God, the man could kiss. Whether it was gentle and affectionate or uncontrolled and passionate, Tian Di had mastered the skill.

Tian Di shifted.

Jordon's cock rubbed against Tian Di's thigh, making stars form behind Jordon's eyelids. He threaded his fingers into Tian Di's wet hair and tugged.

Breaking the kiss, Tian Di mumbled, "I love when you do that."

"Like this?" Always wanting to please, Jordon pulled his hair again. Not hard, but just enough to get that breathy neediness released from deep inside Tian Di.

A broken "Yeah" ricocheted around the bathroom. Tian Di adjusted his hips, and the position lined up their cocks. A semithrust grazed his cockhead against Jordon's, making the stars burst.

Cupping Tian Di's ass helped keep Jordon upright. Wait, he had two hands on Tian Di's naked butt in his hotel shower? *Holy fuck!* Either he would be changing his sheets or the God of All Things Gay decided to grant him all his fantasies at once.

Rubbing his hands over the firm muscles of Tian Di's finely sculpted ass made Jordon want to work with clay. Maybe he should—

An anxious thrust accompanied by a needy moan yanked Jordon back into real life. Instinct and sensation overrode the surreal.

Jordon wrapped his hand around both their cocks and tightened. He gave a long stroke, forcing his cock to slide against Tian Di's.

Tian Di gasped. "I love being with you."

Jordon's confidence built. He trailed his mouth from Tian Di's lips, along his jaw, down his elegant neck, and licked.

"You drive me insane," Tian Di muttered and shivered. He grabbed Jordon's ass, drawing him closer.

"Good." Jordon teased a particularly sensitive spot on Tian Di's neck until he got a whimper of surrender. The yearning, laced with such hunger, went right through him.

Tian Di groaned. "Please."

Taking mercy on him, Jordon bit, marking Tian Di as taken. An overwhelming need to possess this man, any part of him, made him suck harder. *Mine!*

Jordon fondled Tian Di, teasing him with anticipation.

Tian Di covered Jordon's hand with his so they stroked together.

The urgent slide of wet skin on wet skin became heated. Jordon's erection rubbed against Tian Di's, catapulting him to the heavenly realm, but Jordon craved more.

"God! Not touching you all day…." It put Jordon on the crazy side of had-to-have-now. He kept jerking their cocks with Tian Di.

Groaning, Tian Di agreed, "I know."

Jordon tucked his head onto Tian Di's shoulder for a moment, afraid, terrified, of where they were heading and how this might end. Everything they were doing was probably irresponsible for Tian Di's career, though nothing could have stopped Jordon from wanting to selfishly follow what this was between them to its conclusion.

The man who haunted his dreams, who had sung him songs, and who had lived up to and exceeded all the expectations, was with him. Jordon's heart expanded and made him want to believe this was more than a physical happy ending. Could this, just maybe, be more of a happily ever after?

Groans of physical need echoed off the marble as they stroked.

Tilting his head back put Jordon's mouth just a kiss away from Tian Di's.

Days seemed to crawl by until Tian Di pressed his mouth to Jordon's, and that connection was enough confirmation.

"Almost there," Tian Di warned.

Hands joined together, their tugs became urgent.

Jordon's balls tightened further. The delightful pressure couldn't be contained and radiated out from his core.

"Yes." Jordon shot. Everything intensified when Tian Di grunted and came with him.

They clung, stroking each other and themselves through climax and back down to earth. Fists still wrapped around their shafts, they tried to catch their breaths as the warm water washed them clean.

Tian Di's sweet laughter echoed.

Pulling back, Jordon asked, "What?"

"I think I like showering with you."

"Me too. I could take a shower like this every day for the rest of my natural life and never be sick of it." What was he saying?

Tian Di smiled brighter than the sun. He took Jordon's face in his hands and pressed their lips together. "Me too."

Jordon ducked his head into Tian Di's wet shoulder. Happy didn't even cover how those words made him feel.

Eventually they stepped out of the shower. Jordon took a towel and dried Tian Di.

"You don't have—"

"I want to." It was that simple. Jordon wanted to take care of Tian Di in every way possible.

Tian Di grabbed a towel and gently patted Jordon dry.

Jordon left a towel around his waist as he led Tian Di out of the bathroom and tucked him into bed. He made him tea and then crawled in beside him.

Propping himself up on a pillow, Tian Di nestled Jordon under his arm and sipped his tea. "Thank you."

A rightness settled over Jordon.

Tian Di finger-combed Jordon's hair until Jordon almost fell asleep.

"I really hate to do this, but I need to go pack for Beijing." Tian Di slid from the bed and pulled on his jeans.

"You can borrow my clothing for the show." Jordon tried to pull him back into bed.

Tian Di snorted. "How I wish I could cuddle around you and go to sleep. And let you wake me up in the middle of the night. But I need to get ready for the trip."

Jordon's well-meaning "I understand" was accompanied by a hug that evolved into another round of kisses that pulled Tian Di back into the bed.

With a long sigh, Tian Di stood again. "I have to go."

Frowning, and maybe even pouting a little, Jordon peeled his hands off of Tian Di, lay down, and yawned. "You're right. I shouldn't make it harder…. That's what he said."

TIAN DI chuckled. He'd never been with anyone so willing to laugh and find joy in everything. "You make it very hard. All the time… that's what I say."

Jordon snorted.

Tian Di hated to leave Jordon, but he needed to pack for the trip. Sighing, he snuggled Jordon beneath the covers, hoping to quench his need to crawl back into bed with him. "I promise you, I wouldn't go unless I had to. I'll see you tomorrow on the bus to the airport."

"I'll text you sooner. Okay?" Jordon bit his lip and stared at him.

Tian Di kissed him tenderly, trying to convey all that was in his heart. At the risk of sounding like a lovesick fool, he begged, "Please do. Even though it's only a few hours, I'm going to miss you like crazy."

He snuck out of the room and got on the elevator. Once the doors closed, he exhaled. Whew, no brothers had appeared. Tian Di didn't like the secrecy, but if Jordon needed to keep things quiet, so be it.

His phone buzzed with a text from Jordon. It read, *Thanx for the great day. I want to fish from whatever tree you pick!* The message was signed with a heart and an artist emoji.

He texted back, *We will find the best tree together*, and signed the text with a heart and a microphone.

The elevator doors slid open. Angel Luv sat at the bar, nursing a drink.

Tian Di should move quickly, and maybe if he were lucky—

Angel waved him over. "Let me buy you something to drink."

There was no refusing this. He'd been caught. "Tea?"

"Ah, still in instrument-protection mode?" Angel grinned at him over a glass of amber liquid.

"What?"

"Nothing…." Angel ordered a hot tea as Tian Di slid onto the stool next to him.

The bartender set a teacup and pot in front of Tian Di, and Angel still hadn't spoken.

Tian Di should convey how grateful he was for the opportunity the Dark Angels had handed the members of Made in China. "The band appreciates being able to open for the Dark Angels. It's an honor."

Angel scoffed. "You know it's all a game."

True. "Well, I appreciate you helping us like this."

"But? I can hear your question. Go ahead and ask me?"

There seemed to be no escaping Angel's study of him. Tian Di hated he could be so easily read. "Why would you bother?"

"I can tell you it's because we've been there, and we were, but really, it's because we can and should. You and the band are talented and deserve to be heard. We just happened to be in a position to make that happen. You've been given the chance; make the most of it."

"Thank you." Tian Di sipped his tea.

Angel spun the ice cubes in his glass. "You're wearing one of Jordon's shirts."

Looking down—and he tried not to feel like he'd been caught stealing pork buns—Tian Di admitted, "Yeah."

The silence stretched between them until Tian Di cleared his throat, hoping something brilliant would fly out of his mouth.

Angel shook his head. "You waiting for me to warn you off him? Or threaten you about how your relationship with him could destroy Made in China? You'll be waiting a long time."

Tian Di stared at him.

"His brothers might kill you, though. Look, my band freaked when Darius and I got together. You've just got to remember it's your life, and there should be more to it than music."

He sat there trying to process what this superstar told him.

"I'm going to head upstairs to what's more important to me than music. But you do you...." Angel left him.

Tian Di turned his ring around his finger. A vision of Jordon flashed through his brain. He slipped the ring off and stared at the musical note. Then he put the ring on the other hand.

CHAPTER 11

A CHIRP woke Jordon. He stretched and reached for his phone. Tian Di's text read, *You up?*

Jordon giggled, adjusted his cock, and sent a devil emoji along with *Very.*

Tian Di responded immediately. *I think you're flirting with me.*

Always. Jordon felt a familiar lightness of spirit he usually only got when lost in art.

How long do you have before you see your brothers?

An hour.

In that case, after I do my stretches, I'm going to take a shower and pretend you are with me like last night.

Jordon gripped his cock in one hand and typed with the thumb of his other. *That's the hottest thing anyone has ever said to me!*

Every time I think of our shower I get hard....

Dot. Dot. Dot. Was Tian Di going to touch himself? *Do you mean...?*

Tian Di sent a demon emoji and *I'm going to call out your name when I cum.*

Holy fuck! Tian Di was going to jerk himself off while thinking of Jordon. Thrill and arousal battled for words.

Jordon needed to clarify. *You're going to think of me and get off?*

Yes!

He sent a devil emoji, heart eyes emoji, and *Wish you were here to kiss.*

Jordon gave his cock a slow stroke at Tian Di's *Me too. Care to join me in the shower? You can think of me touching you until I make you cum.*

Wishing he could think of something hot to say, Jordon settled for *Okay.*

Fifteen minutes later... warm water, soap, and the image of Tian Di made for a very satisfying shower.

After he got dressed, Jordon had to ask, *Did you?*

Call your name? I did.

God. You're hot. Can't wait to see you.

So are you! See you soon.

JORDON WHISTLED his way into the private breakfast room. His brothers and their other halves sat at a long table facing a row of windows. A table of covered silver serving trays, a fancy coffee maker, and juices lined the opposite wall.

Zack sat next to Andrew, and Dusty buttered toast for Justin, the love of his life. They all turned around to study Jordon.

Would they see a difference in him? He nixed dancing to the music in his head, as well as greeting them with his traditional "Morning bros and their hoes" comment that begged to be spewed out; instead he swapped the immature and sexist quip for a simple "Morning."

"What are you so happy about?" Zack asked, like Jordon's good mood broke some law.

His heart shouted, *Tian Di! He's the most wonderful man in the world!* And if Jordon hadn't misunderstood the "whole climbing the right tree" analogy, then Tian Di just might be Jordon's boyfriend. He wanted to paint murals of happiness and love all over the world. Tian Di made him excited to be alive. Not ready for what the truth would bring, Jordon went with "Nothing."

Zack glanced at his phone. "Well, you're late. We ordered pancakes for you, but they might be cold."

Totally worth the fantasy of getting off while your boyfriend—hee hee, boyfriend—is jerking off to you. Jordon smirked. "Thanks, but why did you order for me if I wasn't here?"

Zack answered, "'Cause I've been doing it since we started touring. You used to get mad if I didn't."

"I believe you accused us of trying to starve you." Dusty chuckled, possibly remembering how Jordon would simply snarf food off their plates until his arrived.

"True. And I appreciated it, but from now on I can order myself." Jordon said the words with a smile, but Dusty's gaze narrowed on him. He was finally trying to implement his therapist's suggestion of finding ways he could take responsibility back. "What?"

"Nothing." Dusty shook his head and put a smile on his face that didn't cover his confusion.

He slid into the empty seat next to Justin. "How's our next story going?"

Justin's lilac-colored T-shirt and purple leather bracelets stepped into the realm of the genderbending wear he favored, though not so far that his simple black jeans didn't pull the outfit back into the jurisdiction of China's acceptability.

A knowing look confirmed Justin knew Jordon was avoiding dealing with his brothers, and as always, he willingly played along, giving him a bit of safe haven. "Our next manga story is coming slow, but volume sixteen of my series is flowing nicely."

"No worries. Let's just get the general idea down, and I'll work on the storyboard while you get the dialogue together. I can make adjustments post dialogue."

Justin frowned. "Are you sure? I know you like—"

"Totally fine." Jordon was too happy to let a small snag in their flow get him down. If a deadline slipped... oh well. The world would keep turning.

His phone chirped with *Miss you.*

See you soon! He signed his text with a heart-eyed emoji.

Dusty craned around Justin, attempting to look at Jordon's cell phone. "Gwen?"

A lie itched his tongue to avoid dealing with fallout. "No. Tian Di."

"Tian Di?" Zack growled. "Why is he texting you? How does he have your—"

"I didn't realize it was your business?" Jordon tried not to respond with aggression, though the line between "stay out of my business or I'll rip your motherfucking head off" and assertive seemed fragile and faint.

"Everything about you is my business," Zack decreed like he had for years.

Justin leaned toward Zack. "It's actually not."

"But—" Zack deflated and his gaze darted to Dusty, then lingered on Jordon. He swallowed and then leaned into Andrew.

Megan breezed in. "Morning, Davis and Nikeman crews."

"Morning, Megan," Jordon said, maybe a bit too loud.

"Darling Jordon, thank you for the comforters. They were a lovely surprise. I can't wait to use them."

His brothers had texted their thanks, but Andrew added his: "Very thoughtful."

Justin bumped into Jordon's side. "Thanks. Makes me feel even guiltier I'm late with the story."

Jordon rolled his eyes. "No big."

Megan tapped her aqua talons on the table. "I'll schedule to have them shipped home. I can—"

Shaking his head, Jordon said, "No need. Everyone should just bring them to the concierge. They'll ship them home."

"What?" Dusty asked.

"What?" The shock on everyone's faces reinforced what Jordon's therapist had told him. He needed to expect people noticing the difference in him and not knowing how to take the change. Jordon altering his behavior meant they'd need to adjust their perceptions of him and it wouldn't happen overnight.

Zack stared at him. "You took care of that?"

"Yes, all by myself. I'm having them shipped to the studio for easy pickup." Geez, it wasn't like he brokered a Middle East peace deal. He laughed, but it was kind of sad how surprised they were. Though taking this little bit of responsibility was a step in the right direction.

"Dust, our little boy is growing up," Zack snarked.

Jordon's pancakes were cold, so he waved the waiter over. "May I have two scrambled eggs, toast, and bacon?"

"Of course," the waiter said. He returned with the food almost immediately.

"So you've been spending a lot of time with Tian Di," Dusty stated.

With a mouthful of bacon, Jordon nodded and crunched.

Dusty sat straighter in his chair, appearing to get ready for a lecture, grilling, or both. "I—"

"Oh, Dusty, would you help me do a walkthrough of our hotel room? I'm sure I forgot something." Justin stood.

Dusty showed his intelligence by letting his fiancé drag him out of the breakfast room.

Zack took over where Dusty left off. "Well, now that the tour is starting, Tian Di won't have a lot of time for you."

Andrew inhaled sharply and stared at Zack.

"I mean he'll be busy, right, and we can start hanging out again." Zack didn't read or chose to ignore Andrew's reaction and his.

Jordon didn't think Zack tried to drive daggers into his heart, so he simply said, "I think Tian Di will still find time to hang out with me, but you're right. You and I haven't seen each other much."

Zack's mouth dropped open.

"I miss you too. See you in a bit." Jordon stood and gave him a hug before leaving the room.

JORDON MADE sure his bags were loaded onto the bus, though he couldn't deny the opportunity to drink in the sight of Tian Di through the bus window. The man casually sat on a damned tour bus, but he looked like a prince receiving accolades from his subjects.

When he noticed Jordon gawking at him, Tian Di grinned and waved.

Jordon's heart somersaulted.

"Jordie!" Zack ran out of the hotel. "Where's your stuff? I went to your room, and you were gone."

Pointing at his bags, Jordon said, "I packed myself."

"All of it? Do you have your—"

Jordon pulled out his passport. "I really am an adult."

"Hmph." Zack piloted him onto the tour bus as though he required assistance navigating the steps.

Tian Di gave Jordon a mischievous smile.

Jordon started to sit next to Tian Di, but Zack chirped, "No need to share. There's plenty of room on the bus."

Zack steered him into another seat.

Glaring at Zack did nothing. *Why am I letting him control me? I'm an adult. If I want to sit with Tian Di, I will.*

Jordon flipped Zack the bird, got up, and plopped his ass right next to Tian Di. The warmth of pressing against the man's side burned through him, settling the nerves that had been stirred by Zack.

"Hello," Tian Di said.

Jordon decided to go bold and whispered, "I came super hard thinking about you."

Tian Di touched his heart as a blush tinted his cheeks a dusty pink. "I think Indigo heard me in the shower."

"Why, what did he say?"

"Nothing, he simply high-fived me."

Jordon chuckled. "Nice."

Tian Di smirked and pointed at Jordon's shirt. "Lick Me, I'm Delicious. Is that a suggestion?"

Excitement and nervousness skated through him. He'd always wanted to try that. "Maybe... at some point."

Zack poked in between the two of them and asked, "What are you two talking about?"

"What's your deal? I'm talking to Tian Di." Jordon glared, pissed at himself for letting Zack's appearance stop him from grabbing Tian Di's hand.

"Yeah, but about what?" Zack probed.

"Nothing." Jordon resisted the urge to smack Zack. He was an adult....

"Oh, 'cause—"

Josh tapped Zack on the shoulder. "I'm sorry to bug you while you're trying to insert yourself where you don't belong, but could Robin speak to you about your crew?"

Zack stood upright, focusing his attention on Josh. Funny but predictable how he went red alert on all things roadie related. He took his job super serious. "My crew... yeah, of course. Robin, what's going on?"

Josh steered Zack back to his own seat, which was close enough to Robin to speak. "Well, I just think they need to double-check my secondary keyboard. I know I don't use that one until the second half of the show, but—"

Breathing a sigh of relief, Jordon glanced over at Tian Di.

Tian Di wore a small secretive smile and held his hand open.

Jordon didn't wait. He slipped his hand into Tian Di's. A completeness filled him.

The hand holding his felt different. Studying it, Jordon asked, "Where's your ring?"

Tian Di cleared his throat and raised his other hand. "I moved it."

What did that mean? Was he saying he was open to being married to more than music?

A thermos was thrust between them, and Indigo asked, "You want some tea?"

Tian Di glared at Indigo. "No, thanks."

"You should protect your instrument." Indigo shook the bottle.

Glaring, Tian Di asked, "Did you poison it?"

"Of course not." He stared at Jordon, then directed his gaze back to Tian Di. "Make sure you don't either."

Guilt swamped Jordon.

"Subtle much?" Tian Di said to the vanishing Indigo.

THE DARK Angels exited the bus and tramped up the jet's steps, heading to Beijing without much fanfare. They'd boarded a private plane like this one a thousand times over the years.

Jordon hung back and fell into step with Made in China. Excited bits of Mandarin bounced around the group.

Jin grabbed on to Styx's arm and whistled.

Indigo slapped Styx on the back and spoke to him in Mandarin. Tian Di translated for Jordon. "He says he's going to take some promo shots and will send one to Styx's father."

"Why?"

"Last year, Styx almost had to leave the band, but Indigo got him out of a forced marriage and future family obligations with money, along with promises of fame. These pictures will give Styx's family face."

Jin gave Styx's arm a quick squeeze and nudged him toward the steps.

Made in China's success meant more than just living their rock-and-roll dreams of fame. Each of them needed the band to succeed for personal reasons.

Was his relationship with Tian Di putting that in jeopardy? Tian Di's smile chased most of the guilt from Jordon's head.

Indigo took pictures and videos of each of the guys mounting the jet stairs. He had them turn around on the top stair and wave, as if a huge crowd sent them off.

Angel stuck his head out of the plane to call down to Indigo, "Your dad would be proud, Indigo."

Indigo shrugged and snapped a picture of Angel. "It's a great photo op."

Angel gave a quick wave and ducked back inside the plane.

Jordon offered, "I'll get you going in."

Indigo handed him his camera. "Thanks. Just press here. Hold the lens straight. I can edit the pictures later."

Jordon did as instructed and then entered the plane.

Zack waved to Jordon, gesturing to the empty seat across from him and Andrew.

Tian Di smiled at Jordon. He sat across from Robin.

Robin grinned and guided Jordon into the seat next to Tian Di as if he were unaware of Zack's calling out Jordon's name. "There you are. I was telling Tian Di I had downloaded *Lace & Frills* on my iPad. You guys will really love the animation."

Robin skirted back to Josh, who immediately grabbed him into a hug as if he needed to scent-mark Robin as his, or perhaps he was simply looking for any excuse to touch him. Maybe for the first time ever, Jordon understood Josh's need.

Trying not to glance at Dusty, Jordon failed.

Dusty's eyes narrowed like he wanted to say something, but Justin cuddled into him. "Dust, have you seen the bathroom?"

"What? No, but it's probably like all the other jet bathrooms, right?" Was Dusty being dense on purpose?

Justin trailed a purple-painted fingernail along Dusty's neck. "I think you should take a look at this one."

His big brother actually blushed. Jordon could almost see the lightbulb over Dusty's head turn on.

Justin winked at Jordon as he strutted toward the back of the plane.

Dusty tripped past to follow his fiancé, not even sparing Jordon a look.

Robin engaged Zack in another conversation with Indigo about roadies.

Divine intervention needed to be appreciated. Jordon kissed Tian Di's shoulder and then snuggled close, with the excuse of seeing Robin's iPad screen, as well as sharing earbuds.

ONCE THEY landed in Beijing, Jordon grabbed his bags and slid in Tian Di's taxi.

Tian Di grinned. "Indigo and Li told me I can relax until dinner. Would you like to see something in Beijing?"

Zack's text buzzed Jordon's phone. *Want to go to the National Museum?*

Nah, but I'll see you at dinner. To Tian Di he said, "I'd love to."

After a quick stop at their hotel, Jordon and Tian Di caught a taxi right outside. "You said you've been to the Forbidden City already."

"Yeah, on a trip here a few years ago. Zack took me to the Beijing art museum and the Great Wall."

"Would you enjoy seeing the Temple of Heaven? This is the temple complex where the emperors of the Ming and Qing dynasties went to pray."

"I've seen pictures of the primary-colored holy buildings, but I never made it to the Temple of Heaven. I'd love to go with you."

Tian Di spoke to the driver and the taxi zigzagged through traffic.

Pointing, Tian Di said, "You changed your shirt."

Jordon grinned and looked down at his pink shirt, which stated "I Like Boys" in white letters, and shrugged. "I thought this would be less suggestive."

Tian Di snorted.

ONCE THEY were inside the compound, Tian Di played sexy tour guide. His deep, rich voice swirled around Jordon, making him want to kiss and cuddle Tian Di. "They started building the Temple of Heaven complex in 1406 and finished in 1420, which fell in the Ming Dynasty. The emperors came here to pray for gratitude and good harvests."

Yet again Jordon was impressed by the facts Tian Di had at the ready.

Tian Di gestured to the grounds. "The entire complex is based on the cosmic laws of the time."

"How do you mean?" Jordon studied the red circular buildings, topped by a black shingled roof with yellow, blue, green, and red trim racing around the balconies of different floors.

"The most powerful number is nine, so everything is laid out in multiples of nine. Though one hall has twelve inner columns that represent the months, and twelve outer ones that are for the twelve hours of night and twelve of daylight."

"Interesting. Many artists rely on mathematical equations to create artistic symmetry, but these builders took that concept a step further here."

They hiked numerous white steps to reach the Hall of Prayer for Good Harvest.

"This is the largest hall and was made completely without nails."

"The craftsmanship is incredible." Jordon couldn't take it all in.

"Make sure you step all the way to the other side of the doorjamb with your right foot. Don't let it touch." Tian Di, ever the gentleman, making Jordon's heart flutter, held out his hand to assist Jordon over the threshold.

Not for the first time Jordon asked himself, *how can Tian Di be real?*

Jordon made sure to clear the two-foot-high stumbling block. "At the Forbidden City, they said this was a barrier against floods, and we were told if we stepped on it, we'd be inviting obstacles into our path."

Tian Di nodded.

"You and I don't need anything else in our path." Jordon didn't even think about how that sounded.

Tian Di nodded. "Agreed. I'll be right back."

He purchased a bundle of joss sticks, walked to a space in the row with praying people, and lit them. Raising the incense bouquet between his steepled hands, he waved the sticks until they smoked. He put the incense high against his head. His hair fell around his face as he offered what seemed like a heartfelt prayer. He bowed three times to the temple altar, then repeated the bows in all four directions. Lastly, he planted the smoldering joss sticks in the bronze urn and gestured toward the door with his head.

Jordon followed him outside. "What did you pray for?"

Tian Di smiled at him and led him off to the side of the building. "Us."

"Us?"

Nodding, Tian Di whispered, "I love you."

"You what?" Jordon's cry drew some attention, but the tourists soon resumed their tourism.

Tian Di stared deep into Jordon's eyes and articulated each word. "I love you."

Joy ripped through Jordon.

He hadn't concealed how he felt but wasn't sure if he should, though one look at Tian Di's sincere and vulnerable expression had him blurting out his own truth. "I love you too. I know it's selfish with the danger to your career, and crazy 'cause we've just met, but I do."

They stared at each other for a long moment. Jordon swallowed hard. He wanted to hold Tian Di. Megan and his brothers had warned him against any public displays of affection. They were frowned on in China, but at a temple, they were forbidden.

However, where there was a will, there was a way. He suggested, "Selfie?"

Tian Di's eyes sparkled with understanding. He threw an arm around Jordon and dragged him close.

Jordon breathed him in as he pretended to fuss with the camera. To be close enough to melt into him was everything.

"Ready?" Jordon asked when he couldn't justify prolonging the activity any longer.

Tian Di purred, "Yes," then planted a soft kiss on Jordon's cheek.

Jordon clicked the picture.

With his thumb, he caressed the skin around Tian Di's index finger.

Tian Di took Jordon's hand and returned the gesture that felt much more like a promise when he vowed, "Someday."

JORDON COULDN'T stop smiling. Tian Di loved him. He loved Tian Di. His brothers, Tian Di's singing, his art, and living half a world apart seemed like distant issues. They needed to figure out a way to make it work.

They spent the rest of the afternoon meandering around the temple complex and trying not to kiss.

Jordon showed the taxi driver the text Zack had sent him with the address of the restaurant where everyone was meeting for dinner.

Tian Di slid his hand into Jordon's, and they grinned at each other all the way to the restaurant.

Jordon helped Tian Di out of the taxi and paid the driver.

After giving the waitstaff their names, they were marched down a long corridor toward a private dining room. The closer they got to the end of the hall, the more the colors dimmed and the music changed to gloom and doom. But that was silly.

Jordon opened the door and stopped short.

Tian Di stumbled into Jordon.

Every conversation in the private dining room stopped. All heads turned to study Tian Di and him.

Zack waved Jordon to the empty chair next to him.

Indigo called out, "Tian Di, come sit with your band."

They were being separated. Their places on opposite sides of the table weren't just symbolic, but a representation of the literal gulf between them. *Geez, love made you uber dramatic.*

Sighing, Jordon leaned into Tian Di so he could get one last touch as he passed. *Desperate much?*

Zack frowned at Tian Di, then asked Jordon, "Did you have a nice day?"

"Yeah, we went to the Temple of Heaven." Jordon allowed his gaze to find Tian Di's, and he couldn't stop the smile from morphing his face.

He loves me. Tian Di loves me. I love him.

"You missed Styx eating a live scorpion," Zack informed him.

"Ew! Thanks, brain bleach please."

Zack snorted. "I ordered you beef with broccoli."

"Um, I thought we had this discussion." Jordon would not make a scene, but fuck!

Rolling his eyes, Zack said, "No for the table. I made sure we ordered one plate of the beef with broccoli. I wasn't sure if you'd like anything else that was being ordered. Though the chicken with scallions and ginger is delicious."

Right, at these things usually the plates are ordered at the beginning. Easy to jump to conclusions but he guarded that boundary. Go him. Defender of independent food ordering. "Oh, um, thanks."

Angel was at one end of the table telling a story about their first troubled tour. Dusty and Darius added bits, and Josh reined in their embellishments. As funny as the tale was, Jordon kept staring at Tian Di.

His movements were fluid. He was simply beautiful and graceful, but it was more than that. The realization coldcocked him in the face. Tian Di was the living embodiment of everything Jordon could have wanted in a partner, and he loved Jordon.

Zack grabbed Jordon's napkin and elbowed him. "You do know you shouldn't be drawing this in public, right?"

Jordon stared at what he'd created. He had penned Tian Di sprawled out on a grouping of pillows. His long hair fanned out and the look on his face....

"I didn't realize I was drawing." Sometimes pencils seemed to appear in his hands.

"Well, you might want to keep your drawing fugues PG-13," Zack said, with way too much censure for it to be a suggestion.

The food arrived piping hot, so Jordon pulled out his chopstick fan and attached the device.

"Ha, ha, ha. That's too funny. You guys are cut from the same cloth," Darius cried out.

What? Jordon glanced around and saw Tian Di had a fork in his lo mein that rotated with a press of a button.

They shared a grin across the table.

Tian Di said, "A gift from my sister."

Jordon chuckled and tilted his head toward Zack. "Christmas two years ago from my brother."

ZACK AND Andrew escorted Jordon to his room, which happened to be two floors up from Tian Di's. He was surprised when they didn't try to lock him in. "We'll be right next door."

As soon as the door shut, he texted Tian Di. *Want company?*

Definitely! I have a big shower you might be interested in.

Jordon's cock didn't need to be told it should harden. He tossed a clean T-shirt, underwear, socks, and his toiletries into his bag.

He opened his door with all the stealth he could manage and booked it to the elevator.

Jordon made it to Tian Di's hallway, but someone paced in front of a door. *Craptastic!*

Why did it have to be Indigo's father? He was probably there for the concert, but why was he in front of someone's door? "Um, hi, Mr. Song."

The man jumped and whispered, "Oh. Hello, Jordon. Is everything all right?"

Jordon dropped his voice too. "I'm… um, yeah. When did you get in?"

Mr. Young stepped away from the door he was standing at. "Just a little while ago. I wanted to surprise Indigo and see the band."

Not sure what to do, Jordon said, "Nice. I'm sure they'll appreciate it."

"Well, have a good night." Mr. Song glanced at the door one more time and took off down the hall like his ass was on fire. Using a keycard, he opened a door and slipped inside.

What the hell?

Tian Di's door cracked open. "You wanna come… in?"

Jordon grinned. "Definitely."

CHAPTER 12

"*Wǒ cào!*" Tian Di peeked from behind one of the curtained walls to view the Beijing National Stadium.

"Fuck me is right." Indigo stepped back from the curtain and let the panels fall closed.

The view of the stadium made Tian Di lose his breath. It held eighty thousand people, and unlike today's sound check, every last seat was filled.

Tian Di put his hand over his mouth and breathed in and out slowly. When his heart had stopped trying to beat its way out of his chest, he confessed in a whisper, "I never dreamed this would happen."

Indigo's confident facade cracked. "This is pretty quick for Made in China to be here. Usually there's more of a buildup with more time to gather fans. We owe your boyfriend a debt."

"Jordon didn't do anything other than show people the video Sebe had us make." It was important to Tian Di that Indigo understood.

"Yeah, yeah, but without him falling in lust with you strutting around the stage, that"—Indigo pointed to the curtain—"wouldn't have happened this fast. Fact."

"That's not why I'm with him."

Indigo snorted. "No shit. He's adorable, sweet, and talented. And if he's anything like his drawings, you're lucky to have him between the sheets."

"Hey!" Tian Di growled.

Indigo rested a finger against Tian Di's mouth. "Shhh, it's less than an hour before the show. You should be in vocal rest."

The asshole was right. This was the biggest show Tian Di had ever done. He had taken Indigo's advice about protecting his voice and he hadn't spoken above a whisper all day. For the last hour, he'd only been mouthing his words.

He frowned as loud as he could and grimaced.

Putting his hands out in front of him, Indigo tried to calm him down. "I meant no offense. I was pointing out Jordon's too cute for anyone to think you're with him as a thank-you."

Tian Di needed to let it go. Now was not the appropriate time to strangle a bandmate. Time to change the subject, he mouthed, "I remember watching the opening ceremonies for the Olympics in Beijing with my sister. I never even hoped to sing in the Bird's Nest."

"Well, you are, to eighty thousand people. Tonight!" Indigo might have been trying to be endearing, but he failed in a spectacular fashion.

And the nerves threatening to kill him where he stood returned. Tian Di huffed out a silent "Thanks."

Indigo smacked him on the back. "You'll be fine. But we've got to figure out a way to ease Styx and Jin into this."

They jogged down the stairs to the dressing room. Tian Di zigzagged around the racks of clothing, equipment, wires, groups of people gossiping or gushing, and roadies hurrying around.

Indigo held open the dressing room door, forcing Tian Di to face the guys first.

"So?" Styx tapped out a beat on his thigh that probably left bruises.

Tian Di glanced at Indigo, hoping for rescue.

Indigo shrugged. "In truth, it looked like nothing special. Basically the same as sound check… only more seats are filled."

"I heard it was a sold-out show," Jin groused. "During sound check my hands shook to the point I would have lost the guitar if it wasn't strapped on me."

"Well, Jin, thankfully you're into guitar bondage." Indigo waved off Styx's would-be retort. "Hey, didn't you like driving past the signage with Made in China billed with the Dark Angels? The Dark fucking Angels… tell me your parents didn't flip, Styx."

Tian Di would never admit it aloud, but it might be a good strategy on Indigo's part to relax Jin by pointing out the benefits of this gig, even with the stress.

Jin glanced over at Styx.

Styx had a ghost of a smile on his face. "Yeah, they were heading to the town's center with that picture to show everyone."

Li cleared his throat. "Though there's a lot of people, almost every ticket holder is here to see the Dark Angels, not Made in China."

Indigo pouted. "Killjoy. I don't know about you guys, but that reality doesn't steal the magic of this for me."

Li continued, "I'm trying to point out there's no pressure, because we're a bonus. The crowd expects us to suck, and if we don't, they'll think we're even better than we are."

Tian Di smiled and mouthed, "This is more success than I'd ever imagined. By the way, I texted my sister a pic of the marquee. Her response back was a simple squeal. We can do this…. Shall we head upstairs?"

The members of Made in China followed Tian Di. They stood at the curtains, listening to the audience scream.

"Dark Angels! Dark Angels!" The audience chanted.

Indigo rolled his eyes and put his hands on his hips. "Still isn't stealing my happy. We are going to own that stage—Dad, what are you doing backstage?"

The band's attention turned to the man who appeared to be an older version of Indigo. The man shared the same height, build, and fluid movements with his son, he just had shorter dark brown hair.

"I wanted to wish Made in China a good show." Mr. Song Young shook Styx's, Jin's, and Tian Di's hands. "I'm Indi's father. Very nice to meet each of you."

"What are you doing here?" Li gave him a quick hug. "Indi said we wouldn't see you until after the concert."

"Eh, I couldn't wait." Mr. Young shrugged. "How are you boys doing? This is by far the biggest show you've ever done, so any mistakes will be multiplied." Did Song Young think that was a helpful reminder?

Jin groaned. "I'm going to be sick."

Tian Di tried to give the music production god a smile that said, *I'm ready*, though he probably failed.

Styx's drumsticks faltered, and then he stopped tapping his sticks all together. He moved closer to Jin. "It's going to be all right. Besides, you didn't eat lunch."

A wide-eyed stare passed between them, and then Jin said, "And it's a good thing."

"Less to throw up," Tian Di whispered to Jin.

Jin gave him a small grin and readjusted his guitar strap.

Indigo folded his arms over his chest and glared at his dad.

Li answered, "We're fine."

Song Young shook his head. "No, if you are, you're insane. It's a sold-out show. This is one of the biggest venues on the tour."

Styx gaped at him with bug eyes.

Jin whimpered and grabbed Styx's arm.

Tian Di enclosed his arms around himself and wished he could hug Jordon right now. Fear slithered through him.

Song patted Styx on the shoulder. "You should be terrified."

"Nice pep talk, Dad. Time to alter your boy-band chat, though." Indigo rolled his eyes and patted his father on the back. "Guys, where he's going with this vomit-inducing speech is to embrace your fear. Make the terror work for you. I'm scared shitless, but it won't rule me. I'm going to dance fire over my keyboard, and fuck anyone who doesn't like our music. Hmmm, that doesn't translate well in Mandarin… but you get the idea, right?"

Tian Di got it, and his band needed the concept. "Yes. We've worked for this, and it's ours."

Li's uncle slipped out of the shadows to say, "Made in China will be epic. Have a memorable show, guys. See you after the performance."

Song stared after him as Tai-hua left backstage.

"Dad. Dad? Dad!" Indigo waved a hand in front of his father's face.

"Sorry, yes?" Song hauled his eyes away from the path Tai-hua took.

"Dad, I checked the tea. They did get Longjing processed in Hangzhou, and we had blue teacups with koi on them."

Smiling, Song said, "Good."

Styx scrunched his face and turned toward Indigo. "I still don't understand why you added those bizarre things in our contract, Indi."

Indigo grinned. "If those small details are honored, then other more important things like how our instruments are set up, or how the lighting is controlled, will happen as they should."

Styx murmured something to Jin, and soon both of them were chuckling.

"Dark Angels. Dark Angels. Dark Angels."

Indigo smacked everyone on the back. "We're going to show these impatient bastards why they'll be lining up for us next year… or the year after, right?"

"Right!" Made in China shouted as a group.

Where was Jordon?

"Dark Angels. Dark Angels. Dark Angels."

Two minutes until go time, and unsurprisingly, the crowd continued chanting for the Dark Angels.

Tian Di started to pace. He had to go out there and try to convince them to give Made in China a chance over their boos and disappointment.

Indigo wrung his hands and repeated, "This is perfectly normal. It doesn't matter. Don't let it get into your head."

Jin paced and Styx air drummed.

Angel Luv appeared and slapped Song Young on the back. "I got this."

What?

Dusty rushed out to the top of the stairs. "What is that asshole doing now?"

Angel flung open the curtains.

The crowd erupted in chaos the moment Angel's foot hit the stage.

Indigo snorted and pointed to the stage monitor. "Doing what he does best."

Dusty stood next to Tian Di and glared at the monitor.

Angel snatched a mic and asked, "Lights?"

When he was drenched in a spotlight the entire crowd seemed to lose their minds. The decibel increased tenfold, and everything from bras to flowers flew onto the stage. "Pretty Ones. My Pretties…."

Tian Di studied how he aroused, and calmed, the crowd with nothing but attitude and a few words.

Hands in front of him, Angel requested silence, and got quiet with a few exceptions of "I love you, Angel!" being shouted.

Tian Di needed to learn this kind of crowd magic.

"Made in China… is the Dark Angels' gift to you."

More bellowing echoed through the arena.

Dusty huffed out his breath, folded his arms, and admitted, "They do love the idiot. I'll give him that."

Tian Di mused, "Love? More like worship."

"My Pretty Ones, the Dark Angels really want to share Made in China's music with you. You up for that, Pretty Ones?"

Angel got on top of the crazy, slowed the direction, and steered the audience's attention to where he wanted their focus. "Oh, I know many of you are *up*! Right!"

Tian Di turned to find Jordon half-hidden by a clothing rack. Just seeing Jordon made everything all right. He hurried over to him and whispered, "Come to wish me luck?"

Jordon wrapped an arm around his waist and gave him a quick hug. "You don't need luck. You, and Made in China, are incredible."

"I missed you today." Tian Di hoped Jordon heard him.

Jordon pressed into him. "Me too. I spent the day with Zack, and drawing you."

The feeling of affectionate arousal replaced the doubt and worry. Tian Di grinned and whispered, "Am I clothed?"

"Somewhat… by the way, I love this androgynous look you've got going on. It's working." Jordon ran his fingers over the silk under the guise of straightening the fabric.

He enjoyed Jordon fussing with his long bloodred silk jacket embossed with golden plum blossoms. The jacket skimmed the top of his knee-high boots. Tian Di muttered, "Indigo said because you can't see my pants, many might mistake me for a woman."

Jordon's eyes sparkled with naughtiness, igniting heat inside Tian Di as his hands traced down Tian Di's sides. "Well, they're in for one hell of a surprise…."

Angel waltzed through the thank-yous from Made in China and patted Tian Di on the back.

Tian Di mouthed, "Thanks, Angel. We really appreciate—"

He grabbed Tian Di's hand and touched his polish. "Hey, those are some rocking nails."

After Tian Di and Jordon had spent themselves loving each other, Tian Di couldn't sleep. Jordon had taken the opportunity to paint abstract designs in primary colors on his nails, including his toenails.

Tian Di grinned but didn't say anything other than "Thanks."

Angel was astute. "Jordon, why don't you do my nails?"

Jordon pressed his lips together for a moment and then said, "I guess you never asked."

Zack appeared out of thin air, the way a skilled roadie could, and asked, "When did you have time to become a nail tech, Jordie?"

A twitch under Jordon's eye was the only indication of his anger. Jordon shrugged. "Yeah, nail painter to the rock stars."

Angel nodded. "Which is why I don't know why you haven't done my nails…."

"Time to go," Indigo announced.

Jordon grabbed Tian Di's hand and squeezed.

Styx gave Jin a hug and stormed off onto the darkness of the stage.

Jin readjusted his guitar strap. He stood in place, and then jumped in place a few times. Giving a thumbs-up, Jin bounced out clutching his guitar.

Indigo got close to Li and said something.

Li yanked Indigo's hair. "Later." He kissed Indigo's neck, and he swaggered out onto the stage.

Smirking, Indigo adjusted the front of his pants, shrugged at Tian Di and Jordon, and followed.

"I'll see you after?" It shouldn't have come out as a question, but Tian Di's insecurity climbed back to the surface.

"You're damned right you will. I love you." Jordon tugged him into a hot kiss.

Tian Di pressed against him before stepping back. "Love you too."

"Kill it for me." Jordon's smile filled Tian Di's soul with calm.

"I will… and I want to see those pictures." Tian Di noticed Zack across the stage, glaring.

"I could use a model." Jordon beamed and gave him a nod.

"Anytime, but first I'm going to go do this." Tian Di gestured toward the stage.

Jordon laughed. "I suppose you must."

Tian Di allowed Jordon's love to wrap around him and fill him with strength. He stepped out into the performing abyss.

Wǒ cào. I got this. Just sing for Jordon.

As the lights came on, Tian Di kept his head down but put a little swivel in his strut. He ignored that the crowd's applause was one tenth of what Angel Luv got. Tian Di would claim it as his own and build on their good will.

He grabbed the bejeweled mic. The band waited for Tian Di's signal. Several whistles cut through the audience.

Tian Di raised his head and Indigo's keyboard gave him the notes he needed. He belted out a love song with a mix of Mandarin and English lyrics in a very deep voice.

The crowd gasped.

Tian Di didn't give them any time to adjust, he used the cascading confusion to win them while their defenses were down. Once the initial puzzlement about his gender was absorbed, some of the fans sang along, but more importantly he had everyone's attention on Made in China.

The song ended in strong applause. Tian Di waved for their silence and took the opportunity to speak to them. "I want to thank Angel Luv for that incredible introduction. We're extremely honored to be touring with the Dark Angels. Please show your appreciation for the Dark Angels."

The crowd predictability went wild.

Tian Di indicated a song order change and ignored Indigo's head shake.

"We're going to keep things going with 'Evolution.'" He harnessed the audience's energy and took them into the harder rocking song meant to feed the crowd's mood and keep the elation high.

As he finished, Indigo gave him a nod of approval, and he caught Jordon backstage cheering. He almost felt like the rock god Jordon drew.

Their set flew by, and much quicker than expected, he marched off the stage, flanked by the rest of Made in China to cheers from the audience.

Jordon flew into his arms and hugged him. "You were amazing. So good."

"Really?" Tian Di could hear the roar of the throng and had felt they were with the band every step of the way, but Jordon's opinion was more important than everyone else's.

Jordon kissed Tian Di's cheek. "Absolutely! I think they want an encore."

Indigo tugged Tian Di out of Jordon's embrace. Out of the corner of his eye, he saw Jordon's big brother glowering at him. They definitely would have to deal with Jordon's brothers sooner rather than later.

Song Young stalked over to Made in China. "Made in China has the mythical *it*. You grabbed the audience immediately and didn't let go. Now get back out there and give them a little more."

After a double encore, the Dark Angels lined up to congratulate them with high-fives and backslaps.

When Tian Di got to Dusty, their eyes met. Instead of tapping his shoulder with a drumstick like Dusty did everyone else, he stated the obvious. "We need to talk."

Tian Di inclined his head. "We do. Have a great show."

"Always." Angel shouted as he pulled Dusty away, "Get out there, drummer boy. Give me a strip tease to enter on."

Dusty smirked, saluted, and hit the stage.

Angel gave Tian Di a shrug. "I gotta regain the audience. You did good making them yours." He followed his band out to the stage.

The Dark Angels roared louder than the audience with one of their most popular rock anthems.

Turning, Tian Di found his *boyfriend* and rushed to him.

The tension in Jordon's body would have been a giveaway even if the grimace on his face didn't scream "problem."

"Jordon?" Tian Di asked everything in that one word.

Jordon shook his head. "They both know."

"You good?"

"No… yeah. I mean, it's not a surprise. I'm spending every second I can with you, and I can't keep my lips off you."

Tian Di shrugged. "I don't mind that one bit."

Jordon looked around and then pressed his mouth against his for a quick kiss. "I've got to tell them about us and also about Japan."

"It's going to be okay. We're going to pick the right tree, and we can make this all work."

Jordon's chuckle faded into a groan, which sounded a lot like doubt. "I hope so."

Tian Di had to find a way to show Jordon they would be all right, because they were good together and loved each other.

As Tian Di tugged Jordon downstairs under the stage and into Made in China's dressing room, he fleshed out an idea that had been in the back of his mind. Their assigned dressing room wasn't fancy. The sofas, chairs, and tables had seen some use, but the fact that they had a dressing room at all meant the band had made it to the big time. And the best thing by far was the two individual bathrooms with locking doors.

Tian Di pulled Jordon into a bathroom with red walls and black fixtures.

"Wow, even the toilet is black," Jordon muttered as he looked around.

There was a shower stall, but there wasn't time. Tian Di slid the lock in place.

"What are—" Jordon's question died as Tian Di pushed him against the glossy vanity.

"I'm relaxing you, and reminding you of a reason we're worth fighting for." Tian Di teased his hand down the front of Jordon's pants.

"Oh my God." Jordon pressed against the attention Tian Di provided.

"Not the time for teasing, only pleasing." Tian Di unzipped Jordon's jeans and slid his fingers into them. He bypassed Jordon's pretty green jock and pulled out his cock.

Tian Di gave Jordon's beautiful circumcised cock a nice slow stroke. He might be biased, but he loved Jordon's shaft.

"I like that you get hard for me." Tian Di rubbed his thumb over the glistening mushroom head.

Jordon groaned. "What are you doing?"

"Am I doing it that badly?" Tian Di purred. He continued using his fingers to spread the precum around the head of Jordon's cock.

Jordon opened and closed his mouth a number of times. "No, oh. No, you're not. It feels incredible."

"Good, because sex is part of how I want to show you I love you. I do, you know, so much." He nuzzled Jordon's neck and gave him another tantalizing stroke.

Jordon bit his lip as if he could stop the moan that echoed off the bathroom walls. "I love you too, but—"

"Good." Tian Di would never get enough of feeling Jordon's erection throbbing in his hand. He was careful not to pull the skin on Jordon's shaft the wrong way since he didn't have foreskin.

"You know some people don't consider what we're doing sex." Jordon worked Tian Di's zipper down.

That was an odd comment. "This is whatever we want it to be. It's just about us. I'm loving you...."

"I want to love you back." Jordon wrestled Tian Di's leather pants and underwear down to his thighs. "Mm, nice."

Tian Di jutted out rather obscenely, albeit proud.

Jordon stared down at him and closed his hand around Tian Di's shaft. With no hesitation, he rolled Tian Di's foreskin over the head of his cock. He adored how Jordon handled his cock like he owned Tian Di's cock, and in a way, he did.

Allowing himself to be pulled into a thorough kiss, Tian Di stroked a bit faster. Maybe someday soon Jordon would let him suck, but now he just wanted to kiss him and make him come.

The bathroom shook a little as the Dark Angels' music started up again, adding a dose of reality to their private little adventure. The crowd's enthusiasm rebounded through the bathroom.

Jordon pulled back and glanced at the ceiling. "I can't believe we're doing this here."

"You like it?"

Nodding, Jordon added, "Yeah, it's mega hot... anyone could just walk in."

Tian Di had locked the door, but public sex did add a bit of naughtiness to what they were doing. "Would you like someone to walk in and find you like this?"

Jordon groaned. "Oh God. I'm backstage at a concert.... Mm, doing this."

Tian Di followed that thread of what sounded like a highly desirable fantasy and, in between pressing kisses along Jordon's neck, added, "You're in my dressing room. Are you my groupie?"

Indigo had taught him that English word, and Tian Di loved saying it. The word felt good in his mouth.

"Yeah." Jordon twirled his hand in Tian Di's hair and yanked.

Tian Di growled. He loved the tight pull on the nape of his neck. The move never failed to send fireworks of arousal throughout his body. "That's right. But I'm also the man who loves you."

"I love you more than I thought possible." Jordon pushed himself into Tian Di's hand while tightening the hold on his hair. "More. Please, more."

Tian Di had a hard time keeping a grip on Jordon when he started writhing. "You want me to make you come... backstage?"

Jordon gasped, "Fuck, yeah."

The stadium broke into applause. "Hear that? They're clapping for you."

Tian Di caught himself moaning because Jordon's relentless strokes were bringing him close to the point of no return. Breathing hard, he got swept along with his own words. If Tian Di wasn't careful, he'd come before Jordon.

Redoubling his own efforts on the upward stroke, Tian Di twisted his palm over the head of Jordon's cock.

Jordon groaned.

He loved that arousing sound. "You going to lose it in a rock star's bathroom? How many groupies have come in here?"

"How many rock stars?" Jordon whimpered.

In one last-ditch effort, Tian Di asked, "You going to come, right now?"

"Yes!" And Jordon did.

Tian Di stroked him through his orgasm and then joined him in release. The waves of pleasure dragged him under as he shot in time with Jordon's tugs.

Jordon sagged into him. "I think I like being your groupie, and—"

Jordon's cell vibrated.

Sighing, he grabbed his cell. "It's Zack. Let me text back, otherwise he'll be calling me. I'm sorry I—"

"Go ahead and answer him. You don't want him to worry." He just needed to make sure the Davis brothers knew he loved Jordon.

He cleaned himself and refastened his pants.

Jordon rezipped his pants and washed his hands. "This thing of keeping tabs on me never bothered me before. To be honest, their texts reminded me when to eat, and when to sleep. When I'm working I can get lost. But now it's… I don't know."

"They raised you and want to protect you. And I know you want to be treated like the man you are." Tian Di understood why Jordon felt stifled.

"I don't want to be the little pain-in-the-ass Jordon. I'm an adult, and it's time they started treating me like one." After a frown, Jordon added, "Granted, I need to continue acting like one, but I'm changing how I'm behaving. They need to get with the damned program."

"Maybe being honest with them and telling them what bothers you, and maybe sharing your success as Sakura Rose, might help them see how independent you really are."

Jordon said, "Yeah, it's not like I don't want them in my life. I don't need them in my business constantly. I wish they could see me as who I am and not the person who thought it was easier to have them take care of everything."

"You are a phoenix." Tian Di wanted to encourage him without pushing him.

"Though after this discussion about us and Japan, ashes might be the only thing left of me." Jordon sighed.

"No." Tian Di would make sure that wouldn't happen.

"I'm being dramatic. It's time I deal with them, and they need to start seeing me differently."

TIAN DI followed Jordon back upstairs to the backstage area. Watching Angel work the crowd was nothing short of amazing.

Finally the Dark Angels sauntered offstage, waiting to do an encore. Mayhem swallowed them for a few minutes.

Tian Di and Jordon stood off to the side and clapped.

Dusty hustled over to them and stopped short. "You've got dressing on your shirt." He reached out to touch Jordon's shirt.

No!

Jordon jumped back from his brother.

Angel sauntered over to them and stayed Dusty's hand. "Dude, that's not dressing."

"What?" Dusty looked positively puzzled.

Angel held out his fist to Jordon. "Way to go, little man."

Jordon froze, and his eyes looked like they might pop out of his head.

Zack appeared out of nowhere and glowered at Tian Di. "So, what now, Jordie? You're such a sex pixie you can't wait to jack off until later?"

Did he think Jordon had been alone?

Jordon smirked as he wiped off his shirt. "And you're a lobotomized fuckwit. After the show, I want to talk with you and Dusty."

"Absolutely." Dusty nodded, and he headed back out to the stage.

Zack opened his mouth, then snapped it shut, gave him a nod, turned on his heel, and stalked off.

THE JOY and electricity of Tian Di's first successful arena show drained while he and Jordon waited to speak with Dusty and Zack.

Jordon paced in place, shifting foot to foot. The little muscle under his eye twitched. He kept looking around.

Zack hurried past them but took the time to shake his head at Jordon like he had done something terribly wrong and disappointing.

"What is your problem, Zack?" Jordon asked with a frown.

Glancing around, Zack stomped back to them and requested, "We'll talk later."

"Hey, let's go downstairs." Tian Di led Jordon back downstairs and into the Dark Angels' dressing room.

He and Jordon sat on one of the sofas.

"By the way, I see what you mean about not being treated like an adult. However you decide to handle this, I support you."

Jordon slipped his hand into Tian Di's, and somehow, with an unsure smile, Jordon made the world brighter. "Thank you. That means a lot."

"It's going to be okay" was the last thing Tian Di said, because band members and various other people filed into the dressing room.

People milled around.

Dusty darted into the dressing room. "I'm going to grab a quick shower."

"Take your time." Jordon's voice squeaked.

Tian Di held back a smile as Dusty's fiancé tried to slip into the bathroom unnoticed, but the Dark Angels' bass player ratted him out. "Where are you going, Justin?"

With a smile, Justin used his fingerless gloved hand and gave Josh a middle finger.

Josh snorted. "Is that an offer? I don't think Dust would like that."

Dusty threw his sweaty T-shirt at Josh and pulled Justin into the bathroom with him. The door bolt slid into place before Josh could pull it open.

Zack dropped into a nearby chair, crossed his arms, and glowered at Tian Di.

Tian Di chose to remain silent, though he wanted to tell Zack there was no need for the posturing.

Jordon looked back and forth between them like they were in a perverse ping pong match. He cleared his throat. "So, um, wasn't Made in China great? Zack? Zack!"

"Ow. No kicking, you damned brat," Zack snarled as he rubbed his shin.

"Then answer me." Jordon opened his eyes wide. "Um, I'm sorry. I shouldn't have kicked you. That was childish."

Zack rested against the back of his seat to study Jordon. "You've been acting weird since you got here. Did aliens do a swap?"

Jordon inhaled and exhaled deeply several times. "Made in China was good, weren't they?"

Huffing out an angry breath, Zack admitted, "Yeah, Made in China did well, from what I heard." He shrugged almost in an apologetic way at Tian Di. "There was drama around Jin's second guitar, and I... it doesn't matter. You guys killed it. For your first big show, Made in China probably did better than any other of the opening acts the Dark Angels have ever had."

Tian Di didn't let his shock show, but those were strong words of praise, even with the undercurrent of misgivings coming off Zack in a torrential downpour. "Thank you. We hope we can live up to the honor the Dark Angels have allowed us."

The conversation ground to a halt.

Jordon and Zack stared at each other.

Tian Di failed to think of something to say to end the bizarre contest.

Zack frowned, opened his mouth, and shut it as Dusty reentered wearing jeans, rubbing his hair with a towel.

Dusty snapped the towel, catching Angel in the ass. "Hey, can you guys head over to the other dressing room. I wanna—" He nodded his head toward Tian Di, Jordon, and Zack.

Angel followed Dusty's gesture. "Sure." Angel clapped. "Pretties, let's move this party next door."

Everyone else followed Angel out like he was drunk and dropping yuan.

Justin kissed Dusty right on the mouth. He whispered something that ended with "later."

Dusty had a bemused smile on his face while he watched Justin exit.

The door clicked shut.

Pulling on a fresh T-shirt, Dusty fell into the space next to Zack on the sofa.

The only thing breaking the silence was the laughter from the other dressing room that filtered through the air vents.

Dusty and Zack narrowed their focus on Jordon as if they compelled him to speak. Only great restraint allowed Tian Di not to squirm. He didn't know who was scarier, Zack or Dusty. He kept reminding himself they *all* loved Jordon.

Tian Di made a mental note that he and Jordon needed to coordinate better as a couple. He was here to support, however Jordon chose to handle this situation. Knowing Jordon's wishes might have helped.

Jordon pressed closer to Tian Di.

Tian Di was glad he'd taken Jordon for some private time, because the way Jordon's tension coiled up, he might have exploded otherwise.

Jordon ended the staring contest. "I see people in colors."

"This… this isn't about Tian Di being Asian," Zack sputtered.

Jordon shook his head and waved Zack off. "No. I mean… I see the colors of people's essence. Like Dusty's all protective blue unless he's with Justin; then he's tinted in purples and indigo. Zack's golds mixed with metallic silver, and when he's with Andrew he goes a leathery bronze. I'm reds and oranges, but you two only see me as bubblegum pink."

Within two beats, Zack snorted. "What?"

The comment seemed to spur Jordon, making him pour out his words. "I love Tian Di, and I'm going to Japan to meet my publisher at one of their events."

"Well, that's a lot to unpack." Dusty leaned forward and studied Jordon.

"You love him? You don't even know him." Zack pointed to Tian Di.

Jordon snarled, "I know everything that matters."

The pause turned into silence with only frustrated breathing accenting the air.

Dusty broke the quiet. "What publisher? I thought Megan hooked you into a house in New York for the Dark Angels manga?"

"She did. This other publisher is for Sakura Rose." Jordon stared at them as if he could will them to understand.

"Sakura Rose? Who the hell is Sakura Rose?" Zack demanded with anger, frowning at Tian Di.

Jordon pointed to his chest. "Me. I'm Sakura Rose."

"What?" Dusty stared at Jordon, then Zack, and then back to Jordon. His face scrunched with bafflement.

"I'm Sakura Rose. I write for Kin Jirareta Ai Press." Jordon held his chin higher in defiance.

Zack shook his head. "Why? For how long?"

Jordon opened his mouth, but nothing came out.

Dusty tilted his head. "So you've been drawing, I'm assuming, not just manga, but yaoi? Why didn't you tell us?"

Jordon thrust his finger at Dusty. "Because of that face. Right there! I didn't want to hurt you."

Dusty gathered his damp hair and secured it with an elastic band into a tail. He stared at Jordon and finally asked, "Why would that hurt me? Us?"

Jordon's head dropped. "I didn't think a Japanese press would take my stuff, but I wanted to try. I don't know. I guess I didn't want to disappoint you. Besides, you have the Dark Angels and Justin. Zack, you have your crew and Andrew. What did I have? Nothing."

"What?" Zack cocked his head.

Jordon slipped his hand into Tian Di's. "I wanted something for me. I—"

Slapping his thighs, Zack shook his head. "You... you have us. You've always had us."

"I want more. I needed to succeed at a publishing house that wasn't arranged by my big brother's manager!" Jordon raised his voice.

"Have you?" Dusty's calm question seemed to ease Jordon. "Succeeded?"

"Yeah, I think I have." Some of the stiffness in Jordon's body relaxed.

Tian Di wished he could hug Jordon or somehow make this situation easier.

Zack interjected, "Of course you did. Your art is amazing. You're probably the best artist they have."

"What?" Jordon stared openmouthed at Zack like it was the first time he'd heard that.

Dusty tapped Jordon's knee. "Good for you. Congratulations. You've got to know how extremely talented you are."

Tian Di's heart soared as Jordon's face lit up. He added, "Your brothers are right. You are incredible. You know I'm your biggest fan."

Zack growled low in his throat. Dusty kicked Zack's foot, and he started coughing like he'd just been clearing his throat.

Jordon exhaled like he had been holding his breath for years, then turned his attention back to his brothers. "My publisher invited me to this big dinner... and I'm going to attend."

"When is it?" Dusty seemed to always be the practical one.

"This weekend." Jordon dropped the words like they were hot.

Zack waved them off. "No problem. There's no show this weekend. I can get Tamaka and Ralph to cover the transfer of equipment to the next venue, so I can take you."

Jordon stiffened and shook his head. "No. How about you do your job, and I'll do mine."

"But how will you get around, communicate, get to where you need to be?" The worry in Dusty's tone was real and couldn't be discounted.

Zack folded his arms. "Yeah, you couldn't even get to the Albany airport for your flight without a mishap. How are you going to get around Japan?"

"I screwed up the dates, but I got here, didn't I? There was a problem, and I dealt with it."

Zack *tsk*ed. "You can't just go to Japan by yourself."

Jordon frowned, then opened his mouth. Nothing came out but a huff of air.

Then scoffing at his brother, Jordon glared. "Excuse me. You were two years younger than I am when you joined a *whip me, beat me* club."

A what? Not the time to ask, but what?

"Safer than you getting lost in Japan—alone!" Zack made a point, but Tian Di didn't know what it was.

"I can manage. If I get into trouble, do you have no faith I can get out of it?" Jordon pinned his gaze on both his brothers.

Dusty wiped his hands on his jeans. "Look, Jordon, I swear I'm working hard on not treating you like a kid because you're right, you're not, but Japan is tough. To be honest, I don't know that I'd be all that comfortable going alone. Remember when I took you and Zack, we had a tour guide for most of it. There are parts of the country where English is hard to come by, and getting around can be problematic."

Tian Di nudged Jordon and softly offered, "If you want a translator, I'm fluent in Japanese."

Turning to Tian Di with a big smile, Jordon said, "See, yaoi is educational. You wouldn't mind coming with me?"

"Always." Tian Di couldn't help the double meaning, and judging by Jordon's grin, it wasn't lost on him.

Though catching the grimace on Zack's face, the wordplay wasn't wasted on him either....

Jordon's smile was big enough to compete with the sun. "So it's settled. Tian Di will join me, and since there's not another show for a week, maybe we'll do a little touring."

What? Tian Di would support Jordon in whatever way was needed, so he nodded.

Dusty folded his arms over his chest. "Jordon, I know you're working on setting boundaries, and Zack and I probably need to work on dealing with it better than we have, but don't taunt."

Jordon pressed his lips together and squeezed Tian Di's hand hard. "Going away with my boyfriend shouldn't be taunting or pushing any boundary. The only one to set these boundaries would be me or him, so—"

Zack pointed a finger at Tian Di. "Oh, you think you're just going to go away with him. We haven't even gotten to *Tian Di* yet."

Tian Di didn't allow the irritation and anger at Zack's tone to affect his expression. He simply waited, meeting Zack's glare with calm serenity.

"Where do you get off taking advantage of my little brother? Who do you think you are? Sweeping in and taking him to Japan! Do you think it'll help your career?" Zack's voice rose as the accusations built.

Tian Di tried to formulate a considerate and kind answer because "fuck you" wasn't a good response.

Jordon's bitter laugh startled them all. "No, actually both of us know I could hurt his career. A Chinese singer with a gay lover is sort of a death knell. Top it off with knowing that one nod from the King of the Drums over there, and Made in China's music becomes a death march into the void of notes never sung. Fucknuts, I'm lucky he even gave me a second look."

Zack frowned and his hands squeezed into fists. "How long has this even been going on?"

"Why is it that important?" Jordon's voice rose to meet Zack's.

"I want to know how long he's been using you." Zack spoke through clenched teeth as he looked between Jordon and Tian Di.

Jordon closed his eyes for a moment, then asked in a quiet voice, "Using me? Is Andrew using you?"

Zack hit the chair's armrest. "No! How could you say that?"

"I know it sucks, right? Don't you see that's what you're doing to me?"

"Jordie, you know I'm not trying to hurt you. I just... this is hard for me." Zack's voice broke toward the end. "So how long?"

"We've been seeing each other since the party." Jordon appeared to be daring Zack to take issue.

"Well, that's not long," Zack pointed out, like the time frame mattered.

Jordon's grip on his hand started to hurt, but Tian Di wouldn't let go. "We love each other."

Zack rallied and waved off Jordon. "I've heard from you and your puppy love."

"Why don't you respect me?" Jordon's words held so much pain they threatened to break Tian Di's heart.

"What? I do!" Zack shook his head and denied what he couldn't admit to himself.

Jordon huffed out a breath and explained, "I shared with you that for the first time ever I'm in love, and you dismissed me."

"No… I mean… I didn't mean to. I'm sorry. It seems sudden." Zack grasped at understanding as if he were trying to save rice from the rice cooker, burning his hands as he failed to pull out a single grain. "What about you, Tian Di?"

Trying to find his center, Tian Di was thrown for a moment by Zack's almost-gentle question. "Your brother is simply the best person I've ever met. I love seeing the world through his unique artistic perspective. He fascinates me, he's kind, his work speaks to me on a very basic level. I know we haven't known each other long, but I love him with all my heart."

Zack shook his head as if he were attempting to make room for all this information that didn't fit. "Maybe this is just infatuation…."

"Why would you say that?" Jordon glared. "'Infatuation' says the guy who fell in love with Andrew without saying two coherent words to him. What, should I wait and play around for years before going back to who I love?"

Zack grimaced. "How do you know this is even real?"

Jordon shook his head in the exact manner of his brothers. "You're about as useful as a weather rock."

Tilting his head, Zack squinted at Jordon. "A what?"

"When the rock is wet, that tells you it's raining." Jordon grinned big for a second, clearly enjoying his own quip more than anyone else in the room.

Tian Di fell a little bit more in love with him in that moment.

Zack groaned. "I'm serious. How do you know this isn't just a weird romantic insta-love that wouldn't survive the real world?"

"How do you know it's real with Andrew?" Jordon threw the question back.

True, how did anyone know if love was real? He glanced at Jordon and his heart screamed, *"Because it is."*

Dusty pressed his lips together and remained silent.

Jordon and Zack both looked at their oldest brother.

Leaning toward Dusty, Jordon said, "Dust, even though I was young, I know how much you went through to be with Justin.... Zack, I remember that day in the diner."

Zack exhaled hard. "Jordie, we know how hard and painful love can be, which is why we're worried. We don't want you to go through what we did."

Jordon shrugged. "Yeah, but if someone's worth fighting for... you do what you have to do."

"You're right," Zack conceded.

Dusty cleared his throat. "Jordon, I promise we're going to keep trying to see you as an adult and not the kid who would insist on wearing the Burger King crown through the McDonald's drive-thru."

Jordon snorted. "Come on, though, that was the ultimate in irony."

Tian Di made a note to check the word irony because that didn't seem to fit.

Zack's head hit the back of the couch. "I'm trying, Jordie, I am, but it's hard for me."

"Yeah, well, it sucks for me," Jordon said with just the right amount of bite to get Zack's attention.

"You're right. I'm sorry. I'll try to stop being an ass." Zack frowned.

Dusty stood and pulled Jordon into a hug. "Justin keeps telling me I need to stop being an overprotective ass fighting everyone, including you, to keep you safe. There is no safe in this world. You're an adult and need to make your own decisions."

Zack nodded. "But maybe you should have a safeword, and you use it when you don't like what me or Dust is doing. Once I hear that and I'll stop."

Safeword? Another word Tian Di needed to look up.

"Nope. Not a chance." Jordon was quite definite on that. "You're going to have to listen to my words and respect them."

Zack pushed off the sofa and yanked Jordon into an embrace—or a headlock. From Tian Di's angle, it was impossible to tell.

But the daggers in Zack's glare thrown at Tian Di were sharp and not subject to misinterpretation.

CHAPTER 13

JORDON MOANED as he snuggled into the warm body cuddled next to him. He smiled before he even opened his eyes to find Tian Di grinning at him.

More love and affection pushed into Jordon's bursting heart. How could he have gotten so lucky? "*Zǎo ān*, my love."

Tian Di skimmed some wayward hair out of Jordon's eyes. "Morning to you, my love."

My love.... Jordon's heart sang at those words directed from his very *own* love. Happiness burst through him. This was nothing short of a miracle.

He pressed a kiss to Tian Di's cheek. "Shower?"

"Yes." Tian Di raced to the bathroom with him. After using the toilet, he washed his hands and put toothpaste on Jordon's brush.

When Jordon was done at the toilet, he washed his hands and accepted his toothbrush. Damn. "Thanks."

"I know this will probably sound crazy, but I love we have kind of a morning routine." Tian Di's eyes had grown a bit misty, confirming Jordon wasn't alone in the overwhelming sensations that spun around them.

The domestic perfection of sharing a bathroom triggered a surreal wonder Jordon hoped would never end. Putting toothpaste on a toothbrush might be a small thing, but it was so much more. To have someone care for him, and to be able to take care of them, was something Jordon always hoped he'd have.

Jordon cleared his throat. "It's not crazy. There's an artist, Pieter Bruegel the Elder, who I never appreciated before."

"What did he paint?" Tian Di glanced at Jordon in the mirror.

"Everyday scenes of life. But right now, experiencing the most mundane things with you, even brushing my teeth feels like it's nothing short of a miracle. You've given me a better perspective and appreciation of everything. Thank you."

Tian Di adjusted the water and stepped into the shower. He held the shower gel like an invitation. "Shall we get dirty before we get clean?"

With an offer like that? "Definitely."

Jordon accepted some soap. He was aware of the time, so he got right to business. Wrapping his fist around Tian Di's cock, he started stroking.

Tian Di rewarded him with a surprised grunt that turned into a long moan. He stabilized himself against the wall and grabbed Jordon's erection with sexy determination.

Leaning forward, Tian Di's and Jordon's mouths met in a delicious, minty kiss.

Damn, Jordon was so close already. First orgasm of the day always happened way sooner than he expected.

"I'm going to come," Jordon moaned, and came.

Tian Di purred and thrust into Jordon's fist until he grunted moments later.

The water rinsed away their cum.

Tian Di rested his head against Jordon's. "I love you, and I adore taking showers with you."

"Yeah?" Jordon searched Tian Di's face for any need unmet, and only found his lover grinning and relaxed. Though how long would he be satisfied so easily?

He kissed Jordon on the nose. "Best way to start the day."

Jordon felt his worry untwining.

"Although I think any way we start the day would be the best way, as long as I start the day with you." Tian Di's words wedged into Jordon's brain, making him happy.

The only response Jordon had was to press his mouth to Tian Di's. He clung, trying to put all the love in his heart into the kiss so he didn't say something cheesy.

After their shower, Jordon dried Tian Di's back and rubbed the excess water out of his long hair before he used the towel on himself.

Tian Di scrunched product into Jordon's hair, then smoothed some onto his own. He bent over to dry his long hair.

Jordon took a peek at the view. Damn! Even Tian Di's feet were lovely. His legs were toned, though not overly muscular. It would be seventh heaven to sculpt him.

He enjoyed watching Tian Di shrug into one of his T-shirts. "It looks good on you."

Smoothing his hands over the cotton, Tian Di said, "Thanks. Now are you sure you're okay? I don't have to go to the band meeting. I can postpone the guys—"

"No! If anything, you should be early to any band meeting and stay late from now on. I don't want us being together impacting you or Made in China in a bad way. We have to show everyone it's not going to affect your dedication to your career."

Tian Di gave him a nod. "You're right. But what about you?"

"I'm fine. I'm going to pack for Japan." Though just saying the words whipped terror through him.

For some reason diarrhea of the mouth had struck him last night. He'd be meeting with his publisher, though he hadn't thought through the implications of what going on vacation might mean. Didn't that imply taking things to the next step… sexually?

Added to that, he'd bet visitors in the shape of overly protective brothers, or their agents, would be appearing soon.

Jordon sighed. "This whole setting boundaries and trying to hold them is draining. Although when I look at you, it's totally worth it. You deserve a partner, not someone everyone feels they need to babysit."

Tian Di stalked over and surrounded him with his arms, making him feel supported, loved, and not smothered.

After a hug that could have doubled for a rub-off session, Jordon walked Tian Di to the door. "Go to your meeting, and I'll see you afterward."

With another three kisses, Tian Di slipped out the door.

Even though he knew Gwen was sleeping, Jordon texted, *He's perfect! Tian Di will be coming to Japan with me as a translator & then for a short vac!* He signed off with a kiss emoji and the artist emoji. Maybe she'd have advice for him.

He checked his messages. Oddly enough, nothing from Dusty or Zack. He was not quite sure how he felt about that. Was it possibly progress, or were they ignoring him?

Jordon texted Robin, *If you got any time, stop over.*

Within two minutes there was a tapping at his door.

"Hey, that was quick." Jordon let Robin in.

Robin hugged him and then grabbed Jordon's face to stare at him. "Are you okay, sweetness?"

"Yeah." Jordon frowned and took in Robin. He wore a soft teal jersey on top of a dark teal T-shirt and black jeans, making him look casually pulled together by a stylist. His normally pristine mane of blue-green hair was held down by a scrunchy hat. "I didn't mean to drag you here."

"No problem. Now catch me up on your world." Robin led Jordon to his roundish hotel love seat, which attempted to be modern but got lost with the dated plaid pattern that fought the stripes scattered throughout the room.

Jordon filled him in on the brotherly discussion, ending with "And somehow I invited Tian Di to come away with me for a couple of days after my publisher's event."

"How romantic! Why does this upset you? I'd thought you'd be excited. It was a bold move on your part." Robin plucked a long strand of dark hair off Jordon's T-shirt.

"I know; *too* bold." Jordon dropped his head back onto the love seat.

"What do you mean?" Robin searched Jordon's face.

"Going away to another country implies… *things*." Jordon tried to control the panic beginning to surge.

"Have you talked to him about—"

A knock at the door interrupted him.

Robin smiled. "That's probably Josh. He was still sleeping, so I left a note and slipped out. I can tell him—"

Jordon hurried to the door to let him in. "No, it's okay. You guys are a twofer."

"Is Robin—" Josh looked over Jordon's shoulder and smiled at Robin. "Hey, I got your note. I wanted to know…."

There was nothing Josh wanted to know; he simply wanted to be with Robin. They were rarely outside of touching distance.

Jordon put Josh out of his misery. "Why don't you come in?"

"Oh, um. Great." Josh patted him on the back and rushed over to Robin. He sat next to him, nuzzled his neck, and then kissed him on the cheek.

"We were talking about the drama that is my life," Jordon grumbled as he dropped into the uncomfortable, striped armchair. Why did hotels insist they could tie together different patterns if they were in the same color? No, it made for chaos, which would be fine if it didn't look so much like Jordon's life.

Josh eyed Jordon quizzically. "Your brothers giving you shit about Tian Di? He's a nice guy, by the way. I've asked around about him."

After biting back the snarky remarks about Josh scent-marking his territory, Jordon squished comments on Josh's stalkery habits. He was crushing this maturity thing! Proof Jordon could be an adult with the best of them... and, well, there were just too many responses to choose.

Jordon sighed. "It's not only their reaction to me having a boyfriend. I asked Tian Di to come away with me without thinking about what he thinks that means we'll do...."

Josh looked clueless and turned to Robin for a translation.

Robin tilted his head toward Jordon, asking permission.

Fuck it all anyway, or not. Jordon shrugged. "Whatever."

"Tian Di and Jordon have never—"

"Does he want to?" Josh asked Robin instead of Jordon.

Jordon answered, "I haven't asked. We've done stuff, but he's a guy. Of course he'd want to fuck. Everyone wants to fuck."

Robin rested his hands on his knees. "Careful with the stereotypes. You're a guy, but you don't want to...."

"He doesn't?" Josh looked from Robin to Jordon and back again to Robin. "Jordon, you don't want to?"

There the issue was in neon. Jordon didn't want to fuck or be fucked. The whole idea was a boner kill. Now hugging, kissing, touching, and being touched registered an "Oh hell, yes please!" on his sex-o-meter. And as for oral, he couldn't wait to suck and be sucked, but not—

"Just eat salad," Josh declared, like this was supposed to make sense.

"Excuse me? Nothing exciting ever happened that started with eating salad." Jordon wanted to make light and maybe backpedal.

"It keeps things clean." Josh imparted this wisdom to him like he was sharing a secret magic trick from the Book of Anal Sex.

Jordon was tempted to ask *what* things, but stopped before he could form the words—*ew*!

Josh read Jordon's hesitation. "It's natural to be nervous your first time, and—"

"I'm a sexual side." There, Jordon admitted it aloud, but he got none of the relief one supposedly got from revealing their deepest secret.

"A what?" Josh's face scrunched.

Robin smiled at Jordon and then turned to Josh. "Side means Jordon isn't a top, bottom, or versatile."

Josh shifted closer and his brows drew together as he studied the mystery that was Jordon. Geez, any more intense and he'd whip out a magnifying glass. What? Did he now think Jordon some kind of mystery to puzzle out, like those word games he played on his phone? "You're not straight, are you? I was at your coming-out party. Wait, I mean, if you are, that's fine… I just—"

"Um, no. I'm not, nor have I ever been, straight." Jordon had no clue where Josh got his ideas from… though maybe that wasn't fair. Not any of the gay men he knew admitted they didn't want anything to do with anal intercourse.

Robin smiled and shook his head. "A sexual side is someone who enjoys all kinds of things, just not intercourse."

"So, um, asexual?"

Jordon tried not to get frustrated. "No, asexual means the person doesn't experience sexual attraction. Though they may or may not engage in sexual activities."

Josh waved his hands in front of him for a moment. "Hey, don't take offense. I'm trying, but hell, I don't even know where I fall in terms of orientation."

"You're Robin-oriented. I'm good if you want to just leave things at that." Robin nudged Josh.

Jordon wanted Josh to understand the way Robin did. "Look, I love everything I've done so far with Tian Di, but what if he wants, like, *more*?"

"Talk to him—"

Another knock at the door interrupted Josh's way too practical response.

Jordon's room was in danger of becoming Grand Central Station. Everyone wanted to catch the crazy train to Jordon Davis's show-and-tell of his sex life, or his lack of….

Not sure whether it would be one or both of his brothers, Jordon opened the door cautiously. "Oh, hey, Justin."

"Hi…. Oh, hi, everyone." His brother's ambassador waved to Robin and Josh over Jordon's shoulder. "I don't want to interrupt."

"Nah, come on in." Jordon dragged the rolling chair from the desk and sat, gesturing to Justin to take the striped chair.

"I love how the lace accents your jeans," Robin exclaimed.

Justin touched the red lace peeking through the tears in the upper thighs of his jeans. They must have been attached to some kind of lingerie. "Thanks."

Silence.

The guys all took turns looking at one another, then at Jordon.

Finally he could take it no more. Jordon broke. "I'm an idiot. I invited Tian Di on vacation, and I don't wanna fuck."

Justin waved him off. "You shouldn't do anything you're not comfortable with. I'm sure he doesn't expect—wait, Tian Di's not trying to force—"

"No! Of course not. But me. I don't want to fuck or be fucked." When no one said anything, Jordon tried to lighten the mood. "I'm waiting for the rainbow police to break down the door and snatch my gay card."

Epic fail.

Robin frowned at Jordon. "No, there are plenty of guys who are gay or bisexual who don't have anal sex. Just 'cause you're gay doesn't mean you have to want something in your butt."

Justin traced the patterns in his lace. "You know, your brother and I… it took a long while before we ever even tried…."

Josh recrossed his legs. "I heard he called Darius for advice."

Really? First Jordon heard of this. "Yeah, and what wisdom did Dare impart to him?"

Josh snorted. "Lube. Lots and lots of lube."

Justin chuckled with a smirk.

Robin added, "I think that was for a different issue. Your brother wanted to have intercourse but was hesitant, whereas you don't."

"Oh, so you don't want it either way." Justin nodded a bit vigorously. Maybe if he bobbed his head enough, he'd find enough space for the "don't want to have anal sex" concept. "That's called being a side, right?"

"Yes." Jordon shouldn't be surprised Justin knew the term, since he was the one Jordon always went to with personal questions.

Justin picked at his red nail polish. "My therapist suggested I look at various ways to express sexuality. I guess she wanted to show me it's okay not to want certain things, and that there's no right way to find gratification, but in my case, even after everything, I still wanted to do *that*...."

Robin rose to his feet and gave Justin a quick hug before Justin's words even burrowed their way into Jordon's brain.

Unlike Jordon, Justin hadn't been rescued. He'd been raped and badly beaten. His recovery had taken years. The experience left him unable to truly trust anyone until Dusty. Justin had shared his story with Jordon to convince him to tell the police everything he knew about the guy who attacked Jordon.

"I'm fine." Justin ended the hug and sent Robin back to Josh. He plucked at the stretchy red lace on his thigh. "The important thing is that you and Tian Di are doing things that make you happy and satisfied. Whatever that means."

"As long as children and animals aren't involved," Josh declared.

What? Did he honestly think he needed to set those kinds of limitations? What the fuck?

Jordon couldn't help himself. "So, I guess *baby animals* are definitely a hard line for you sexually." He waved off Josh's ludicrous suggestion. "Sorry. I—"

"Ha-ha." Josh gave him a look similar to the ones he'd give Dusty when he'd made a jackass remark.

Jordon ran his fingers through his hair. "Look, we haven't even had oral sex, so I don't know what I was thinking by inviting him."

"Do you want to have oral sex?" Robin asked.

At the same time, Josh asked, "So you want to play inhale the python with Tian Di?"

A smirk ruined Jordon's attempt at deadpan. "Inhaling the python.... Zack refers to charming the snake. Gwen calls it kneeling at the altar of knob jobs."

"Nice. How about penilingus?" Josh chortled.

Robin's eyes widened. "Or making mouth music...."

Justin held up his index finger. "My mother explained oral sex to me by using a Popsicle, so for years I thought of it as sucking the penisicle."

Good thing Jordon wasn't sipping a drink. He'd have spewed soda everywhere.

Josh folded his arms across his chest. "How about sampling the sausage? Or nibbling the worm... blowing the love whistle... getting a throat culture—"

Robin's sharp inhale stopped Josh's endless list. "Okay, okay. Jordon, do you think you want to explore that with Tian Di?"

Hell to the yes! Jordon nodded.

"Not to pry, but have you ever?" Justin asked.

Pressing his lips together, Jordon frowned and shook his head. "Nope. Never got that far. Probably the only person this century to make it to twenty without oral sex."

Justin cleared his throat the same way Jordon's big brothers did before they gave a lecture. "Well, since you've never had other sexual partners, Tian Di's safe. According to the CDC, there's little to no risk of contracting HIV through oral sex."

"You could use a condom, and Tian Di should get tested if he hasn't been already," Josh suggested.

"Are you going to tell me the safest sex is abstinence? Or knowing you, next you'll tell me how to treat his dick like an ice cream cone melting in the sun. Though believe it or not, I have a pretty good idea about how dick sucking works." Jordon could get a PhD in porn.

Josh sighed. "Hey, bud, just trying to help."

"I know." And Jordon did understand, though sometimes the fact these guys had known him since he was ten didn't make things easy.

"Do only what you want to do, and don't feel pressured to do something you *think* you *should* do." Josh held out his fist like fist-bumping was still a thing.

Jordon bumped his fist so Josh could put it back on Robin's thigh.

Robin smiled and pointed to the nightstand. "I see you still wear your retainers."

"Yeah, sometimes. After straightening my teeth, I should wear them more," he admitted. He was still pissed that Dusty wouldn't let him get regular braces with Pride-colored metal.

Robin's eyes sparkled. "When you're ready for advanced BJing... wear those. They give you different surfaces and—"

Jordon smirked. "Sounds like you're speaking from experience."

"Perhaps." Robin winked, and Josh actually blushed.

"I'm just going to say one more thing." His de facto brother-in-law met Jordon's gaze. "Dusty didn't want anal sex either, because of my history, but I ached to be with him that way. Though if he decided he never wanted to have intercourse, we'd have found a way to satisfy that need in me. That's what you do when you're in a relationship. You talk and figure out ways to make each other happy."

"Yeah, I know." If that was true, why did Jordon have so much doubt eating a hole in his heart? Would not wanting to have anal be a deal breaker and ruin everything between him and Tian Di?

Justin patted his shoulder. "Just remember, it's okay if you decide you want to do it. It's fine to never have anal sex. It's okay to decide you want to later. Relationships with people we love evolve, grow, and change."

"Though I don't think for me this is a changeable fact." The admission came easier now that he had confessed his feelings aloud.

JORDON HAD almost finished packing. He'd divided his clothing for Japan from the clothing that would go back to Shanghai, happy he would be able to get everything for Japan into a carry-on and a suit bag. Now he'd have to deal with the things left hanging in—

A sharp knock made him jump.

Had to be Zack. Jordon opened the door.

Typhoon Zack raged in. "I simply can't believe you fell for a singer. I love Angel and all, but you know what he was like, don't you?"

Duh! Jordon folded his arms and glared at his brother. "Get out your dumbrella, because the stupid is falling thick. Angel Luv and Tian Di Zhao are both phenomenal singers, but that's where the comparison begins and ends."

"I'm serious." Zack let out an exasperated sigh.

Jordon zipped the last of his packing cubes and placed them in his carry-on. "Great to meet you. I'm Jordon. Now go fuck an artichoke."

Zack squinted and then grimaced. "Any way you do that... that would hurt... a lot."

Ignoring other suggestions pouring into his brain because they were less than mature, Jordon pointed to the two larger suitcases. "Can you take these suitcases to Shanghai with you?"

"Of course." Zack opened Jordon's largest suitcase and started to pack the hanging items.

Jordon stopped him. "I've got it. Really. I can pack my own shit."

Zack hesitated in letting go of the hangers, then released them into Jordon's custody. He sighed. "Okay, fine. It's a habit. Don't have kittens; I don't know if they have an SPCA here in China."

Jordon growled. He set the clothing on hangers into the suitcase and folded them over. It might take more room, but it made for easy unpacking and fewer wrinkles.

"I just don't understand why you'd go for someone like him." His older brother stood with his arms folded across his chest and scrutinized the packing proceedings, waiting for Jordon to screw something up.

"*Like* him? What's your problem with Tian Di?" Jordon got right in Zack's face.

Zack started pacing. "I don't know him. You don't really know him. You've never even had a boyfriend, but you meet him and boom—that's it. You love him?"

"Yeah, I do."

Zack dropped into the chair. "Oh, Jordie. He lives halfway around the world from you. He's a singer! How can this possibly work out?"

"I don't know. But goddamn, I really want it to." Oh, geez. How pathetic did he sound?

Slapping his hands down on his thighs, Zack said, "I just—"

Knock. Knock. Knock.

"That's probably Drew." Zack flew to the door and let in his other half.

Andrew took Zack's face in his hands, pressed their mouths together for a moment, and rested his forehead against Zack's.

Zack took a couple of deep breaths. He stalked over to the love seat and sat down.

"Jordon, I'm sorry for the intrusion." Andrew appeared as sincere as ever.

"Nah, it's all good. Have a seat." Maybe Andrew could control Zack or at least make him sing a different song.

Jordon continued to pack.

"How do you know you love him? You don't even know him." Zack's tone was considerably calmer.

Andrew leaned back on the love seat and folded his arms over his chest. "Zack, is that a fair question?"

Zack snarled. "What don't I like on my pizza?"

"If you want me to back off, you know what has to be done." Andrew's voice dropped an octave or two.

What the fuck?

"Mushroom, dammit! Mushroom." Zack bit out the words like the fungus had done him wrong.

"What code word fuckery is this noise? You can take your safeword shit somewhere else." Jordon had enough to deal with.

"Why can't you understand, Jordie? I don't want you to get hurt." Zack's voice broke and he used his hand to cover his face.

"That's life… isn't it? Hurt happens." Jordon didn't mean to be so matter-of-fact, but it was the truth. Life hurt and all anyone can do is survive.

"I don't want that for you." Zack struggled to get the words out.

Fuckery fuck!

Zack glanced at Andrew, and something seemed to pass between them. Andrew squeezed Zack's hand and kissed his palm. The grimness vanished, and Zack straightened.

Jordon sighed and sat down hard on the bed. "All my life I've longed for the kind of love and support you and Dusty both have. I'm building that with Tian Di. Why do you begrudge me the possibility of having that?"

"I want you to have that, just… why a singer? Have you been blind these last few years?"

Just when Jordon thought he'd made progress. "I don't care that Tian Di's a singer. I care what kind of person he is and how he makes me feel."

"It's too soon—"

"You can't make my decisions for me. I love him, Zack. Truly, with my whole heart. Maybe it was a crush before I knew him, but now I love him. I know it's new, but he's mine and I'm his."

"Yes, but—" Zack grabbed Jordon off the bed and death-grip hugged him.

Jordon didn't need much of a memory to recall the shit Andrew had put Zack through, even though the guy had tried to make up for the years of stupidity between them. Hell, he even collared Zack. But there was a part of Jordon that would always hate Andrew for the agony he'd caused his brother.

Hugging him back, Jordon whispered, "You survived... and Tian Di is much less of an asshole than—"

Out of some misplaced duty, Zack smacked Jordon in the back of the head.

Jordon cuffed him back and ducked away. He was an adult, but some things learned early in life didn't change with Adulting 101. Zack whacked him. Jordon hit back.

Zack placed his hands on his hips. "I can't help but feel this relationship is too quick."

Shrugging, Jordon repeated Robin's words to him, "Love doesn't go by any clock."

"But—"

"In some ways, I've known him forever. We click. He understands me. I have to see where this goes. I don't want any regrets." If blunt honesty didn't penetrate Zack's overprotection, nothing would.

Zack inhaled quick. Direct hit. Andrew had made decisions for Zack under the guise of not wanting him to regret committing too young, and they both wound up regretting the years they weren't together.

"He's good to you?" Zack studied Jordon.

"Very good. He loves me. I just want to spend time with him, and I miss him when we're not together... like part of me is missing."

Zack sighed. "I guess I should get to know him better."

"You should. He's a great—" *What in the Mother of Monet was Zack thinking?*

Zack pulled out two strips of condoms from his back pockets. "Glow in the dark, ribbed and lubed—"

Jordon was one part horrified, one part thrilled. This was Zack's attempt at a blessing. Should he fill him in there wouldn't be much fucking, if any? Which could be the end of things.... "Um, thank you... that's a lot of condoms... how exactly do you intend on getting to know him?"

Zack snorted. "Nice. But seriously, has he been tested?"

"We haven't—"

Zack held up his hand. "Before you do, you need to."

Funny how everyone just assumed anal had to be part of the deal. Well, for most guys, it probably was.

CHAPTER 14

"WELL, THAT took longer than expected." The gauntlet of Japanese customs had mentally drained Tian Di. Standing in line gave him a flashback of waiting outside his father's office until he was buzzed in. Once when he was twelve, his father had forgotten all about him, and Tian Di had been left there for half a day.

"Compared to my last commercial flight, this was easy. Let's get SIM cards." Jordon shepherded Tian Di to an airport shop. Even though Tian Di was there as a translator, he could tell Jordon had something to prove. With hand gestures and pointing, Jordon was able to purchase two SIM cards all on his own.

A warm feeling bloomed in the center of his chest as Jordon took care of him. Tian Di happily handed his cell to his boyfriend.

Jordon opened Tian Di's phone, popped out the SIM card, and put in a Japanese one. He did the same to his own phone, then stowed their original SIM cards in a little baggie he had ready.

Accepting his phone back, Tian Di gave a slight bow. "*Arigatou gozaimasu.*"

"You're welcome." Jordon grinned and returned the bow. "Let me just text my brothers and Gwen to say we arrived."

"Sure." Tian Di texted his band and his sister to let them know he'd landed.

Since they only had carry-on, Tian Di started to head straight for the taxi queue, but Jordon pointed out a man with a "Mr. Davis" sign and the publishing house logo.

"Welcome to Japan. I'll take you to the Prince Hotel. The publishing dinner is at 8:00 p.m. tonight." The driver took the luggage and directed them to an underground parking lot.

Jordon grinned as he slid into the back of a town car. "Swanky, and all for us."

Tian Di pushed in close to Jordon. "You deserve it."

On the sly, Jordon slipped his hand into Tian Di's and squeezed. "I doubt that, but this is uber cool nonetheless."

Leaning in, Tian Di whispered, "Being with you makes my face hurt from smiling so much."

Jordon grinned. "Me too."

Tian Di rubbed their palms together. The contact seemed to ease Jordon, allowing him to relax against the seat.

The car zoomed past the skyscrapers, shops, apartment complexes, and people. Tian Di had been to Japan a few times but always forgot how underdressed he felt with everyone in suits and ties. He was glad that, before they left Suzhou, Indigo had reminded the band to always pack their suits, just in case they needed them for any leg of the tour.

The driver carried their bags to the bell desk.

Jordon gave the woman at the front desk his passport.

She stared at the name, checked the computer screen, and then called over someone else.

The newcomer said, "Excuse, Mr. Davis, I'm sorry. But this reservation is for Zack Davis."

Tian Di stared at him.

"Oh, right. I think the name my publisher had on some of my files is incorrect." Jordon pulled out the invitation letter with all the information.

The driver made a call and handed over the cell phone to one of the hotel staff. Within a minute of nodding, he returned the phone and turned to Jordon. "I'm terribly sorry. Here's your room key, Mr. Davis."

Tian Di didn't mention he'd be staying with Jordon, to avoid the hotel changing them to a room with two beds.

Jordon palmed some bills and passed the tip when he shook the driver's hand.

The driver denied the money twice before accepting and departing.

"Why did they have your brother's name on the reservation?"

Jordon shrugged and followed the bellhop pushing their luggage on a cart. "I was young when I submitted my work. When they accepted it, I panicked. I wanted to be taken seriously so sent a picture of Zack's driver's license and a blurry picture of my passport."

"So they would think you were older?"

"Yeah, I never thought it would matter. I had a pseudonym. Dumb, though I thought the accountant who does the Japanese taxes for me had fixed the issue that first year, but I guess not everyone was made aware of the correction."

"I'm sure you're not the first." Tian Di followed Jordon and the bellhop into the hotel room.

The room wasn't much more than a bed, small desk with a chair in the corner, and a tiny white bathroom. Everything appeared clean. Showering might not be as much fun as it usually was, because the stall didn't look like two people could fit.

The bellhop unloaded the cart, setting their baggage on the well-used suitcase bench. He opened the nondescript yellow blackout drapes and explained in Japanese how the air system and lights worked only when the room keycard was inserted in the slot near the door. Then he demonstrated, and all the lights in the room came on.

Tian Di went around the tiny room turning off the excess lights. The window let in enough to fill the area.

Jordon trailed to the door with the bellhop and tipped him.

As soon as the door shut, Jordon stepped into his embrace.

Tian Di kissed him on the mouth. That was better. "Not touching you is hard."

"I know." Jordon melted into him.

"Do you want to check out Otome Road?" Tian Di suggested, although putting the bed to use was an appealing option as well.

Jordon popped his shoulder off of Tian Di's shoulder and stared at him. "The center of the yaoi universe. Hell to the yes!"

"This hotel is right in the heart of the Ikebukuro district." Tian Di opened Google Maps. "The Animate store is the start of the land of yaoi."

"Let's go." Jordon dragged Tian Di out of the room and into the elevator.

People strode down the street with purpose.

Jordon smiled at him. "Now this is a pace I understand."

They jumped into the pedestrian parade and headed toward paradise. "Hong Kong moves more like this too. Quicker than Suzhou."

Jordon pointed to a café across the street. "What's that?"

"A Danso café. Women dress up as bishie boys."

"Interesting. I need to send this to Gwen." Jordon snapped a picture, typed something, and sent the text to Gwen.

Blip.

She texted back, and Jordon held the phone out for Tian Di to read. *I wonder how many of those servers are actually transmen?*

"What does she mean?" Tian Di's question fell out of his mouth, but he was with Jordon, so questions were okay. It was liberating to have someone who didn't see questions as problems.

"Transman is short for someone who was assigned female at birth but whose gender identity is male."

"What do you mean *assigned*?"

"Doctors can only try to identify body parts; they can't know gender identity." Jordon gestured below his waist and then pointed to his head.

"Try to?"

Jordon continued, "Yes. Did you know about one out of two thousand babies are born with genitals that aren't typical? Surgery used to happen sometimes without even telling the parents. Now, many parents choose not to have the surgery performed on their babies."

Tian Di had heard of a word to describe this. "Inter... the word is trapped between languages."

"Intersex," Jordon supplied.

Nodding, Tian Di continued, "Yes. Intersex. That's the word.... In Hong Kong, we have a pink season, which is supposed to celebrate and promote understanding of gay, lesbian, bisexual, and transgender people. It's an uphill battle because many people, like my mother, refuse to admit we exist."

Jordon leaned into Tian Di for a few steps. "I'm sorry. I know how shitty that feels."

Tian Di no longer felt isolated. "Yeah. I will say, as much as Indigo bugs me, living with him and the rest of the guys has been good for me. And now I have you, and well...."

"You totally do." Jordon sighed. "But it's still painful that I can't hold your hand right now without causing a stir. I guess, from what I understand, Japan is starting to have a better understanding of gay and lesbian people. Gwen said they did pass a law that allows people to have their gender changed on their family registry, but it's called the gender identity disorder law."

Why was that bad? "Oh, and the word *disorder* is negative?"

Jordon nodded. "It can be. Though I think folks need a diagnosis for any kind of treatment here."

"True, and in Hong Kong you need to have surgery before your gender can be changed on legal documents."

"What? Not every transgender person wants affirmation surgery. Not everyone needs or can have surgery." Jordon sighed.

"I didn't know that." Tian Di never had anyone talk to him about these issues. The closest he got was listening to Indigo throw sexual innuendos around.

Jordon continued to walk. "Change is slow, and progress is rarely a straight line. But I have to say, sometimes I think the focus on harmony can limit the ways people can express themselves."

"Hmm, I do know it's hard to be different." Tian Di touched his own clothing. He wasn't transgender. He didn't identify as a girl, but sometimes he didn't feel all that male.

Jordon nudged into him. "I love everything about you. I love you for you."

Tian Di had gotten a lot of censure for wearing his hair long and for clothing that wasn't considered manly enough, though he'd learned people were less vocal if his look inclined toward cool and aloof. Thankfully, the androgynous look had come back into style.

As they walked, Jordon stuck his hands into his pockets. "I'm always surprised at how much fan mail I get from people thanking me for giving them characters they can identify with... some fans I've communicated with for years, and several have come out as transgender to me. They say yaoi gave them a safe space to explore themselves and who they are."

"I guess I'm not the only one taking solace in the pages of your manga." Tian Di followed signs to Sunshine City and pointed to the large building. "Animate."

Jordon squealed and sped up. "Fourth floor, here we come."

He laughed because Jordon's enthusiasm lifted Tian Di's spirits. "Fourth floor?"

Jordon held the door for him. "That's where the yaoi lives."

The directory showed the fourth floor was dedicated to girls' comics, including BL.

Jordon stood in the lobby area and gazed at the advertisements covering the walls. "Now, is it true no one knows the word *yaoi*?"

"It's BL or Boy's Love here."

Jordon seemed to ponder this and finally said, "A lot of folks in the West get confused by calling the genre 'Boy's Love,' because they think the comics are for pedophiles. Add scenes where characters act immature and are drawn—"

"Oh, you mean when the characters appear as children because they are acting like children?"

"Right. Though most Americans would freak if they knew the age of consent in Japan is thirteen. Granted the age might be higher based on prefectures, but still."

"Consent?" Tian Di wracked his brain to figure out the concept he missed. Indigo had mentioned *consent*, but he'd forgotten to look up the word.

"Being able to legally say yes to sex."

"Oh, okay. It's fourteen in China and sixteen in Hong Kong." Tian Di lowered his voice to fill Jordon in. "For a woman to receive anal sex it's twenty-one."

Jordon squeaked, and then forced, nervous laughter followed. "Umm…. So I guess in Hong Kong if I was a girl I couldn't legally have intercourse yet."

There it was. Tian Di hadn't been imagining things. Jordon became twitchy and pale anytime certain kinds of sex were mentioned, and he went to great lengths to avoid the subject. Tian Di had always assumed the reaction was inexperience, but maybe this reaction was something else.

He pulled Jordon over to the side of the hallway to let a group of schoolkids pass. "What's wrong?"

Shaking his head, Jordon wouldn't make eye contact and backed away. "Nothing. Nothing. Umm… it's just weird; I mean odd. Dammit! I can't help but to get tangled in my Western filter."

"What?" Tian Di was positive that wasn't the issue, though he'd let the subject go for now.

"Everyone makes judgments through their own experiences, background, values, how they were raised—you know, all that. I call this a filter, like a lens you view the world through. And when I label something that is outside my experience weird and odd, that's me judging something based on my American way of thinking. Something I try not to do, at least not since I've met Gwen."

Tian Di tilted his head. "Why?"

"Because she'd kick my ass if I didn't acknowledge it." Jordon chuckled.

"Thank you for explaining it to me." He wasn't sure he completely understood, but he got Jordon's general meaning. However, that still didn't explain the nervousness. He added, "You know you can tell me anything, right?"

Jordon's head hit the wall behind him. He opened his mouth but then snapped it shut. Nodding, he grabbed Tian Di's arm and pushed him toward the steps. "Come on, boys in love await."

Tian Di studied Jordon. Maybe he imagined Jordon's discomfort, or it could just be worry about the event tonight, unless, well, maybe Jordon—

Jordon took that moment to turn and smile at him. No, Jordon really did love him, of that he had no doubts.

Fighting to stay in the present, Tian Di turned his attention to their current adventure and followed Jordon.

He hiked the yellow steps of Animate with his boyfriend, who happened to be the artist of his favorite BL of all time. And they were in the flagship Animate store. Life was incredible.

Oh, and he was lead singer in the opening act for the Dark Angels.

He stumbled on a step.

Jordon was right there to catch him. "You okay?"

Tian Di nodded. His priorities had really reordered themselves.

They trudged past hentai posters of ample-chested women with big eyes and parted lips. Tian Di found the ones tangled in tentacles a bit disturbing.

Jordon stepped onto the fourth-floor landing and gasped. "Heaven."

BL manga, yaoi merchandise, DVDs, and accessories filled in every possible place along with *doujinshi* and cases of character figurines. All in one place. As a teen, Tian Di would have passed out with the overwhelming joy, and being here would have given him an instant erection.

Grabbing Tian Di's hand, Jordon exclaimed, "I'm surrounded by love. This is incredible."

His boyfriend didn't appear aware of the women and schoolgirls herded into groups, all staring at the abnormality of having two guys enter their domain. The younger ones giggled behind their hands, but most stared until the yaoi claimed their attention yet again.

Jordon pressed a quick kiss to Tian Di's cheek and rushed headfirst into an aisle. Moaning, he ran his fingers over the plastic-covered books and slid one off the shelf to study the cover.

Three hours later....

TIAN DI decided as much fun as it was digging through massive amounts of BL, watching Jordon captivated him completely. His "ohs" and "ahs" did things to Tian Di's heart and delicious things below the waist.

Jordon carried a tower of manga, along with a basket filled with figurines and limited-edition items.

He hated to yank Jordon away, but the time on Tian Di's cell said they didn't have a choice. "Unfortunately, even though we're not even halfway through this floor, I think we need to head back to the hotel soon."

"What? Oh yeah, right." Jordon's voice was husky as he added one more book to his pile.

Tian Di leaned in and read some of his choices. "*Target in the Viewfinder, Yellow, Super Lovers, Ouran High School Host Club, Love Stage, Gravitation, Crimson Spell, Loveless, Junjo Romantica*, and a *Yuri on Ice* DVD. Why are you buying them here?"

Jordon shrugged. "I guess I've always wanted to get my favorites in Japanese from the Animate store."

"But I think you forgot my favorite."

Checking his pile, Jordon asked, "Which?"

Tian Di searched and, two aisles over, found the Sakura Rose section.

"Wow." Jordon ran his finger along the spines of his own manga. "This is incredible."

Tian Di snapped a picture of Jordon in front of his section of mangas.

Grabbing a few of his titles, Jordon held them and posed.

A staff person appeared out of nowhere and reminded them, "Photos are forbidden."

Tian Di clicked four pictures before he nodded and held up his hands to indicate he'd take no more pictures, though he was thrilled to get the ones he'd taken.

Jordon added one of his manga to the pile. "My publisher still hasn't sent me a copy of this one."

They meandered to the payment area via the yaoi merchandise aisle. A couple of phone charms, a messenger bag with popular characters on the front flap, and a dog tissue holder were added to the need-to-have pile.

Jordon paid for his purchases.

Tian Di grabbed a couple of the bags.

Not being able to wait, Jordon snatched his copy of Sakura Rose out of the bag and removed the plastic. "I'm too curious to wait."

Two uniformed staff people surrounded him. "No. Do not open. Please out."

The staff repeated their diplomatic way of tossing them out of the store in English.

"We should go." Tian Di could feel his face heating up.

"Oh wow! The story came out better than I hoped. I had a hell of a time with this storyboard." Jordon ran his fingers over several of the pages. "What? Oh my. I just wanted to—"

The staff walked them to the stairwell. "Please. Leave."

Jordon laughed. "Wow, kicked to the curb for the crime of opening my own purchased manga."

He was fascinated by Jordon's lack of concern. "It doesn't bother you, does it?"

"No, does it bother you?" Jordon bounced down the stairs.

Did it? "If it were me, I would be red-faced—I mean, embarrassed— but if I really think about it, no harm was done other than not following a rule you didn't know about." If Tian Di were honest, he was tired of following rules and traditions that made no sense.

"Sorry if I embarrassed you." Jordon frowned.

Tian Di waved him off and wanted him to smile. "I wonder if they had known you were opening your own book if they would have acted differently."

On the way back to the hotel, they sat down and ate a couple of slices of pizza and a Mirinda orange soda. "Ah, a true Japanese meal."

Tian Di tried not to laugh. "And for dessert, shall we get some beef tongue ice cream?"

"Ew! No. I'll play the ugly American card to opt out of a bovine tongue-flavored cone."

Once back in the room, Jordon checked the time. "I guess we should get ready."

Needing to take the worry off of Jordon's face, Tian Di reminded him, "Japan's a very environmentally conscious country. I think it would be frowned upon to waste water."

"The stall looks tiny, but since I've already ripped the fabric of society at Animate, I think I should respect all other laws." Jordon peeled off his T-shirt. "But we only have time for, like, you know, our regular shower, right?"

Tian Di nodded.

And Jordon exhaled harder than normal but unzipped his pants in a hurry.

JORDON GROWLED at his cell phone after texting his brothers that he was fine three times, then tossed it on the bed. He seemed more agitated after the shower than before. He kept fussing with his shirt, his tie, his hair.

Tian Di brushed Jordon's hands away and straightened his suit, then ran product through his hair and kissed him until Jordon melted against him. "You look handsome. They'll love you."

Jordon shrugged. "Thank you for doing this with me."

"Of course." How could he make this easier on Jordon? Trying to think of ways to avert potential problems, Tian Di suggested, "To keep matters simple, I can introduce myself as your assistant or translator."

"But—"

This wasn't America. "I know you're not ashamed of me or of us, and neither am I. But just like you don't want our relationship to hurt me, I feel the same. Let this be about you as an artist."

Jordon sighed. "I don't like it, but fine."

Tian Di smiled with more confidence than he had and guided Jordon downstairs to the ballroom.

As soon as Jordon gave his name to one of the doorkeepers, she jumped out of her chair. "I'm terribly sorry about the confusion around your name when you were checking in. I hope you were not embarrassed by my mistake."

"Not at all. The fault lies with me. My apologies." Jordon took the name tag that read *Jordon Davis*. He smiled and gestured to Tian Di. "This is Tian Di Zhao. He will be acting as my assistant and translator."

"Very good." She quickly made Tian Di a name tag and swept them inside the ballroom. There were about thirty round tables perfectly set and scattered across the plush red carpet. Chandeliers dripping with crystals diffused a soft light across the ballroom.

The hostess led Jordon directly to a group of two tall men and one petite woman. "Excuse me. Allow me to introduce you to Mr. Davis and his assistant, Mr. Zhao."

The woman introduced the tall man in the elegant navy suit with a lighter blue shirt and a blue tie as "Mr. Sato, your assistant editor."

Jordon exchanged business cards, a handshake, and bow. "Mr. Sato, nice to meet you. I saw the pictures you posted from your Kyoto holiday. They were quite artistically taken."

Mr. Sato looked to the assistant, who translated Jordon's words, and nodded. "Thank you."

The translator said, "Mr. Davis, may I present Ms. Ito, your editor."

Jordon exchanged name cards with her and stared down at the cardboard rectangle. He shook hands and executed a bow. "It's very good to meet you. Thank you for the book recommendation about the Edo period. You were correct. I never realized the impact that time had on drawing today."

"Mr. Davis, it is a pleasure to meet you. I am happy you enjoyed the book." She spoke with only the slightest accent.

The translator paused dramatically before introducing Jordon to Mr. Miyazaki, head of Kin Jirareta Ai Press.

Jordon bowed. "Mr. Miyazaki. It is a pleasure to meet you. Thank you for the opportunity you've given me."

"I still recall how Ms. Ito put you forth as a new artist with such strength." Mr. Miyazaki shook Jordon's entire body with a firm handshake.

"It's uncommon for me to feel so passionately about an artist's work. Mr. Davis impressed me and my staff by sending me six completed stories as well as his own popular series published in America. This is why I fought strongly for us to publish him."

Mr. Miyazaki frowned for a moment. "It would have been more compelling to build on your already embedded fan base by using the same name, but Ms. Ito convinced me it wouldn't be necessary."

"Lucky for me, I was correct. As Sakura Rose's numbers suggest." Her expression reminded Tian Di of his sister. It showed she was more than aware of her worth and merely tolerated the figurehead's position of power.

Jordon gave her a dazzling smile. "I appreciate the chance you took on me. Thank you for inviting me to this event."

"Enjoy the evening," Mr. Miyazaki said in an almost dismissive fashion as he turned and stalked to another group.

Ms. Ito smirked. "Find me a bit later. I would like to discuss the next few stories with you while you're here."

"Of course." Jordon smiled.

Tian Di and Jordon were shown to their table. "Will you need me to stay with you and translate?"

Shaking his head, Jordon gestured to Tian Di. "No, Tian Di will assist me. Thank you for allowing me to distract you from your other duties."

Her eyes lit a little too bright. "It was no trouble. I will have another place setting added to the table. Anything you need while you're here, I'm—"

"I appreciate the offer, but Tian Di will make sure I have everything I need."

Just like that Jordon stopped Tian Di from eating vinegar. Any jealousy he had vanished.

The woman nodded and backed away.

Tian Di whispered, "I definitely will make sure you have *everything* you want or need."

Jordon's green eyes had grown huge, and his mouth dropped open. He might have been trying to say something, but only a squeak came out.

"Are you okay? Here, drink some water." Tian Di handed him the goblet from the table.

Jordon drank some and with trembling hands put it back on the table. "I'm fine."

He was anything but…. Maybe it was just nerves.

People started to fill in around their table. They were all around their early twenties, all pretty, and if catching snippets of their conversation counted, each one was interested in Jordon. Apparently being daughters of executives in the main publishing house got them prime seats. Every one of them seemed to be major fans of Sakura Rose and American men.

After the introductions and name card exchanges, Jordon took charge of the conversation and made sure everyone was included. He asked the quietest woman at the table, "Where would you set a BL story outside of Japan?"

Her eyes lit, and without hesitation, she claimed, "China."

"China?" Jordon asked, and the rest of the group murmured.

"The culture is different, and I think Chinese men are… lovely." She ended on a bold statement as she gave Tian Di a small smile.

That was very sweet. Tian Di inclined his head, but then returned to hanging on every word Jordon uttered so no one was led on.

Between the salad course and the main course, a woman with a rainbow ribbon loop pinned to her dress said, "Sakura Rose, I truly love your work. I especially like that your stories allow us a better understanding of… what does Tricks call it?"

She glanced around the table for help. Each of the other women shied away from the question like it was a bug. Tapping her ribbon, she said, "Like this."

Jordon grinned. "The gays of the rainbow."

She earnestly nodded. "Yes, reading him helped me understand about…." She gestured to Jordon to help her.

"Um… other orientations," Jordon supplied.

"Yes, that's the word. *Orientations*. Not just men who like men, but women who like women and people who like both."

"That's wonderful to hear. I think the sports manga have really impacted BL in a positive way. I want to contribute to the progress."

TIAN DI stayed glued to Jordon's side throughout the evening. If Tian Di wasn't already hopelessly in love with Jordon, he would be tonight, watching him charm not only the executives, but to take time to care for others. Tian Di had the most amazing boyfriend in the world.

"They're worshipping you like a rock star," Tian Di whispered. He was happy they appreciated Jordon.

Jordon chuckled. "You'd know. Let me get you a drink. Preference?"

"Surprise me." Tian Di watched Jordon order them two flutes of champagne.

The woman on his right stopped her conversation and asked quietly in fast Japanese, "Why is your boss bringing—"

Jordon brought Tian Di a drink.

Jordon touched his hand and smiled. "I'm going to speak to Ms. Ito again. Do you need anything else?"

"No, I'm fine. Thank you." Tian Di turned back to the woman who questioned him.

"Ah, I see why he's bringing you back drinks." The woman's conclusion was correct.

He wasn't sure if he should attempt to dissuade her, so he opted to change the subject. "Tell me, do you live in Tokyo?"

TIAN DI practiced his Japanese on the women around the table. Once he submerged himself in the language, the words came back.

He fended off another question about Sakura Rose. "I'm not sure what will happen with the storyline next. I believe he is speaking with his editor, Ms. Ito, right now."

One woman waxed poetic. "Such luck to know what the next adventures will be while we have to wait."

A collective sigh turned into smiles when Jordon returned.

Jordon crashed down into the seat and inclined toward Tian Di. "Dude, you're never going to believe this. They want me to speak. Should I get that woman who helped before?"

Tian Di grinned. "Do you think I'm shy?"

The bark of Jordon's laughter startled some around the table. "No, I guess not. After Beijing, this is a small audience for you."

Tian Di asked, "What do they want you to talk about?"

"Ms. Ito didn't say."

"Well, that makes it easy. When?"

"Um, now." Jordon gestured to the frantically waving translator standing with Ms. Ito.

Tian Di stood. "After you."

Ms. Ito waited at the podium. "Greetings. Welcome to the tenth annual gathering of Kin Jirareta Ai Press. I'm Ms. Ito, and I'd like to thank the artists for leaving their storyboards, the editors for leaving their storylines, and the fans for setting aside their reading tonight to celebrate with us."

Tian Di whispered a basic translation to Jordon. He added, "Remember, that feeling you think is nervousness is really excitement."

Jordon groaned quietly.

Ms. Ito continued, "Tonight I would like to introduce the artist responsible for one of the fastest-selling and most popular series Kin Jirareta Ai Press publishes. Please welcome Sakura Rose."

"You're up." Tian Di gestured for Jordon to climb the stage steps.

The crowd rose to their feet, applauding Jordon, then finally sat back down.

Tian Di raised the mic to his and Jordon's height and brushed a hand across Jordon's for a moment to remind him he wasn't alone. "Thank you for the warm welcome tonight, and thank you for allowing me to be part of the Kin Jirareta Ai Press family. I'm honored to be an artist with this incredible publishing house."

People applauded after Tian Di translated.

"We are all dependent on the eyes of our editors and assistant editors to protect us from ourselves. A special thanks to Ms. Ito and her team from shielding the world against my mistakes, plot holes, and storyboard disasters."

The audience chuckled after the translation.

"Our press is named Kin Jirareta Ai, or Forbidden Love. It is my hope someday that there are no forbidden loves… only love."

Tian Di had to swallow hard before he translated.

Everyone shot to their feet, and Jordon ended his speech on the perfect high note.

"*Ai wa ai.* Love is love."

CHAPTER 15

IDK what to do. I love Tian Di. I don't want to lose him! Jordon texted Gwen.

If he'd ditch you over that F him! Gwen was never one to suffer compromises well.

Gwen! Jordon needed to get a grip. Tian Di didn't seem to be that type of man but....

Anal Ease or just tell him yr not into fuking. But talk to him. Gwen signed her text with a happy face with whirling crazy eyes.

They'd been going around in circles dozens of times, and Gwen kept ending in the same spot.

Jordon sent a thumbs-up.

Zack's text flashed across the top of his screen. *Where will you be 4 this vac? How long?*

Not sure yet. Yeah, that would go over well with his schedule-happy brother—liking everything to be scheduled.

What? Why not? If he doesn't want to go with you, I can still be there by 3pm.

Shit! The organizer from hell knew the flight schedule? Of course he did. Jordon hurried to text. *We haven't talked about it yet.*

Can't you talk to him?

Jump to conclusions much?

Sorry.

He's sleeping right now.

In your room?

Duh! There was a long pause that held all the unfair censure Jordon could take. Jordon fired off, *He's my bf!*

Make sure you use protection.

Argh! Should be sufficient to let Zack know what he thought about that!

You call me if you need me. Anytime. Zack's words screamed how far out of his comfort zone he was.

Of course. Later. Jordon tried to set his phone aside.

Call me or text me.

Jordon texted, *Got it. Having fun here. Later.*

He felt trapped in an Edvard Munch painting. The expressionist painter who put *The Scream* on canvas had a way of giving life to the anxiety and angst that streamed through Jordon's body. Trying to set and hold his new boundaries was exhausting. No wonder he'd never done this before.

A soft snore from Tian Di's side of the bed made Jordon's fret turn to the possible ways Tian Di would react to Jordon's not wanting to have sex. Or maybe he should just suck it up and do it. *That's what he said....*

Tian Di rolled closer, and in his semiconscious state, tucked the blanket around Jordon, making a burst of affection replace the doubt. Tian Di cuddled into Jordon's back. His morning erection couldn't be missed, bumping against Jordon's ass.

And all Jordon's ill feelings resurfaced. Jumping out of bed, he hurried into the bathroom and used the toilet. He brushed his teeth, turned on the water, and stepped under the spray.

As he rinsed the shampoo out of his hair, Tian Di joined him in the shower. "Morning, my love."

Jordon opened his mouth to a minty kiss. Tian Di swept his tongue past Jordon's lips, and Jordon's toes curled in response. Everything stood up and took notice. How did a kiss chase away his crazy?

Tian Di traced the probably dark circles under Jordon's eyes. "You didn't sleep well. Are you still keyed up about last night?"

"I don't know." Jordon rinsed off.

"You were amazing. Everyone loved you. So sexy.... Mmm, maybe I can relax you?" Tian Di skimmed his hand down to Jordon's stomach en route to his erection. He wrapped his hand around Jordon's shaft and gave a moan-inducing stroke.

Tian Di's dick grazed across Jordon's ass once again, terrorizing him with what should be happening on this vacation. Sex was what boyfriends did. They should have used all the condoms Zack had given them by now... well, at least most of them.

No, he should tell Tian Di first. Jordon whirled around before his dick deflated. "Um, yeah. How about later? First let's figure out what we want to do and head out."

If Tian Di wasn't happy with the change of plans, he didn't say. He shampooed his hair. Though shampooing one's hair shouldn't be an erotic act that could sell tickets. Every elegant movement enchanted Jordon, made him wish he'd have shut his damned mouth and had fun in the shower.

Maybe he should—

"Could you hand me a towel?" Tian Di asked as he shut off the water.

Refusing to whine, Jordon dried Tian Di and then used a towel himself. He followed Tian Di out of the bathroom to their suitcases.

"Where should we go?" Tian Di passed Jordon a pair of green underwear.

Jordon tried not to drool as Tian Di pulled on a red pair of boxer briefs. The material clung to his ass in just the right way. "I don't know. Any ideas?" Jordon tossed Tian Di one of his painted T-shirts and put on one of Tian Di's.

"Have you been to Kyoto? We're too late for cherry blossoms, but Philosopher's Path is still lovely in the mornings."

"I went on my first trip here. Though I don't mind going back if you want to go. It's gorgeous there. So much to draw." Tian Di handed Jordon a pair of black jeans and nabbed a pair for himself.

"Huh, where's someplace neither of us have gone so we can explore it together?"

Jordon swallowed hard. Was this his way of suggesting they should—

Tian Di grinned. "Have you ever been to Jigokudani?"

"Where?" Jordon glanced up from putting on his socks.

Tian Di disappeared into the bathroom and came out with a bottle of mousse. "I do love the natural wave of your hair," he muttered as he pushed product through Jordon's hair. "Jigokudani is where you can see the snow monkeys of Nagano."

"I've seen pictures where they're sitting in the hot springs and snow is falling. That would be great, but would they still be there this time of year?"

After a quick Google search, Tian Di grinned. "The monkeys, which are actually macaques, are there year-round. Apparently, the park provides food."

Some weird fact tickled Jordon's brain. "Wait, isn't that where the Hokusai Museum is? In Nagano?"

Tian Di danced his long elegant fingers over his phone. "Yes. We could see the snow monkeys and the museum. Have you ever stayed in a ryokan?"

The excited question made Jordon glad he could say "Nope."

Dusty had wanted to stay in one of these traditional Japanese inns during their trip. They looked cool, with tatami mat floors, sliding papered doors, and futons on the floor for beds. Though at sixteen, sleeping on the floor and using communal baths had made Jordon dig his heels in and flat-out refuse.

A few clicks later, Tian Di's smile liquefied any of Jordon's reservations. "We could stay near the park in a ryokan. I heard they even have some with private outdoor onsens."

Jordon wanted to ask if they had Western bathrooms, but didn't want to appear a prima donna. Besides, for Tian Di, he would sleep on the floor and use a squat toilet for a night or forever. Whatever would make him happy. "Um, we could do that."

Tian Di placed the call and made the reservation.

"Use my credit card. I asked you on this trip." Jordon handed over the plastic magic.

Shrugging, Tian Di whispered, "Fine, but I'm getting the train tickets and all of our meals."

"Sure."

"I held the room with the card, but we have to pay cash." Before Jordon even told him, he didn't have that much Japanese yen on him, Tian Di said, "We can stop at an ATM at the train station."

"Great. We should text our siblings the plans." Jordon ignored the gnawing in his gut. He texted, *Heading to Nagano! Snow monkeys and Hokusai museum.*

An immediate *Be safe* from Dusty and a *Have fun call if you need me* from Zack followed.

Dusty texted, *Miss you.*

Tears sprung to Jordon's eyes. Geez, he was a twit. He'd only been gone a couple of days, but in Davis time that was a long time. *Miss you 2*, he texted as quickly as his fingers let him.

Zack's text read, *Take pics… if you want.*

Jordon snapped and sent a selfie of him smiling.

Tian Di finished texting his sister and pulled him into a tight hug. He didn't say anything and he didn't have to.

THE TRAIN ride to Nagano flew by. Jordon leaned into Tian Di and whispered, "You're the best travel companion ever."

"As are you." Tian Di continued to read him articles about the snow monkeys in his deep voice. If the whole singing thing didn't work for him, he could definitely get voice work.

Jordon clicked around and found cute videos from the park visitors of the monkey drama. "Tian Di, look at this!"

They watched the videos until the train pulled into Nagano's station.

Tian Di got off the train and turned to offer Jordon his hand.

Jordon accepted the assistance and felt loved by the consideration. "Thanks."

Tian Di found an information desk and asked some questions in Japanese. He led Jordon to a ticket window, where they purchased a Snow Monkey Pass. "I found this tip online. This pass includes unlimited use of the bus, admission to the park, and free use of certain trains."

They boarded the bus and Jordon pressed in close to Tian Di. The contact made him cozy and more than a little bit aroused.

Tian Di smiled. "I'm glad we're doing this together."

Firsts were a big deal. He should just let Tian Di fuck him. They were in love; it couldn't be terrible, right? *Fucknuggets!* Why did the thought make him feel sick inside? He heard the voice of his therapist in his head saying, *"You're not listening to yourself."*

"Hey, you okay?" Tian Di caressed his arm.

"We should fuck." Jordon's words squeaked out too loudly. There, he'd said it.

Tian Di looked around and then whispered, "I think the transportation authority of Japan would frown on doing that activity while riding their bus."

Jordon's laughter barked out. He shook his head, not letting Tian Di play the suggestion off as a joke. No, he could do this... he would do this. Jordon was all in, and this would prove how serious he was about Tian Di. He vowed, "Tonight."

The unreadable expression Tian Di wore made Jordon feel distant, but this was the next step in their relationship. Right? Maybe anal sex wouldn't be so bad.

Even if it was, he said it, so everything was settled. No backsies, as
Zack would say. They'd do *it* tonight.

JORDON AND Tian Di trudged a few blocks from the bus stop and hiked
along a dirt path, following signs for the Jigokudani Monkey Park. Jordon
switched his knapsack to his other shoulder. "I guess it was a good thing the
Prince Hotel let us stow our carry-on with them."

"Everyone said that would make staying at this ryokan easier, since
there's no road for a taxi." This was one of the first things Tian Di had
said since Jordon had blurted out his unromantic, blunt, and possibly
insulting suggestion of what their evening's activity should be.

God, he was such a cocksocket. Maybe he should—

Tian Di pointed to the traditional wood house. "There it is."

The differences in the ryokan's wood coloring suggested the
building had expanded from a house to an inn and had sprawled out over
the generations, with each adding a few more rooms or some more space.

Opening the door, he let Tian Di into the wood lobby.

A smiling man greeted them.

Tian Di's Japanese greeting got a smile, and the man directed his
questions to Tian Di.

Jordon didn't mind playing an ornament, and he let Tian Di fill out
all the paperwork, while the apparent owner photocopied their passports
and took a stack of Japanese yen for the room.

He wandered over to the display case of basic toiletries and candy.
The ryokan charged quite a markup. Lube. Did they have any Anal
Ease? *See? Fucking is such a bad idea.* No lube! Dammit, he'd figure
something out.

The man waved Jordon back and led them through a wood-paneled
hallway. He pointed to the communal bathrooms, which Jordon hoped
they wouldn't have to use.

Ha, Jordon was worried about using a public restroom? Considering
what he was willing to do for Tian Di, he almost snorted.

God, this just seemed all kinds of wrong.

The man opened a door, stepped inside, and flipped on the light. He
pointed out how the lock worked on the outside door, and then took off
his shoes and slipped on a pair of red slippers.

Tian Di pointed to two more sets. "The blue ones are for guests."

Jordon put on a pair of the slippers and placed his and Tian Di's shoes in a low cubby.

The man slid the papered screen open.

Jordon followed Tian Di and stepped inside. *Serene* was the first word that came to mind. The pristine room had tatami mat floors and white walls. A low, dark wood table and two cushions was the only furniture in the room.

The man talked to Tian Di in Japanese, probably pointing out the amenities of the room.

Peering out one of the two windows, Jordon saw that their room overlooked the ryokan's public hot springs. The windows were cracked open just enough to allow in a cool breeze that made the curtains dance. Several monkeys sat on the rooftops and surveyed Jordon, probably looking for a handout.

Tian Di translated, "The owner recommended we don't open the windows more than halfway, because the monkeys will enter."

Jordon cranked the windows closed a little more before turning away. He could've sworn the monkeys gave him a pout. He smiled at the only picture in the entire room—a copy of Hokusai's *The Great Wave*.

The man continued to chat with Tian Di. Maybe he was telling him where they could get some lube… or not.

He slid another door open to an all-white room containing a mirror, a sink, and a Western toilet. Thank the Great Cockasarus, 'cause squatting over an Asian toilet wasn't in Jordon's skill set, and ugly American or not, he'd like to keep it that way.

The memory of Dusty taking him and Zack to the countryside in France wormed its way to the surface. They'd stopped at a rest stop. Jordon, much to his mortification, recalled racing out of the bathroom saying, "Someone stole the toilet. There's just a porcelain hole in the floor."

Talk about embarrassment. But he was still glad there was a sit-down here.

Their host went to the far wall and slid open another door to a small but perfect paradise. He pointed to the crocs in blue by the door and said more things to Tian Di in Japanese.

Would any of this talk result in the lube they would need later… the lots and lots of slick Jordon would need to endure this… endeavor? If there wasn't a separate gift shop, how long did Amazon Prime take?

God, why had he said anything? What had he been thinking? He really did need to know if they even sold Anal Ease in Asia.

Tian Di caressed his arm and then translated. "These are outside shoes to navigate the garden, or you can walk on the pebbled path for a foot massage."

Jordon nodded. He tried to focus on how the tiny gray pebbles could feel like anything other than stepping on Lego blocks again and again. A gentle breeze called his attention to the corner of the garden. A weeping willow's branches draped low, swaying in the wind as it created a privacy wall of leaves. A wooden awning over the onsen had been artfully designed to give cover from weather while still remaining in harmony with the rest of the space. Steam rose from the sunken gray rock-hewn onsen, which was the size of twelve bathtubs.

On a simple rock bench sat plastic bowls, body soap, and washcloths. Maybe Tian Di would teach him how to take a proper dip in their hot spring.

"The owner wants to know if we want dinner in our room or—"

"In the dining room." Jordon's voice jumped two octaves higher into the emergency range. "I mean… it's probably very atmospheric."

Was that even a word?

Tian Di frowned and dipped his chin. He spoke to the man, who slid open another door and pointed to the two navy robes hanging inside.

He bowed and left.

Jordon rushed to the closet for something to do. "Look! There are monkeys on the robes."

"You're adorable." Tian Di lifted Jordon's hair and pressed his lips to the back of Jordon's neck.

Jordon moaned as shivers of want ran through him. He rested against Tian Di. This position made Tian Di's erection nestle into Jordon's ass crack. Spinning away, he clung to a monkey robe as if it would stop him from drowning in his own stupidity.

"Um, I didn't see them at the front desk, but maybe you have to ask for them. I bet they sell these." *Along with Anal Ease.* Jordon rambled unable to shut his mouth. "We should check."

"If you want, we can take an onsen before dinner. The owner reminded me it was customary to wear our robes to the dining room."

What? "Sure."

"Maybe the onsen will relax you." Tian Di kept staring at Jordon. Yeah, to him, Jordon must appear a puzzle.

With a couple of pieces missing.

JORDON FOLLOWED Tian Di outside to their private oasis. He shucked off his clothing and tried not to perv on his boyfriend. "Teach me the art of an onsen, *senpai*."

Busying himself with folding their clothing, he strove not to drool as Tian Di stripped his clothing away in what appeared to be more of a dance. Dammit, Tian Di was scorching hot.

Tripping after Tian Di's lithe form convinced Jordon he needed Michelangelo stat. Someone needed to capture his form in sculpture, and Jordon could never be that talented.

"There's various ways to prepare for an onsen, but the idea is you get clean before you get in. And if you prepare the right way, it will help you to adjust to the hot water before you get in."

"So where's the bag of rice?" Jordon had always drawn his characters washing with the bag of rice before they stepped into the bath.

"Are you hungry?" Tian Di's lips twitched.

Jordon giggled, then restrained himself. He started to chuckle, because Tian Di strained to keep a straight face, which made his eye twitch. "Starving, but let's onsen first."

"A bag of rice is a thing of the past. Unless you're at a posh spa, usually it's a washcloth and soap, but let's simply take a shower." Tian Di pointed to the handheld sprayer in the corner. He nabbed some chopsticks from his bag, and twirled his hair up into a bun.

Jordon longed for a pen to draw him.

They soaped up and rinsed off.

Tian Di set the washcloths to the side. "Since it's only the two of us, I don't think we need our privacy cloths. Usually you would use them to protect your modesty."

Jordon was embarrassingly erect. Argh, he totally should have taken Tian Di's offer and gotten off this morning, because right now he could hang his privacy cloth on his jutting pole and there would be no hiding, only highlighting his state.

"Take this bowl and pour water from the hot spring over you. Using the onsen water helps you get used to the temperature. You can add cold water from the faucet under the shower spray if you need to make the water cooler." Tian Di demonstrated and then refilled the bowl for Jordon.

Tian Di gently poured the hot water, and splashed down Jordon. The water burned but aroused as rivulets cascaded down his body.

They repeated this process several times until Jordon almost begged for his cock to be put out of its misery with less teasing and more direct attention.

Tian Di stepped into the onsen and sat on the smooth rock edge.

Jordon copied him. Damn, Tian Di's gorgeous cock was erect and begging for some attention as well.

Fuck, he really wanted to reach out and take care of Tian Di's erection and his own. He could stroke them both off, and he'd bet within two minutes they'd need another shower.

Although staying horny would help him *do* things....

Taking Tian Di's offered hand, Jordon stepped farther into the hot spring. Was this what a lobster felt like being lowered into a scalding pot? Hot water lapped higher and higher on his body as they shuffled down the slope.

"Have a seat."

Jordon sat next to Tian Di on a stone bench that submerged him to the tops of his shoulders in near-boiling water. His muscles unwound and tension disappeared, only because there was no choice. He splashed the hot water on his face to wash away the sweat beading on his forehead.

Tian Di rested his head against the edge. His eyes were closed, and several long pieces of hair dipped into the water.

Jordon planted his mouth on Tian Di's, and then pulled back. "You know I love you, right?"

Wrapping his arms around Jordon, Tian Di kissed his neck. "Yes. And you know I love you?"

"Yes."

Tian Di stared into his eyes. "No matter what."

Jordon wasn't so sure. Here was the perfect time to talk to Tian Di about his feelings and worries, but the words eluded him.

After a few minutes of heavy silence, Tian Di broke the stifling quiet. "We should get out. Too long in here can make you dizzy."

They dried off. Tian Di held out the monkey robe for Jordon.

"We're really supposed to wear these for dinner?" Jordon slipped into his and held Tian Di's for him.

Tian Di spun into his and kissed Jordon on the nose. "Yes, but if you're not comfortable, we can—"

"No, that's okay. I can do this." Wearing a robe to a restaurant was different, but he was here for new experiences. He needed to learn to deal.

They scuffed down the wooden hallway in their slippers and entered the restaurant. Jordon envisioned this on a storyboard and smiled.

Some guests dined in robes and some were in clothing.

The waitress seated them at a table in the middle of the dining room and asked questions in Japanese. Tian Di translated, "Do you want your sake warmed?"

"Um, I don't know. You choose. I'm not much of a drinker." Jordon glanced over at Tian Di.

He replied to the waitress, and after she left, he told Jordon, "Usually if the sake is a very high quality, you'd want the sake chilled. But tonight, warmed will be nice."

Jordon nodded. What did he know?

The waitress returned, carrying two wooden trays, and set one in front of each of them.

Jordon stared down at the food. Raw fish over rice, a pile of Zack's worst food nightmare—straw mushrooms—a couple of carrots, three asparagus stalks, and a dead bug. *Say what now?*

A quick check on Tian Di's tray said the corpses were laid to rest on their dinner trays on purpose. Out of the corner of his eye, Jordon saw a woman pick up her own bug with chopsticks and take a bite.

Jordon gagged into his napkin and tried to pass it off as a cough. "Sorry."

"Pickled crickets aren't for everyone." Tian Di turned his chopsticks around and removed the dead bug from Jordon's tray with the backs.

"You eat them?" Trying not to be horrified, and wondering what a cricket-flavored kiss would taste like, Jordon gagged again.

"I don't like the taste." Tian Di set Jordon's bug next to his own and covered them with a large carrot circle, creating a bizarre orange cricket grave marker for the cemetery on his plate.

The artist in Jordon wanted to take a picture, but the six-year-old inside him kept chanting that bugs didn't belong on dinner trays.

Their waitress returned and poured sake into brown earthen cups with artfully uneven glaze. Jordon searched for the imperfection with which Japanese artists intentionally mar their creations. He found the small nick on the base of the cup.

He copied Tian Di, holding the filled cup in his open palm.

"It's tradition not to set the *ochoko*—or cup—down until you finish the drink."

"*Kanpai*," Jordon toasted.

"*Kanpai*." Tian Di drank the sake like a shot.

Jordon had never had sake, but when in a ryokan…. He pounded the liquid in one go and swallowed. "Tastes like warm, sweet rice juice with a kick."

The waitress rushed over and refilled their cups. She said something to Tian Di and took their sake carafe away.

Tian Di shook his head. "I was scolded for not refilling your cup immediately."

Jordon recalled that was how some of his characters would get very drunk at work events—the social grace of refilling the cup again and again and again. The heat of the sake spread from his mouth and throat outward.

"*Kanpai*."

Tian Di arched an eyebrow but didn't say anything.

After a couple of minutes, Jordon proclaimed, "I feel loose in my shoulders."

"Onsen or sake?"

"Both…." Maybe getting a little tipsy would help. Still holding his cup, Jordon whispered, "I love you. Thank you for being in my life. *Kanpai*."

Tian Di's smile ignited him more than alcohol. He raised his cup but didn't down the drink.

The waitress returned with more sake and filled Jordon's cup.

Not wanting to be rude, he held the cup properly and drank.

After refilling his cup once more, she clapped him on the back and said something sounding like praise.

Jordon drank. His worries became further away and not nearly as important as before the sake.

She poured again, and he drank what she poured him.

Wait, weren't the sake cups supposed to be placed in wooden boxes or something? Jordon wanted to ask, but he'd have to use a lot of words and his mouth felt lazy.

Tian Di said something to the waitress, and she took her hand off Jordon's back by way of running her fingers through his hair.

Jordon ducked away from her and swayed. How many cups had he drunk? Four or five, and did it matter? He giggled, covering his mouth.

The waitress reappeared with two large bottles of cold water.

Tian Di opened one and poured a large glass for Jordon.

"Thank you, kind and gentle sir." Jordon smiled and then attempted to eat some fish, but the chopsticks made the task difficult. His coordination might be off. Besides, Jordon didn't want raw fish.

"I have a few protein bars in my bag you can have later." Tian Di finished the last of his fish.

Jordon stared down at his tray of raw fish and the disks of future bug burials. Were carrots now forever ruined? "I don't want to eat this."

His worry was quiet, though lurking in the background.

"Come on. Let's get you back to the room." Tian Di helped him stand.

"Do you think I'm drunk?" Jordon asked through snorting giggles. He allowed Tian Di to guide him down the empty hallway.

"Is that a question?" Tian Di looked around and then gave him a quick kiss on his cheek.

The hallway hadn't been crooked on the way to the restaurant. "Tian Di, someone must have stretched the hallway."

"I guess the walk after the sake feels longer going back to the room." Tian Di took care of the door and steadied Jordon as he tripped up the step.

"Someone stole our table, just like the French toilet...." Jordon cracked up more at Tian Di's confused and slightly concerned expression. The low table and cushions were gone. In their place were two futon mattresses and two snowy white quilts.

"It's the Case of the Missing Table." Jordon giggled. He crashed down onto the futon.

Reality. Time to do this. He gathered his focus and wrestled to balance on all fours. Pushing his robe out of the way proved impossible because the fabric kept falling back into place covering his ass. He fell face-first into the pillow.

Damn. Ha, ha, ha. "I feel like I'm a cow being tipped."

"What? Why would you give money to a cow?"

"No, not money to a cow." It was too much to explain, so Jordon just snorted. He struggled back onto his hands and knees. Trying and failing once again to pull his robe over his ass. Tian Di would have to take care of the robe.

"Jordon, what are you doing?"

Jordon kneeled and waited. Eventually he looked back at Tian Di. "I'm ready. Condoms are in my bag."

"For what?"

He screwed up his face in an effort to brace himself for the onslaught. "You know. The fucking. I can do this. Go ahead. Just do it."

CHAPTER 16

WHAT IN the world? How drunk was Jordon? He was on all fours in front of Tian Di, demanding to be penetrated.

Tian Di lay down next to the love of his life and stared at Jordon's expression of fierce determination. He skimmed a hand over Jordon's back. "You're trembling."

"I'm not." Jordon swayed. "Go ahead. I can do this."

"I have no doubt." Tian Di had to figure this out.

"Good. Do it," Jordon demanded, wiggling his backside.

Tian Di wasn't sure of the answer to the question, but he had to ask, "Why do you keep insisting I do something you clearly do not wish to do?"

"Let's get this over with," Jordon spilled out with alcohol-lubricated honesty.

Tian Di pulled him down to the futon and swaddled Jordon in a blanket. "Ah, the slurs of sake truth. Is this why you got drunk?"

The silence went on for a long time until Jordon sagged and huffed out a defeated "I guess."

"We don't have to do anything you don't want to do." Tian Di snuggled closer to a pouty drunken Jordon.

"Use condoms to fuck," Jordon slurred.

"Always." Tian Di's sister had drummed that into his head.

Jordon yawned. "Good."

Tian Di grabbed a bottle of water he'd brought back from the restaurant. "Here. Drink some, and then you can tell me why."

"Why what?" Jordon tried to push out his lower lip but failed and started giggling.

"Why did you get drunk and start insisting we do something you don't want to do?" That might be too complex a question for Jordon to process.

Jordon drank the entire bottle—probably more to stall his answer than out of thirst. "This is what boyfriends do. They have sex."

What? "We have sex every day. Sometimes more than once."

Truth be told, Tian Di couldn't believe his luck in finding such an affectionate lover. Unlike some of his past relationships, Jordon seemed fixated on Tian Di's pleasure and always made sure he was satisfied.

Jordon's eyes were glazed over. "Yeah, but that's not real sex."

Not real sex? "What does—"

A snore ripped through the room.

Tian Di stared at a sleeping Jordon. His mouth turned down in a frown.

Rearranging the blankets around Jordon, Tian Di combed his fingers through Jordon's hair until he snuffled. Jordon's lips turned into a small smile, and he cuddled into Tian Di's side. That was better.

How could Jordon think they weren't having sex? *Real* sex? Certainly, it felt like amazing sex to Tian Di. It was probably the most physically satisfied he'd ever been, and they hadn't even gotten to his favorite: Mouth sex.

When in doubt, google it out. *Why was he quoting Indigo?*

Tian Di grabbed his phone, clicked around the internet, and tried not to wince. Instantly, there were too many sites depicting anal sex. Japan wasn't censored like China, and he wasn't sure if that was a good thing or not. The video of two men sandwiched into one made his buttcheeks tighten.

Not that he wouldn't have anal sex with Jordon, but he found the whole process could be messy, painful—though he'd do it if Jordon wanted to. Maybe with Jordon the entire experience would be better?

After a couple of minutes of determined searching and adjusting the key words, he found less porn and more how-to sites. One started off by stating not all gay men liked anal sex. The website pointed out other ways of enjoying intimacy. *Manual? Ah, manual that must be with hands—and oral, of course.* The site also said men enjoyed intercrural sex and frottage. *What are those?*

Tian Di followed the first link for intercrural sex, glad he didn't have to try to pronounce the word. He read that intercrural was when someone wanted to thrust between their partner's legs or thighs. They put lube on their partner's thighs and rutted to happiness. That might be nice. No need to stretch anything out, and holding Jordon tight was always great. He started to harden over the thought of sharing that with Jordon.

Ignoring his body's responses, he focused. Now, what in the world was frottage? Oh, yes. Dry humping and rubbing against each other. Tian

Di was a definite fan. Maybe intercrural was frottage with more direct thrusting?

He clicked back to the main article, which ended with "anal sex is *not* mandatory to have gay sex," and saved the link. Maybe he could show Jordon.

Tian Di curled into his lover. Horny, but mentally exhausted, he let sleep take him.

SMALL KISSES rained down on Tian Di's neck. "Mm, this is a nice way to wake up."

No verbal answer, just lips pressed to the pulse point on his neck.

"How's your head?"

The kisses stopped. "It's pretty good. I thought I'd have a headache, but I don't."

Tian Di had to get Jordon to talk to him. "So about last night—"

"Let me go to the bathroom first." Jordon darted out of the room.

Nature called Tian Di, so when Jordon exited, he entered. He came back to an empty room, but the garden door was ajar.

Tian Di peeked out. Jordon was rinsing off soap. The scent of summer roses in full bloom wafted through the air. He enveloped Jordon in a fluffy towel and took a quick shower himself.

Jordon dried him.

"I'm not drunk, and we can do it right now. I'm ready." Jordon's voice cracked a little.

"Why do we have to do *it* that way?" Was that too honest of a question?

Jordon shrugged. "Um… we're boyfriends."

"Will you stop loving me if we don't?" Tian Di's heart pounded. Would Jordon turn out to be like the first man he'd been with and say yes?

"No! Course not." Jordon crossed the room and sat on the futon. He draped the comforter around him.

Tian Di joined him. "Talk to me."

"I'm a side." Jordon pronounced this revelation with such misery it sounded like he was confessing to having an incurable illness.

"I'm not sure what that means." Tian Di combed his fingers through Jordon's wet hair.

"I've never fucked or been fucked, and I don't think I would like it. The whole idea is just, like, a big no to me. But I can do it, and I can do it with you."

"But you said you don't want to do that. So why are you trying to force yourself to do something you're uncomfortable with?"

"I love you, and I want to make you happy."

"I am happy." Wasn't Tian Di clear enough? He took Jordon's index finger and ran it over where his musical note ring used to be.

Jordon dropped his head onto Tian Di's shoulder. "Long term, I mean. You're not going to want to stay with me."

Tian Di wanted to deny that inaccuracy, but he needed to understand why Jordon thought that. "Why not?"

"Because you must want to fuck—be with someone that way, right? And I don't think I do."

Odd how a piece of him wanted Jordon to keep believing that, because there were expectations around the act. "I've done that before…."

Jordon raised his head and stared. "And you liked it, right?"

"It was okay. I did it more for the other man than for myself." Tian Di needed to be honest, though he left out the parts of feeling blackmailed and used.

Jordon stared at Tian Di and frowned. "Yeah, but what if we never did that? Wouldn't you miss that?"

"It wasn't—I love being with you, and what we do means so much more than anything I'd done before." He shoved his cell phone at Jordon. "Take a look at this article. Read how it ends."

Jordon scrolled through the article and sighed. "Yeah, I know that, but—"

"I love you. You. And if you want to do that, we can, and if you don't, we don't have to…."

Jordon got quiet and stared into Tian Di's eyes. "And I really love you."

The connection was heart-stopping. In that moment, he had total clarity. He'd do anything for this man. "Good. We should be able to tell each other everything."

"I'll try. Look, there's a piece of me that feels like I should try, you know? Like maybe I'd love anal sex." Jordon's voice grew softer, and he grimaced.

Tian Di nodded. He wished he could take away the sadness from Jordon's eyes. "And maybe we will someday. Maybe we won't. But you need to hear me, what I am saying. I am having great super satisfying sex with my boyfriend."

Jordon sighed, reached over to his knapsack, and pulled out his iPad. He tapped on the screen, and then handed the device to Tian Di. "I always had this image of how sex was supposed to be."

Tian Di stared at the iPad and read the picture's title, "A Princely Deflowering."

Jordon pointed to the drawing of a grinning man engaging in vigorous anal sex with another man. They both looked like Jordon. "This is what I always thought sex would be like for me. Every dirty magazine and porn site always has guys taking dick up the ass. I thought, I'm gay, so I'll love it. There has always been a piece of me that wasn't into the idea, which confused me. I even started experimenting with myself. I tried my fingers, dildos, you name it, and I searched to find the pleasure of penetration. But I just didn't like having something inside me, so then I thought maybe I wasn't a bottom—"

"Bottom? I've never heard this term."

"Oh, sorry, right. That I didn't like to receive. I might be a top. You know, the one giving." Jordon demonstrated by poking his index finger back and forth. "I played with a Fleshlight, thinking—"

"Flashlight?" Tian Di failed to understand how a torch light would be sexy, though he was positive Jordon could make anything hot or adorable.

Not laughing at him for not knowing, Jordon found a website on his phone and handed it over to Tian Di.

The video started with a canister that looked like a flashlight. A man inserted a banana into the opening and jammed the fruit in and out. "Oh, I see. You put yourself inside and thrust."

"You don't think that's weird, do you?" Jordon's cheeks had tinted to a bright pink.

"No, I don't. It might be interesting." Should he tell Jordon what he liked to do? First things first—he needed to understand what Jordon meant. "Do you think you're a top?"

"I don't think so, 'cause while I liked—" Jordon mimicked holding the Fleshlight, and moving the imaginary device back and forth. "—I didn't enjoy thrusting into it. When I pretended to fuck someone, the whole activity just felt wrong… like too rough or something."

Tian Di wanted to make sure he didn't misunderstand. "This is what you mean when you say you're a side?"

"Yeah." Jordon seemed to be searching Tian Di's face for rejection.

His honesty made Tian Di tug him into a kiss. He tried to convey love, affection, and friendship with his lips.

Jordon moaned and deepened the kiss until they pulled back from each other, a little breathless.

"You like manual?" Tian Di hoped he used the word correctly.

"Yes."

"How about the other stuff? The website said frottage, mouth, and inter… inter, you know."

"Inter-however-you-say-it." Jordon shrugged. "I might enjoy that, since it's more like rubbing and not quite fucking. I don't know. And, well, we sort of did the frottage thing on the first day we met, and yeah, I loved it."

Tian Di tried not to sound too hopeful. "Mouth?"

"Um, well, I've never…. But I've always, always, always wanted to try. I'm pretty sure I'd love that." Jordon's gaze didn't meet Tian Di's, and the pink flush on his cheeks deepened to a shade of red. "You've probably—"

"Some."

Jordon nodded. "Blowjobs look really hot."

Tian Di couldn't resist. "You want to see something?"

Jordon pulled back and squinted his eyes. "What?"

The worried expression made Tian Di question whether he should continue. "You shared something with me, and I'd like to share with you. If me showing you this bothers you, I can stop."

"Okay." Jordon agreed a little too fast.

Tian Di did a quick version of his stretches. "You probably don't remember last night's conversation."

Jordon grimaced. "Oh, no. I don't. What did I say?"

"Nothing bad. I think you were trying to talk about using condoms during sex." Tian Di's muscles felt loose from the onsen, but he continued stretching.

"That's funny. I guess score a win for Dusty and Zack's sex-safe talks. Just so you know, I've been tested for STD... sexual transmitted diseases. I don't have any."

"Good. I go to my sister's doctor in Hong Kong for tests. There have been no issues." Wanting to put Jordon's mind at ease, Tian Di added, "I haven't been with anyone in about eight months, and my last test was after the testing windows."

Jordon's gaze followed every stretch and position Tian Di twisted into. He eventually said, "Good to know if we ever did do *other* things...."

"Like mouth sex...."

Grinning, Jordon snorted. "Yeah, mouth sex. Would you think it's safe without condoms?"

"Yeah." When he felt limber enough, he unknotted the towel he'd tied around his waist and lay on the futon. He put a pillow under his head, and did the final loosening of his muscles. He kicked off the floor so his feet hung behind his head. His semihard cock dangled over his mouth, and he glanced at Jordon.

Jordon licked his lips. "Holy mythical cocksucker. Can you really suck yourself?"

Tian Di rolled his foreskin down and flicked his tongue across the tip of his own cock. A tingle of lust slid through him.

"That's—" Jordon panted. "—amazing."

Encouraged, Tian Di rocked and took the top of his fully hardened cock into his mouth.

"This is wild. Holy fuck. My boyfriend can suck his own cock." Jordon's words were as far from censure as Tian Di could imagine. They might even hold pride in his kinky ability.

Tian Di added the slightest amount of suction and sucked in more.

Jordon's moan echoed off the walls and went straight to Tian Di's pleasure center. He loved performing, and to show Jordon something he'd never demonstrated for anyone felt incredibly freeing.

"God, Tian Di that's so fucking hot." Jordon shifted closer, licking his lips and skimming a hand over Tian Di's ass.

Tian Di pulled off his cock and offered, "You want some?"

Those green eyes Tian Di loved so much got huge. Jordon gasped. "Really?"

Trying not to beg or to scream *yes*, Tian Di managed to get a "please" out of his mouth.

Jordon caught his gaze and gave him a semiconfident half smile. He scooted to Tian Di's side and leaned over. His breath ghosted across the shaft.

Breathing became almost impossible.

Jordon's mouth almost touched Tian Di.

Tian Di's voice was shot, but he encouraged Jordon. "Go ahead."

"Like this?" Jordon asked, then swiped his tongue tentatively over the tip.

"Jordon," Tian Di hissed.

"Yeah?" Jordon jerked back like he'd done something wrong.

"More, please. It feels so—"

Jordon wrapped his hand around Tian Di and held him to his mouth. He lashed his tongue around the tip and down along the shaft. Holding the cock to Tian Di's mouth Jordon asked, "Sharesies?"

Excitement crashed through Tian Di. Jordon wanted to pass his cock back and forth like a lollipop.

One groan later, Tian Di licked his own cock, then Jordon lavished attention on him. He kissed Tian Di's cock and licked again.

"Your tongue." Tian Di moaned.

Back and forth they licked and kissed Tian Di's cock until he was on the edge of mindlessness.

Pulling back, Jordon asked, "Can I be greedy?"

"Greedy?" Tian Di had no clue what he meant.

Jordon unfolded Tian Di's body so he lay flat. Leaning over, Jordon flicked his tongue across Tian Di's lips until Tian Di arched toward Jordon's kiss.

"Mm, yes. I don't want to share anymore. Can I be greedy and try to suck you off?" Jordon asked the question like that might be a problem.

Arousal warred with affection as Tian Di pulled him up and kissed Jordon's mouth. "Be as greedy as you want."

Wrapping a fist around Tian Di's shaft, Jordon trailed his mouth down to where Tian Di longed for Jordon to be.

Jordon enveloped him and slid his lips halfway down the shaft.

Tian Di let out a whimper. It had been too long since he'd been in someone else's mouth.

Jordon stole a look at him and smiled around Tian Di's cock.

And this wasn't just someone, this was Jordon. Nothing had ever been this sweet or this good. Tian Di relished the unique pleasure of being connected with his love. Everything they did together reinforced that they belonged together.

Jordon pushed down farther, started coughing, and pulled off, gagging a little.

Oh no. Tian Di half sat up. "You okay?"

Frowning, Jordon wiped his mouth. "Yeah. I can't go that far down."

"That's okay," Tian Di reassured him. Maybe they should—

Jordon pushed him back down and slipped his lips back over Tian Di's cock and sucked.

Tian Di had no words, and probably no voice, so he threaded his fingers through Jordon's hair to convey his enjoyment of the attention.

His lover seemed curious in his oral exploration. There was no rush to get Tian Di to hurry or to climax. Jordon licked and sucked here and there, giving loving attention to every centimeter of Tian Di's cock as if to mark every part of him as taken. All the attention added to his arousal.

After pulling his mouth off Tian Di, Jordon flicked his tongue around the shaft from the top to the root. He paused to ask, "Am I doing all right?"

Tian Di hissed, "Yes."

Jordon winked and returned his focus to Tian Di's cock. He slid his mouth over the top and sucked, all the while keeping eye contact.

"Getting close," Tian Di gasped. Everything in him tightened and coiled.

Heated excitement passed through their gazes.

Jordon combined bobbing his head with sucking and stroking.

Tian Di fought to hold on to the edge. "I'm going…."

The gentle vibration of Jordon's moan tossed Tian Di into the abyss. Waves of ecstasy crashed into him, and he came.

He shivered with completion as he watched Jordon swallow and wipe his mouth.

"Was that good?" Jordon asked with concern.

Tian Di stretched his hands above his head. "Amazing. I can't believe that was your first time."

Jordon smirked and appeared adorably proud of himself. "I'm a quick study."

"Hey, anytime you want to practice…." Tian Di tucked the hair covering Jordon's face behind his ears. "Did you like doing that?"

"Yeah. A lot."

Good. "That's one of my favorite things to do."

"So you like that better than—"

"Is it bad if I say yes?" He totally did. The wet sucking did him in every time.

Jordon combed his fingers through the strands of Tian Di's hair. "Um, no. Is that why you got flexible enough to do it yourself?"

Tian Di shrugged. "I didn't think I'd have a boyfriend anytime soon, so in a way I guess I did. It lets me suck and be sucked."

Jordon shifted restlessly. "Oh, you like sucking too?"

Energy flooded Tian Di's system, and he shoved himself into a sitting position. "Love it. Since I've been sucked, can I have a turn at sucking?"

A squeak came out of Jordon. "Hell yes." He whipped away the comforter that had hidden his erection.

Excitement tripped through Tian Di at being able to give this to Jordon.

He bent over Jordon's middle, his face close to Jordon's reddish, throbbing cock, and he blew a stream of warm air. No foreskin obscured the mushroom head. All of his beautiful cockhead was visible... accessible.

Jordon wheezed and his toes curled. "Never had one. I'm not going to last."

Tian Di kept their gazes locked, tracing a slow lick from Jordon's balls to the tip, and grinned. "Think of pickled crickets."

"Ew! No. Yuck." Jordon's chuckle ended in a groan.

Tian Di slid halfway down the shaft, enveloping Jordon's cock in his mouth. He cupped Jordon's balls and lightly squeezed, tugging gently.

Jordon threw his head into the pillow and arched his back.

Tian Di accepted the invitation. He wrapped his hand around Jordon's cock and started sucking him off. There was no time for teasing, no buildup, just direct attention of a sucking mouth on a cock.

Jordon strained and trembled—as if he had any hope of not losing all control.

"Tian Di," Jordon gasped, filling Tian Di's mouth.

Timing his sucks and strokes to Jordon's release, Tian Di swallowed everything Jordon gave him. When there was nothing left, he applied firm pressure with his tongue on the underside of Jordon's circumcision scar and licked.

"Mmmm," Jordon moaned.

Tian Di kept spit-shining Jordon's cock.

Eventually Jordon requested, "Come here."

Tian Di studied Jordon's grin. "Did you like that?"

Jordon's eyes were glazed over, and he grinned. "I bet you can taste the answer."

Chuckling, Tian Di licked his lips and gave a sly smile. "I'm going to say you did enjoy that."

Jordon nodded with enthusiasm and cuddled for a few minutes.

Dare Tian Di ask? "Do you think that could be called sex?"

"Absolutely." Jordon gave him a lazy smile. "I know I have goofy ideas sometimes."

"I don't believe that. I think many people don't consider anything other than intercourse with the opposite sex as sex."

"So you're okay having sex with a side?"

Tian Di stretched and cracked his back. "I'm excellent having sex with my incredibly hot artist boyfriend, who I love to the extreme."

"I love my sexy rock-star boyfriend completely." Jordon yawned and snuggled into Tian Di.

A couple of hours sleep later, Jordon closed his hand around Tian Di's erection. "Hey you up?"

Tian Di snorted. "I think you know I am."

"Maybe we could experiment with other things that the website suggested men can do together."

Tian Di stopped nodding like he was trying to detach his head from his body. He swallowed and tried to find his voice. "Which way?"

"You choose."

There was no question about what he wanted to try. "Would you like to try the inter—how do you say it?"

"I don't know. I'm a lover, not a linguist." Jordon paused and stared at Tian Di with a big smile on his face.

Tian Di apologized, "I should be getting a joke, but I'm not."

"Dumb *Star Trek* funny."

"Oh." Tian Di smiled. "That was a space show."

"You want to go between my thighs?" Jordon slid one finger through two held straight out.

Guilt started to chew a hole in Tian Di's mind. "Is that okay?"

"Sure." Didn't sound as positive as Jordon looked.

"We don't have to try it." Tian Di shouldn't have asked.

Jordon laid a hand on Tian Di's thigh. "No, I want to, and we can always stop, right?"

"Yes. If you don't like how something feels, we don't have to continue." That was a small comfort.

"Same for you. We need to be able to explore things, and some we might not like as much as—"

"Mouth sex," Tian Di supplied in the hopes of getting Jordon to smile. Success. Then worry crept back in. He had never asked anything of his lovers before. Maybe because they wouldn't have gifted him with much. "I feel selfish."

"Don't. I want to explore all the sex with you." Jordon grinned and gave his own hardening erection a slow stroke. "Come on, let's try this."

Tian Di retrieved a bottle of oil from his bag. Jordon's wide eyes and open mouth suggested he should explain. "I brought this thinking we might want to give each other massages."

"Well, this is a massage of sorts. A thigh massage...." Jordon rubbed his thighs together and chortled.

"Ha-ha." Tian Di kept control of his laughter for about two seconds. He fell onto Jordon and started tickling him.

Jordon giggled, rolled toward him, and tried to scuffle off the futon. "Ha, I've two older brothers; you never give up the high ground."

Tian Di landed on the floor with a naked Jordon on top of him. Jordon captured Tian Di's hands and held them over his head. "Mmm, I like this position."

Heat flashed in Jordon's eyes as he shifted. His erection pushed through Tian Di's thighs, and he froze.

Tightening his thighs, Tian Di pressed against Jordon's erection.

On a broken moan, Jordon kissed and hugged Tian Di, and wiggled his butt.

Tian Di cupped Jordon's ass and helped guide his movements.

Jordon squirmed back.

"What?" Tian Di hoped he didn't do anything wrong.

"Hey, this is good and all, but you were supposed to do *my* thighs," Jordon reminded him like he'd forgotten.

Tian Di nodded. "Did you like it?"

"Hell, yeah. I think I'm going to need a few hundred turns doing that to really decide, though. But you first. Where's the oil?"

"Here." Tian Di massaged Jordon's calves and worked his hands around Jordon's knees. He poured some oil on Jordon's thighs and couldn't stop from rubbing his balls. They were right there, and now they glistened like his thighs.

Not being able to resist, Tian Di licked at the drip forming on the tip of Jordon's cock. Since his lips were right there, he put his mouth over the top and sucked.

"Holy fuck," Jordon hissed out.

Tian Di grinned. He could happily suck Jordon off.

"Come here. I promise you can do that later… like as much as you want." Jordon was the voice of reason.

"Yes." Tian Di didn't know what he was agreeing to, but he poured some oil on his cock and stroked the glistening liquid in.

Jordon lay there, blond hair fanned out across the pillow, lips kiss-swollen and mouth sex ready.

Tian Di covered his body.

Wrapping Tian Di in an embrace, Jordon whispered, "I think we're going to like this kind of sex. I love hugging you tight."

Tian Di wiggled around until his body aligned with Jordon's thighs like he'd seen in the pictures. He pushed through and his cock made space between them.

Jordon found the place on Tian Di's neck that made him insane and nuzzled.

"Yeah." Hot and getting breathless, Tian Di thrusted.

Sparks ignited.

Jordon grabbed his asscheeks and added downward pressure. "You like it?"

"It's the best parts of intercourse." Tian Di wasn't sure if Jordon understood him between all the groaning. His dick was being dipped into pure pleasure. Hot, slick, and Jordon.

"We should call this outercourse." Jordon kissed him.

Tian Di humped faster. "I think I'm going to call this way very good."

Jordon tightened his thighs and squeezed rhythmically. "Do you like this position better or worse than mouth sex?"

Tian Di was slipping into ecstasy. "It's different. Love it. Love your mouth… too far away. I want to kiss you. Need to come."

Their mouths met and merged in a sloppy kiss. Jordon swept his tongue in and played with Tian Di's.

Fuel added to the fire.

Jordon started moaning and writhing with Tian Di.

As Tian Di shifted, he realized he rubbed across Jordon's erection, and the friction almost did him in.

He focused and kept moving in the way that made Jordon groan the loudest.

Jordon's squirming intensified. He clutched Tian Di's ass hard and jammed him down.

A long groan ended in Jordon's gasp, "Coming."

Holding Jordon's trembling body as he released his frustration was erotic. Being so close to Jordon, heavenly.

Tian Di buried his face in Jordon's neck and thrust faster. His body spiraled tight.

Jordon murmured, "I came for you. Come for me."

And Tian Di did. He gave Jordon everything in him. In that moment he could have died and been content with his life. He coasted down from a high and snuggled into Jordon.

"I think I need to—"

"Yes." Tian Di helped him stand.

"Reality." Jordon scrunched his face. He pushed off the futon and tottered his way to the outside shower.

Tian Di followed him into the courtyard and found a nice warm-water setting for them.

As they rinsed off, Jordon asked, "Should we take an onsen?"

"That would be lovely."

Tian Di began the pouring of the onsen water over him.

When they were finally settled into the hot spring, Jordon rested his head on Tian Di's shoulder.

Tian Di asked, "What did you think about *outercourse*?"

"Hot and sexy. You?" Jordon grinned.

"Same. I like holding you close."

Jordon smiled.

AFTER THE onsen, Tian Di went to his bag. "I know we haven't had breakfast—"

"But we had lots of protein." Jordon snorted.

"What?" What was Tian Di missing?

"The mouth sex... cum contains protein," Jordon whispered.

"Oh!" Tian Di laughed once he got the joke. "Are you going to keep calling it mouth sex?"

"Yes, of course." Jordon nodded.

Tian Di held out a box. "I thought you might like to try these."

Jordon stared down at the monkey chocolates. "If I wasn't already in love with you, this would do it. Chocolate, it's not just for breakfast anymore."

CHAPTER 17

"I'M A goddamned adult! And I don't have to check in all the time." Jordon tried to quiet his voice to a more mature volume but failed. He plopped back down on the futon with his cell phone. Why had he even left Tian Di's snuggle?

Tian Di rolled onto his elbows, the comforter slipping, exposing his shoulders and chest. "You okay?"

Jordon growled and waved his cell.

"Which brother?"

"Zack is going off the rails. Can't I have one day I'm not tethered to my phone? He acts like I've been kidnapped and he hasn't heard from me in weeks." Jordon kissed Tian Di's full, plush lips. Yesterday he had needed to lose himself in all things Tian Di.

They'd spent the entire glorious day exploring the numerous ways a side can have fantastic sex. Jordon didn't think they got through 1 percent of all the activities he wanted to try. He'd come to terms with a lot yesterday. Shouldn't he be allowed to burrow in with his boyfriend and play?

"Didn't you text him yesterday at dinner?" Last night, Tian Di had dragged him off the futon and into town. Apparently protein bars and ejaculate weren't enough to keep hunger at bay.

"Yup. Though this morning he sent me a text detailing, not asking, mind you, all the scheduled activities for every day off he has on tour. He's even started to purchase tickets for museums and city combination tickets."

"Did he do this in the past?"

Jordon frowned. "Yeah, I guess, but that was before."

"Maybe he misses you." Tian Di might be too reasonable.

Jordon wanted to stay pissed. "I miss him, but he needs to respect me and my time."

"Have you told him that?"

Sighing Jordon admitted, "Not in so many words. I guess I need to do that."

Tian Di gentled a hand down Jordon's back. "Is there anything I can do?"

How did one shoulder squeeze let Jordon know everything would be okay? "Nah, I need to text him back."

"I'm going to speak to the owner and confirm we won't be having dinner here tonight, but we'll be staying until tomorrow."

"Great, thanks."

Tian Di gave him a toe-curling kiss that made Jordon want to rethink their plans for the day. Did he really need to see the snow monkeys? He had seen the pictures. Before he could suggest more futon tricks, Tian Di dressed and slipped out of the room.

Another text vibrated his phone, making him glare at Zack's new words. *I scheduled the early morning tea and temple tour in Penang.*

He texted, *That's two months from now!*

Of course. Zack found nothing insane about planning that far in advance.

U have to ask me. Was that blunt enough?

Why??? I've never asked U before.

Well, that was a reality-based boot to the head. The truth bomb was Zack had been scheduling and arranging activities for Jordon since they started touring with Dusty.

Why is this a problem, now? Zack didn't have to say since Tian Di. The accusation came over the text loud and clear.

Jordon punched the pillow and then counted to ten. He reminded himself he was an adult, and if he wanted to be treated like one, he needed to act like one. He texted, *Zack, from now on I'd like if we talked before U schedule things.*

Jordon had allowed Zack and Dusty to micromanage the details of his life. It had been easier. All three of the Davis brothers had grown used to this dynamic. He understood they wanted to keep him protected, but now the overprotection felt like control.

What? Don't U want to hang out with me anymore?

His brothers had done everything for him, and he'd let them. But now it was time to adjust the boundaries. *Emotional blackmail much?*

Argh! Sorry. I'm trying... and failing. I'll work on talking to U about things I just assumed before. I miss U Jordie.

I love hanging out with you, but coordinate with me so I can plan around other things I need to do.

W/ Tian Di, Zack texted back.

Anger flashed through Jordon. He typed, *YES and with Justin. I do WORK even though you don't consider my art a real job.*

I totally do. I'm proud of what U do and all U have accomplished.

Really? Never felt that way. Though in truth, Jordon had never asked anyone for feedback on his art.

Yes!!!!! BTW I'm reading your Sakura Rose manga.

And? A nauseated shudder went through him at the idea of Zack gawking at the sexually explicit images that came out of his brain.

Excellent!!!!!

Wow. *Thanks.*

Though that Tricks is mega filthy in a good way. It's a great story.

Thank you. We good?

I'm a planner. Can U take a look at the things I scheduled & tell me if I should cancel/reschedule?

That's fair. *Of course.*

It's weird, U know.

What?

U having Tian Di. I guess I'm trying to get used to the idea of you being old enough to have a boyfriend. Let alone you having a serious one.

Jordon had been okay with Dusty's dating. When his older brother found someone who made him happy, Jordon thought that was super cool. But when Zack started seeing Andrew, Jordon had hated it. Not just because Andrew had been an asshole and didn't deserve Zack, but because Jordon was afraid he wouldn't matter to Zack as much.

Jordon texted, *U know I love U fuckhead.*

Yes, A-hole. I love U 2, Zack responded, then asked, *Are U having a good time?*

Leaving out the amazing incredible sex, Jordon texted, *Yeah, great! We're seeing the monkey park & museum today.*

Good. Send some pics.

Jordon texted, *What R Yr plans today?*

Doing some stuff w/ Andrew.

Knowing better than to ask what that might entail, Jordon texted, *Have fun*, and signed with an artist emoji.

U 2. Call if you need me.

He fell back onto the futon. *Ouch!* This sucker wasn't nearly as comfortable when Tian Di wasn't there to snuggle with.

Setting boundaries, and keeping them, exhausted him. Jordon didn't want to hurt Zack or Dusty, but he needed to do this for him. His therapist told him creating new neuropathways could make you feel drained. He was grateful they'd been there for him when their mother turned him out, but he was an adult now. A different dynamic needed to be built.

Even though it was awkward and felt kind of shitty, setting boundaries was important. Adulting 101 lesson of the day: it was healthy to realign previously set limits.

A few minutes later, Tian Di came back. "We're all set. I think I avoided insulting the owner by explaining I'd take you to the restaurant my sister recommended."

"Playing the sister card, well done." Jordon slipped his arms around Tian Di and breathed easier. "Ready for the monkeys?"

"That's not the question."

"What's the question?" Jordon loved how Tian Di tried to keep a straight face, though his laughing eyes screamed that a joke was in the works.

"Are the monkeys ready for us?" Tian Di's voice remained serious as he locked their room.

Jordon snorted and trailed after Tian Di. "They're not, but who could be?"

Tian Di chuckled, stepped outside the ryokan's front door, and took a deep breath. "Not too hot today."

Spying some clouds, Jordon worried. "I hope it doesn't rain."

Tian Di shrugged. "Eh, if it does, we'll deal with it."

Jordon let that thought sink in at a philosophic level. Things happened, and people just dealt with what life threw at them. He could deal with rain. If he got wet, so what? It might be romantic to kiss in the rain.

"This way." Tian Di pointed out the path toward the Jigokudani Snow Monkey Park.

As they trekked, Jordon found the vivid greens of the forest fascinating. "Look at all the shades in the leaves. There's jade, malachite, midnight green, sea green, and—get ready for it—"

Grinning, Tian Di said, "Forest green?"

"You totally stole my thunder." Jordon shoulder-bumped Tian Di.

The path ended in a paved area. On one side was a rock wall with different levels of flat ledges. Groups of macaques congregated and lounged in the sun. On the other side was the man-made hot spring pool, rimmed with rocks, that was in all the pictures of the snow monkeys of Nagano.

Three monkeys were submerged to their necks in the steaming water. One surveyed Tian Di and Jordon, and the other two had their eyes closed. A couple of monkeys ran around the rim of the pool, clearly not following the "no running in the pool area" rule.

"Look at him." Tian Di pointed to a relatively young monkey who hopped into the water. He held his hands delicately above the water, took a few tentative steps, and darted back out.

Jordon enjoyed taking in the cool factor of being someplace he'd heard about. "Aw, poor thing. Maybe the spring is too hot for him."

Tian Di pointed out five monkeys sitting in a row on the rock wall, grooming each other. "The monkey version of Made in China—Ew." One of the monkeys found a tasty bit in the other's fur and ate it. "I'll assume that's a twig and not lice."

Jordon didn't dissuade him of his false belief. He directed his attention to a female resting on a lower rock. "Look at the mommy monkey feeding her baby."

"The baby is staring so lovingly at his mother. That's so sweet." Tian Di threw an arm around Jordon's shoulders.

The touch helped keep the bitterness from stealing Jordon's bliss. His life might not be perfect, but it was pretty damned fabulous.

"Do you mind if I draw?" Jordon started dragging out his sketch pad and pencils.

"Of course not." Tian Di moved closer to the hot spring and started reciting words to Made in China songs.

The way the light played off Tian Di's face and hair was too glorious for words, but not for drawing. Each line Jordon set down attempted to capture a hint of the magic that was Tian Di.

After he had Tian Di on the page, he expanded the picture to include the hot spring and some of the monkeys. When he was happy enough with the image, he picked the red pencil to sign the page. He scrolled the word *To* and stopped because he could no longer draw for a mysterious figment of his imagination. Not when Tian Di—

Screech! Argh! Chaos broke out in the hot spring. Some monkeys jumped out of the water and others moved to the side.

Tian Di jumped closer to Jordon. "What was that?"

Shoving his sketch pad and pencils into his bag, Jordon stepped directly in front of Tian Di. What was happening?

The question was answered by the rowdy group of adolescents chasing one another over the top of the rock wall. One of the biggest monkeys stomped out of the hot springs and stood on the rim. The male, based on his anatomy, didn't look amused.

He shrieked, displaying his teeth.

Jordon shifted his position and inserted himself between Tian Di and the angry monkey.

The chastised monkey rebels sat down on a rock ledge near the top of the wall and shut up.

The male gave one warning screech and returned to his bath.

Tian Di kissed Jordon's cheek. "Thank you."

"For?" Jordon cocked his head.

"Protecting me."

"Oh." He hadn't realized he'd done that.

"You're so cute when your cheeks get all pink like that. Just like a character in one of your manga drawings." Tian Di grinned.

Jordon couldn't even give him a mock frown. He shrugged and said, "Let's take some pictures."

Tian Di sent one to his sister.

Jordon sent Zack and Dusty one of himself, with the monkeys enjoying the hot springs in the background.

Zack texted, *Send 1 of U & TD.*

"Um, Zack requested a picture of us together."

"My sister asked for the same thing." Tian Di waved his cell.

Jordon sniffed.

"What's wrong?"

"This is another of Zack's olive branches. His way of telling me he's going to try to accept that I'm an adult and that I have a boyfriend who's very important to me."

"All that from just a text?" Tian Di was either impressed or concerned, Jordon couldn't tell.

"It's Davis-speak."

They took several poses and chose to send a smiling picture, one of them making silly faces, and his favorite pose of Tian Di kissing Jordon's cheek.

Dusty and Zack both texted back *Great pics.*

Tian Di looked at his phone and gave a rueful chuckle.

He didn't want to pry, but Jordon was damned interested to know what got that response. He promised he wouldn't push if Tian Di didn't want to answer. "What?"

Tian Di thrust the phone close enough for Jordon to read the translation of the text in question. *He's the one.*

Well, fuck! "Is she right?" Jordon stared into Tian Di's eyes, knowing the answer in his own heart.

"My sister's never wrong." Tian Di's sincerity made Jordon joyful.

Jordon did a little victory dance, ending with a fist pump.

Tian Di laughed. "Since I keep gushing my love at you, it shouldn't be a surprise."

"You haven't gushed in the last two hours. Now if you want, we can head back to the room." Jordon wiggled his eyebrows like a perv. Though he doubted his body would cooperate.

Laughing harder, Tian Di waved Jordon off. "No, after all day yesterday and this morning, I think we need a little break."

Jordon pulled out his sketch pad and red pencil. He stared at the *To* he'd written for a moment and then added Tian Di's name. Then he signed it *With Love, Your Future Husband.* He closed the pad before Tian Di could see what he wrote.

"What did you write?"

"I'll show you someday." Jordon tucked his sketch pad away.

Tian Di scrutinized him.

"Oh my God, look at him." Jordon pointed to the monkey dangling from the park camera. He kept swinging under the device and then putting his face to the camera lens.

Laughing, Tian Di took out his phone. "I've got to get some video of this."

Jordon laughed. "Mr. Curious is going to freak out the people who tune in to the park's monkey cam. The eye of the monkey sees all."

"You want to take a few more pictures and head to the museum?"

"Sure." Jordon took some more snaps, focusing in on the colors in case he wanted to paint this experience.

Tian Di glanced away from his cell. "I found the bus route that drops us two blocks away from the Hokusaikan Museum."

JORDON WAS impressed by the Japanese transportation system. Their bus was clean, quick, and efficient. Compared to Albany's CDTDA buses, it was like traveling first class.

Tian Di paid the museum admission and pointed to the Japanese sign. "Sorry, the sign says no photos."

"Bummer," Jordon grumbled and tucked his phone into his bag.

Skimming the museum pamphlet written in Japanese, Tian Di said, "They said this is a small museum, so they rotate what they have of Hokusai's works. He was very prolific, and is believed to have produced thirty thousand pieces of art—can you imagine?"

"Incredible. I can't wrap my head around that number." Jordon whistled as they meandered down the hallway toward the galleries.

"Do you ever feel intimidated by other artists?" Tian Di studied him.

Jordon paused outside the first gallery and thought about it for a moment. "Some artists cut more prolific artists off at the wrists. They criticize them for not taking the time or care with their work, but not me. We're all adding art to the world, and I'm honored to bear witness to their talent."

Tian Di nodded. "I feel the same way. The guys keep comparing me to Angel Luv or to other singers. I have my own style, and I don't begrudge Angel his success or Symmetry's domination of the Asia charts. I'm thrilled for their music because they're bringing happiness to the world through song."

Jordon smiled. "I'm glad you're not jealous or petty, 'cause insecurity coming from the singers of other opening acts in the past was horrifying. One singer purposefully tampered with Angel's pants so his zipper came undone during a performance."

Tian Di's eyes got huge. "No! What happened?"

"He made it part of the show. Of course, that was the last time the opening act performed. Megan, the manager, was not amused and dropped them."

Tian Di chuckled. "That's crazy."

Jordon gestured toward a colorful placard on the wall. "Hey, does that sign mean Hokusai's Thirty-six Views of Mount Fuji are on display now?"

"They are. We're catching the exhibit a week before they rotate those pictures out." Tian Di pointed the way.

Stepping into the gallery was like a punch in the gut to Jordon. Views of Mount Fuji filled every wall.

"Oh my God." Jordon stumbled to the center of the room, then turned in a tight circle to take in all the paintings.

Tian Di handed him a napkin.

"Thanks." Jordon shook his head, wiped his eyes, and stepped closer to the works.

Tian Di stood next to him. "Each painting has Mount Fuji in it. Where is it in this one?"

Jordon pointed to the almost hidden mountain. The paintings showed the perspective of Mount Fuji close and far, seen through towns, from the water, part of the action, and not. "Mount Fuji remained a constant. Hard to believe such beauty is a volcano. The last eruption was in 1707."

Pointing to a sign, Tian Di translated, "Mount Fuji is the most climbed mountain in the world. One hundred thousand visitors trek to the top yearly."

"In a future story, I have one of my characters making the climb to be at the summit for the honorable rising of the sun."

Tian Di's mouth dropped open. "Which character?"

"You want me to tell you?"

"Indigo would accuse me of totally fanboying on you, but yeah, who?"

Jordon chuckled. "Tricks, but I'm not going to say who he might or might not be with."

"You're cruel," Tian Di accused, with a grin on his face. "Would promises of mouth sex sway you?"

Jordon smirked. "Don't I have those promises anyway?"

Tian Di rolled his eyes. "Yeah, of course, but who?"

Jordon laughed and spun in a circle, gesturing to the masterpieces. "Which is your favorite painting?"

Surveying each painting again, Tian Di chose *The Great Wave*.

"Why?"

Tian Di pointed to the big, blue, white-capped waves with the boats being tossed in their wake. "I know it's the most popular, but I like how it reminds us to live. That big wave is coming for us all. We need to enjoy life and learn to surf the waves life throws at us."

"Wow, that's deep. Are you a singer or a philosopher?"

"A little of both. What's your favorite?"

Jordon led Tian Di to his choice. "*Umezawa Manor in Sagami Province*. I like how the two cranes fly off by themselves."

"And the five that are eating or fishing aren't concerned, because those two aren't leaving forever. They will return. Independence doesn't have to mean alone." Tian Di made his point.

Jordon ran his fingertips over Tian Di's forearm in a light, almost appropriate, public display of affection. "Exactly. My therapist called that interdependence. It'll just take some adjusting for me and my brothers."

They came to another placard in Japanese with no English in sight. Tian Di translated, "He started this series when he was seventy years old. There were ten more paintings that surfaced, but then the printings of them stopped."

Jordon meandered through the other paintings, just drinking in the brilliance. "I appreciate that you don't rush me, but are you bored? I know I go pretty slow at times."

"Not at all. I find seeing art through your eyes has given me a better appreciation of the world."

"What do you—oh, Tian Di. Look at these illustrations he did." Jordon rushed over and studied the images.

Tian Di squeezed his shoulder and stood close to him. "This right here is what I mean."

Huh? Jordon stared at him.

"I've never given a passing thought to the illustrations in books, and now I can't believe I've missed such beauty. I see colors, buildings, and even lines differently. My enhanced vision has enriched my singing."

That puzzled Jordon. "How?"

"When I'm singing lyrics about inky black streets, I try to taste the depths of color now that you've shown me what exists. I'm more aware of everything around me. I hope you always want to share art with me… including who Tricks might be with during the honorable rising of the sun."

Jordon snorted.

Tian Di leaned in and added, "And the mouth sex. I always want to share the mouth sex with you even if you don't tell me."

Nodding, Jordon grinned. "Wonderful. I love the mouth sex, and yes, we should call oral sex that forever. Come on, let's look at the paintings he did in his late thirties. They were under a different pseudonym."

Tian Di translated the placard. "His names were Sori and Hokusai Tokimasa, though I guess you read that. This is the series of beautiful ladies."

As Jordon strolled past at a snail's pace, he shook his head. "Look at the lovely long necks and tiny hands. A sign of what beauty was at the time."

"The hair styles are so elegant." Tian Di mused, "The lines remind me almost of manga drawings."

"They do. I studied his use of defined lines when I was fourteen. Art books are great for learning about an artist, but nothing beats seeing the actual paint strokes." Jordon could feel the influence seeping into him, possibly refining his own techniques.

"I truly love you," Tian Di whispered with such reverence Jordon was confused.

"I love you." Jordon looked around. "Why are you saying that? Don't get me wrong, I always want to hear that."

"I just wanted you to know I appreciate you and adore everything about you. Seeing you in a museum is just... well, it's amazing."

"It's probably like when I watch you turn into a rock god onstage." As if Tian Di didn't always inspire Jordon to see his sexy star appeal. Hell, Jordon could barely stay off his knees around him. "Although that's only one part of you and only one part of why I'm in love with you."

SHOVING A power bar into his mouth on the way to the museum might have broken the rules of Japanese etiquette about not eating outside a restaurant or home, but it did nothing to stave off his hunger. Jordon asked, "How about an early dinner?"

"Sounds good. The yakitori place is within walking distance. Shall we?" Tian Di led the way through a downtown area with shops and some restaurants.

"This is much lower key than Tokyo."

"No neon to burn out your retinas." Tian Di glanced around. "I like the slower pace at times."

"Me too."

"This is the restaurant." Tian Di held the door for him.

There was only a long bar table with a display of fish tanks, glass refrigerated sections, and twelve stools. The table separated diners from the cooking area. There were various grills and hot surfaces along with baskets filled with fresh vegetables and produce.

Tian Di greeted the only person in the restaurant—apparently the chef, based on his attire.

Jordon bowed with Tian Di and let himself be led to the barstool at the end. He parked himself.

After about five minutes of discussion with the chef, Tian Di turned to him and said, "I ordered."

"Thank you. Seemed like it wasn't easy."

The chef banged down a teapot and two cups.

Tian Di poured tea into the cups. "It's done."

The chef served them each a single tempura shiso leaf.

Jordon nabbed the leaf with his chopsticks and bit into the vegetable. Light, crisp deliciousness exploded in his mouth. He stared at Tian Di. "This is incredible. I want, like, a thousand of these."

Tian Di laughed as a plate with one tempura shrimp and a single yakitori chicken skewer with green onion was placed in front of each of them by a grimacing chef.

Jordon whispered, "Why is the chef angry?"

Tian Di gave one of his rueful smiles and shrugged. "There's no love between China and Japan and in some cases a deep-seated hatred due to the war. And some of the older folks still hold a grudge against Americans."

Shaking his head, Jordon said, "I didn't feel that in Tokyo or on my last trip."

"No, the bigger cities or ones more dependent on tourism see travelers as a good thing. But we might be the first foreigners he's seen in a while."

The chef shot them a frown over his shoulder, suggesting he might have heard and understood more than Tian Di expected.

Jordon offered the grumpy man his most charming smile and proclaimed, "Oishī. Arigatōgozaimashita."

The chef's eyes got wide, and he gestured to the food. "Eat, eat," he demanded in English before turning around to create more food magic.

Tian Di leaned into him for a moment. "Well done."

Pleased he may have moved them off the chef's poisoning for sport list, Jordon asked, "I did say delicious and thank you, right?"

"Yeah, you were the model ambassador," Tian Di reassured him.

"Well, even with the hate, this food is incredible!" Jordon took a picture and sent it to Zack.

Zack sent him one of squirrel fish. Jordon turned his phone around to show Tian Di. "I told him I didn't know he liked squirrel."

"Nice."

Jordon displayed the second picture Zack sent of the fish bones. "I'd say he did."

"You seem better with your brothers."

"I know everything won't be all fixed overnight. I know I need to hold tough on the boundaries. I think now that they know what I'm trying to do, they'll even help me."

"Your brothers love you, and I bet they will. They want the best for you."

"I know. Though it's hard to break out of the roles we've played for years, but we're making steps toward that."

"You need to keep telling them what you need." Tian Di added, "And me. You can tell me what you need as well. I'll do everything I can to give it to you."

Jordon spoke the truth. "You. I only need you."

"Done," Tian Di vowed.

CHAPTER 18

TIAN DI must have stepped into a dream. He and the most wonderful boyfriend in the world had gotten back two days ago from an incredible trip to Japan. Jordon had even opted to stay with him in Suzhou instead of going to Shanghai early. Between laundry and bouts of loving mouth sex, they only had enough time to pack for the next leg of the tour and catch the bus to Shanghai with the band for their next show.

Hard to believe, but in a few hours, he would perform in the Shanghai Mercedes-Benz Arena. Not to mention that right now he and his band were hanging out with the legendary Dark Angels as if it were commonplace.

"Who knew this arena had an ice rink in the basement?" Jin, who opted to stay off the ice, propped himself on his elbows against the railing next to Tian Di.

"Not me. I thought the text invitation to a skating party was a joke," Tian Di answered in his preshow whisper.

Jin nodded. "Yeah, me too."

"Jordon assured me it wasn't. I guess the Dark Angels always do things as a group every couple of weeks to blow off steam and reconnect." Tian Di tightened the scarf around his neck and e He rubbed his hands together against the cold of the ice rink.

"Seems to be working," Jin mused as Josh and Robin flew by, grinning as they raced each other around the rink.

Jordon slid over the ice, executing a perfect turn in front of Tian Di, and blew him a kiss as he skated backward.

Tian Di tingled and threw him a kiss back. If this was a dream, he never wanted to wake up.

Jin pointed at the duo laughing and effortlessly skating backward. "And who would have thought Angel Luv and Dusty Davis were such good ice skaters?"

"I guess because their hometown is in upstate New York, they learned to skate. Jordon said the winters are cold, and they get lots of snow and ice."

"I can't imagine freezing weather like that." Jin hugged himself tighter inside the puffy jacket the arena had provided.

"Yeah—look at Jordon. He glides over the ice like he has wings." Tian Di couldn't help but admire Jordon's fluid movements.

"As Indigo would say, you're drooling," Jin spoke in English, carefully pronouncing each word.

He shrugged and confessed, "I can't help it."

Jin smiled and then a comfortable silence settled over them as they watched.

Tian Di's phone buzzed with his daily reminder to run through Made in China's song lyrics. He might not get stage fright, but he lived with the terror of forgetting the words.

"Go ahead. I don't mind." Jin understood what the special alarm meant.

Tian Di scrolled through the words on his phone and read the words, "Neon-lit streets only highlight my loneliness and doubt."

Jordon shook his butt to the new song blasting out of the speakers and waved his hands in the air. He skated by Tian Di, singing with all his heart. His smile never failed to make Tian Di's heart expand with even more love, reminding him some of the lyrics were distant memories now. He was no longer filled with doubt and loneliness, but with love and happiness.

"Jin, come on, I know you only have eyes for Styx, but Jordon is stunning, and he's such a good person. I love everything about him. He is my idea of the perfect guy." He spoke soft but slow, to ensure his words would be understood.

"I agree with you."

"What—*Zack*? Oh, sorry, I thought Jin…. Sorry." He remembered to lower his voice back to a whisper when he got to the second *sorry*.

Zack stood where Jin had been.

Dusty appeared on his other side, slouching against the rail. "You really do adore him."

Tian Di wasn't going to front. "How could I not? Look at him."

If Dusty stared any harder, Tian Di might burst into flames. Hopefully, Tian Di maxed out the man's truth-o-meter.

Zack usually convicted him with his gaze. It always felt like the guy was trying to figure out how many years Tian Di deserved behind bars—but not right now.

Trying to think of something to say, Tian Di whispered, "Jordon skates beautifully."

"We taught him," Dusty and Zack said in unison.

Zack laughed. "Well, that's not quite true."

Dusty covered his face. "That's right. I gave him skating lessons for Christmas when he was eight because he wanted to skate—"

"In the Olympics, if I remember right." Zack laughed. "Though, I think it was the costumes he liked. All frilly and sequined—"

Shaking his head, Dusty said, "No, he loved skating. The costumes were just a bonus."

"Argh." Indigo clutched the railing for dear life and slip-walked past them.

"You need some help?" Dusty hurried to the ice entrance.

Li slowly took one hand off the rail and waved Dusty off. "Thanks, but I've got him."

Tian Di didn't think that was true, since Li did not have much more stability than Indigo.

Dusty almost reached them.

"Just a bit farther." Li pointed to the exit. The gesture cost him his balance, and he toppled over, landing on Indigo.

"We don't have ice in LA for good reason." Indigo laughed and rolled on top of Li. "Though maybe ice skating isn't that bad... as long as I'm on top."

Jordon and Angel skated to Dusty and helped guide Indigo and Li off the ice.

As if Jordon heard the wishes Tian Di made, he slid to a stop in front of Tian Di, gripped him by the hair, and pulled him into a very loving kiss. Mmmm, good thing they had the rink to themselves.

Tian Di was positive he would never get used to Jordon's affectionate, loving, and very sensual kisses.

Jordon rested his forehead on Tian Di's before he asked, "Were my brothers grilling you?"

Tian Di shook his head and whispered, "No."

Jordon snorted, sounding very much like Zack.

THE DRESSING room Made in China was given had uncomfortable, stiff fancy sofas and chairs scattered about, along with six lighted makeup mirrors. There was a buffet of sandwiches, cookies, tea, sodas, chips, and various candies. The offerings were probably scrumptious, but Tian Di didn't eat before performances.

"Indigo, if I smacked you in the face, it wouldn't interfere with your keyboard playing hands, right?" Tian Di growled. He didn't know how to throw a punch, but he could learn.

"What?" Indigo held out his hands. Why did Indigo have to play a jackass constantly?

"I put up with a lot, but I will not tolerate anyone being disrespectful to Jordon." Tian Di raised his voice above a whisper.

"Dude, calm down. Vocal rest. I'm just asking him if you were the first Asian he's hooked up with, or is he a rice queen?"

"I don't know what a *rice queen* is, but I can tell by your face you're being, as you say, all kinds of wrong." Tian Di bit out each word in English so Indigo wouldn't be confused.

Jordon touched Tian Di's mouth, reminding him of his voice, and then ran a hand down his arm. "Hey, it's okay. Indigo is trying to be funny. Failing, but he's just teasing. Indigo, Tian Di is my first boyfriend, and I love him, so I guess I'll never know if I'm a rice queen."

"See? Jordon knows I mean—ow! Where the fuck are you... oh. Okay." Indigo allowed Li to drag him into one of the dressing room bathrooms.

Jin and Styx sat on the sofa, drinking tea and talking about one of the Western television shows Indigo made everyone watch as a band.

Tian Di leaned toward Jordon and mouthed, "What is a rice queen?"

Jordon rolled his eyes. "It means a lot of things, but the term can describe someone who has a fetish for Asian men."

Glaring at the bathroom door, Tian Di silently bit out his regret. "I should have smacked him when I had the chance."

"Nah, I think that was Indigo's way of letting me know he's watching out for you." Jordon was always too sweet.

Tian Di drank the rest of his tea. "I don't need him protecting me from you. From him, maybe, but not you."

Jordon refilled Tian Di's teacup. "I know, but he's doing the same thing my brothers have done to you."

Sipping the warm tea, Tian Di mouthed, "Thanks. Oh, about that. They weren't grilling me, but I thought I was talking to Jin about you, but Zack slipped into where he'd been and—"

"Ah, maybe that might explain this?" Jordon showed Tian Di the recent texts from Zack.

Tian Di read them.

Ur BF doesn't suck.

Then Jordon had responded, *Yes, he does.*

And Zack texted, *TMI.*

Tian Di pointed to *TMI* and gestured for an explanation.

"Too much information." Jordon shrugged. "Well, you do suck."

Tian Di ran a hand over Jordon's crotch. He loved Jordon's cock. "If it wasn't so close to showtime, I'd provide evidence."

Jordon wiggled and moaned. "How about as soon as you're done with the show?"

"Before the after-party?" Jordon cupped Tian Di, making him gasp. "Before, definitely before the interviews, or right—"

A knock sounded on the door, and a roadie stuck her head in and shouted, "Ten minutes."

"Well, that cuts off any other ideas we might have had." Jordon took his hand off where Tian Di preferred it and stuck out his lower lip in an adorable pout.

Tian Di couldn't resist and put that pout to use. He gave him a kiss on the mouth.

"Later." Jordon pulled Tian Di to one the love seats.

Tian Di sighed as he sat down. He scrolled through his cell phone, skimming the words of the songs.

Knock! "Two minutes!"

Indigo burst out of the bathroom. "Hey, Jordon. You know I didn't mean any harm, right?"

Jordon nodded. "You're just looking out for your boy. I get it. But I promise you, this isn't me fetishizing anyone. I love him."

"Yeah, I guess we've all got gay Asian boyfriends... except for Tian Di." Indigo drummed his blue nail-polished fingertip against Tian Di's cheek. "So maybe you're the one with the fetish."

Ignoring the jackass, Tian Di swatted Indigo's hand and cuddled into Jordon.

Jordon snuggled back into him and whispered, "Hey, if this is a fetish, I'm good with that."

"AND THERE'S your evidence. We both suck." Tian Di might have said that a little too loudly on their way back into the main dressing room from the bathroom. He had dragged Jordon in there as soon as he was done with the show.

Indigo clapped. "You guys timed that perfectly. We should get to the interview."

Jordon's cheeks tinted pink. Maybe from Indigo's attention, or maybe from their mouth sex, but either way, Jordon was all his.

"Come on. What room is the interview in?" Indigo rallied the band to their feet.

Li checked his phone. "In the basement, right next to the rink."

Made in China and Jordon got into the elevator and made their way to the interview. They stood outside in the hallway waiting for the Dark Angels to finish with the reporter.

Indigo peeked in. "Shit! We should have thought of that."

"What?" Li pressed his face to the door window. "Wow."

Tian Di wanted to understand, but no one said what they saw. He took his turn peering through the glass.

The Dark Angels sat together with a reporter, but it was their choice of clothing that sent a thrill through Tian Di. Someone had apparently convinced them to wear Made in China T-shirts. Dusty even had on a Made in China bandanna, its letters in Mandarin, wrapped around his forehead, holding back his damp hair.

Tian Di glanced at Jordon, who looked away. Ah, he'd come to an agreement with Sebe about the shirts and might have had a hand in this too.

Indigo growled, "Damn, I wish we had Dark Angels shirts. Is the merchandise for the show still out?"

Jordon waved the members of Made in China to step away from the door and over to him. Opening his overstuffed messenger bag, he pulled out five T-shirts. "Zack said you guys might want these but not to give them to you unless you asked."

"You're a lifesaver." Indigo grabbed a Dark Angels T-shirt and swapped it for the one he was wearing.

Tian Di grabbed one and mouthed, "Zack?"

Shrugging, Jordon smiled.

Jin took a T-shirt and asked in English, "Did you make the Made in China T-shirts that the Dark Angels are wearing?"

Jordon nodded. "I drew the designs Sebe asked for, and he did everything else."

"Thank you, Jordon." Styx pronounced each word in English with careful precision.

The door opened, and the Dark Angels poured out into the hallway. The members of the Dark Angels saw the shirts Made in China wore and grinned. Everyone hugged.

"You know this is kind of history-making, don't you?" Indigo asked.

Angel Luv smirked. "Every night the Dark Angels perform, we're breaking rules and rewriting history."

"I always thought it was shitty that bands don't always act like family. All bands are related through lyrics and united by music." Dusty's words gave Tian Di chills.

Josh pointed to his shirt. "Wearing these were totally Dusty's brain giant. It's why we keep him around. Sometimes he has good ideas."

"Hey, even a broken clock is right twice a day." Dusty made eye contact with Tian Di.

Tian Di touched his heart; he got the message. This was Jordon's older brother accepting Tian Di as Jordon's boyfriend. Maybe Davis-speak could be learned.

No one had to tell him the Dark Angels were special, and not because they were rock legends.

"Okay, okay! Enough with the huddle cuddle." Josh pulled away, and Robin with him, breaking up the group hug.

Angel snorted. "Afraid of losing rock-star points?"

"Nah, man, there's things I want to do before the after-party." Josh led Robin away.

"Or someone he needs to do." Indigo cackled.

Dusty slapped Tian Di on the back. "Go wow the reporter with your interview skills."

Tian Di swallowed hard. "Thanks."

THE BAND crushed onto one of the couches, with the reporter from the international magazine, *Shanghai Music Scene* peering at them from a chair.

"And that's how we decided on the name Made in China," Indigo finished the tale of the band naming.

The reporter turned to Tian Di and asked, "Since you weren't there in Beijing on the Great Wall, did you feel left out of the decision?"

Tian Di's turn to show the band's united front. "I was new to the band and trusted the band to make the right decisions. Besides, I love the name."

"There's no friction in the band?" *Argh, so the reporter wanted to play like that.*

Tian Di countered with a smile.

"Not the kind of friction you're talking about." Indigo flirted with no one in particular.

Shooting Indigo a "not the time or the person" look, Tian Di drew the reporter's attention back to him. "Indigo means any friction within the band is not necessarily a bad thing. We have a chemical reaction when we all come together."

Indigo snorted.

Tian Di spared Indigo the glare his snort deserved and then cast a shy look at the reporter. "We know each of us brings something necessary to our music, and when we combine our efforts, well, I think it can be amazing."

The reporter's mouth dropped open, and his pen slipped out of his hand.

Li grabbed the pen off the floor and gave him a rock-star smile. "Sir."

"Um, yeah. Thanks." The reporter took the pen back but appeared dazzled by Li, staring for longer than necessary.

Indigo gave a small head bow, acknowledging their performances. Subtlety was king in Asia. Maybe Indigo would believe them and try getting with the program of delicacy and finesse.

Shaking off his bemusement, the reporter glanced over to where Styx was trying to hide and said in Mandarin, "I know you and Jin are just learning English, so thank you for doing an interview in your second language."

Styx gave him a smile and Jin added, "No problem."

The reporter grinned back and asked in Mandarin, "You two grew up together in… where again?"

Jin threw an arm around Styx. "Yintang. We've been best friends for longer than I can remember."

The way Styx unconsciously melted into Jin before sitting straight spoke of more than a lifelong friendship.

An arched eyebrow reached to the reporter's hairline. "I take it you've been playing together for a long time?"

"Yeah." Styx gave yet another one-word answer in English.

Tian Di nodded, encouraging Styx to say more, but he didn't.

The reporter asked, "So, someone special back home?"

Jin glanced over at Indigo and then repeated the scripted words they'd decided on in English. "The girl Styx was supposed to wed is happily married to someone else now."

"Aw, that's tough." The reporter frowned, but Tian Di would bet all his yuan that would be a direct quote.

He had to admit, Indigo's idea had been nothing short of genius. With a few words, Styx's appeal would rise as the heartbroken jilted lover. Indigo spent a long time explaining to Styx's father how branding Styx this way would increase his popularity and Made in China's. This also added another layer of protection against Styx's matchmaking mother.

Jin shrugged. "Besides we're enjoying being bachelors for now. We've got our music—"

"And each other. We don't need more." Styx's tone made the statement in English a declaration.

Jin beamed and shoulder-bumped him.

Indigo might have muttered something obnoxious and Tian Di ignored him.

"Since we're talking about broken hearts and love, how about the rest of you?" The reporter went from sympathetic to "give me the dirt" in record time.

Tian Di did his best to call a blush to his cheeks and not look at Jordon, who milled around in the shadows, pretending to talk to the Dark Angels' manager.

The reporter shifted forward. "Li, Indigo, and Tian Di, what about you?"

Indigo gave an overcompensating smirk. "What about us?"

"Well, the Dark Angels are all in relationships, albeit with each other. By the way, does that pose a problem?"

"What do you mean by that?" Indigo's tone warned the reporter he really didn't want to go down that path.

The reporter shook his head. "Our readers want to know if you guys are in relationships. Indigo, are you?"

Indigo puffed his chest up. "We have lots of relationships."

Based on the way Li's smile dropped, he understood what the plural of the word meant.

The reporter's expression remained the same, so he didn't, which was probably for the best. "Tian Di?"

The band decided they wouldn't lie, but they would take some cover behind vagueness. "Yes."

"Marriage plans?"

Tian Di called on superhuman resistance not to look at Jordon. "I hope so."

Crash!

"Sorry." Jordon grimaced and picked up a beaten and tattered, but thankfully empty, guitar case off the floor.

AFTER THE reporter left, Indigo asked, "Tian Di, was that a proposal or what?"

Tian Di glared at Indigo and then grabbed Jordon in a half hug. "Come, let's go to the after-show party."

Jordon beamed at him. "Sorry for making a disturbance."

"No worries." Tian Di pulled him into a kiss he hoped confirmed his desire that they were headed toward marriage.

They all meandered down to the after-party, which was held in a large ballroom flooded with people.

Jordon whispered, "Go be a rock star. I'll be hanging out in the back. Mingle."

Sighing, Tian Di participated with the rest of Made in China, accepting congratulations on a great show. He endured numerous discussions with Chinese businessmen interested in how Made in China could make them richer.

Enough already. Tian Di needed a bit of peace.

Everyone was busy—Indigo and Li having a discussion with the Dark Angels' manager, Styx chatting with Dusty, probably about the new drums he wanted to purchase, and Jin talking with Josh and Darius—so Tian Di took his chance and made a break for it.

He found Jordon in the back corner, sitting at a table by himself, sketching.

"I escaped." Tian Di slid into the seat next to him.

"Hey, you. Here." Jordon handed him a cup of warm tea.

"Ah, thanks. My cords are beat." He drank the tea quickly.

Jordon refilled his cup.

A nervous slither crawled through Tian Di. Since they were headed to Hong Kong next, he had been kicking around an idea for the last couple of days. "Um, so we have a break in the tour between Hong Kong and Singapore."

Jordon closed his sketch pad and gave him a small smile. "Yeah, the Dark Angels decided they wanted to enjoy this tour, so they had Megan spread the shows further apart than normal to allow them time for side travel."

The schedule was inconvenient as hell for Made in China, since they didn't have the discretionary funds the other band had, but the opportunity was worth the cost. They planned to commute to the apartment when the schedule made sense to do so, and stay cheap when they were stuck in a tour location longer.

"I guess Dusty and Justin wanted to see Singapore, while Dare, Angel, Josh, and Robin really want to go gambling in Macau." Jordon paused but then pushed through. "Any thoughts?"

He and Jordon were still in the new-boyfriend phase, where neither wanted to make assumptions or ask for too much. Tian Di looked forward to moving past this hesitation dance.

"Um, well… I was wondering if…." This was Jordon. Tian Di could ask for what he wanted. "I would like to introduce you to my sister."

Jordon's whole body vibrated, and he bounced in his chair. "Of course. I'd love to meet her. She's in Hong Kong, right? Is she like you? Or—"

Tian Di needed to manage Jordon's excitement with reality. "But my parents will demand a dinner and, well, you know, they might be… rude."

Jordon gestured to his chest and joked, "I'm from New York. Rude doesn't bother me."

"This would be the first time I've brought anyone home… ever. It could be… unpleasant." Tian Di didn't know what to expect and didn't want to understate the potential for disaster, but he really wanted Zhang Min and Jordon to meet.

Jordon pressed his knee against Tian Di's. "Hey, I'd walk on broken glass for you."

"It might feel like you have by the end of the visit." Fury burned through Tian Di that his family wasn't more accepting.

Jordon took his hand. "I wish I could kiss your mouth right now until you remember what's important. They don't need to accept you. I do. I love you. I want to meet your sister, and I want your family to know I'm crazy in love with their incredible son."

KNOCK. KNOCK. Knock.

Jordon stopped pulling off Tian Di's shirt and exhaled hard. "Sorry."

Tian Di trudged over to the door after Jordon put his T-shirt back on. It was a little frustrating. After an extremely long after-party, he'd finally gotten Jordon alone. All he wanted to do was kiss and touch and celebrate all things Jordon with a slow round of mouth sex.

Tian Di opened the door. "Hi."

Dusty clutched his phone in one hand. "Hi, um. Is Jordon in there? He's not in his room, so I figured—"

Stepping aside, Tian Di waved Dusty in.

Justin stayed at the door and mouthed, "Sorry."

"Does this text mean you're not going to tour Singapore with us?" Dusty stood in front of Jordon and appeared honestly perplexed.

A rush of familiar emotions rained down on Tian Di. He hated to drag Jordon away from his brothers, but he didn't want to be separated from him either.

Jordon's expression screamed how much he loathed disappointing his brothers, but there was also a resolve. "I'm hanging out in Hong Kong a few days after the concert, which is why I sent the text letting you know."

Dusty stepped back like he'd been punched. "Why? Where are you staying? Do you have a hotel yet? Things book quick there, and—"

"I'm staying with Tian Di and his sister."

Dusty did a full stop. His eyes got wide. "Oh. Of course."

"I want to meet Tian Di's family." Jordon restated his plans.

"But I thought—" Dusty snapped his fingers. "I know! We'll just stay until you're ready to go to Singapore."

Guilt slashed through Tian Di. Dusty was grasping for salt running out of a bag.

Jordon shook his head. "Dust, I…."

Tian Di hated seeing Jordon torn. "Jordon, we can postpone you spending time with my sister so you can hang out with your brothers—"

Jordon stared at him. "No. I want to be with you."

It didn't have to be a choice. Tian Di said, "You can. Maybe we can—"

Zack poked his head into the room. "Dust, maybe the kid wants to see where Tian Di is from without his brothers."

Dust stumbled over to the dresser and sat. "Oh, yeah. Right. Yeah. No worries. We'll see you in Singapore still, right?"

Jordon's face fell. "Of course. We don't have exact plans yet, but I'll be there. It's not like I'm running away from home."

Tian Di was ripped open by Jordon's broken laugh.

Dusty's expression said he couldn't tell the difference between different plans and total abandonment.

Tian Di had to take that frown off Jordon's face. "Hey, why don't we meet for dim sum before you head to Singapore? And I can show you the highlights of Hong Kong."

Zack's and Dusty's faces lit with the Davis smile.

Jordon turned to stare at Dusty, then at Zack. Then he gave Tian Di a big grin that told him he had done well.

Zack took two steps into the room to drape an arm around Tian Di's shoulders. "Sounds great. Hey, how do you say 'no mushroom' in Mandarin?"

CHAPTER 19

HONG KONG reminded Jordon of an Asian version of New York City—a force to be reckoned with all on its own. The skyline stunned him, with skyscrapers sweeping down to the water. Not to mention, this was where Tian Di had grown up.

Tian Di stumbled out of Made in China's first television interview.

Jordon nabbed him in a quick embrace. "You did great." The weary expression Tian Di gave him compelled Jordon to say more. "Not that I'm judging you, but I considered myself an expert on your public persona. As your biggest *stan*, I might as well confess I used to watch your interviews on Youku for hours at a time."

"Stan?"

Jordon could kick himself for using Zack's word. "Um, it means stalker fan."

"Oh, a combination of the words. Got it." Tian Di cocked his head with a smirk. He accepted the cup of tea Jordon handed him. "You are a wonderful stan."

Jordon attempted but probably failed at a glare, because really, who could cast aspersions on such a lovely boyfriend? "Look, maybe the whole being in love with you cancels the stan thing out. I, for one, think we can bypass the creepiness of me trolling websites to stare at you."

Tian Di chuckled. "Well, I am your stan. I love your work… though I didn't go on websites to ogle you."

"Fine, fine. Let's ignore the fact that there were no websites with my picture for your whack-off pleasure."

"Whack-off pleasure?" Tian Di arched his eyebrow.

Fuck, where're my pencils? I need to get this on the page. Jordon gestured the universal jerkoff sign.

Tian Di leaned in and tilted his head. "Wait, you—"

Groaning, Jordon closed his eyes. "That is so not the point."

"No? Because that's kind of—"

"We're both creepers and therefore perfect for each other. Let's simply leave the discussion at that." Jordon wiggled his eyebrows. "Anyway, you did well in the interview. Really."

Tian Di exhaled hard. "Thanks. This isn't only an internet show, but something everyone I know might see."

Meaning Tian Di's parents. Jordon wished he could make the uncertainty on the home front easier, but years of experience told him some things didn't work out that way.

"It might be dumb, but I like that Zhang Min makes sure our parents are well aware of the band's successes. I like them knowing I'm doing what I said I would."

Jordon longed to kiss away all Tian Di's problems. "I'm very proud of all you've accomplished. I want to sing from the rooftops how freaking awesome you are."

"Speaking of singing, I've got to head over for sound check. Come on."

TIAN DI checked his cell phone again. He mouthed, "Where is she? She said she'd be here by now."

"I'm sure she's just been delayed by security." Jordon tried to reassure him again. "Do you want me to go check?"

"I—Zhang Min!" With a big smile, Tian Di shook his head at Jordon. He pulled Jordon over to a shorter, female version of himself standing next to a backstage clothing rack.

"Tian Di! Shhh, your voice." She closed the space between them and flung herself at him.

Tian Di caught her in his arms and closed his eyes. He whispered in her ear, "It's like holding everything good in Hong Kong. I missed you so much."

"Me too. Thank goodness for Skype, but nothing beats this." She looked him up and down and then squealed before hugging him again.

It was an hour before the show, and most of the people backstage were not from Hong Kong, so they barely noticed the unusual physical display of affection.

Jordon couldn't help but be pleased that Tian Di didn't follow the tradition of no physical contact other than a handshake. Handshakes between siblings were wrong. If Jordon tried to give Zack a handshake, his brother would smack him in the head before hugging the life out of him. He'd definitely do the same, only maybe a double whack.

When Tian Di finally released his sister, he turned to Jordon, beaming. He mouthed, "Jordon Davis, this is my big sister, Zhang Min Zhao."

She lowered her eyes and held out her hand.

Jordon shifted his gaze to the floor and shook her delicate hand. "Very nice to meet you, Ms. Zhao."

"Very nice to meet my brother's *friend*." She smiled, looking him in the eye with the same sparkle Tian Di had. "Please call me Zhang Min."

He pulled out the wrapped present he'd tucked into his bag. "I'd like you to have this."

"No need for presents." She put both hands in front of her to ward off the gift. "It is not necessary."

"Please. It's only something small." He held out the gift, red-wrapped with a gold ribbon. "I made this for you."

Jordon had filled a book with sketches of Tian Di and used a photo of Zhang Min from Tian Di's cell phone as a reference so he could include her in some of them. He turned a few of the stories Tian Di told him about growing up in Hong Kong with his sister into pictures.

She protested one more time before she accepted the gift with both hands. "You did not have to do this, Mr.—"

"Please call me Jordon." He hoped to eliminate her sounding like she was talking to Dusty instead of him.

She put the present in her bag. "Thank you, Jordon. Though I should be the one kissing your hands for all the pleasure you've given my brother."

Jordon stared, and when he opened his mouth, only a squeak came out. *Say what now?*

Tian Di, without missing a beat, mouthed, "That's what he said."

Jordon never expected to be in the role of corrupter, but he was more than a little proud of the sauciness that rolled off his boyfriend's tongue.

Zhang Min covered her mouth, and her eyes got huge. "Tian Di, you are getting dirty just like his books. I love it! This is going to be fun."

TIAN DI'S prestage ritual adjusted to add a big hug for his sister.

Jordon was ridiculously happy seeing them together.

After the sisterly hug, Tian Di grabbed Jordon in an embrace. He added a small private kiss to Jordon's neck, and his hand found Jordon's ass for a quick good-luck rub.

Jordon shouted over the drumbeat, "Good skill. Have fun."

Tian Di took the stage. As usual he glided to the spotlight in a demure fashion.

Made in China slayed the opening and brought the crowd to their feet halfway through the first song.

Styx gave Tian Di a soft back beat as he introduced the band. "On bass guitar, we have Li Zhehao. Jin Lan is on lead guitar. Styx Wong keeps our beat. Indigo Song plays the keyboards. And I'm Tian Di Zhao. We're Made in China."

The crowd applauded. "I love you, Tian Di" was screamed out.

"And Made in China loves you too," Tian Di smoothly depersonalized the affection. "Now how about we show you our love?"

Video monitors played upgraded clips of their original video of "Evolution." The band flashed across the screens in traditional robes until the lights cut out and the recorded music feed died. Styx, Jin, Indigo, and Li picked up the driving beat live.

Zhang Min leaned toward Jordon and shouted above the music, "Seeing his videos and performances online doesn't compare to him live. I still can't believe that's my little brother out there."

Tian Di strutted to the center of the stage and sang "Evolution."

Jordon dragged his eyes away from the rock god commanding the stage and smiled. "He's amazing. The crowd loves him."

Zhang Min screamed, "Yes!" She began bouncing in time with the music.

The song ripped the crowd open and rocked them to their core. Gone was all pretense of the shy man who had been on the video monitor, and left was the singer who could make Jordon cream his jeans without even trying.

Zhang Min was a damned good dancer. Jordon was right there with her, letting the music free him. They danced through the rest of the show.

"We're going to close out the show with a new one." Tian Di soothed the audience with his voice and slow movements.

God, how did Jordon get this lucky? Hearing Tian Di's sultry voice had always made Jordon breathless. Reality hit him again. That singer was his boyfriend. *Holy fuck!* But Tian Di was so much more than a scorching hot rocker; he was playful, fun, enjoyed all the best sex acts—

Tian Di started singing. "Priorities and loss. Retelling time of broken steps—"

From the opposite side of the stage, Angel Luv stepped out from behind the curtain and sang, "Locked doors and stilted knocks."

The video monitors showed Jordon the bemused smile plastered on Tian Di's face.

What the fuck? Why was Angel out there with Made in China?

The crowd roared with pure madness.

"Hi, I hope you don't mind if I interrupt…," Angel Luv purred.

It was like throwing red meat to starving predators. The zoo lost their mind.

The Dark Angels' singer swaggered to center stage, drank in the audience's love for a moment, and then silenced them. "Hey, Pretty Ones. Shhhhh, let me ask Made in China a question?"

The audience hushed.

Angel swiveled toward the band. "Guys, I was wondering, would any of you mind if we make this last song a duet? What do you think? Would that be all right?"

Tian Di blinked several times, but he rolled with this new scenario. "I'd be honored to sing with you. Who wouldn't?"

Angel sidled closer to Tian Di. "I was hoping you'd say that."

They shared a smirk, because really, what else could Tian Di have said?

Zhang Min tapped Jordon on the arm. "Is this planned?"

"Um, no." Jordon held his breath.

"Son of a cocksucker. Angel Fucking Luv is brilliant." Megan appeared between Jordon and Zhang Min. Megan grinned at Zhang Min, and then she snatched the backstage pass hanging around Zhang Min's neck and examined it. "You're Tian Di's sister?"

Zhang Min nodded.

Jordon's attention was divided between watching the quiet discussion onstage and the conversation happening around him.

"I'm Megan, the Dark Angels' manager. After this little duet goes viral, I believe your brother and Made in China will be getting quite a few calls. Make sure you put in a good word for me. I'd love to manage Made in China." Megan nudged Jordon. "You too, honey."

"Of course, Megan." Jordon couldn't tear his gaze from Tian Di.

"Pretties. Pretty Ones!" Angel spoke to the crowd. "Have you heard this man sing?"

Lots of hoots and hollers came from the audience.

"I just had to harmonize with him."

Holy shit! How did Angel even make that sound dirty?

"Though, Pretties, keep in mind, we've never practiced this, so cut us a bit of slack."

The audience applauded.

Angel wiggled his eyebrows. "But no beating me with it. You know Dare frowns on such things… unless he's shall we say, involved…."

Hoots and hollers roared along with their agreement.

Tian Di and Angel conferred for a minute and then spoke to the rest of Made in China.

Even though Styx looked like his head might explode, he counted them in.

Angel and Tian Di's voices harmonized beautifully, sending chills through Jordon. "Priorities of love or loss. Retelling a time of broken steps, locked doors and stilted knocks. No way in and no way out."

Jordon let the melody sweep him away until Megan elbowed him. She pointed to the video monitor. "Look at the crowd."

Almost everyone had a cell phone trained on the duo. If even a small fraction uploaded to social media, this duet would go viral. Made in China and Tian Di would definitely be getting lots of offers.

"Fuck me. Angel Luv just gave Made in China a gift of a lifetime. Nice to have met you, Zhang Min Zhao, but I've got to get on this now." Megan vanished.

Angel threw an arm around Tian Di like they were old pals. They sang heartfelt words prioritizing love over everything. The song ended with them singing in perfect synch, "Don't waste time. Life doesn't last…. Chase love down and hold it fast."

Everyone was on their feet screaming.

Jordon let loose a few whoops. Goddamn, Tian Di had claimed his rock-god status, and all Jordon wanted to do was play attentive groupie.

Zhang Min asked, "Do you think Made in China will really get a record deal?"

Fuck! Jordon needed to keep his lustful thoughts about her brother to himself and focus on answering her question. "A record deal? Definitely. Probably more than one."

"Do you think that Megan will be representing Made in China?"

"I don't know." He looked over at Sebe. The little dynamo was young but very capable. "Though Sebe might think he needs someone to supervise."

Zhang Min laughed. "Tian Di has told me about him. He acts much older than seventeen."

JORDON COULDN'T stop smiling as he followed Tian Di and Zhang Min into her town car. He was exhausted but full of energy after a relatively quick stop at the after-party.

"Home, please," Zhang Min told the driver. Then she turned to Tian Di and Jordon to gush. "The concert was incredible."

"The Dark Angels are always great," Tian Di said.

Zhang Min made the sibling "I shouldn't have dropped you when you were a baby" face. "I was referring to Made in China, and you. You were amazing."

"Thank you," Jordon huffed out. "I've been trying to tell him Made in China is one of the hottest bands out there."

"And after that little duet, you're going to be all over social media," his sister said with the full confidence her marketing background allowed.

The driver whisked them through the wet streets of Hong Kong. It must have rained during the performance.

Zhang Min pointed to Jordon as she addressed Tian Di. "You need to listen to him. He knows."

Tian Di shrugged, though his pursed lips couldn't prevent his smile. "I'm glad you liked the show."

"I loved it. And you, baby brother, were meant to be onstage."

Jordon nodded. "He's a rock god."

Tian Di snorted.

His sister smirked and shared a fist-bump with Jordon. "I like Jordon. You should keep him."

"That's the plan," Tian Di said as they pulled into the drive of a luxury high-rise.

They hadn't talked about the future directly, but Jordon was totally on board with finding a tree to fish from, no matter what that meant. Tian Di was his and he was Tian Di's.

Tian Di gave Jordon a peck on the mouth when the driver became distracted with getting their bags out of the trunk.

Jordon grabbed some of their bags, and Tian Di got the others. They rode the elevator to the twenty-eighth floor with Zhang Min.

"I made up the guest room with extra towels for the two of you." Zhang Min appeared to be sending sibling telepathy to Tian Di.

"Thank you." Tian Di touched his heart.

She waved him off. "What? You thought I would have you sleep in separate places? I'm not Mother."

Thank Monet's Mother, Jordon would be sleeping next to Tian Di. He had gotten used to having a bed partner and the domestic bliss of living together, albeit in hotels and out of suitcases, but it melted his heart and centered him nonetheless.

Tian Di looked a bit misty-eyed.

Grabbing Zhang Min, Jordon gave her an awkward hug and mumbled, "Thank you."

THE NEXT morning after an abbreviated shower, Jordon sat at Zhang Min's sunny breakfast nook in her kitchen overlooking Repulse Bay. He'd made strawberry crepes, but he was positive they weren't as good as Dusty's—although Tian Di and Zhang Min liked them well enough, since they didn't reject the idea of a second batch.

"I've called for the car to take you to the house." Zhang Min frowned.

"Wait, you're not coming?" Tian Di closed the book of sketches Jordon had given Zhang Min, and he grimaced.

"I wasn't planning on it." She stared at him. Jordon didn't have to hear their sibling telepathy to see "little brother begging older sibling to save him from the evil parental units."

She rolled her eyes. "Fine, only 'cause Jordon's going to tell me who Tricks is ascending Mount Fuji with…. Right, Jordon?"

"Um…." A big sister bullying him felt the same as a big brother pushing boundaries. But he had his own skills and pulled the little brother wiggle out of thin air. "You wouldn't want me to ruin the story for you, Zhang Min."

Tian Di chuckled with his sister, and they both exclaimed, "Yes, we would."

ZHANG MIN'S driver pulled up to the gleaming steel gates. A gate? Why hadn't Tian Di told him how rich his family happened to be? Didn't matter to Jordon, but it was odd.

He glanced at Tian Di, who studiously inspected the pink flowering bushes.

Jordon touched his knee to Tian Di's. When Tian Di looked at him, Jordon smiled and grabbed his hand.

Tian Di leaned in. "I didn't say anything because it has nothing to do with me."

Squeezing his hand, Jordon pointed out, "It's part of who you are."

The car rolled forward as the gates opened, revealing a house made of harsh angles of glass and steel. Instead of being structurally appealing to the artist in him, Jordon couldn't help but wonder about growing up in a building that was so cold and uninviting.

Jordon tightened his hold on the bag of eight gifts. He'd wrapped each one in the lucky colors of red and gold. Eight was the number for prosperity, which was what he hoped to convey. It had taken him two days to gather all the presents.

Before heading to Hong Kong, he'd dragged Tian Di on a gift accumulation detour. He picked up tea in Hangzhou, purchased rice wine, and had even given up one of his boxes of chocolate monkeys from Nagano. The next day they headed back to the Suzhou government shop, which had produced a silk scarf, an embroidery with two dragons surrounding a ball representing the world, and two pairs of silk slippers. He added a picture he had drawn of the Zhao family, rolled up and tied with a red ribbon.

Tian Di, his sister, and Jordon stood on the front porch. Zhang Min took a deep breath and rang the bell.

Jordon squished his need to hug them both. The fact they had to wait like strangers on the porch killed him. More strong gratitude swamped him for the love his brothers had lavished upon him, which helped to heal the wounds his mother had sliced into his heart.

Zhang Min and Tian Di had banded together. It had been them against the world. He stood closer to them so they might feel like they had another person on their side.

The metal door swung open and a woman in her midforties peered out. She didn't smile during her intense inspection. Then she sighed and shook her head. "I see you still haven't cut your hair, Tian Di. And Zhang Min, why do you insist on wearing that dress? It looks like an old rice bag."

Zhang Min smoothed down her dress, Tian Di touched his hair, and Jordon wanted to give the critiquing witch a throat punch.

"This is my mother, Mrs. Zhao."

This was the woman who'd brought Tian Di into the world, so Jordon owed her for that, if nothing else. He shook her hand, then held out the golden gift bag to her. "Mrs. Zhao, please accept this as a small token of my appreciation for having me over."

After she did the customary dance of refusing his gifts, she snatched the bag out of his hands. "Thank you for your kindness. I look forward to opening this later."

A man appeared in the doorway.

Tian Di introduced Jordon. "Jordon Davis, this is my father, Mr. Zhao."

"I'm pleased to meet you, Mr. Zhao." Jordon might have shaken hands a little too hard, because Mr. Zhao grimaced.

Mrs. Zhao guided them into a formal living area done in rose and creams. The room was filled with antiques and fought against the structure's angles. "Please, have a seat."

Tian Di's father said, "I have a conference call. If you'll excuse me," and he disappeared.

Zhang Min rolled her eyes.

"What do you do, Jordon?" Tian Di's mother asked.

Clearing his throat, Jordon said, "I'm an artist."

She cocked her head to the side and repeated, "An artist?"

"Yes."

Her "hmmm" said volumes on how unworthy she thought him.

"He's one of my favorite artists of all time," Tian Di groused.

Hearing Tian Di stand up to his mother and try to protect him made Jordon feel loved.

"Oh, so he draws those silly magazines."

Zhang Min growled. "Mangas are not silly."

Mrs. Zhao ignored her daughter and narrowed her focus on Jordon. "Do you have a girlfriend, Jordon?"

Jordon glanced over at Tian Di, not having a clue how to answer. Tian Di's mother had been told they were seeing each other. He expected she'd avoid the subject, but her pathological denial threw him. Did she think he would deny being with her son?

Tian Di cleared his throat. "Jordon's my boyfriend, Mother. You know that, because I told you."

Mrs. Zhao grimaced and fluttered her hands about. "Please stopping saying that."

"Why? It is the truth." Tian Di glared at her with angry defiance.

She fussed with her napkin. "Some truths are best left undiscovered."

Tian Di winced. Her arrow obviously pierced her son's heart.

That didn't stop her. "If I had known you wanted a Westerner, there's many expat girls. I know some from America, Germany—you name the country."

Covering his face with one hand, Tian Di appeared wiped out by the exchange.

Enough! Jordon couldn't take more of this. "I'm afraid that won't work, Mrs. Zhao."

"Whyever not?" The innocence in her tone made Jordon's blood boil.

"I love your son, and I want to spend my life making him happy." Jordon wanted to make that clear.

Mrs. Zhao stared for a moment and then proclaimed, "Well, I need to go check on the meal. Please excuse me."

Did he just screw everything sideways? He was afraid to look at Tian Di.

Zhang Min threw her arms around him. "Thank you."

Jordon hugged her back and found the courage to peek over at Tian Di.

Tian Di sat back with his hands behind his neck, grinning at Jordon.

Eventually Zhang Min released him from her sisterly strangle hug.

Jordon stared at Tian Di and couldn't help but share in the mysterious smile. "What's with the smile?"

"You stood up to her, confessed your love for me, and made her speechless in the process. You did all that in less than five minutes. You're amazing, and you're mine." Tian Di crossed over to him in two strides and gave him a toe-curling kiss.

JORDON FOUND himself seated at a round table across from Tian Di in an elegant red-and-gold dining room. He was sandwiched between Zhang Min and Mr. Zhao.

"Tian Di, your sister said your band did well." Mr. Zhao stated it like Tian Di would deny all knowledge of performing.

"It was a good show." Tian Di glanced at Jordon. "Jordon's brother is the drummer for the band we opened for."

"Convenient."

Jordon put on a happy face to overcompensate for the grimness of this family dinner. "It is. I found Made in China's music way before this tour. Your son's vocals drew me in and held me hostage."

"I've never heard him." Mr. Zhao glanced toward the door. "Ah, here's the shark fin soup."

An unsmiling woman with a tight bun and a pristine uniform carried a covered tureen. She ladled out bowls for everyone.

Jordon forced himself not to think of all the finless sharks floating belly up for this soup. They were honoring him… or maybe just trying to scare him off with a show of wealth. If that was the case, they should bring it on, because money was simply paper with art on it. Wealth didn't impress or alarm him.

Mrs. Zhao pointed at the bowl in front of him. "*Si hah.*"

Zhang Min leaned in to him. "She means try it."

He tasted the gelatinous liquid. The soup had a delicate flavor that was almost lost to the texture. Somehow it managed to be chewy and a little crunchy at the same time.

Jordon complimented Mrs. Zhao. "It's delicious."

Dinner was a banquet, and the food kept arriving. The next course was abalone stew in oyster sauce with Zack's worst nightmare—straw mushrooms.

As the courses kept coming, Jordon tried a little bit of everything, not wanting to be seen as bad mannered, though the tension in his stomach made everything difficult to get down, let alone enjoy.

Mrs. Zhao glared at her daughter. "I spoke to Margaret's mother yesterday. She's a grandmother again. When are you going to find a man? You're not getting any younger."

"Mother, please." Zhang Min set her chopsticks down on the red ceramic koi chopstick rest.

"What? It's true." Mrs. Zhao turned to Jordon. "What would your mother think if you weren't going to give her grandchildren, Jordon?"

Tian Di's gasp echoed off the golden walls of the dining room.

Jordon wondered how he didn't gush blood from that remark. Mrs. Zhao cut him on so many levels, and while doing so, she denied who he was at his very core.

"I don't think she would care all that much." If Jordon was brutally honest with himself, even with years of therapy, that still sucked monkey balls.

"I wouldn't be too sure. Women wait all their lives to be grandmothers. To see the family name carried on."

"Mrs. Zhao, my mother kicked me out when I was sixteen for being gay. She no longer acknowledges me as her son. So even if I were to adopt or find a surrogate to carry a biological child, as far as I'm concerned, she doesn't have any right to be a grandmother to any of my children, or my brothers'."

Mrs. Zhao's mouth opened and shut. Jordon imagined she looked like the finless sharks in their death throes.

He understood he'd ripped the fabric of her societal expectations, but he was already doing so by loving their son, so he'd go for broke. "Can you imagine a child being kicked out for just being who he is? I don't know what I would've done if it hadn't been for my brothers."

Mrs. Zhao stared at Jordon and then spared Tian Di and Zhang Min a glance. Then she stared down at her plate. "That is rather terrible, Jordon. I'm sorry for your loss."

Jordon reached across Zhang Min and held out his hand to Mrs. Zhao.

She studied it before tentatively taking his offered hand.

He shook her hand and added an awkward bow. "Thank you, Mrs. Zhao. Thank you."

The new course arrived, allowing the moment to end. A platter of fresh lobster pieces, roast duck, and some other meats Jordon couldn't identify were delivered to the lazy Susan in the middle of the table.

"Yes. Er, *si hah.*" Mrs. Zhao pointed to the food.

Tian Di gave Jordon a smile, and that was enough to get him through the next course.

Mrs. Zhao steered the conversation toward safer subjects like politics and world issues that had no clear solution.

The meal ended with a serving of fried rice and longevity noodles.

Mr. Zhao turned to Jordon right when he was slurping one of the extremely long noodles with less-than-expert skill. "I understand you publish with Kin Jirareta Ai Press."

Slurp, slurp, slurp. How long was this thing? As soon as Jordon had the last of the noodle in his mouth, he nodded. After he swallowed, he said, "Yes, sir."

"I have a meeting with a potential customer."

Not sure where this was going, Jordon said, "Oh."

"Yes, his daughter, I understand, is a big fan of yours." Mr. Zhao made the statement like Jordon knew all about the fan and her father's potential connection to the Zhao family business.

Tian Di stared from across the table. "How do you know that?"

Mr. Zhao smiled grimly. "You'd be surprised at the things I know."

Tian Di slapped the table. "You can't just use Jordon this way."

Shaking his head, Mr. Zhao said, "It's nothing more or less than I'd ask of your sister's husband."

"If she had one," Mrs. Zhao added as if she were compelled.

Jordon recognized the impending request for assistance for what it might possibly be—a bit of acceptance. "How can I help, Mr. Zhao?"

"If you'd be willing to meet his daughter for tea at the Peninsula, I'd be grateful," Mr. Zhao stated with the appropriate level of humility. Was this the olive branch of peace, or would the patriarch of the family beat Tian Di with it somehow?

"I'd be happy to do that for you. May I suggest Tian Di should accompany me." Before Mr. Zhao could object, Jordon pointed out, "You may not realize it, but your son is a rock star, especially after the concert here last night."

During the dessert of fresh seasonal berries and sweet, hot red-bean soup, Mr. Zhao focused on Tian Di. "Will you be on that entertainment TV show tonight?"

Tian Di narrowed his eyes. "Yes. They interviewed us before the sound check last night."

Jordon tried not to go all dreamy but couldn't help it. "Tian Di did a magnificent job. He answered all the questions while still giving an air of rock-god mystery."

Zhang Min choked on her laugh and shoveled some berries into her mouth.

"What Jordon means is the interview went well." Tian Di downplayed his success.

Mr. Zhao shifted forward. "I understand your bandmate Styx was a bit camera shy."

"How did you—" Jordon stopped himself.

Tian Di stated, "Jin, the guitarist, covered for him, and it worked."

"Well, this Styx needs to stand on his own better. One can't always depend on one's significant other to bail them out." Mr. Zhao made the pronouncement as if it were law—and wait, he not only knew but acknowledged Styx and Jin were together? Wow, this man was connected to things Jordon might not want to know about.

Everyone dropped their heads and stared at their fruit.

Except Jordon, who shook his head. "I don't know if I agree with that, Mr. Zhao. I'd bet your lovely wife would stand up for you. I know Tian Di's always got my back, and I'll always have his."

Mrs. Zhao and Zhang Min gasped. Tian Di gave Jordon a wide-eyed stare.

Mr. Zhao studied him for a moment and barked out a laugh. "I think I will enjoy having you around this table in the future, Jordon."

"Thank you, sir. I appreciate that." Not quite sure what to make of the sudden acceptance, he'd count this turn of events as a win until someone told him differently.

After tea, Zhang Min, Tian Di, and Jordon said their goodbyes and escaped.

Zhang Min and Tian Di fell into her town car. Jordon slipped in behind Tian Di.

"Home," Zhang Min told the driver.

As they rode past the gates, Tian Di blew out a breath. "Whew, we survived."

"Speak for yourself." Zhang Min gave him a side-eyed glare and dropped her head to the back of the seat.

"You still my boyfriend?" Tian Di laid his head on Jordon's shoulder and even batted his eyelashes. His tone held a note of teasing but with an undercurrent of worry.

Jordon hugged him tight. "You can't get rid of me that easily. And wasn't it you who taught me that if it rains we'll deal with it?"

"My parents are more like a typhoon—"

"Life is going to throw some stupid at us, but we'll handle it together." Jordon wanted him to understand.

Zhang Min *awwe*d them.

"Besides, parents love me. How can they not?" As long as they weren't his own, of course.

Tian Di didn't say anything, but he slipped a hand into Jordon's and squeezed. And it was everything.

THE NEXT day, Zhang Min's driver dropped Jordon and Tian Di at the entrance of the Peninsula Hong Kong. Two bellmen swung open the doors so they could enter.

Afternoon tea was held in the hotel's white lobby. The ceilings soared high above them, and pillars surrounded the room. Each was highlighted by gilded artistic details on top, and the design edged and crisscrossed the entire ceiling. Tall potted plants scattered through the lobby gave a sense of privacy. A five-piece band played classical music on the balcony overlooking the room. If the Peninsula was going for lush elegance, Jordon would call this success.

A petite woman in a sleeveless red dress waved to Jordon and Tian Di.

"That must be her," Jordon said as they zigzagged their way over thick-cushioned gold rugs to her.

She held out her hand. "Hello, I'm Ashmi Duàn."

"Jordon Davis. But please call me Jordon." He hoped that cut off the need for formal surnames being used. "And this is—"

"Oh, I know Tian Di Zhao. I was at the concert last night with my girlfriend. Front row. Center." She stared at him. "You are extremely talented."

"You're very kind. It is very nice to meet you, Ms. Duàn." Tian Di shook her hand.

After a long moment, she gestured for them to join her at the shiny cherrywood table. "Please take a seat, and please call me Ashmi. I ordered the Peninsula Classic Afternoon Tea for three. You'll just need to pick your tea."

A waiter arrived with a tier of plates holding an incredible selection of finger sandwiches and tea pastries, along with warm chocolate-chip scones, clotted cream, and a mix of berry preserves.

She handed them an extensive tea menu.

Jordon was a little overwhelmed by the five pages of choices and wished Justin or even Andrew were here to help him navigate the options. "What are you going to have?"

"I usually order rose tea. What kind will you have?" Ashmi asked.

Jordon surveyed the tea and decided, "I'll have the same."

Tian Di smiled. "Rose tea is my favorite."

"I didn't know that." Jordon grinned at learning a new detail about his boyfriend. There were so many things they had yet to discover about each other, and he couldn't wait.

The white-gloved waiter came back and poured tea into the cups via the silver tea strainer to catch any stray leaves or rosebuds not staying in the pot. The scent of roses wafted through the air, reminding Jordon of their outside onsen in Japan. The waiter replaced the pot on the silver rest so there were no drips on the pristine tablecloth.

Throughout the ritual, Ashmi kept staring at him and Tian Di.

After one sip, Jordon inclined his head toward Tian Di. "Before we go, remind me to nab two bags of this tea and strainers for Andrew and Justin. I think they'd love it."

As soon as the waiter vanished, Ashmi asked in a low voice, "Are you two together?"

Jordon opened his mouth, but what could he say?

She shook her head. "I won't out you. I'm gay too. When I said 'my girlfriend,' I really mean my *girlfriend*. We've been together for three years."

Staring at Tian Di, Jordon was pretty sure he heard the man's thoughts. Couples communication was indeed a thing. "Thank you for sharing that with us. We're not hiding our orientation, but right now we're not announcing it."

"I won't say anything, but to know people I admire are like me… matters." Ashmi dabbed her eyes with a tissue.

Crazy pressure started to surge in Jordon. Tian Di used his foot to touch Jordon's, and the connection calmed the rage of nervousness.

"So, Jordon, I'm a huge fan. Can you sign these for us?" She pulled out five books.

"Of course." He dug around his bag for his gold pen.

"When did you start drawing?" Ashmi's question put the afternoon back on track.

DUSTY AND Justin altered their plans and decided to go to Macau to cause trouble with Angel and Darius, taking Zack and Andrew with them. Jordon took the time and consumed the Hong Kong Museum of Art, the shops on Cat Street, Stanley Market, and had lots of fun with Tian Di and Zhang Min doing everything and nothing. Now Jordon and Tian Di headed over to the Celestial Court to meet his brothers and their significant others for dim sum.

Outside the restaurant, Jordon answered a call from an unknown number. "Hello?"

"Jordon. This is Mr. Zhao. Tian Di's father."

Why in the world was he calling? Was he going to warn Jordon off his son? And how did he get this number? "Hi. I hope you're well."

"Yes, I am. I wanted to thank you. That must have been quite a lovely tea. Chairman Duàn said his daughter was thrilled and didn't stop talking about you or my son. I don't know what you said to his daughter, but we won their business."

"Mr. Zhao, I didn't say anything to her about your business." Was that what he was expected to do?

"Ah, very smart of you." Mr. Zhao sounded unduly impressed by Jordon's lack of business knowhow.

What in Michelangelo was this?

"You and my son make quite the power couple. Extend my thanks to him as well. And if you have time before you go to the next stop on the tour—Singapore, I believe—please come back for dinner." The call disconnected.

Jordon stared at his cell phone.

"What?" Tian Di glanced at Jordon's phone.

"That was your dad. He thanked us for getting him Ashmi's father's business and called us a power couple."

"A power couple?" Tian Di shook his head.

"Come on, let's power through some dim sum, then some."

"What?"

"Dumb joke."

TIAN DI had arranged for their group to have a private room so they could enjoy a meal in peace.

After they ordered, Dusty asked, "What the hell did you think when Angel joined you onstage?"

Tian Di grinned. "I'll never know how he learned the words. Though at the time, I was too stunned to think. I just sang."

"Damn good thing you did. I heard Megan barely got ahead of the media storm." Zack chuckled.

"It's good to know Angel still has some influence." Dusty chortled, and he began tapping out a soft beat on the table.

Tian Di toyed with his napkin. "I'm very grateful to Angel and all of the Dark Angels for using your power to assist Made in China."

Dusty stopped drumming. "Oh, I almost forgot. Tian Di, Megan asked me to pass on to expect a text tomorrow morning. She'd like you to go back to Suzhou for a few days. For some promo shoots of Made in China before you head to Singapore."

"Oh… really." Tian Di looked at Jordon.

"Really. You'd be surprised what she's capable of doing. Made in China made a great decision taking on Megan as your manager."

"I guess." Tian Di took a drink of tea.

Dusty clapped Jordon on the shoulder. "And, Jordon, no worries if you want to go with Made in China. We'll catch up with you in Singapore. Oh, but seriously, make sure you read the travel notes on Singapore. I don't want you getting caned."

Zack snapped to attention. "Caned?"

"Not in a good way." Andrew arched his eyebrow, then whispered into Zack's ear until he fanned himself.

"You promise?" Zack demanded.

Andrew gave a single nod.

Jordon didn't want to put those puzzle pieces together, so he glanced around the table filled with some of the best people in his world.

After a while, his brothers and their partners were laughing and enjoying the evening together.

As the evening progressed, Jordon felt an enormous wave of happiness. Maybe it was the sips of beer he was stealing from Zack's bottle.

Boundaries didn't have to mean walls. If anything, the ones he'd set with his brothers allowed him to have more freedom. He didn't feel trapped by their protectiveness anymore, only cared for.

He loved the people around the table so much, and as an adult, he needed to tell them. Tapping on his teacup with a chopstick focused everyone's attention on him.

Jordon raised his cup of tea. "I want to thank everyone here for being a part of my life. Dusty, you always took care of me and Zack, especially after Mom didn't want us. Hell, even before that, you practically raised me. Thank you for always being there for us."

"Always, you know that," Dusty reassured him.

"Justin, you may be Dusty's fiancé and my writing partner, but you're more like a brother to me... just much less annoying than the two I have."

Everyone laughed.

Jordon continued, "You brought happiness to the Davis clan... as well as your own brother, Andrew. Andrew, I know you and I haven't always gotten along—"

Zack snorted. "Understatement."

Jordon ignored the peanut gallery. "But you truly are specially made for Zack, and I'm grateful to you. Besides, you might be growing on me."

"Thank you, Jordon." Andrew gave him a warm smile.

"Zack, I can't thank you enough for all the rescuing you've done, and all the museums you've gone to with me over the years. Thank you for being one of my best friends."

Nodding, Zack fist-bumped with him. "Don't mention it. No, seriously, if that gets around, I'll lose my roadie street credit."

Jordon laughed. "Cute how you assume you have street credit."

Zack gave him the middle finger.

Turning to the love of his life, Jordon held out his hand.

Tian Di grabbed on and rubbed their palms together.

"I saw my brothers find their other halves, but I never thought I'd find mine. Tian Di, you fit me perfectly. I can't even begin to tell you how much you mean to me. I just plan to show you over the next hundred or so years. Your love has let all my reds and oranges shine through. I love you. I love all of you."

Everyone hugged and drank tea.

"*Búyào mógu*," Zack whispered to Andrew.

"Um, Jordon, why does Zack keep whispering *no mushrooms* in Mandarin to Andrew?"

"No reason we want to figure out. Trust me. It would then require brain bleach." Jordon grinned.

CHAPTER 20

AFTER THE Suzhou promo photo session was complete, Made in China had a few days before they needed to head to Singapore. Tian Di suggested Jordon take another class with Chin Yu Fan. This time the first hour was a pure battle of wills between Jordon and Chin Yu. Neither wanted to give a centimeter.

"No, no, no." Chin Yu Fan clapped her hands.

Jordon jumped away from his painting, almost losing one of the paintbrushes he clutched in his fingers. "What?"

Tian Di steadied Jordon and wished he could do more than watch the struggle.

"You." She took away both his paintbrushes and drew a free-form lotus. It looked nothing like the picture she'd wanted Jordon to copy.

Jordon smiled, pointed to her proving-a-point version, and then gave her a thumbs-up. "Well done, Fan lǎoshī."

"No." Chin Yu X-ed out her drawing.

Jordon turned to Tian Di. "I need you to translate."

"Sure. Go ahead."

"Fan lǎoshī, I respect you as a teacher and a new friend, but most of all as an artist. I want to learn, but I need to do some things my way."

Tian Di wasn't sure of the reception Jordon's remarks would get, but he translated faithfully.

Chin Yu glared at Tian Di like it was his fault. She said in English, "Americans have too much freedom."

Jordon cocked his head. "Please tell Fan lǎoshī I can work within limits. I've learned boundaries can allow me to find more freedom and happiness, but I want to help set the limits."

Tian Di translated because he didn't know how much English Chin Yu Fan understood.

She shook her head and then stared at Jordon. In Mandarin she said, "I don't know how to teach someone so independent."

Translation duties completed, Tian Di added, "This is really new for her."

Jordon nodded. "Please tell her I appreciate all she's taught me so far, and I'm honored she's willing to share her talent with me. Try to explain I'm not looking for independence so much as… respectful interdependence."

For Tian Di, that drove home the point of everything Jordon was doing with his brothers. The boundaries weren't to keep them out, but to allow Jordon freedom to do his own thing without being smothered.

Chin Yu Fan stared at both of them longer than was comfortable, but finally gave a nod and resumed the lesson.

Tian Di was impressed with the agreement Jordon struck with Chin Yu. She expected Jordon to draw something her way until the image was flawless, and then on a separate sheet of paper, she allowed him to outline the picture with his unique flair. Over the next two hours, Jordon created one reproduction of a dragonfly landing on a fully opened lotus and another with two dragonflies and two lotuses partially closed. He painstakingly applied color and water to the page.

Chin Yu Fan sang a never-ending chorus of "*gānzào*" and "*bú ganzao*" as she micromanaged the amount of water Jordon used.

But in the end, Jordon had created two gorgeous pieces.

"*Xiè xie*, Fan *lǎoshī*." Jordon shook Chin Yu's hand.

"Anytime, Jordon," Chin Yu said with much sincerity. To Tian Di she demanded, "You bring him back. He's a good student. I have more to teach him."

LATER WHEN they were recovering from what Jordon had called a bout of afternoon delight, Tian Di contemplated how Jordon worked hard to be the man worthy of him. But what about him? "You said you loved that I allowed you to become a phoenix."

Using strands of Tian Di's hair, Jordon painted invisible designs over his naked chest. "Yes, I appreciated you seeing me for me."

Maybe it was dumb, but Tian Di was glad he could be stupid in front of Jordon without losing face. He needed to say what he was thinking. "Well, you've always been a phoenix, but I love watching you spread your wings. Seeing you has inspired me. I want to become the dragon you deserve."

Jordon groaned and struggled to sit upright. "What do you mean? Is this a sex position? Because I'm still recovering, but—"

Tian Di laughed. "Jordon, I love you. You're so silly. It is not a sex position, but later we can find one, and you can name it the dragon."

Jordon held his hands up as if speaking to a crowd. "I am the phoenix, namer of sex acts."

"That's right, you are." Tian Di just wanted to tickle him, then slip back into a nice, slow round of loving him, but he should do this while he had strong intentions.

Probably reading the change in Tian Di's expression, Jordon asked, "So how are you going to become the dragon? Sounds serious."

"I watched you change how you interacted with your brothers and even Fan lǎoshī. I need to alter how I interact with my mother."

Jordon's emerald eyes widened. "What do you mean? You can't change her."

Tian Di pushed himself to a seated position. "You're correct. I can only change how I interact with her, and what I'm willing to tolerate to do so. A dragon is persistent and bold."

"Dragons are also heroic, noble, intelligent, and filled with goodness. All of which describe you. You're already a dragon. Sounds like you need to let her know who you are." Jordon gave him an affectionate kiss, then pulled on his jeans. "I'll hang out in the living room."

"You don't have to go."

"Oh, I'm not going. I'm looking forward to naming the Dragon with you. I'll do a bit of drawing while you work on changing the tone of your interaction with her." Jordon pulled on a T-shirt and shut the door behind him.

Jordon was right. This needed to be done alone. Tian Di found his discarded clothes and slipped them on. He made his bed, then skyped his mother's number.

"Tian Di? Is everything okay?" Her surprise at the call reinforced that he didn't reach out to her often.

"Everything is fine. I wanted to check in." He pushed away the guilt.

She tilted her head and stared at the screen. "That's kind of you. I'm fine."

"Good. Good."

His mother touched her heart. "Oh, wait! Are you calling to tell me you've found a girl you want to marry?"

Anger knocked guilt out of the way. "Mother, I'm gay."

"I know you say that, but—"

"There is no *but*! I've always liked guys. I will always be homosexual, meaning I am attracted to men." Tian Di growled. Maybe this was hopeless.

There was a long pause, and he expected she would say she had to stir the dumplings or check on something. Instead she proclaimed, "I like Jordon. He's a nice boy."

"He's a man. I love him, and he's it for me, so I'm happy you like him."

She couldn't have stared at him harder if he had erupted into spontaneous dance. Granted, he'd rarely been so bold and direct with his words to her. A shiver of fear slipped through him, but he didn't let her reaction stop him.

He asked, "Do you think it was right his mother kicked him out of the house at sixteen?"

She gasped, and her hand fluttered, then came to rest over her heart. "No, of course not. Do you think I'm a monster?"

He didn't answer, even though he thought no such thing. She was set in her ways, but she wouldn't abandon him… completely.

His silence kept her on the defensive. "It's terrible, a mother doing that to her son. That poor boy. Thankfully he had brothers. By the way, your sister showed me a movie where that happened. The poor child was so distraught he took his own life."

Score for Zhang Min. She always helped him by paving the way with their parents.

Though he couldn't let his mother distract him from his point. "Do you realize why I don't come home much or call?"

She hesitated. The knowledge was there in her hurt expression but was quickly replaced with pretend understanding. "You're busy. Trying to be a singer… with your band."

"Mother, I have to deny who I am in order for you to see me and to spend time with me. I need to stop doing that."

His mother shook her head as if she could prevent his words from penetrating into her brain. "What do you mean? I don't—"

"By asking if I found a girl. When you complain about my hair and my appearance, it hurts me. You have never supported my singing."

"I'm just trying to make you better."

"That's what I'm talking about! You can't justify this behavior. It's simply not right."

She waved him off. "You're overreacting. You always tend to do that."

He clenched his fists in order to keep his voice controlled. "Only because you push and push, hoping I will break. Well, I won't, and you can't bully me into the family business, and your criticisms of me don't convince me; they only slice and make me feel terrible."

"I don't want you to feel bad. I want to encourage you to have a better life. That's all I've ever done with you and your sister." She sighed with her burden of being the unappreciated parent.

Tian Di growled. He wouldn't let her muddy the water by bringing Zhang Min into the conversation. "Finding a girl won't make me better. Picking on my appearance won't make me different. I've let your harmful criticism go for a long time, but I won't do that anymore. I can't do that to Jordon. It's not right."

"What are you saying?" His mother glared at the screen, but her voice broke.

This was it. It might not be what he intended, but he'd worked himself up, and there was no turning back. He was exhausted dealing with his family's treatment. No more.

"Mother, you have a choice. Either you can accept I'm gay and Jordon is my boyfriend, or you can pretend I'm dead."

A sharp intake of her breath wheezed over his speakers. "Tian Di, never say that. There is no choice."

"Yes, there is, and it's yours to make."

"You are my sweet little boy who loved rose tea and cookies...." She covered her face.

"Is this goodbye, then?" His heart would break if she said yes, but so be it. He could no longer endure a thousand cuts a call and tens of thousands during a visit. The abuse needed to stop one way or another.

"No. Never." She shook her head.

Inside him was the little boy who craved her acceptance and would settle for a single serving, but the man he wanted to be for Jordon had to have more. "Then I need you to start accepting me for who I am."

She shifted away from the computer and stared at him as if seeing him for the first time, or maybe looking for a loophole.

He would show her no weakness in his resolve.

"I hope you and Jordon come home for the Spring Festival." She looked right and left, then whispered, "Your father quite likes Jordon. He says he has fire like a Zhao."

High praise. Tian Di could only agree. "He does."

"You know your father and I were younger than you when we had Zhang Min?"

What? Did she not hear anything—

"Jordon mentioned surrogacy. He will make a good father. Do you suppose he would let me help interview the surrogates with you? There's a good clinic here in Hong Kong, and—"

Tian Di's head hit the desk. Indigo would say out of the pot and into the fire.

"Tian Di. Tian Di? Tian Di!"

He raised his head. "Yes, Mother?"

"Even though Hong Kong doesn't allow two men to get married, if you were married overseas and came back to live in Hong Kong, the government would recognize your marriage. Jordon would be allowed your benefits."

His benefits… right. If Tian Di worked for his father. "I will not be joining the family business. I—"

She waved him off. "Fine, but after you marry, we could come back to Hong Kong for a reception, and—"

"In one call you've gone from pushing women on me to planning my wedding reception with Jordon?"

"I only want your happiness." She tapped her finger against her chin. "Never mind, Tian Di. I can probably discuss this directly with Jordon. He's quite reasonable and, I bet, has an eye for detail. Artists are special that way."

"Mother." Drowning in love was still drowning.

She smiled sweetly. "No worries, my darling boy. There is no rush. The waitlists are quite long at the suitable reception venues anyway."

Tian Di stared at the insanity that was his mother. "I love you, Mother."

"I look forward to seeing you in a few weeks."

"A few weeks?" *So soon?*

"Yes, your father is taking me and your sister to one of your shows." She touched the screen. "Thank you for calling me. I look forward to hearing from you… and Jordon, soon."

The chat ended. What had he done? Some dragon he was!

He powered down his computer and went into the living room.

Jordon sat cross-legged with his sketch pad amid a rainbow of colored pencils.

"Can I see?" Tian Di pointed to the picture.

"Of course. It's not done yet." Jordon handed him the sketch pad.

A multicolored dragon with shimmering scales curled around a tree. He cuddled a long-tailed rainbow bird perched on the branch. The dragon held a fishing pole and was reeling in two fat goldfish. In the corner of the picture, black letters scrolled in English.

> *Dear Tian Di,*
> *I used to write to my future husband, but since I now know your name....*
> *We will find the right tree to fish from*
> *And we'll live happily ever after.*
> *Your Future Husband,*
> *Jordon*

Tian Di pulled Jordon off the floor and into his arms. "I love you so much."

"You okay?" Jordon studied him.

"Better than okay." Tian Di captured Jordon's mouth to prove he was just fine. Dreams of what their happily ever after would look like chased through his mind. His laughter broke the kiss. "Though I think my mother wants our reception in Hong Kong."

Jordon tilted his head and smirked. "Oh, um, okay. I guess we're bypassing a long engagement."

Tian Di shook his head. "Nope. Apparently all the suitable reception places have long waitlists... but probably not as long as the fertility clinics in Hong Kong."

Jordon's face scrunched, and then he laughed. "She does know I can't get pregnant, right?"

Tian Di chuckled. "I think so, but that's not going to stop her from demanding a grandchild from you."

"Looks like you had a good talk with your mother." Jordon smiled.

"I worked myself into an ultimatum of accepting me or pretending I was dead. She countered with same-sex couples getting rights and benefits in Hong Kong if they married overseas."

"And babies?"

Tian Di demonstrated his mother's logic. "Marriage equates to children."

Jordon took his sketch pad back and dropped it to the floor. "I'm impressed. She moved right past acceptance and backflipped into how she gets a grandbaby from you."

"From us." Tian Di skimmed his hands down to Jordon's ass and pulled him closer. Jordon had already started to harden. He squeezed and kneaded Jordon's ass. "Do you want to go figure out the sex position that you will name the Dragon?"

"I've given the matter some thought." Jordon nabbed his sketch pad off the floor, flipped a few pages, and turned it over.

"Oh, well. Yeah." Tian Di got even harder studying the depiction of Jordon sucking him while he sucked Jordon.

His body had memorized the delicious slurp of Jordon's mouth and the lick of his tongue. Actually, every part of him begged to experience the sensation of being sucked again. But the joyous look of completion on Jordon's face made Tian Di guide his lover back into his bedroom.

"I think mouth sex is so good I'll make you roar." Jordon's eyes flashed with promise and determination.

Tian Di asked, "Do dragons roar?"

Jordon locked the door and stalked across the small space. He pushed Tian Di back onto the futon. "I don't know, but let's find out."

EPILOGUE

"DRAGONS DO roar." Jordon smirked as he wiped the corners of his mouth.

Applause filtered through the closed door.

Tian Di threw a pillow at the door.

"What? A good performance deserves applause," Indigo called out.

Jordon's cheeks were pink, but he shrugged. "I agree with that."

"Want to see if phoenixes roar?" Tian Di asked—as if he didn't know the answer.

Jordon shuffled closer to Tian Di's mouth. "Yes, please."

Z. ALLORA never expected to share her words with anyone, but things don't always work out as planned. Growing up in Upstate NY, she was a tomboy: playing basketball in the park, twirling a rifle in color guard, but composing stories filled with angst in secret.

She didn't always believe in romance, although before giving up on it completely, she took out a personal ad in a college newspaper. On October 20, 1987, at 5:08 PM, she found what she didn't think existed, and married her best friend five years later.

A bit of an overachiever, Z. received three bachelor's degrees (Psychology, English, and Philosophy) and a master's degree in Psychology. She loved enhancing the quality of life of people in her residential and day programs, but her love's job swept Z. overseas to Singapore, Israel, and China.

While living in China, she discovered M/M romance and a new world opened. The magic of the genre gave her new insights about herself and those around her. When she saw protests in Malaysia by parents who genuinely believed watching a singer could make their children gay, the ignorance was too staggering to ignore. No longer content to keep her words to herself, she published her stories hoping to add another voice to foster understanding and to promote equality.

Z. believes each of us is wonderfully unique and deserving of a happily ever after. Regardless where we are in the infinite spectrum of gender identity, orientation, or sexuality, our differences and similarities should be both respected and celebrated.

However, Z. will never apologize for having too much yaoified smexy goodness in her books. She teases that plot is simply the words between the sex scenes (though that's a bit of an exaggeration). Sex is one of our most important and basic forms of communication, and she feels it's a vital part of understanding her characters.

Z. Allora truly believes this rainbow romance is changing hearts and minds, and will continue to speak out for love for all of us.

Email: Z.AlloraHappyEndings@gmail.com
Facebook: Z Allora Allora
Website: www.zallorabooks.com
Blog: zallora.blogspot.com
Dreamspinner Press: www.dreamspinnerpress.com/books/z-allora-637-a
Queer Romance Ink: www.queeromanceink.com/mbm-book-author/z-allora

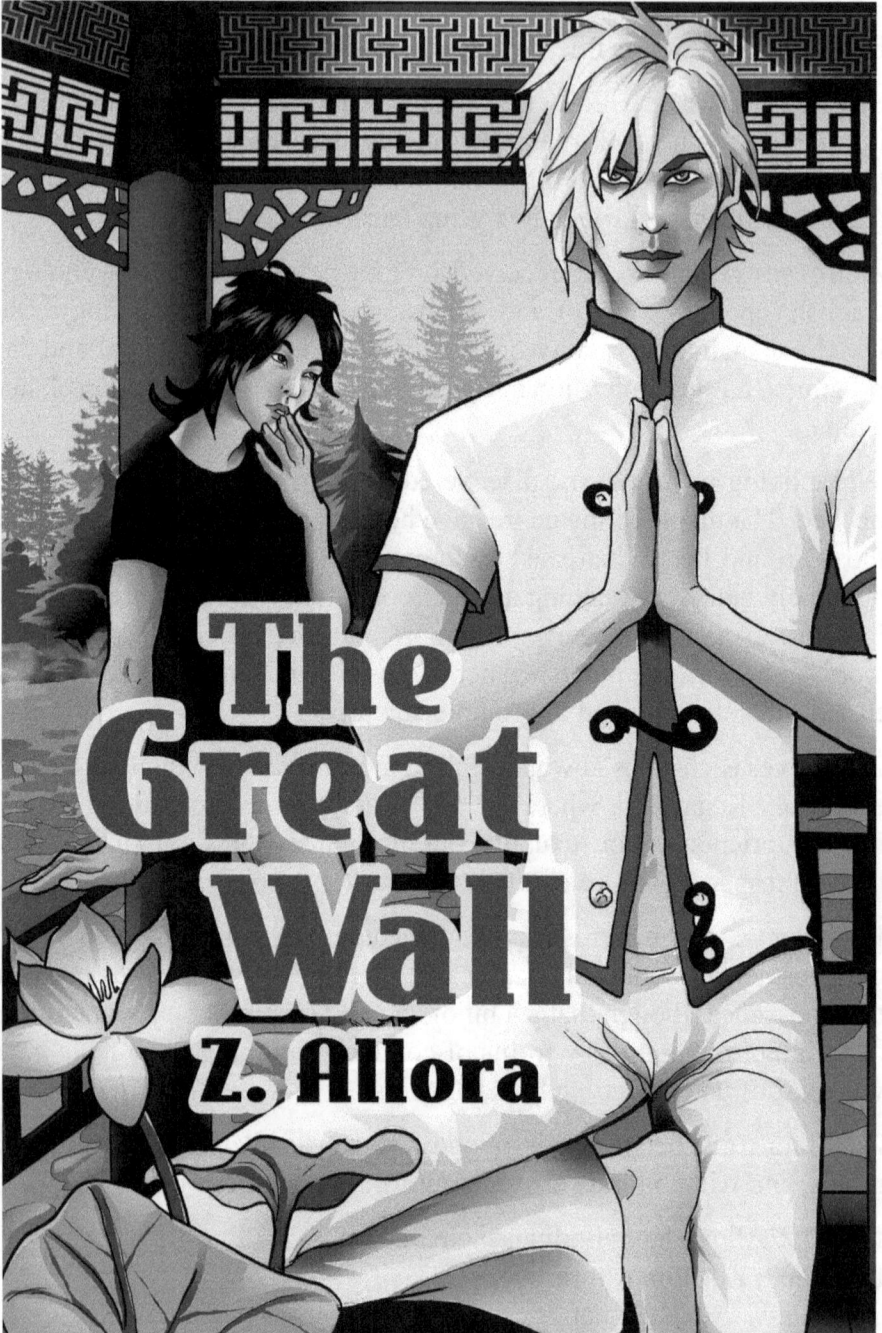

Made in China: Book One

Destiny will be decided by a battle between heart and mind….

Jun Tai "Styx" Wong loves two things: playing the drums, and his best friend, Jin. But being a good Chinese son means he can't have either—he'll have to marry a girl of his parents' choosing and settle into a traditional job. His move to the bigger city of Suzhou is both a blessing and curse, as living with Jin makes it harder for Styx to suppress his desires. Nearly dying while trying to eradicate his feelings serves as a wake-up call for Jin, who takes extreme measures to keep Styx safe from harm.

When given a second chance at life and happiness, will Styx be able to claim the future he wants with Jin, his bandmates, and his music? Can love and hope grow with the constantly looming threat of Styx's parents ordering him home? Great things await—if Styx finds the courage to break down the wall that stands between him and everything he wants.

www.dreamspinnerpress.com

Z. ALLORA

THE CRAVING

The craving is an undeniable urge that drives K'Dane citizens to find their life mates—if only to sate their uncontrollable physical longings.

Thrilled at being named a Chosen, Phoenix Dotir leaves K'Dane to become an artist-monk who will create dimensional art capable of changing worlds. Living by the monastery's Principles of Purity will surely help him overcome the craving. But he never accounted for star chaser Zadra Solav.

Zadra doesn't believe in rules and makes his own future. Fate separates him from the man he loves, but one touch renders him helpless to his own desires. Bonding with a monk is forbidden, and Zadra's family sends him to deep space to avoid disgrace. Unable to give up, Zadra must find a way to reunite with his Chosen.

Tormented by enforced separation, Initiate Riva Quinton struggles with his vow of chastity and risks all to rescue his lover. Together with his Eros, he stows away onboard a star craft to follow his heart.

Four men defy destiny and tradition for love… but their love is a crime punishable by death.

www.dreamspinnerpress.com

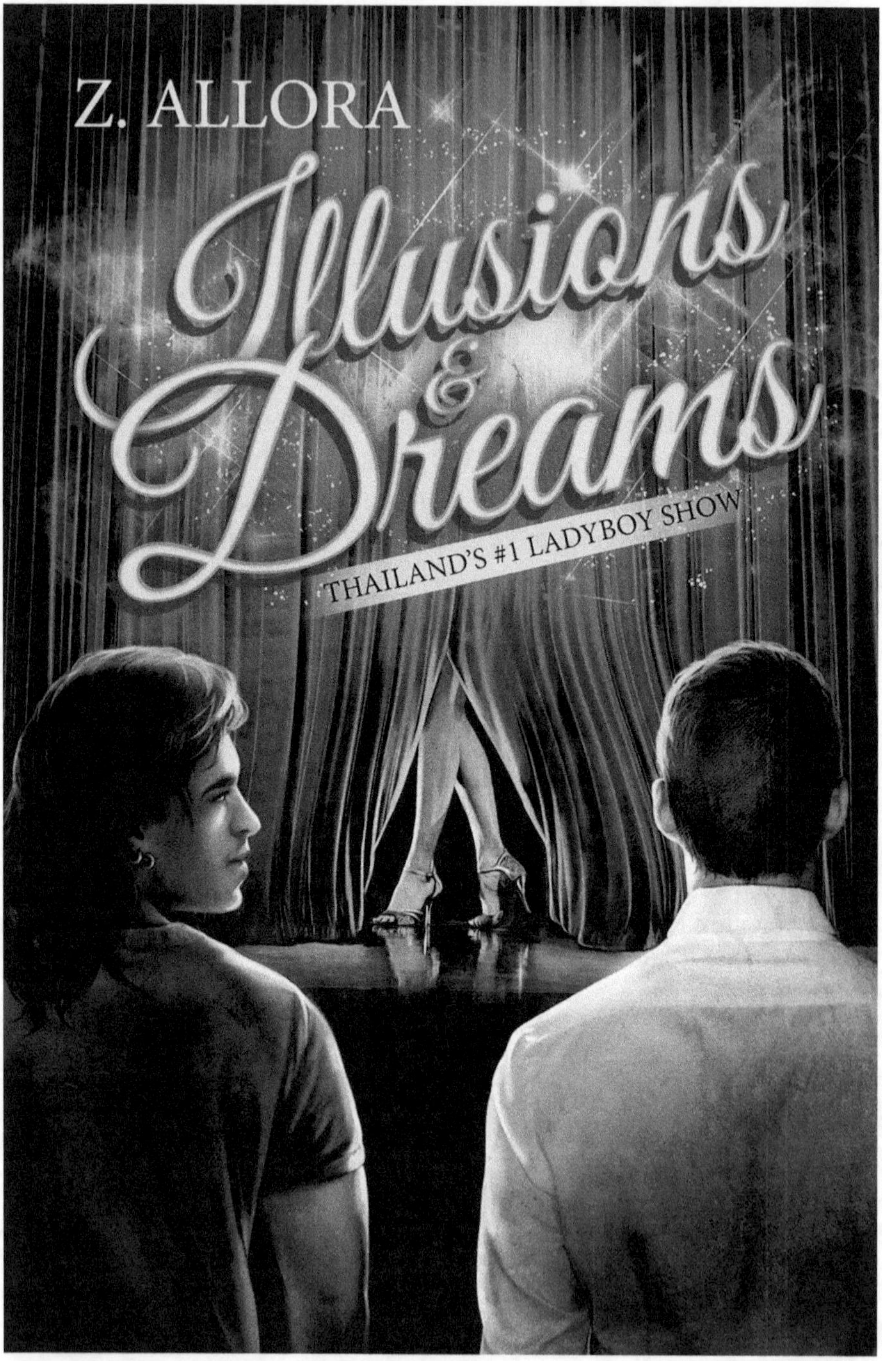
Z. ALLORA
Illusions & Dreams
THAILAND'S #1 LADYBOY SHOW

After Randy Camster failed at marriage, his life centered around work, TV sports, and listening to his friend Jake complain about how Randy's lack of a sex life will be the downfall of mankind. Not true! Well, not totally. Randy has just never understood the fascination with sex… until ladyboy performer Lalana Dulyarat shimmies into his world via an Internet ad for Thailand tourism. After that, it doesn't take much for Jake to convince Randy to take a Bang Cock vacation.

Finding an adorable little imp named Boon-nam wasn't on Jake O'Neil's itinerary. Gay, straight, and undecided, Jake has had 'em all, but never a virgin aching to explore her new body after successful affirmation surgery. Talk about pressure. And what's with everyone warning him not to break Boon-nam's heart? His is the one in danger.

Jake's openness about sexuality has always made Randy wonder if he is too focused on gender. Lalana is even more beautiful in real life than he'd hoped, but she's keeping her "male parts" and has no intention of ever having surgery. Does it really matter? A return ticket to reality awaits. The clock is ticking on the two couples' hopes for love, unless they can find a way to span gender, culture, and half a world.

www.dreamspinnerpress.com

The
LiBRARIAN'S
RAKE

Z. ALLORA

Opposites might attract, but is acting on that attraction wise?

Librarian Tristan Cooper can't steer clear of sexy, motorcycle-riding bad boy Phillip—the man is hot—but Phillip is bound to find quiet, bookish Tristan boring, like all Tristan's boyfriends. Tristan yearns to explore his wild side, the part of himself he's only allowed into his fantasies, and maybe rakish Phillip is just what he needs to feel free.

Sexperienced hairdresser Phillip is more of a believer in happy endings than happily ever afters. Experience has taught him not to hope for more—until he meets sweet, vulnerable Tristan, who seems genuinely interested in his heart. But Phillip can't trust enough to see himself as a man Tristan might want for more than a night.

With the help of a pair of matchmaking grandfathers, Tristan and Phillip might find the courage to step beyond their comfort zones and discover what has been missing from their lives....

www.dreamspinnerpress.com

Entwined Dreams: Book One

Rejected. Heartbroken. Devastated.
Zack Davis wanted to serve only one man, Andrew Nikeman. He was denied because Andrew thought he was too young and because their brothers were together. So Zack crushed his submissive tendencies and focused on being the perfect Dom, giving every sub he played with something he couldn't have.

After years of denying his submissive side, Entwined's charity auction "Are you Dom Enough to be a sub?" gives Zack an excuse to get a little of what he's always craved.

Andrew doesn't know when his infatuation turned into more, but it kills him to see Zack with a constant parade of submissives. He'd refused to jeopardize his brother's relationship or become Zack's regret; however, Zack isn't a kid anymore, and his brother's relationship is unbreakable. Now Zack's popularity and success as a Dom might ruin Andrew's dreams of collaring him, but he can't wait any longer to confess his feelings or he risks losing the man he loves forever.

www.dreamspinnerpress.com

Secured
and Free

Z. ALLORA

Entwined Dreams: Book Two

An abusive Dom robbed Orion Gordon of his love of BDSM, destroying his confidence and leaving him unsure he'll ever find peace through submission to another. Still, deep inside, his longing continues.

Marcus Sadir loves Hunter Dixon, yet he can't be the one thing Hunter truly desires: a sub to control. And Hunter can't find satisfaction in the sadistic aspects of the BDSM lifestyle, while Marcus thrives on inflicting and sharing pain. When Marcus convinces Hunter they should find a third on a permanent basis, they discover Orion might be the key to bridging their differences and joining them on a deeper level.

But they must help Orion move past his trauma enough for him to enjoy new facets of BDSM and kink again. Their journey toward becoming whole—together—won't be without challenges. Can Orion trust enough to try again?

www.dreamspinnerpress.com

www.ingramcontent.com/pod-product-compliance
Lightning Source LLC
Chambersburg PA
CBHW070052030726
47506CB00002B/443